AGAINST
THE WALL
HIGH STAKES

DEE J. ADAMS

Books by Dee J. Adams

The Adrenaline Highs Series

Dangerous Race

Danger Zone

Dangerously Close

Living Dangerously

Imminent Danger

A Little Danger

Always Dangerous

The High Stakes Series

Against the Wall

Over the Top

Out of the Blue

ACKNOWLEDGMENTS

I have to thank the usual suspects...Kate Willoughby and Lynne Marshall. Ladies, I can't tell you just how much I appreciate your ears and ideas, your good advice and honest critiques. You've made me a better writer with each book.

Thanks to Julie Goldstein for so many hours of work. You are amazing, talented and beautiful, and you're my friend for life. You've been one of my biggest cheerleaders and I can't tell you how much it means to me.

A giant thank you to Melissa Johnson, who once again made my story stronger and thought of things that hadn't crossed my mind. Watch out, I'm not letting you go.

Thank you to my family for years of support as I've juggled writing and life. Sean, Katelyn, Malcolm, Eileen, Carol, Thom, Evelyn, Marion, Sam, Sue, Heather, Barry, Robin...and all my cousins from the East Coast to the West Coast, you all have been so supportive and I love each and every one of you.

DEDICATION

This one is for Sean.

Thanks for the idea to "just write it down."
It's all your fault.
None of it would've happened if you hadn't believed in me.
Life with you has been one awesome ride
and I couldn't imagine taking it with anyone else.

Love you.

CHAPTER 1

THE GUN WOBBLED IN Tanner Bryant's hand as he wiped the sweat trickling in his eyes. His thudding heart drowned out the sound around him. All day, he'd been calm, and cool, exacting every move. Everything had gone as planned until now. The longer he waited on the rafters, the more his nerves frayed. Only a few house lights lit the large soundstage where a half built movie set waited to be finished, and darkness kept him hidden this high up. He'd heard some rustling a while back and caught sight of a giant rat scampering by on an adjacent beam. He'd seen bigger.

Dammit, he shouldn't have taken so much time to learn Juneau's schedule. All of a sudden the man had hired more bodyguards as if he knew Tanner wanted a piece of him.

Tanner focused on the scene twenty feet beneath him. He couldn't hear what the girl was telling his target, but he didn't care. Her gestures and position pissed him off. Thirty seconds ago, he'd had a clear shot, but now, little Miss Muffet stood in his way. She was just an itty-bitty thing, not tall, not wide, but he didn't trust his aim and didn't want to hurt her.

But he did want to hurt the man next to her. Desperately. He wanted Maurice Juneau to suffer. Painfully and for an extended period of time. Tanner didn't need Juneau to know who had shot him. It just mattered that the man felt pain. Juneau was smart. He might actually figure out who pulled the trigger if he learned Tanner had been released from prison. Oddly, that thought did give Tanner a sense of power. The pond scum had ruined Tanner's life and it was only fair that Juneau knew it was him.

But, it wasn't a prerequisite.

Tanner shifted on the catwalk. Three minutes ago, his whole body ached from being in the same position for so long. He'd gotten on the studio lot by hiding in the back of flatbed truck loaded with sets. Hiding under a black tarp had been easier than he'd expected. Waiting for Juneau had scraped his nerves raw, but now that he had the man in his sight, all his aches faded. The bastard had aged in seven years. The gray in his hair proved it.

Tanner almost didn't care if he went back to prison. Didn't care what his life might be like after shooting this man. He only had to pull the trigger to get satisfaction. Well, pull the trigger and hit his mark.

But no. Instead he had a little wisp of a she-thing gesturing and flailing, trying her damnedest to get Juneau's attention. The asshole had been on the phone almost from the minute he walked onto the stage with the girl at his heels like a frantic puppy. Almost as if she knew Tanner was about to strike and wanted to save the black-hearted son of a bitch. That was impossible. Tanner had never seen her before. Didn't know who the hell she was. His nerves were finally getting the better of him if he thought anyone knew he was here at all, much less what he was doing.

Juneau's small office staff was supposed to be gone. He was supposed to have wrapped his last film and sent everyone off for a couple days of R & R, so who the hell was this girl?

She edged left and Tanner adjusted his aim, and just as quickly she moved right.

Damn her.

She moved left again and this time Tanner pulled the trigger. He felt the kick of the Glock in his hand at the same time a Town Car entered the huge elephant doors of the stage. The shot rang out and Juneau ducked. Fuck. He missed. The girl jumped a mile and spun around.

But Juneau ran and Tanner kept firing, nearly choking on the taste of failure. The car door opened and the bastard dove in, leaving the girl in the dust as she sprinted after the speeding black car.

Scrambling down the wall ladder, Tanner already set his sights for the next opportunity as he ran for the door. He may have missed this time, but Juneau wouldn't be lucky forever. A last glance over his shoulder froze him. His heart beat frantically, screamed for him to run. The girl had stopped and moonlight shining from the doors illuminated her silhouette and white T-shirt. A white T-shirt that was quickly turning red as blood ate up the cotton from the top of her shoulder. His stomach lurched.

Holy shit, he hadn't missed after all. He'd shot *her*.

Tanner stood, horrified at what he'd done. She'd paid a price meant for someone else and he couldn't leave her. As if realizing something was wrong, she looked at her shoulder and wobbled on her feet. Sirens sounded in the distance and snapped Tanner back to life. Whisper quiet, he sprinted toward her. Twenty feet away and she saw him, stumbled as she took a step back. She looked deathly pale as she clutched her shoulder with the opposite hand.

She tried to say something even as her eyes widened and her mouth dropped open. She'd spotted the gun in his hand. Knew he was the one who'd shot her and tried to run.

Shit, now he was really fucked. Tanner grabbed her around the waist just as her noodly legs buckled beneath her. She hardly weighed a thing, a hundred pounds at best. But getting out of here wasn't going to be easy with the extra dead weight on his hands.

Tanner hefted her in his arms, checked that she wasn't leaving a trail of blood behind them and raced for the side door. His escape golf cart waited for him. Was a golf cart really going to get him out of this? He might've laughed if he hadn't been in so much trouble. But he hadn't laughed in so long he wasn't sure he knew how.

This late at night the studio lot was empty. A big white moon and a few dozen stars lit up the warm California sky, and Tanner kept her on his lap as he started the cart and raced toward the back lot. He'd done his homework, knew there were places to hide, ways to escape. Security here didn't scare him. Not yet anyway. These guys didn't compare to the prison guards he'd dealt with for so many years. Hell, the giant rats scared him more than these guys.

But just the thought of prison had him pushing the golf cart to its limit. He was *not* going back to prison. Not because of Juneau. Not for any reason. He'd spent enough wasted years behind bars. He'd rather spend his life on the run than in another dank cell.

After pulling the golf cart into an alley on New York Street, Tanner cut the motor. Down the small road, he spotted a dark pickup truck. Without too much thought, he lifted his load—she was still out cold—and eased toward the new wheels. He passed by a deli, dry cleaners and ice cream shop. Up close the store façades looked as fake as they really were. Tanner squinted in the moonlight when he reached the driver's side door. Unlocked. *Yes.* He quickly deposited the girl in the passenger seat and jumped behind the wheel. It only took a minute to hot wire the old truck and then he was moving toward the gate. He'd never hot-wired a car before. Funny, the things a guy learned in prison.

He spotted a baseball cap on the dashboard and slid it over his head. He covered the girl with a windbreaker that was bunched up and tucked beside the seat. Gate security waved as he passed them. "Have a nice night," he called through the closed window. He took a right onto the street and checked the rearview mirror. It didn't seem as if security knew of the incident. Maybe the blazing sirens had been from a car on the residential street along the studio.

Suckers.

Tanner kept an eye out as he drove through Burbank and made his way into Hollywood and his fleabag hotel. Ten minutes later, in the middle of Sunset Boulevard traffic, he released a sigh and finally looked down at the female lying in the passenger seat.

If her shaggy, short dark hair was any indication, she'd had a hell of a day. But then again, he'd capped it by shooting her. He winced. Damn, he'd screwed this up. To top it off, she looked like a damn innocent kid. She couldn't have been more than twenty-one. Her pale skin gleamed in the moonlight. She had a cute little pert nose that matched the rest of her. Cute. Pixie. Just like her haircut...and her shape. Everything about her screamed cute, innocent and shouldn't have been shot.

Swallowing back the panic, Tanner focused on the road. He had to make this right. He of all people knew what it was like to be in the wrong place at the wrong time and he'd be damned if he didn't do all he could for this girl.

Pulling over, he stopped the car. What had he been thinking to take her? Sure, she'd seen him before, but now...now she'd know where he lived. Fuck. He wasn't good at this on-the-fly shit. It had taken a lot of planning to be at the stage, lure Juneau and hatch an escape route and now he'd gone totally off-roading.

He should dump her. She hadn't come to and maybe she hadn't really seen him. It had been dim on that stage…

One more look at her shoulder had him moving again. No, he couldn't shoot her then abandon her. That was low, even for him. Despite not hearing his mother's or sister's voices in seven years, they still rang very clearly in his head. *"You did what to that poor girl? Then you left her?"* Their disappointment would be clear not only in their voices, but in their eyes. Tanner ruthlessly shoved back the picture. More and more he'd been thinking about his family, and it only made him feel worse. He'd hurt them enough already, no reason to compound the pain.

Another few minutes and he'd be home…well, not home, but someplace to crash and hide for the night. A place where he could think about the next step and take care of his…hostage. Crap, now he had a hostage. She wasn't just a girl or woman or lady. She was a hostage.

Nice going, Tanner. Way to fuck up your life even more.

CHAPTER 2

JESSIE ST. JOHN DIDN'T open her eyes. She wanted to, but something was very wrong and she needed to piece together what had happened first. Street noise drifted to her ears; cars, trucks and occasional pedestrians talking loudly. Where was she? Time to backtrack. Where had she been before this? Talking to her boss, Maurice, where he'd blown her off. She'd been his assistant for three years and he still treated her like dirt. He took credit for her good ideas and blamed her for his bad ones. Things had certainly gone bad tonight. She concentrated, tried to focus on the last thing she remembered. Wow, she had a headache. Her shoulder hurt too. That was because...she'd been shot?

Oh, God, she'd been shot! Everything came back with a flood of memory, but Jess kept her eyes shut. Where was she? Then she remembered... *He'd* taken her. The shooter had picked her up as if she'd been a rag doll—which she'd turned into when her legs had given out—and carried her out the door like a caveman. Her heart pounded furiously in her chest. God, please don't let him be watching her. She strained to hear anything, but unlike outside, the silent room gave no sign of life. She was on something soft. Probably a bed. Maybe a sofa. The air smelled stale. Definitely not a hospital. No, he wouldn't have snatched her just to deposit her in a hospital. He could've left her behind if he wanted her to get medical attention. He took her because she'd seen him. Oh, boy, had she seen him.

Tall, about six feet four inches of long, lean man. More muscle than she'd seen since glimpsing the cover-boy model calendar her brother had bought her last year, and short dark hair so thick she

6

doubted he'd ever lose any of it. His face had mesmerized her. Scared her. Hard, dark eyes glittered as he'd moved toward her. Lines lightly creased his eyes and mouth and a prominent nose, that might have been big on another man, fit his face fine.

She'd tried to speak, tried to run. The gun in his hand had terrified her, made her realize that she had indeed been shot. God, that stuff only happened in the movies. But he'd scooped her up and wimp that she was, Jess had simply lost consciousness. She'd been known to pass out when something scared her. Her body would shut down as it had tonight. What a wuss. Her little brothers still teased her about it mercilessly.

Thinking about her brothers brought the urgency back. She had to get out of here.

Jess's shoulder throbbed as she listened harder for noises, but the street sounds still dominated the room. She must be above it somehow, on a second or third floor. Deciding she couldn't play possum the rest of her life, Jess opened her eyes to a dimly lit room. A naked bulb cast the only light. A battered television rested on a scarred dresser against the wall and mini fridge sat under a counter with a sink. She turned her head a fraction to the side.

He was there.

Staring at her as if he'd been waiting for her. She hadn't heard him make a sound. Hadn't been aware of him in the slightest. It seemed ridiculous, because now she was totally aware of him. Of the space he occupied and the way he watched her. Why would he be looking at her as if *he* was afraid of *her?*

"I wasn't sure if you'd ever wake up." His low voice held a hint of humor. Could he possibly think this was funny? When she didn't respond he continued, gestured to her shoulder. "It's not bad. More of a scratch. If I'd known that, I wouldn't have hauled you out of there the way I did, but you were bleeding a lot and..." He trailed off, clamped his mouth shut.

That was almost reassuring. Maybe he'd let her leave. Jess lifted the collar of her shirt and glanced at the bandage. But this wasn't her shirt. He'd replaced her T-shirt with a much bigger one. It was brand new and all black. One of his? Oh, God, he'd seen her practically topless. Heat warmed her cheeks as she rose up on her elbows and scooted back against the wall, trying for any amount of distance. She ignored the burn in her shoulder. "Not a problem," she croaked. She forced herself to look on the bright side…at least she was wearing clothes.

He was young-ish, which had nothing to do with whether or not he was a psycho. If she stayed calm and made no sudden movements, maybe she could just walk out of here. She eased her legs from beneath a polyester bedspread, but he halted her progress with an outstretched arm.

"What do you think you're doing?"

Okay, shoot. Maybe not so easy to just walk away. "It's just a scratch, so I thought I'd…you know…go home." Yeah, right. She wouldn't dream of running straight to the police or even think about giving them a perfect description of this guy. She'd go right home. Do not pass Go, do not collect two hundred dollars.

The thought of home jolted her back to her situation and her heart pounded harder. As long as her family wasn't there, she didn't have a home. Sure, she had an apartment, but the home she grew up in, the home where her parents and brothers lived had been her safe haven. But not anymore.

His cold smile pulled her out of her thoughts. "I can't let you go. Not yet anyway. How old are you?"

What? What did it matter how old she was? She'd already proved she was a total wimp by passing out, so maybe it was time she showed a little backbone. "It's none of your business how old I am. How old are you?" she snapped back, unable to hide the growing frustration and anger building under her skin.

"Twenty-seven," he answered. He looked older… Like ten years older. "I know." He nodded as if she'd said it aloud and she was sure she hadn't. "Prison will do that."

Great. Prison. The man was an ex-con. Or worse, maybe an escaped convict. But she'd had her ear to the news nonstop in the last twelve hours and hadn't heard anything about anyone escaping from prison. Still, a fresh flurry of panic bubbled in her gut. What was she supposed to say now?

Forty-eight hours ago, she'd been juggling her job and the production coordinator's job, wrapping the last film, returning equipment rentals and dousing fires from accounting. She'd been waiting for a chance to be part of the production team and hadn't complained about the workload. But now her life had spun so far out of her control she didn't know what to do first.

Information. She needed information to figure out how dangerous this man was. "How long were you in prison?" *Stupid question.* What if he hadn't had a woman in so long that he now wanted to take what was in front of him? When would she learn she needed to think before speaking?

"Seven long-ass years," he told her. He wasn't looking at her like she might be breakfast, lunch or dinner, so Jess took a little solace in that.

She could ask him what he was in for, but fear kept that question buried. Murder? Rape? She swallowed and went in a different direction. "When did you get out?" Fair question seeing as how he'd broken the law with a bang, no pun intended.

"You ask a lot of questions," he said, voice low and eyes narrowed. "Maybe you answer some of mine and I'll answer more of yours. How old are you?"

"Fine." What did it matter? "Twenty-six." As of yesterday. *Happy birthday to me.* This was not the kind of surprise she'd been hoping for. In fact the last twenty-eight hours had turned her life upside down. She didn't have time to be sitting here with this guy, playing whatever game he had planned. She forced back a shudder.

He leaned forward, elbows on his knees and dragged a hand through his hair, mumbling and swearing something incoherent under his breath.

Jess surveyed the rest of the room. Along with the one double bed she occupied and the scratched dresser and old television, there was also a chipped desk in the corner. The dirty beige carpet desperately needed a cleaning, the walls needed painting and the air needed freshener. It was your basic fleabag motel.

He still had his head down. Maybe she should bolt now. While he wasn't paying attention and his guard was down. Jess looked at the door across the small room, gauged her chances of making it outside. No way. He was too big. He'd catch her in a second. She could scream. He didn't have the gun in his hand and as she looked around she didn't see it anywhere. Maybe that's what she needed to do. Just scream loud and long. Jess took a breath, ready to howl for all she was worth when he looked up. He pounced on her so fast she didn't know what happened. One minute, she was about to scream her head off and the next he had his hand over her mouth and his body covering hers.

He stared at her, nose to nose as he pinned her shoulders and head against the wall and her lower body on the bed with his...very muscular self. "I don't recommend that course of action," he said in a deadly quiet tone. "I didn't mean to shoot you. I wasn't aiming for you, but don't be mistaken... Just because you weren't my target doesn't mean I won't keep you quiet until this is over. I need to figure out what I'm going to do, but if you can't keep your mouth shut, I'm going to do something you'll be extremely uncomfortable with. Do you understand me?"

Jess stared into his hard, dark eyes and swallowed. Fresh panic set in and her pulse hammered. The edges blurred and a wave of dizziness made her stomach turn, but she willed herself to stay conscious. She concentrated on the bite of his fingers against her cheek and took a deep breath through her nose. The faint scent of soap lingered under a hint of masculine sweat. Blinking, she cleared her vision. She couldn't afford to be gagged or tied. Her best bet was to make him think she'd be compliant. The more he trusted her, the better chance she'd have to escape. Jess nodded. At this point she'd have done just about anything to get him off her. He was strong and heavy. Not an ounce of fat on him.

"I'm going to get up now," he told her. He leaned close to her ear, his body rubbing up against hers as he shifted. "Don't make me do something I don't want to do." The threat was as clear as the thick ridge in his jeans and Jess shuddered when chills raced across her body.

She nodded again as tears filled her eyes. Dammit. No way would she cry. The past twenty-four hours she'd been nothing but helpless. She'd lost control of everything and now it had gotten worse. Think. *Think.* What could she do to change the situation?

Slowly he eased his hand from her mouth and Jess took a steadying breath. "I won't scream," she said softly. "Just get off me and I won't scream."

He gradually moved away and paced the small room. To say he was on edge was an understatement. Jess heaved a sigh. Her heart still beat a frantic rhythm, but at least she had some space. Now to figure out what he wanted and why. If shooting her had been an accident and Maurice had been the only other person on the stage then at least she knew who this man's target was. "Why were you shooting at Maurice?" she asked.

"None of your business."

"I'd say it's plenty of my business since your bullet hit me."

He turned on her, his face hard, tight. It was the face of a desperate man. Someone at the end of his rope. The look was enough to make her gasp, but she quickly got control of her nerves.

"Look, here's the thing," she said, glancing at her watch, playing it calm—and Maurice thought she couldn't act. Ha. Her clock was ticking and precious time drifted away as every minute passed. "I have something really important to do and I can't spend time locked up here." She stood up slowly, gauging his reactions, but he didn't move. Maybe because she didn't pose much of a threat looking like a ten-year-old wearing her father's top. His T-shirt dropped down to her thighs. Of course he was blocking the door, so he *wouldn't* move. "You have your agenda and I have mine. I know Maurice. I know he's done some bad things and I don't condone them. He's not the first Hollywood producer to run off with people's money and he won't be the last." Jess rambled on. She had no idea what she said as she tried to convince this guy that keeping her wouldn't do him any good.

"C'mon," she implored, gesturing to her shoulder. "I've had worse cuts from falling down. I promise not to go to the cops." And she meant it. She only wanted out of here. When he gave her no response, and seemed inclined to go her way, she tried again. "Why did you shoot at Maurice?" She tried for a smile, tried to buddy up. "If there was a Putz of the Year Award, Maurice would be in the running. I mean, sometimes *I* want to shoot him."

He narrowed his eyes and his face twisted in a grimace. "He took my life." His words came slowly, distinctly, and each syllable filled with malice. "He took my freedom. He took everything that meant anything to me and he needs to pay."

Jess lost the smile. This guy had serious retribution in mind. *Maurice, you idiot. What the hell did you do to* this *guy?*

11

She'd only worked for him a few years. His last assistant had left after Maurice's son died four years ago and he'd hired and fired three other people until she'd come along. She'd heard rumors of his business dealings and had fielded more than one or two angry investors, but it sounded as if he'd hit the mother lode of trouble with the man in front of her.

TANNER RAN A HAND down his face. The motel room was closing in on him, just the way his cell used to. Bringing this girl back here had been a colossal mistake. He saw that now. Anyone would think with a prison record and seven years served that he'd be better at this unlawful behavior, but here he was, fucking up royally.

"What's your name?" he asked as he started pacing again. Funny how even with extra room, he took the same amount of steps as he had in his cell. Four steps in one direction. Four steps back.

She hesitated and swallowed. "Jess. Jessie," she amended as she looked at her watch. "Look, I swear to you that I won't go to the police, but I have to get out of here. I have to find Maurice."

Tanner needed to find him too. "Why do you need him? What's so important?" He remembered how frantic she'd acted earlier. Maybe Maurice had fucked with her life as badly as he'd fucked with Tanner's.

"I can only answer that with a response you might remember." She put a hand on her hip. "None of your business."

Considering what he'd put her through, Tanner almost smiled at her ballsy response. Especially—and also—considering that he had a gun and was twice her size. For a girl who'd passed out cold, she'd recovered her fighting spirit. Running his hand over his hair, he glared at her. "Do you know where he might've gone? Where I can find him?"

Her pretty brown eyes narrowed. "Why? So you can find him and really kill him?" She crossed her arms over her chest and shook her head. "No. No way. I need him alive," she said, suddenly animated and tapping her chest. "I'm not handing him over to you. I don't care what you do to me." Those narrowed eyes widened as he advanced on her and that bravery wilted as she took a step back. But the bed halted her progress and he faced her toe to toe and head to chest. Her head to his chest. Standing this close, he smelled her. A combination of flowers and female perspiration. She wasn't pretty in the classic sense of the word, but she stood out nevertheless. Her pale skin gleamed in the low light, and her short dark hair spiked in every direction. It was her big brown eyes, the color of whiskey that gave away everything about her. Her fear. Anxiety.

Bastard that he was, he played on it. Because that's what he'd learned to do in prison. Take a stand and fight, intimidate, do what had to be done to stay on top.

"I don't think you're in a particular place to bargain," he growled, glaring down at her and not bothering to correct her assumption that he planned to kill Juneau. Although the idea had merit, torturing the man sounded better.

She swallowed. "You n-need me," she stammered. "I can find him. I know where he goes and who he meets. If you want him, you have to play by my rules. But I'll only give him to you on one condition."

Staring into her eyes, Tanner clenched his fists, his frustration eating at him from the inside out. He'd been prepared to do this job solo. He'd had to. The last thing he wanted was to get someone else involved, especially this girl. He didn't care if she was almost his age—she looked like a damn teenager. The more information he got out of her, the more he realized exactly *how* innocent she really was. Not so much in what she told him, but by her body language. Damn, she even smelled innocent and he didn't want to involve her when it came to dealing with Maurice.

On the other hand, she might be good to have around if she knew Juneau's schedule. "How long have you worked for him?" Tanner asked.

She hesitated before nodding. "I've been his assistant for three years and I've started working as a production coordinator."

Tanner remembered Juneau running through a lot of assistants back in the old days. But that had been before the trial. Before Juneau had turned on him to save his son. An old ache flared up at the thought of Alex and just as quickly it turned to a jagged wound, festering with lies and brimming with deceit. It shouldn't surprise him that Juneau couldn't hang onto an assistant. The man was in egomaniac, only interested in his life and image. Of course, that included Alex. Juneau couldn't allow his only son going to go to prison, so Tanner had taken the fall. Now it was time for payback.

So maybe this girl, Jess, might come in handy. Maybe he'd keep her until he had his sights back on Juneau. He sure as hell wouldn't miss the next time and he didn't care what she did or who she told after the fact, because he planned to disappear faster than one of Houdini's illusions.

But Jess was staring up at him as if he resembled the boogey man. Hell, maybe after seven years of hard time, he *was* the boogey man. Prison taught him that everything came with a price. She'd mentioned a condition…well he had one too.

"What's your condition?" he asked, taking a small step and crowding her even more, letting her know who was boss despite the information she had to offer.

"That you d-don't kill him…"

If only. Tanner narrowed his eyes.

"…until I'm done with him," she finished.

Definitely an interesting proposition, but not one he'd jump at without more to go on. Especially since it involved some type of trap. Why would she *agree* to let him kill her boss? Not that she had any say in the matter or that he intended to go that far, but didn't she care about a paycheck?

"Why should I bother waiting?" he asked.

"I told you, I can help you. And maybe you can help me."

Tanner lifted a skeptical brow, but he laid out the challenge. "I don't need your help and what makes you think I want to help you?"

Instead of answering, she swallowed hard. "Do we have a deal?" She stuck out her hand between them. She wanted to shake on it? This little thing had more balls than brains.

"You didn't answer me. What makes you think I'd help you do anything?"

Her mouth parted in a little "oh" but she never uttered the word. Instead, she glanced at her shoulder then back up at him.

"Because you shot me tonight and you feel guilty." She kept her hand out and by God, it was steady. He had to give her credit for that.

Tanner took her hand in his. A mistake. Not only a mistake, but one of mega proportions. Her skin was soft, her hand warm and small in his. Like a jolt of electric energy, he realized he'd been celibate for seven years. Seven of the longest years of his life. He hadn't thought much about it mostly because he'd been too busy planning revenge. Much of that had consisted of strengthening his body and that had been his only relief. Pushing himself so hard that he was too exhausted to think about missing sex.

Goddamn, he missed sex. He missed the taste of a woman. The smell. The little sounds of surrender and need. He missed the feeling of legs wrapped around his hips as he thrust hard and fast. He missed having his cock buried in the tight heat of a woman's body.

Earlier, he'd been too preoccupied to think about the temptation of a female. Sure, he'd looked when he'd changed her shirt, but with her bleeding and his own anger at missing Juneau, his mind had been on other problems.

He was paying attention now. Lots of attention.

Heat rose up from his gut and her eyes widened as if she felt it, or knew. Her mouth did that little "oh" again. Stunned, Tanner looked down at her small hand, still in his. He brushed his thumb over the pale softness of her skin. Her scent, a light flowery combination, climbed up his nostrils and teased his senses.

Her luminous brown eyes widened and she froze, simply quit breathing. Tanner, too, lost the use of his lungs. Sharp bolts of energy ricocheted between them despite the stillness.

He could take her down right now. Stretch her sweet little body across the bed and make her his. Own her. He could relieve the fierce sudden pressure in his jeans. With his hands and his mouth, he could make her feel things she never thought possible. But he never would have thought about forcing a woman before prison and shame swamped him for thinking it now.

Tanner quickly released her hand and stepped back. Hadn't he done enough to her already? Jesus, he must be losing it to consider something so vile. Maybe he couldn't be rehabilitated. Maybe those years in prison had changed him more than he thought and he *was* the lost cause he'd convinced his family that he'd become.

Turning his back on her, Tanner struggled to get his libido in check. Scaring her more than he already had tonight wasn't going to get him anywhere. Shooting her had been plenty, raping her was out of the question.

"I'm sorry," she whispered.

What? Tanner looked over his shoulder. She looked like a kid with her arms wrapped around her waist, but her pert little breasts pressed against his T-shirt and reminded him she was all woman. He focused on her face, sure the question lurked in his eyes. "What are you sorry for?"

"I know you'd rather that I wasn't here and you didn't mean to shoot me. I don't know why you came back for me, but you did and I guess we're stuck together until you trust that I won't go to the cops. And until we find Maurice." She swallowed and averted her gaze. "I just think that maybe it's best if we keep our distance from each other."

"Isn't that big of you," he mocked. He shouldn't vent, but it was easier to be pissed than tell her she was right, because they definitely needed to keep space between them. "Let me tell you something, sweetheart." He advanced and her eyes opened wide. "You don't know shit about me or my situation. You have no idea who you're working for and what he does to the people around him. Don't tell me what to do or when to do it and that includes dictating how close I get to you." Tanner towered over her. A vein in her neck throbbed frantically. He made himself sick with how much he scared her.

Clearly she thought he was going to attack her. Even under the cover of his giant shirt, he saw every muscle strained with tension as she waited. She might've looked young, but Tanner wanted to show her, just once, how he owned her. He wanted to grab her around the nape, tug her forward and crush his lips against hers. Just a taste. Just a warning. He wanted to feel her under him, even if it was only her lips beneath his. He wanted his tongue in her mouth, wanted to know if she tasted as good as she smelled.

He could do it. One kiss and he'd back off.

CHAPTER 3

JESS STOOD FROZEN, HER heart pounding wildly, every muscle tense. No way could she fight this guy off. He was too big. When had her judgment in character gone so completely off track? Just when she thought she had a handle on the man, he popped a vessel and turned schizo. *Prison will do that.* His words rang in her head. What did she expect from a guy out for revenge? Why would he be even-tempered? Or sane for that matter.

He looked scary as hell at the moment. His dark eyes blazed. Fierce. Unstoppable. And very ready to commit some unspeakable acts if she didn't do something to change his mind. She needed to talk…so she tackled the subject that interested him most.

"I think I know where Maurice might've gone tonight," she blurted.

His eyes narrowed. He scanned her from the top of her head to the tips of her toes. His gaze lingered on her mouth and Jess bit her bottom lip, her nerves shot to hell and back. What if it wasn't enough?

His nostrils flared, animalistic.

Though her insides quaked, she stayed outwardly calm. He wasn't an animal and probably not insane. He was a man with a lot on his mind and she needed to treat him like a human being, something he probably wasn't used to in prison. Mostly, she needed to get his mind focused on something other than her body. To do that she had to make him see her as a person, not an object.

"If we're going to find Maurice, I should know your name," she said, trying to put some oomph behind her words. The stronger she sounded the less likely he was to think he could roll over her.

Yeah, right. She may as well have been a leaf on the road and he was the Tuesday street-cleaner. He could blow through her in a matter of seconds. He stared at her as if she'd lost her mind.

"I guess you don't have to give me your real name," she offered. "But I should call you something. I can't just say, 'hey you.'" Long, tense seconds ticked by. She'd stared down her brothers before, but it had never been anything like this. They'd mostly conceded defeat, whether because she was the big sister or they didn't want to face the wrath of their mother, Jess didn't know. But holding her own with this man scared the hell out her. Especially the way his gaze drilled into hers as if he hadn't yet decided if she was dinner…or dessert.

Finally, anger ebbed from his eyes until he blinked away any emotion at all. "Tanner," he mumbled.

Relief whistled through her. Progress.

Tanner. His first name or last? It didn't matter. "It fits you," she said softly. She'd never met a Tanner before, but this man wore his name well. Strong, Male. Competent and in charge. Clearly he wasn't going to divulge another name, but she'd only given one, too, so fair was fair. Not that this situation seemed remotely fair.

"Where is he?" Tanner asked.

Maurice. He wanted Maurice tonight. It shouldn't have surprised her. Just because he'd drawn blood didn't mean he was done for the night…especially since the blood was hers. But her bait had worked. Finding Maurice would get her out of this hotel room. Then she'd find a way to get away from this man permanently.

"He's probably at his Malibu house," Jess answered. That's where he'd run to after every incident…and lately there had been several. Maybe she could ditch Tanner there. Maurice always had a couple of "guys" around. Jess had no clue what they did for a living besides mooch off Maurice. More recently he'd surrounded himself with security. If she could get to him, she'd be okay. Tanner didn't stand a chance against five to one odds.

Tanner snatched a pad of paper and pen from the scratched up desk and shoved it in front of her. "Write down the address and directions," he ordered.

Not likely. Jess didn't take either item. "So you can go by yourself and kill him? Hell no," she snapped. "I told you, I need him alive. I'll show you how to get there."

His nostrils flared again and Jess got the impression he didn't like obeying orders. Especially from someone half his size. God, he really was a giant. Huge shoulders and trim waist. Long muscular legs that filled out his dark jeans to perfection. How ironic that God could create something so ruggedly beautiful on the outside, but mess up so drastically beneath the surface.

"How far is Malibu from here?" he asked.

So he wasn't a Los Angeles native. That worked to her advantage. "Where is here?" she demanded. She had no idea where he'd brought her.

He swore under his breath. "Hollywood."

"We can take Sunset and be there in forty minutes," she told him. "Give or take a few."

"I'll need to blindfold you until we get a few miles away."

Naturally. She shrugged and hid her excitement. More progress. "Why not. I've already been shot. A blindfold is a piece of cake." He flinched, but it was quick and if she hadn't been watching, she'd have missed it.

Fifteen minutes later, sitting shotgun, she was allowed to take off the bandana he'd wrapped around her eyes. She didn't expect to be sitting in a Volvo of all things, and not a sporty one, but a family car. Her mother drove a car like this. A 740 GLE family wagon.

Jess had a sudden flash of memory: her mother driving while Jess sat in the passenger seat, her four little brothers crammed into the back, all fighting over water guns and homemade sling shots. The noise had been deafening, but her mother had been calm and collected. How had her mother stayed so relaxed during the chaos? Jess never figured it out, but at the moment she wanted nothing more than to have inherited her mother's genes.

"Nice wheels," she joked. "Did you get to drive the prison soccer team?"

His deadly glare pierced her before focusing back on the road.

Dumb thing to say, especially to a man just out of prison. "Sorry," she mumbled. "I get nervous traveling with..." Ex-cons. But she didn't say it.

Jess chose to look at the bright side. She needed to talk to Maurice and maybe Tanner's gun would help her get what she needed. Then she'd find a way to save Maurice's sorry ass before Tanner really killed him. There seemed to be some circularity to the evening. Tanner could help her with Maurice, Maurice could help her with her family and she could help Maurice with Tanner. A nice, neat package.

Ha.

What a surreal thought. That Tanner might actually kill Maurice if/when he found him. Looking at Tanner's stone-cold face, mostly hidden in shadows, she doubted she'd be able to stop him from doing anything he wanted. Her shoulder throbbed as if to agree with the assessment. Maybe she couldn't stop him, but Maurice's security team could.

"How much time do you need with Juneau before he's mine?"

Holy jeez! What a question. And he'd stated it so calmly. As if taking someone's life was just another errand in a long day. Of course, if Tanner thought to ask, maybe he had the inclination to negotiate. Maurice had better hope so. So, the time she needed with Maurice depended on how seriously he took the situation. "I don't know."

"Let me rephrase," he said. "*What* do you need from Juneau before he's mine?" The certainty in Tanner's voice freaked her out. He didn't strike her as a man who killed on a regular basis, yet he sure talked like it. What if that was why he'd been in prison? What if he'd killed multiple people? What if Maurice's security couldn't stop him? Bad thought. Because maybe he planned on taking her to Maurice and killing her there, making it seem like some type of work related incident. *Crazy Assistant Attacks Boss And Takes Her Own Life*. Story at eleven. Yikes.

"Did you not understand my question?" he said. "What do you need with Juneau?"

Jess swallowed. This guy wasn't long on patience. Maybe after spending years in prison, his patience had evaporated. If he'd had any to begin with. "Money. I need money." A whole hell of a lot of money.

Tanner glanced at her again, but this time with assessing eyes. He hadn't expected that answer. Good. She wanted to surprise him. Wanted him to know she wasn't a wimp who crumbled at the littlest thing…well most of the time. Most of the time she handled a crisis with calm rational thinking. But her idea of a crisis was a cameraman calling in with car trouble and finding a replacement ASAP. Or making sure the location permits were in order or that a fire marshal was present when incendiary devices were used on the set.

"How much money do you need?" he asked.

Would it matter if she told him? If he knew how much, he might actually spare Maurice, especially if he thought he could get a fraction of that amount for himself.

Jess took a deep breath. "Eight million dollars."

Tanner jerked his head and looked at her. A car horn blared and he quickly corrected the car. "Eight mil." He whistled. "What's a little thing like you going to do with eight million dollars?"

Save her family, but that was none of his business. She'd been warned not to tell a soul and she wouldn't. Not if it meant their lives.

"What does anyone do with that kind of money?" She tried to sound casual, but sounded ridiculous even to herself.

"Depends on who you are," Tanner said. He gave her another hard glare. "Who are you, Jess-Jessie?"

He was mocking her now? "It wasn't enough that you shot me, now you have to make fun of me too?" It was something her brothers would do, but she didn't get any type of brotherly vibe from Tanner. He had her on edge…made her angry. Worse than those two things, he made her itchy. Itchy in a way she couldn't put a finger on. She held back the urge to squirm in her seat.

"I told you," she said, finally answering his question. "I'm his assistant." And someone in a boatload of trouble.

FOR THE HUNDREDTH TIME, Jay St. John surveyed the unfinished basement where his wife and four sons had been tied—and trapped—for the last twenty-four hours. The cement walls had no windows and only one door led to a short hallway and stairs to the upper part of the house. A series of pipes ran horizontally against the walls several inches off the floor and that's where the whole family had been handcuffed. No doubt about it, they were in a boatload of trouble. Trying to loosen the pipe that held him, Jay felt the bite of the handcuffs against his raw wrists and pain sizzled up his arms. The damn thing should give at some point.

His mind had been spinning for hours, trying to figure out who had abducted them and why. Originally, he'd suspected one of his angry clients. As a lawyer, he'd made enough enemies, people not happy with the job he did or a final verdict. But this had been pretty damn extreme. It was one thing to want to hurt *him*, but to grab almost his whole family? That didn't make sense.

Terry shifted and brought his focus back to now. She'd finally fallen asleep an hour ago, her head in his lap. Her cuffs bound her to the same horizontal pipe. He itched to smooth her red hair away from her face, but the restraints made that impossible. From this vantage point, her black eye looked as if she'd gone a few rounds with a heavyweight champ. His sons had similar bruises. So did he. He couldn't have been more proud of Terry, of the boys too. They'd all fought hard until the moment they realized the futility.

"She'll be okay," Eric, murmured, his voice low, but confident. "Remember when she joined that roller derby team a few years ago and got body-checked off the track? She had a huge shiner after that."

Jay looked at his oldest son and forced a smile. The cut over Eric's eyebrow had stopped bleeding, but the trail of blood still remained along his cheek. "Yeah. Good thing it was the end of the season and I convinced her to hang up her skates."

He'd fallen in love with Terry because of her sass. Her attitude and energy drew him like flies to a picnic. She was the only woman he'd ever loved—high school sweethearts in fact—and he'd be the first to admit that their love had grown even stronger through their twenty-seven years together.

Eric stretched his long legs in front of him, rotated his shoulders as best he could and winced before a grim smile curved his lips. "I think the guy that surprised Mom at the door won't ever have kids."

"Yeah." Jay grinned too, picturing Terry kneeing the stranger in the balls and slamming her purse against his head. He'd gone down quicker than a bowling ball in quicksand. At that point the house had been full of men. It had taken five of them to bring down all the St. Johns. It would've taken more if they hadn't picked them off one and two at a time, waiting as everyone got home. But Terry had been just as awesome as the boys, fighting for her family, for herself. Right up until one of the men slammed his fist in her face and she'd crumbled to the floor in a heap. Jay's smile faded and he opened his eyes to banish the memory.

"I hope Jess is okay. You think they plan on bringing her here too?" Eric asked.

"No." Jay shook his head. He'd been considering that idea. "I think we're leverage. I don't know who's taken us, but the longer I mull it over, the more I think Jess is involved. She's the only one *not* here." Once the goons at the house had Terry and the boys, they'd hit the road with six of the St. Johns' in two different vans and a squeal of tires. They would've snagged Jess if they'd wanted everyone, which told him she was being used.

But why and by whom? Who did Jess know who would put all of them in this kind of danger? Only one name came to mind: Maurice Juneau, her boss. Jay had told Jess years ago, when she went to work for the man, that he was trouble. He didn't have solid proof, but he'd worked for Juneau himself long before that and the experience had inspired Jay to shift his career.

Instead of staying in private practice and making money hand over fist, Jay took a job in the public defender's office for a fraction of the salary. Life changed. The household budget got tighter and raising five kids suddenly became a lot harder. Terry took a job as a teacher at the kids' private school and the reduction in tuition was the only reason the kids stayed enrolled.

Yes, life had changed and it was all because of Maurice Juneau.

Though Jay had tried to convince Jess to find other employment, she'd stood firm, saying that this was a great entry level job if she wanted to be in the movie business and that he needed to let go and let her live her life. Despite his protesting heart, Jay had done it. He'd let his daughter go. Let her make her own decisions.

Brendan stirred next to Eric and Jay gestured with his chin to his youngest son. "How's he look to you? I can't see him well enough from over here."

Glancing at his brother, Eric grimaced. "They beat the hell out of him, but I've seen him get the same one or two times before. He's a tough son of a bitch."

"Hey, watch it," Terry mumbled from Jay's lap. "The bitch is listening."

"Sorry, Mom. Figure of speech," Eric said.

"Didn't mean to wake you," Jay murmured softly. "Go back to sleep."

Terry sat up, stretched her shoulders the same way Eric had done. "Not gonna happen," she said around a yawn. "I'm too sore." After craning a look at three of her sleeping and bruised sons, she snuggled as close to Jay as she could and leaned against his side. Beneath the layer of female perspiration, the smell of Terry's jasmine perfume wafted under Jay's nose and he closed his eyes and breathed in his wife. "Okay, anyone get an idea of how to get out of here yet?" Terry asked. "There has to be a way."

"Not with these damn cuffs on," Eric said, rattling his for effect.

"I think we have to wait this out for now," Jay said. "There isn't a whole lot we can do at this point, but we've got to be prepared for any possibility."

"Such as?" Eric asked.

Jay had already spun a few ideas around. "Such as we need to be ready if Jess gets to speak to us. If I'm right and someone is using us to use her, then she'll demand to talk to one of us or all of us. If that happens we need to come up with clues. A way—or ways—for her to figure out either where we are or who has us."

"We don't know either of those things," Terry pointed out.

"Yet," Jay said. "We don't yet, but maybe we will in time, before we talk to her."

"*If* we talk to her," Danny added from his spot along the wall. He sat up and stretched as his brother and mother had. "And that's a big if."

Jay nodded. "Yes, but like I said, we have to be prepared for anything." He paused a moment as he looked around the room. "So what did we see coming into this place?" he asked.

Danny shrugged. "Other houses, hills."

"I saw the pier," Eric said. "You know, the top of the Ferris wheel."

"Yeah, I did too," Jay said, nodding again. "If we can come up with something obscure…something that won't give us away or get Jess in trouble, maybe we can give her enough clues to at least get the vicinity of where we are. If she has the vicinity and knows who's behind this, even if we don't, she'll be able get reinforcements and get us out of here."

"Whoever did this is sure determined," Terry chimed in. "They were ready with the man power and transportation for all six of us. That was one hell of a plan."

The door opened abruptly, slammed against the wall and a man walked in. Terry jumped and straightened. The sound snapped the nineteen-year-old twins awake and they sat up as well.

What caught everyone's attention first was the black mask on the man's face. It covered his eyes and nose in a Batman sort of way. It gave Jay a strange sense of hope that as long as they couldn't identify him, they had a chance of survival.

The designer suit hanging on the man's lean build easily cost three grand. Jay owned a few himself, but they were old. Back when he had his own practice and money rolled in by the wheelbarrow full, he'd splurged on the suits. Those days were long gone. He got the feeling this guy had a closet full. Two men with guns flanked his sides.

"I see everyone's here and accounted for," he said in a voice Jay didn't recognize. "Sorry it took me so long to arrive. I had other business to attend to." He put his right hand in his fancy suit and jingled the change in his pocket. His dark hair had been tamed with gel and the tan on his jaw looked like pure spray on. He perused everyone in the room with sharp eyes. "So. Who wants to die first?"

CHAPTER 4

STREETLIGHTS AND PALM TREES whizzed past as Tanner drove down Sunset Boulevard. Silence loomed in the car. Jess had already told him she worked as Juneau's assistant, but that didn't answer his other question. What did she need with that much money? Or maybe it had nothing to do with need. Maybe it was greed. He'd learned a lot about greed in the past decade. Saw what it did to his best friend and what it did to guys in the pen. How it changed people and made them something different.

Jess wasn't what he first expected. Her baby doll exterior didn't mesh with her backbone. She was scared to death of him. He saw it in her eyes, her mannerisms. The way she bit her lip and stuttered words. But she continually looked him in the eye. Faced him head on. Plus she had an attitude on top of it.

The attitude reminded him of three of his sisters. The naïve, scared part reminded him of the fourth. Not that he wanted reminders of his sisters...he didn't. He had no room for anything but revenge. He had to stay focused.

Prison had hardened him. There was always more to a person than met the eye, so he shouldn't be surprised that Jess—with her peaches and cream complexion—wanted a piece of Juneau's pie. But despite knowing that looks didn't define a person, he'd already judged her. Innocent. It wouldn't be the first time he'd been wrong. Hell, his judgment sucked harder than a category five hurricane.

She hadn't wanted to tell him about the money. He got that. It was none of his business and they probably wouldn't be spending too much time together in the distant future. But why would she be mixed up with Juneau in this way if she'd been his assistant for three years already?

"Are you blackmailing him?" It didn't seem to fit, but anything was possible.

Her jaw dropped as she stared at him. "No," she said, obviously affronted. "I... You don't know... I don't have to tell..." She faced forward, fumed. She played the innocent act like a pro.

Tanner took a closer look, which wasn't easy since he had to watch the road. Her eyes glittered with moisture. "Are you crying?"

She swiped at her eyes. "No." Her adamant tone surprised him.

Every time he meant to catch the little fluff ball, she gave him the warrior. He didn't remember women being this hard to read. Of course he hadn't been around too many women the past seven years. Like zero. Not his sisters or his mother since getting out of prison. He purposely hadn't seen any of his family for more than one reason...his dad being one of them. If he didn't see them, he could pretend his dad was still alive. Tanner quashed the errant thought before guilt swamped him.

Besides, knowing his family, they'd try to change his mind about Juneau. They would've surrounded him with things like love, support and understanding. At least they would have, before he'd turned his back on them. He had too much anger to face any other emotion. They wouldn't understand his rage. His intense need for revenge. Juneau deserved to pay for what he'd done, just the way Tanner had paid for a crime he didn't commit. His family wouldn't understand that. They'd want him to move on. Forget the past, but Tanner couldn't. He lived for the moment when Juneau felt fear. Wanted to see the man's face when he hurt.

"Watch it!" Jess screamed as the car went over the Braille line of the double yellows, and Tanner swerved back into his lane, the street lights coming back into focus. "God, you're going to kill us before we even get to Maurice," she complained. "What is wrong with you?"

Just about everything, but Tanner had no inclination to talk about himself. "If you're not blackmailing him, then what's the deal?" he asked, completely ignoring her question. If she worked with Juneau then maybe they were having, or at some point had, a fling. Maybe someone was blackmailing her. But why? "Are you married?" he asked.

She shot him a glare. "It's none of your business. And no." She wrapped her arms around her middle and her chest rose and fell with heavy breaths.

"Then why do you need the money?" When she didn't answer, Tanner pulled over and shut the car down. Several cars whizzed past. Obviously she had an agenda and he wanted answers. Her timetable seemed a little less flexible than his. Because although he wanted Juneau as soon as possible, he'd rather wait and get it right than screw up a second time.

Jess looked at him, her eyes wide. "What are you doing? We need to find Maurice." She checked her watch. She was definitely on a clock.

"I don't drive until I hear your story. Give it." He shifted in the seat and rested his forearm on the steering wheel.

She blinked, looked like Bambi just out of the smoking forest with no idea where to go or what to do. Yep, she definitely reminded him of Holly. Those big eyes, wide with uncertainty and panic. His youngest sister had taken the brunt of the abuse from her older siblings. Him included. Occasionally he'd stuck up for Holly, but most the time he'd teased her like the others. Tanner shoved the memories out of his mind.

"*I've got time,*" he said, rubbing in the fact that Jess didn't.

Her eyes brightened with unshed tears and the sight rocked Tanner. Made his stomach flip in an odd way. She averted her gaze and stared straight ahead, quickly wiping her eyes, but the damage was done. A strange sensation flexed his heart.

Her jaw clenched and she swallowed hard. In the next instant she opened the door and shot out of the car. Tanner's adrenaline soared as he lunged and caught her back leg. They both tumbled onto the roadside. She struggled beneath him as he grappled for her wrists. Hardly any traffic crowded the road since it was dead middle of the night and the few cars that traveled the street zoomed by.

Tanner's heart thumped hard as he subdued her. "Was it something I said?" he grunted, amused and slightly reverent at her attempt. She finally went limp, her eyes bright with fear as she gasped for air. Breathing hard, Tanner stilled above her. He couldn't ignore the feel of her soft body trapped under his. The way her chest rose and fell with every ragged breath. Nothing sisterly about his thoughts now. Nope, now all he pictured was naked skin and hot sex. He was a frickin' scumbag for feeling this way when she was so clearly messed up and freaking out.

"I can't….please don't…" She couldn't get the words out.

"Shh," he told her. "Shh. I won't hurt you." He wouldn't. He might scare the crap out of her, but he wouldn't hurt her. Not physically anyway. That didn't mean he wouldn't mess with her head. "Tell me why you want that money and I'll let you up." Yes, he was a bastard to the tenth power. Make sure the girl is helpless and go for the throat. Prison had been a twisted teacher.

"I can't." She hiccupped a breath, something close to a sob. Her face contorted into a mask of pain. Something so fresh and real that Tanner felt the ache in his own chest. The foreign feeling wasn't anything he enjoyed or wanted to explore. "I can't," she whispered again.

"Why not?"

She shook her head, refused to look at him.

"What are you afraid of? That I'll tell someone?" He leaned close to her ear, felt her freeze beneath him. Yeah, lying on top of her like this had his cock growing hard. Was that a surprise? She smelled so fucking sweet. At least the lower half of his body was on the ground and not her. "You don't have to worry. I don't know anyone to tell. I've got nobody that wants to talk to me or know me. Tell me your secret, sweetheart. I'll keep it safe." Probably because he wouldn't live long enough to tell anyone, but he'd spare her that information.

Her frantic heart beat hard against his chest, her breath harsh in his ear. "He'll kill them…if I tell." Her words came out on a tortured cry. "He told me he would. I can't say anything, don't you understand. I can't say anything."

Tanner met her gaze. She was for real. Fear and pain filled her pretty brown eyes. "Who is 'them?'" he asked. "Who is going to kill who? Maurice is going to kill someone?" That seemed too far out of Maurice's territory. The man was a scumbag who hired guys to do his dirty work, he didn't do it himself. Jess shook her head, but Tanner grabbed her chin and held her steady. "Tell me, Jess. We have no problems as long as you give me what I want. Tell me."

When she still didn't reply, Tanner ran his fingers through her soft hair and dipped his lips next to her ear. He didn't say anything, he just took in her scent, brushed his lips against the softness of her skin at the edge of her jaw, right beneath her ear. Not a kiss, but a caress. His lips on her skin. Goddamn…she felt so good. His heart roared in his ears. It'd be too easy to forget he'd forcefully tackled her to the ground. Too easy to strip her clothes and his pants and ease the pressure in his jeans, take the edge off his insanity. *God, what was wrong with him?*

He shifted a fraction, like he might move on her and a tiny little catch sounded in her throat. He smelled her fear and had never hated himself more.

"The sooner you tell me what I want to know, the sooner I'll get off you," he murmured, punctuating the words with another brush of his lips along her jaw. "Otherwise…" He let the sentence dangle, made sure his hot breath wafted in her ear, wanted her to worry about the consequences of now.

Desperation clouded her pixie face. "My whole family, okay? He's going to kill my whole family if I don't get his eight stupid-million dollars back! And he means it. I don't have much time."

Since she wanted eight million from Maurice, that meant someone else had her family. An unknown player he didn't want to particularly deal with. As that news sunk in his brain, bright headlights sent a harsh stream of white light over Tanner's head and he glanced over his shoulder to see the flashing reds of a police car.

His luck sucked.

JESS'S WHOLE BODY TREMBLED as Tanner moved off her and pulled her to her feet. One minute she'd been pinned beneath his hard, hot body and the next she stood with his arm draped possessively around her waist, holding her tightly to his side.

The flashing lights of the police cruiser caused a wave of hope to flood her veins. Seeing the police officer rounding the hood of his cruiser with a hand on his weapon sent her stomach into a tizzy. She could get away from Tanner! Run, scream and tell this officer that he had tried to kill her boss tonight and *still* planned on killing him. Hell, he'd shot *her!* But where was Tanner's gun? Would he kill this officer if she said something? He hadn't hesitated firing before so why would he now?

As if reading her mind, Tanner squeezed her waist. The pressure kept her silent.

"Everything okay, folks?" The officer looked older up close. Short salt and pepper hair with matching mustache. With a body still fit and healthy, the only thing that belied the man's age were the dozens of wrinkles around his eyes and mouth.

"Fine. Everything's fine," Tanner answered with another sharp squeeze. "I was trying to help her and I tripped on something…took her down with me. Sorry honey," He looked down at her with apologetic eyes. But there was a warning in his gaze.

The cop looked directly at her. "Anything you want to tell me, miss?" His brows lifted and a tiny smile curved his lips. Her stomach hit the asphalt. Her hopes vanished in a flash. She'd heard the same words from a different cop yesterday. He'd stopped her last night before she'd reached the door to her apartment. The cop had backed her up against the building and told her flat out that if she said a word to anyone, Facinetti would find out and he'd start taking lives. This officer had to also belong to Paul Facinetti. She knew it just as she knew she was safer with Tanner than with this cop.

Was Facinetti having her followed? Testing her? He must be. Making sure she wouldn't talk by sending the men he paid to scare her. He wanted his money and because he couldn't get to Maurice, he was keeping her close. There wasn't a cop she could trust. Because if she talked to the wrong guy, her time frame went to hell and Facinetti would start executing immediately.

Oh God. This guy must have followed them from the studio, but how? Had there been someone on the lot watching Maurice the whole time? Someone who saw what happened on the stage? Facinetti had men everywhere.

Tears pricked at Jess's eyes and just as quickly, anger reared up and made her chest heavy. She blinked back her emotions. "No, everything's fine. I wasn't feeling well and just needed him to pull over. I'm better now."

Tanner looked down at her, suspicion in his eyes. She moved past him and into the passenger seat. "C'mon, let's go. I'm okay." She shut the door, leaving Tanner to wonder if she'd bolt again as soon as he left her side of the car. Clearly he realized he didn't have a choice if he wanted out of here and he hustled to the driver's side and got in. He cranked the engine and a sharp rap on the window made Jess jump a mile.

The officer had his face close to the window and motioned her to roll it down. Jess did, reluctantly. "You sure you're okay?" he asked. "You look like you're bursting to tell me something."

Too parched to speak, Jess simply shook her head. "No," she finally eked out. "Nothing. Everything's fine."

The cop tapped the doorframe with a fist and smiled. "Good girl," he muttered as he straightened. "Drive carefully," he said loud enough for Tanner to hear. "Wouldn't want to see either of you injured on a beautiful night like tonight." A veiled threat if she'd ever heard one.

Tanner rolled up the electric window from his side and glided onto the street without looking back. Jess's stomach turned upside down. "Here," Tanner reached into the back and handed her a bottled water.

Jess gulped a third of it down, trying to calm her pounding heart and run-away emotions.

Now what?

She'd blurted, told him her problem. Fear and desperation had driven her to it. Lying under Tanner had brought a whole new world of problems she wasn't ready to deal with.

He'd tried to kill Maurice tonight. He'd actually shot his gun. Aimed and fired. Facinetti didn't want Maurice dead, at least not until he got his money. He was paying the cop to watch her. Maybe all the time, and he wanted her to know it. So maybe the cop took the opportunity to see whom she'd hooked up with to report back to his boss.

"You want to tell me why you went sheet-white back there?" Tanner asked, glancing at her before returning his focus on the road.

She'd already spilled the worst of it. Besides, the guy deserved to know that if he killed Maurice before Facinetti got his money, Facinetti would no doubt take his revenge out on Tanner's hide. "We're being followed," she said. "I'm being followed. But since you're driving, you are also being followed. You might want to consider letting me off at the next gas station or something." She could call a cab to take her back to the studio and pick up her car. How could this guy want the trouble she'd stepped into just by virtue of working for Maurice? Suddenly she wasn't afraid of him as much.

Tanner glanced in the mirror, made a few turns and adjusted his speed. Jess turned down the visor and looked behind them from the mirror where she saw the cop still following at a distance. After a few minutes, Tanner uttered a vicious oath. "Why didn't you tell me?" he snapped.

She nearly flinched at his tone. "I didn't know until that cop stopped for his visit. But it makes sense. He's keeping tabs on me."

"Why? Who?" Tanner demanded.

She sighed. "You have the right to know since he'll probably kill us both before this is over." More tears pricked her eyes at the thought of her family dying too. Which might happen whether she succeeded or not. "His name is Paul Facinetti and he's blackmailing me. He has my parents and my brothers, and I have to get Maurice to hand over his eight million dollars by midnight Friday. If I don't, he's going to kill one of them each day until he has his money, starting with my youngest brother." Saying it aloud made it all the more real. Made her stomach heave.

Tanner leaned his head against the headrest. "Fuck." The word was short, but heartfelt.

"Tell me about it," Jess muttered. "So you see why you can't kill Maurice. I need to get that money."

"Maurice know all this?" Tanner asked, his eyes narrow and skeptical.

"I wouldn't know because I never got that far!" Jess railed. "I was trying to talk to him when *someone* started shooting at us!" Jess took a deep breath and reined in her anger. She had to remember this man wasn't an ally. She needed to get free of him just as badly as she needed to find Maurice. Just because she'd confided in him, didn't mean she trusted him. Far from it.

Although confiding in him had somehow taken the edge off her fear, which suited her fine.

Instead of the glare she expected, he smiled and Jess's mind pulled a total blank. It wasn't a big smile, but it was lethal just the same. It transformed his face, softened his eyes and made her breath catch in her throat.

Tanner focused on the road. "I told you I was sorry." His low voice resonated in the air, but Jess ignored the way it touched her. No way was she going to let this guy creep under her defenses.

She faced him, her blood pumping hot. "No you didn't! You said you didn't mean to shoot at me. There's a big difference." She faced front and crossed her arms over her chest. The movement pulled the bandage, which made her shoulder ache, which pissed her off. A full minute of silence settled between them until Jess wanted to reach over and strangle him.

This time he looked at her. "I'm sorry I shot you," he said quietly. "I didn't mean to, didn't want to. But I haven't changed my mind about Juneau. His days are numbered." He followed the curves of Sunset Boulevard, his big hands steady on the wheel. "Tell me about this Facinetti. Who is he? Why does he want eight million from Juneau?"

Much to her annoyance, Tanner's sincere apology actually placated her. Any man who could fess up to a mistake won points in her book. Growing up with a bunch of brothers who had a hard time saying, *sorry*, Jess had come to appreciate the word more than most.

She didn't see a reason to keep the secret. Maybe Tanner needed to know what he was up against. "Paul Facinetti owns a casino outside of Vegas. As far as I can tell he's a cross between Steve Wynn and Bugsy Siegel. He's got high aspirations. He invested eight million dollars in Maurice's newest Indy film. It was half the budget. But the star pulled out then the other half of the budget backed out and Maurice had already spent half of Facinetti's money on advances, permits and miscellaneous production costs."

"What happened to the other half?" Tanner asked. "Wait, let me guess. It found its way into his pocket."

Jess nodded. "Probably, yes. I think so. But Maurice is very creative and he's made it look like all eight million is gone. I've checked the projected costs with the actual figures on his budget and it looks hinky to me." She shrugged. "I might only be his assistant, but I'm not stupid.

"Facinetti called Maurice, told him if there's no movie then he wanted his money back. Maurice's response was, 'That's show business, pal. You win some you lose some.' Then he tried to convince Facinetti to invest in another project he's got in the works. Needless to say that didn't go over well with Facinetti. A few days went by and Facinetti called again, telling Maurice that if he didn't get his money back by the end of the week, Maurice would regret it. Maurice said he didn't have Facinetti's money and that Facinetti needed to look up the word *investment* in the dictionary. Maurice then tripled his security. Which was one of the smarter moves he's made because all of a sudden strange things started happening."

"What kinds of strange things?" Tanner asked.

"A break-in at his Beverly Hills house. A hit-and-run car accident. Two guys tried to mug him outside the gym, but Maurice had enough muscle around him and never suffered a scratch."

"So Facinetti got tired of his guys missing the mark and decided to go through you." Tanner shook his head. "Fucker." He paused. "Look, no offense, but why would he think a little thing like you could do what he couldn't do?"

"Because I run Maurice's life, that's why. Not to mention half the business." She'd talked to Facinetti enough for him to figure that much out. "Facinetti must think I have access to his bank accounts or pin numbers or something…but I don't."

He glanced at her as he took another curve on the road. "This Facinetti guy has your whole family?" At her nod he shook his head, his jaw clenched tight. "What happened?"

"We were supposed to meet for dinner Saturday night for my mom's birthday." She didn't mention that it had been her birthday celebration as well. Jess swallowed the lump in her throat. "I don't know how Facinetti would have known." She shook her head, a vision of the house fresh in her memory. "I got to my parent's house and the place was trashed. Every room was upside down, everything broken. There was blood..." Tears threatened, but Jess fought them back. "I know everyone put up a fight. I can't imagine how many men it took to take them all down." She barely got the words out. Her chest constricted with emotion.

"How old are your brothers?" Tanner asked.

"Twenty-one, twenty and the twins are nineteen."

"Hell, your parents didn't waste any time, did they?"

Jess smiled at that usual response. "No, they didn't." Her cheer disappeared just as quickly as it had come. "Facinetti said they're alive, but I know they're hurt." She wiped her eyes determined to hold herself together.

"So you haven't talked to any of them?" he asked.

Jess shook her head as she blew her nose with a crumpled tissue from her pocket.

"That's what we have to do first. Did Facinetti give you a way to reach him?"

"We?" Jess couldn't help but ask. Did he seriously think to help her with this?

"Yes, we," Tanner said. He didn't take his eyes off the road. "I'll help you get the money from Juneau and get your family back safe and in return, you don't say a word when I disappear with Juneau."

A pact with the devil. He still planned on killing Maurice and she'd be an accomplice if she agreed to go along with him. Did she have a choice in the matter? Besides, wasn't there a chance Facinetti might kill Maurice once he had his money? Was that her fault? No. Maurice had dug his own grave.

Still, the part of her brain that grew up with strict morals and clear line of right and wrong screamed that she couldn't keep her mouth shut and be part of cold-blooded murder. But the other part of her brain, the side working on emotion, didn't want to hear the argument. Was Maurice's life worth that of her whole family? The answer was really simple. No. *Hell no.* Did she run the risk of spending years behind bars? Yes. But it would be worth every minute if she saved her family. Maurice stole money just as easily as he peed every morning. He lied about budgets and production costs. He lied about permits and expenses. He was a liar and her family deserved better than to die because of him.

"Deal."

CHAPTER 5

TANNER DID A DOUBLE take. He hadn't expected the almost immediate compliance. He wasn't stupid enough to think he didn't need Jess to help him get Juneau. If a pseudo mob boss, and that's what Facinetti sounded like, couldn't get to the man, then what were *his* odds? At least with Jess, he had a fighting chance. All he had to do was help her first.

Help her get Juneau to unload eight million dollars then rescue her family from God knows where. Yeah, right. No problem. While he was at it, maybe he could climb Kilimanjaro with skates. On the other hand, maybe there was another way to solve their problem. "Did Facinetti tell you specifically that he wanted the money or did he say getting his hands on Juneau would be enough? What if we got Juneau and traded him for your family?"

"I don't know," Jess said, her eyes wide. "I never asked."

"We need to contact Facinetti and get some answers. First we don't do a thing until we've talked to your parents and your brothers. Then we find out if a trade will work instead of the money."

"It might." Jess sounded hopeful for the first time and it gave Tanner a foreign sense of something he hadn't felt in years. Self-respect? Because for the first time in a long time he was doing something right? Hardly. No sense in deluding himself. He wanted the quickest way to get his hands on Juneau and if that meant helping Jess, so be it. He didn't necessarily care if someone else killed Juneau as long as the man suffered. How many different places had Tanner been cornered and jumped in prison? How many punches and kicks had he taken all because prison was a

37

violent place and Juneau had sent him there? He'd just assumed he'd be the one to inflict well-deserved damage on the bastard. But if handing him over to someone got the job done...why the hell not? The justice system sure as hell didn't work and Tanner had no way to prove he'd been railroaded other than the smile Juneau had given him at the guilty verdict and his lawyer's lack of concern.

Jess scrambled, unzipping her small dark backpack. She came up with a card in her shaking hand. "This is his number. I'm not supposed to call unless I have the money."

"Tell him you'll do better than the money and give him the man, but in the meantime, you want proof of life. You want to talk to every member of your family and then you'll bring Facinetti what he wants."

Worry crept into her shining eyes. "What if he hurts one of them because I didn't follow his instructions?"

"What if he's already killed all of them and is waiting for you to do his dirty work anyway?" Yeah, he was pond scum, but she needed to look at all the angles. Tanner's gut turned at the look of absolute horror on Jess's face.

She looked at the card wobbling in her hand. "Pull over," she said softly.

Why? Tanner went with his instinct anyway and eased the car onto the right shoulder. He'd lost their tail ten minutes ago, but still checked the rearview mirror and glanced over his shoulder at the road behind him. Empty.

Jess ran both hands through her hair giving it that electrocuted look before pulling her cell phone from her bag and punching in the numbers. After a slow, deep breath, she hit Talk and the call went through. "If you're wrong... If he hurts them..." Her dark eyes drilled into his, her face lost its pixie quality as tension streamed off her. "I'll kill you."

Tanner believed she might try. He motioned her closer so he could hear the call and Jess adjusted the phone near his ear. He smelled the last traces of her flowery shampoo mixed with a little female sweat. His blood pressure spiked, but he shut down his reaction before it got hotter. He didn't have time to think about what it might feel like to be really close to her. Close enough to get his mouth on her. Closer than he was right now with her knuckles grazing his stubble and her soft breath heating his cheek.

Dammit. Focus, Bryant.

A male voice sounded in his ear. "Ah, sweet Jess. You work fast. What do you have for me?" This had to be Facinetti. Clearly he'd been expecting her call.

Jess swallowed. "I want to talk to my parents and my brothers before I hand you what you want."

"That wasn't the deal and you don't have any bargaining power." Facinetti's tone was low, deadly.

"We never made a deal," she told him. "You took them and told me what to do. Now I'm telling you, if I don't talk to every one of them, I don't hand over the money or Maurice." She sounded as tough as any inmate he'd ever known. "And I've decided that either one will do. I'll either get you the money or the man." She took a steadying breath. The girl had balls of steel. "For all I know you've…" she closed her mouth. Maybe she didn't want to give him any ideas. Tanner didn't blame her. "I talk to them or no deal." Squeezing her eyes shut tight, she bit her bottom lip.

Facinetti paused a long time then finally said, "Hang on. It's going to take a minute." Jess's eyes flashed open and the hopeful look on her face nearly decimated Tanner. Until Facinetti said one more thing. "The next time you call this number, you'd better have my money or I will kill your youngest brother, just as I promised and I'll make the rest of your family watch. Hang up the phone and I'll call you back."

Even in the dark Tanner watched the blood drain from Jess's cheeks. The fear in her eyes multiplied. Cars whizzed past and occasionally rocked them as they waited. Jess stared at the phone as if it might reach out and bite her. The two minutes they waited felt like twenty and when the phone rang Jess jumped a mile.

Facinetti came on the line, his voice cold and heartless. "You've got sixty seconds so make it fast."

"Jess?" a man asked. "Jess? Are you there?"

Tears swam in her eyes and she nodded. "Yes. Daddy, are y-you okay?" she stuttered. That simple little trait was a good tell for Tanner. It was one more piece of information about this girl that might come in handy in the future.

"Yeah, we're fine. Just listen real good to what you're told, understand? Everything will be fine, just listen to what you're told." A sound popped through the phone line and they heard protests and a grunt.

"Daddy?" What had they done to him?

"Jess?" Her mom's voice sounded strong and sure.

"Mom? Are you okay?" Huge tears leaked from Jess's eyes.

"We're okay, baby. It feels like fifteen years since I've seen you." More shuffling happened and a sharp slap popped over the phone.

"Leave her alone, asshole!" one of her brothers called out.

Eyes widening, Jess sat up straighter in the seat, her body a mass of tension. "Eric! Eric, is that you?"

More grunting and scuffling sounds happened before another deep voice spoke. "We're okay, Junior," he said. "Good thing you're not here. You'd be miserable." This time they heard a smack and more protests.

Tears streamed down Jess's face.

"Jess, it's Danny. Don't let this asshole run you round in circles like a fucking merry-go-round." Another smack and the phone moved on.

"Hey, smelly feet, it's Blake." He sounded muffled, almost as if he was talking through a fat lip. "I could really go for a snow cone right about now if—" More scuffling sounded and Jess looked frantic as the voices protested further.

"Goddammit!"

"You son of a bitch!"

"Leave him alone!"

Everyone was yelling something different and Jess looked as if she might implode from the inside out, squeezing the hair at the top of her head like she might pull out a fistful.

Huffing sounded over the line and a man said, "Jess?"

"Brendan?" Jess's voice cracked on the edge of hysteria.

"It's okay, Little J. We're doing what we can, now it's your turn." A loud smack cracked over the wire and Jess fell apart.

"You bastard! Leave them alone!" she screamed.

"Jess." Facinetti's voice came over the line as if he had a smile on his face. "Your family paid a price because of you tonight. Don't make me have to do that again. Next time, they'll have more than a few bumps and bruises and you'll have one less brother."

"You sick bastard." The strangled words crawled from her throat. "I swear to God, you're going to—"

Tanner squeezed her thigh and shook his head when she glanced at him. No need to provoke the guy further. She might want to assassinate the man, but it would have to wait until he didn't have any leverage over her.

"The next time you call, I'll expect a trade. I get what I want, and you get your family." The phone went dead and Jess stared at it, lost in her tortured thoughts.

Tanner didn't want her falling apart any more than she already was. "That's good," he said, gently taking the phone from her grasp as the screen went dark. "They're all alive."

Jess dropped her head into her hands and sobbed, heart wrenching noises that Tanner hadn't heard since he'd been out of prison. The kind of cry that first timers sometimes couldn't hide as they realized what prison really meant. Her despair settled like thick fog inside the car and made his chest ache.

"They all seemed pretty damn tough," Tanner said quietly, a lame attempt to give her solace.

"They are." Jess lifted her head and wiped her eyes fiercely. "They'd be pissed if they saw me crying like a baby."

"You're entitled."

"Let's go." She rolled down her window as Tanner cranked the engine. "The faster we get to Maurice's place the faster I can get them back safe."

"Any idea on how we're going to do this?" Tanner had planned the studio assault to the last detail, but he didn't have a clue how to breach the man's fortress-like house in Malibu. Tanner remembered his one visit from his weekender with Alex...the weekender that changed his life. The giant gated fence didn't allow entry unless someone had a code or was buzzed in, and cameras monitored the estate.

"Yes, I'm going to walk into his house and demand that he fork over that money."

"What if he doesn't?" Despite working for him for three years, this girl apparently didn't know Juneau very well. Or at all.

She shook her head. "That's not an option. He has plenty of money. He has to do this. It's my family we're talking about. Life and death. He'll do this."

Tanner kept his mouth shut. Nope, she didn't know her boss one bit. Hadn't yet learned that the man only cared about himself. It didn't matter. If she could get them in the house, he could take over from there.

THE MALIBU HOUSE HAD never scared Jess before, but tonight it took on a personality of its own. The black wrought iron seemed more like eagle talons ready to yank her off the sidewalk and devour her. Tall shrubs made visibility into the estate near impossible. Dark shadows hid chunks of the property and gave it a haunted feel. Jess fought off a shiver.

She strode up to the iron gate while Tanner hid in the thick bushes. A last minute thought had her twirling the bottom material of Tanner's oversized T-shirt and knotting it at the back. The last thing she needed was Maurice asking her about her change of clothes or the fact that her shirt was suddenly four sizes too big.

Her pulse pounded spastically as she punched in the code and waited for the door to click open. Thank God she hadn't pushed him to get another assistant when she took over the production coordinator job. The new position happened only because Caitlin's husband had a car accident and she quit early to be with him. Knowing that after two weeks, she'd be unemployed otherwise, Jess had just managed to juggle both jobs. She had the codes to all Maurice's homes. Knew how to access each one and lock up when she left. Being his assistant gave her access to almost everything. Just not the things Facinetti had hoped for. She never imagined she'd be using the knowledge for this purpose.

The gate buzzed and Jess opened the door. Security would see her and take little notice. Although it was almost midnight and she rarely came to any of the houses this late, occasionally Maurice needed her to do something last minute during production. He was famous for leaving paperwork behind at any one of his four houses in the Los Angeles area.

Some people had way too much money.

Jess hit the button on the outside intercom and waited for one of the guys to respond. She never hit the intercom, but her excuse would justify it, and if no one answered, then they'd have to try one of Maurice's other residences. A few seconds later, Hector answered and she held in her relief. "Hi, it's Jess. You might want to check the cameras on the back of the estate. I thought I saw someone creeping around." She waited, silently counted to four and motioned Tanner forward. He ducked in after her and the door closed behind them with a click.

"You sure they didn't just see me?" he asked.

"I'm sure. I told you, the cameras only get three parts of the estate at one time. They'll be checking the sides and the back and they won't see us here. They think it's just me. Now remember, don't do anything unless I give you a sign. Once he knows what's going on, I'm sure he'll do the right thing." Jess started forward, but Tanner stopped her with an iron grip around her arm. He pulled her in close, towered over her the way he had earlier.

"This could get very hairy, Jess. Don't fool yourself into thinking that Juneau will do the right thing."

Snatching her arm out of his grasp, Jess took a step back and reclaimed her space. "He has to do the right thing. I won't accept less. This goes way beyond money." She turned and headed into the light of the wide front porch. She stuck her key in the lock and opened the door, aware of the spooky silence in the big house. Maurice had to be here. This was where he came when he had to regroup. She'd never known anyone to spend so much time in all his houses. At first she'd thought it was sweet that he used all his homes on a regular basis, as if he liked them all and couldn't decide which one to live in most. Now it dawned on her that maybe he did it as a form of protection. A way to throw off anyone looking for him.

Like an ex-con recently released from prison.

Jess didn't see how she'd get the money she needed tonight. Could a man really write a check for eight million dollars? She doubted it. She also doubted the chances of Facinetti accepting a check. But Maurice could transfer the funds. She'd call Facinetti and get an account number and have Maurice transfer the money.

Facinetti hadn't said how he wanted his money, but this seemed the most logical.

After letting herself into the house, Jess leaned against the closed door. Finally, she was free of Tanner. The safety of knowing she had Maurice's guys for protection made it easier to breathe. Once Maurice gave her the money, she'd figure out what to do about Tanner, but she'd wait on the off chance she still *needed* him.

Jess headed upstairs for Maurice's office. He'd often told her he rarely went to bed before one, choosing to work in the silence of the night. "Maurice, are you in here?" She opened the door and found him behind his desk.

He quickly rose, his eyes wide, his mouth open. "Jess, are you all right? I mean I knew you would be, but I was still worried."

Right. This from the man who'd ducked out and left her for dead when the bullets had been flying earlier. "How could you know?" she asked. "Didn't it occur to you that I might've been hurt?" She would have loved to mention the fact that she *had* been hurt—shot, no less—but that could bring up too many questions she couldn't answer. "I can't believe you left me." Surprise and hurt laced her tone.

"No one has any reason to hurt you and you're standing here healthy so... Did you call the police? What are you doing here so late?"

"No, I didn't call the police." Why hadn't *he* called them if someone wanted him dead? What was he hiding? "As far as I know no one on the lot knows anything happened." Taking a deep breath, she searched for calm. She liked her boss less and less as the minutes ticked by. "Look, we never finished our conversation before and I really need to talk to you." They had barely gotten started earlier! Maurice hadn't returned her phone calls all day until early evening when he told her to meet him on the stage. When she had, he'd had the phone practically glued to his ear.

He looked at his watch. "It's late, Jess. Just after midnight." He shook his head. "I can't believe you came all the way out here." Maurice came around his desk and tried ushering her out, but Jess pulled away from him.

"I wouldn't have made the trip if it wasn't important. I need you to listen to me." Anger knotted her throat.

Maurice lifted his arms in a gesture of innocence and leaned against his desk. "Okay, I'm sorry. What did you need?"

Eight million dollars, but she sensed the need to work up to the point. "Paul Facinetti. Does that name ring a bell?"

Maurice kept a poker face. "What about him?"

"He wants his money and I'm asking, no demanding, that you give it to him."

Maurice spread his arms, palms up. "You can ask or demand all you want and it won't matter. The movie business is a crapshoot, just like gambling, and I'm sure Facinetti will come to realize it. He took a gamble and lost. The man gambles for a living...you'd think he'd understand the concept of losing money." Maurice shrugged. "Is that all you need?" He moved toward the door again, dismissing her.

Anger and frustration swelled. "No! It's not all I need. You don't understand, Maurice. Facinetti has my family. He wants his money or he's going to kill them, so I'm telling you to give the man his money back. He isn't one of your normal investors and you can't hope that he'll just go away. Give him his damn money back." Jess worked to even out her harsh breathing.

Turning, Maurice looked shocked. "He has your family?" He lifted his eyebrows in a sorrowful gesture. "Jess, I wish I could help, but...the money's gone."

Jess's stomach flipped upside down. He was lying to her face. He had to be. "You have plenty of money, Maurice. Don't give me that crap."

"Seriously. A lot of it went to the permits, greased a few palms. It's mostly gone."

"There's no way you spent eight million dollars on a film that never saw one day of production. I've turned my head for years, Maurice, watching how you played the Hollywood game, but you're up against a man who doesn't want to play. Give him his money."

Maurice came toward her. "If he really has your family, you should go to the police."

The room started to spin. Maurice didn't seem too inclined to jump in and help resolve the situation. "I can't go to the police," she hissed, fisting her hands so tight that her nails dug into her palms. "He has cops on his payroll. Two of them have already made it clear I'm being watched and I have no idea how many more there could be. I can't take the chance he'll find out." Jess blinked back tears. "Look, Maurice, you have to do this. It isn't about the money. It's about my family. It's about doing the right thing."

"Jess, I understand. I really do. But how can I give you something I don't have?"

"But you do have it. You have four houses, cars, money in the bank. Maurice…" How could he be arguing with her on this?

"Jess, you're a sweet kid, but even if I was going to sell one of my houses or a car for you, it would take time. No body's buying anything these days. Even if it happened tomorrow it wouldn't be nearly enough money."

Jess stood there. Stunned. "I can't believe you." The sentence came out in a whisper. "How can you do this to me? I've worked my ass off for you for three years!"

"Look, I've appreciated everything you've done. I'm sure once Facinetti realizes that taking your family isn't going to get him his money, he'll let them go."

"Let them go?" she repeated. "Maurice, did you hear me? I said he's threatening to kill them." Saying it out loud made it that much more real and Jess felt the bottom drop in her stomach for a second time. Panic bubbled in her center.

Maurice just watched her. "Jess, I want to help you…but I don't honestly see how I can. I don't have the money." He shrugged as if their talk was over. "I don't know what else to tell you."

Her eyes widened. "You don't know what to tell me?" She nearly spit the words. Fury joined panic and swept through her hot and thick. Anything she said now would've come out in a stuttering mass of incoherent syllables. Oh, what she would give for some type of weapon. Something to show Maurice she meant business. That would shock the hell out of him. But with nothing to threaten him with she had to move to plan B. Time for Tanner. Tanner wouldn't hesitate to use his gun. She knew that all too well. Once she left and the house quieted down, Tanner and she could sneak back in and take Maurice. Then the man would be in her hands without the protection of his posse. He'd have to cave. Tanner would make sure of it.

"Maurice, you are seriously..." she meant to say seriously lacking scruples and honor, but a sudden commotion broke out down stairs and a bad feeling twisted her already knotted stomach. What if they found Tanner on the grounds? What if their plan to get him face to face with Maurice just crashed and burned?

Out. She needed to get out now. It's what Maurice wanted anyway so it shouldn't be too hard to convince him she was done here...and with him. "Sounds like more bad luck, Maurice. I'll let myself out the back door." Better to stay out of sight as long as possible. He didn't answer as he went behind his desk and shut down his computer. "Consider this my resignation." When she hoped to get some response from the man, he simply flattened his lips and shrugged off her statement. The creep actually thought she'd slip out of his life without another word. He had another thing coming. "I have paperwork you need and research for the next film," she told him. She would've blackmailed him with it, but suspected he'd only laugh at her. "I'll get it to you in the morning, and in return I want my paycheck for the last week. Consider yourself assistant-less."

Jess took little comfort in storming from the room. She peered over the railing as she headed to the back staircase. Two of Maurice's goons had Tanner on his knees, his arms twisted behind his back. He saw her, but didn't make an attempt to speak to her.

Think, think. There had to be a way out of this. She still needed Tanner's help if she wanted to get Maurice, but if Maurice thought she knew Tanner then she wasn't going anywhere either. She doubted Tanner would mention her in any way.

Moving down the hallway to the gym, Jess found a baseball bat in a closet filled with every piece of sports equipment imaginable. Tanner's gun would be in the wrong hands at this point, and a bat was better than nothing. Jess hugged the wall, backtracking quickly to the bathroom next to the office. She closed the door and held her breath, listening for any sound.

The massive gray granite bathroom was about half the size of her apartment. As many times as she'd used this room, she'd never gotten used to its ostentatious amenities. Easily eight feet of wide-open space rested between each wall. Would that help her or hurt her when it came time to listen? She eased toward the door that led to the office.

It took two agonizing minutes of waiting before she heard more scuffling as the men dragged Tanner up the stairs. Jess strained to listen as the struggle continued in the next room.

"Tanner Bryant," Maurice said. "What a surprise. I didn't realize they'd let you out."

"Why? I did most of my time. You made fucking sure of it."

Maurice just chuckled. "I did do that. But a father's got to protect his son. I'm sure you understand."

"I understand I did the time that Alex should've done. I understand you threw me to the wolves to save Alex and didn't bother saying anything after he died."

Information overload. Jess tried to absorb everything, but her heart pounded too hard. Her palms sweat furiously as she gripped the bat.

"I didn't see a point," Maurice said.

"No point in freeing an innocent man," Tanner scoffed. She heard him struggle, heard the muffled sound of a punch and a grunt, squeezed her eyes shut to block it out.

How had this become her life? So much violence and pain. Physical, emotional. Jess had never dealt with anything like this before. Her stomach threatened a revolt and she swallowed convulsively.

"I'll bet you were the one shooting at me earlier, weren't you," Maurice went on to say. "I thought it might be Facinetti again, but it was you."

"Fuck you, Juneau. You've screwed too many people. I'm not the only one you need to worry about. You've fucked over so many people that you've got no idea who wants you dead. Hell of a way to live your life."

Another punch sounded and Jess felt the sting of tears in her eyes. Maurice had let Tanner do time for a crime his son committed. The unfairness made her nausea worse.

"I won't have to worry about you anymore, Bryant. You're

going to be another ex-con who disappeared because he couldn't cut it on the outside. Take care of him," Maurice said. "Dump him in the desert or the ocean. I don't care. I'm heading to the penthouse and I'm taking the other guys with me."

"No problem," one of them said.

"Just don't do it here. There's enough blood on my floor as it is. Clean this shit up. I don't want anything out of place the next time I get back."

Jess heard Maurice leave the room, heard the guys murmuring. She didn't have time to think about the orders he'd given because if she did, she'd lose it. If she didn't act now, she'd be too late. After a flurry of footsteps moving downstairs, she eased out of the bathroom and peeked through the railing. Maurice walked toward the side door toward the garage with his men behind him. She didn't have much time. She had to create some kind of diversion.

Jess went back to the bathroom, closed the door, grabbed the handle and started shaking. "Hey, get me outta here," she called. "Maurice, get me outta here. The door is stuck! Maurice, are you there?" She heard one of the men coming closer. "Maurice, is that you? I thought you got this door fixed."

"Hey, what's wrong?" the guy said.

"The door's jammed. Can you give a hard push and get me out of here?" She held it tight as he tried to jiggle the handle, but when he stopped, Jess stood off to the side with her bat ready, glad the opulent bathroom afforded her room. Two seconds later the door slammed open. The man's momentum brought him forward and Jess didn't waver. Taking a step into the swing, she whaled her bat over the guy's shoulder and he hit the deck with a hard thump. Time sped up and slowed down simultaneously as Jess readied the bat for another shot. But the guy didn't move. He had long dark hair stuffed into a messy ponytail. She didn't recognize him. He must've been a new hire since the threats from Facinetti started. A delayed bout of shakes took over as her arms quivered and her heavy breathing faltered. No time to faint now.

"Rico?" A man's voice came from the office. It sounded like Dev. He'd worked for Maurice for almost two years now. He was a bald-headed giant, and Jess had always gotten along with him. He was quiet, but loyal. "What's up? You okay?"

Panic seized her. What now? Frozen in her spot, Jess grunted then rolled her eyes. Yeah, as if he'd buy *that* response. When she didn't hear anything, she eased out of the bathroom and down the hallway toward the door, her bat ready.

"Let's go, man," Dev said to Tanner. "I don't know your beef with Juneau, but if he says you gotta go, then you gotta go."

Jess peeked in just as Dev raised his gun. Oh, God! She didn't have a choice but to hit him! Tanner's eyes widened, whether because he saw her or because he had a gun pointed at his chest, she wasn't sure. With a surge of adrenaline, she took two big steps into the room and whacked Dev at the base of his skull. A dull thud rent the air. He landed hard on the floor and Jess stared at him dumbfounded. She'd become a one-woman demolition team and this time she'd taken out a man she considered a friend. Not that they were good friends, but they both liked basketball and razed each other about their favorite Los Angeles teams. Another round of shakes took hold and her vision blurred.

"Nice swing."

Jess blinked, cleared her vision as she looked at Tanner. He stood about six feet away from her, a grim smile on his face. He had a split lip and swollen eye. Sweat coated his skin. He took a step toward her and wobbled before correcting himself. Apprehension crept on her slowly as he looked at his side, surprise lighting his face. Blood seeped through his dark t-shirt and he wobbled some more.

Her fault! Dev's gun had gone off after she'd hit him. He wouldn't have shot Tanner in the office, especially after Maurice's warning. It didn't matter now. She'd blown it big time. The room started spinning again and Jess struggled to stay on her feet.

With wide eyes, Tanner looked at her. "Uh-oh." He put a hand to his side and blood quickly trickled over his fingers. "Shit. I hadn't planned on this." Then he fell back against the desk.

CHAPTER 6

TANNER BLINKED AWAY HIS dizziness. Watching Jess sway in front of him worried him more than the stinging in his side. He'd barely felt the shot, so it couldn't be too bad. Still, checking it out now, when Jess seemed as if she might hit the deck, probably wasn't his best plan. He moved toward her, wiping his bloody hand on his jeans and ignoring the pain as it arced up his body and finally screamed into his brain.

Her method of attack had been appreciated, just not well staged. The bozo with the gun probably hadn't intended to shoot him in the office, but Jess's opportunity had been limited too, so he understood her thinking. *Attack while she had a back.* On the other hand, if the guy had intended to kill him here, he'd have a bullet through his heart right about now so her timing worked fine.

As much as he wanted to just leave the house, he couldn't let these two dick heads wake up and sound an alarm. But where could he stash them? "Is there a live-in staff here?" he asked, swiping the man's gun from the floor. Jess kept her gaze glued to his side, her eyes wide. Tanner gently shook her shoulders. "Jess, look at me." Her brown eyes met his, but he saw something besides panic and fear. Empathy? Compassion? Two emotions he didn't want or need. "Answer me, Jess. Does anyone else live here?"

She shook her head. "He has a cleaning crew once a week but they were here yesterday."

"Any idea when he'll come back here?"

"Probably not until late tomorrow at the earliest. Or maybe not for a day or two. He skips between all his houses whenever he wants. Especially lately."

Late tomorrow still gave them plenty of time for what Tanner had in mind. It took him and Jess about fifteen minutes—and more blood spilled than he would've liked—but they got both men into the wine cellar below the house. He gagged them, tied them up and left them for the next person who got thirsty and wanted wine.

Taking her arm, he led her out of the house, checking the yard before he continued. "If you're keeping track it might make you feel better knowing you weren't the only one shot tonight."

"I'm n-not and it doesn't." Her voice shook and she looked damn pale in the moonlight. Her eyes had that extra bright glaze that screamed *freaked out.*

Tanner tossed Jess his keys. She fumbled before catching them. Maybe if he forced her, she might snap out of her little trance. Not that he could blame her for her current state of mind. Tonight's roller coaster had been one big drop and turn after another. "You okay driving?" he asked.

She swallowed. "I can't. I n-need a minute."

Tanner gripped her upper arm, forced her to look up at him. "You did great in there, Jess. Really stellar. But don't fade on me now. We need to get out of here ASAP. Before anyone else shows up. Do you understand me?"

She nodded then glanced at his side. "We need to get you to a doctor."

Did she care or was she trying to find another way to get rid of him?

Tanner didn't want to agree with her, but she was right. He felt the blood dripping into the waistband of his jeans. But he couldn't go to just any doctor. Couldn't walk into a hospital without answering questions or without the cops being called. He ushered Jess to the driver's side and urged her in the seat before crossing to the passenger side and sitting down, taking a deep breath as pain exploded in his side.

Oh, yeah, getting shot sucked.

He reached into the duffle bag at his feet and came up with a ratty piece of paper with a phone number and address. He double checked the numbers and handed it to Jess. "Go here," he told her.

Jess scanned the paper, cranked the engine and made a U-turn. "I can get us headed in the right direction, but you need to plug the address in my phone's GPS to find it."

Tanner had purchased a new Thomas Guide and had practically memorized the damn thing to be familiar with Hollywood and Burbank. Having been in prison for so long made him woefully outdated with high tech equipment, including Jess's phone. He'd wanted to bag Juneau and it took a ton of planning. Figuring out how to get on the studio lot, making sure Juneau would be on the stage... He'd planned everything to the detail. But he hadn't counted on missing his target, getting involved with Jess, taking this side trip *or* taking a bullet. Shit. He pulled out the cell phone wedged in his back pocket and called the number he'd memorized. He could navigate as soon as he made this call.

"This better be good, *vato*. It's after midnight." The man sounded just like his old cellmate.

"Victor, I'm a friend of Chino's. He told me I could call if I ran into some trouble." Tanner waited for the man to make the connection, listened to sheets rustling on the other end of the phone. Moonlight lit the Pacific Ocean and waves crashed silver and black onto the beach to his right. Under normal conditions he might've stopped to enjoy the space, the freedom, but right now his side throbbed with a different need. Maybe one day he'd come back. If he didn't get himself killed before then.

"Bryant?" Victor asked.

"Yeah."

"You been out barely a month, dude. What kinda trouble you in?"

"Enough."

"You know where I am?"

"Yeah. Chino gave me the address. It's going to take me a few minutes to get there."

"I'll be here." The connection ended and Tanner pocketed his phone, feeling the burn in his side with the movement.

"Who's Victor and who's Chino?" Jess asked as she kept a steady speed down Pacific Coast Highway. She was paying attention now, her senses visibly more alert than they were five minutes ago and relief eased through Tanner.

He had no reason not to tell her. After saving his life, he owed her the truth. "Chino was my cell mate. Victor is his older brother. A medic."

"That's lucky."

"If you can call getting shot lucky."

She glared at him before focusing on the road. "I think we're both lucky we're not dead." He liked hearing the snap in her voice. Glancing at him again, she took a steadying breath, as if she needed it for strength. "Why were you in prison?" she asked.

He gave her credit for the question. If he'd been an ax-wielding murderer, she'd probably rather not know. But he wasn't and she deserved some reassurance. She was safe with him. Relatively speaking. "Armed robbery and attempted murder." No need to beat around the bush, since that's what he'd done time for.

"You didn't do it, did you?" Her tone very clearly implied that she believed him innocent, which meant she must have heard his conversation with Juneau.

"A judge and jury said I did. Apparently that's all that matters."

"Not to me," she said.

She barely knew him, but her belief planted a foreign seed of warmth in his gut. Just as quickly as it blossomed, Tanner quashed it. Bitterness rose in his chest. He didn't want her pity. Maybe that's what spurred her sudden change of heart. Why the hell had she helped him at Juneau's house when she could've been rid of him? Instead she'd wielded a baseball bat and saved his life. He should be grateful, but he was pissed. At himself, her, at Alex and Juneau…even his own father. At the whole fucking world. He couldn't face his family and barely tolerated his own reflection. He'd been railroaded seven years ago and all that time in prison had changed him.

"Don't think that I'm some good guy because I didn't commit the crime I was put away for. I'm not innocent. I'm just doing this backwards. I already served the time so I might as well do the crime and Juneau's going to be the victim. I still need you to get to him. I'm still holding you to our deal."

She nodded. "I know. I'm not backing out." Instead of more

questions, she kept a steady pace to Victor's house in Inglewood. With no traffic and the phone's GPS, they made great time. Jess pulled up in front of the house, scurried to Tanner's side and helped him out of the car. His T-shirt and jeans had soaked up a healthy amount of blood, but Tanner had kept pressure on the wound and the bleeding had slowed. Jess wrapped his arm around her shoulders and the contact hit Tanner like a punch. She might be small, but she was strong. Did a damn fine job of taking his weight. Her back and shoulders tensed under his body, but not the way they had earlier. She wasn't scared of him anymore.

He'd have to fix that.

Because he wanted her scared. Scared was better than the alternative. Scared kept people on their toes. Kept a person alive. He'd had to deal with fear every single day in the pen. Wondering if today was the day he got knifed in the back. Was today the day he wouldn't be able to handle an attack? Being scared had kept him sharp and he needed Jess to be in that state of mind. It wouldn't do her any good to think of him as the good guy.

He wasn't, and hadn't been in seven long years.

How had he kept his nose clean his whole life, only to blow everything when he landed in college? The answer blasted in his brain. His family. His older sisters had kept him on the straight and narrow in school. He hadn't thought much about it then, but all those years in a cell had cleared the picture. They'd never bullied, but they'd suggested and guided. They'd helped him make the right decisions. Maybe that was why he'd hooked up with Alex so quickly in college. He'd had the chance to cut loose, to be the life of the party. Those four months with Alex in Los Angeles had been wild. Look where that got him.

A shot of pain took Tanner out of his thoughts as he took the first step onto the uneven sidewalk.

The small house had a weak yellow porch light that threw gloomy shadows across the front walkway. Dark shutters surrounded two front windows and set off light stucco walls. Spring flowers bloomed in the planter boxes surrounding the yard.

The front door opened and a man stood in the doorway. He

was a smaller version of Chino with the same wide shoulders and pit-bull stance. But unlike Tanner's bald cellmate, Victor had jarhead stubble and a dark mustache.

"Bryant?" At Tanner's nod, he held out a hand and Tanner took it. "I'm Victor," he said. "C'mon in. I've got a room in the back. Let's see what you've got going on." He led the way through a small, homey house, past a den and kitchen until they reached another room full of medical supplies. A gurney occupied the far corner and shelves stacked with equipment covered the walls. He turned on bright overhead lights that made the space resemble a treatment room.

"Have a seat." He gestured to the gurney and Tanner eased onto it. "Take off your T-shirt," he said, glancing over his shoulder.

Tanner hadn't wanted to with Jess standing there, but he couldn't really argue if he wanted medical attention, so he stripped off his T-shirt.

Her eyes widened in her pale face and she quickly turned away. It could've been the wound that had her squeamish or the handful of scars that marked his chest...all courtesy of a prison stay. The day he lost count of the times he'd been forced to fight was the day he decided Juneau had to suffer. Tanner took his first look at the wound. Not as bad as he'd first thought. The pain had ebbed to a dull throb. The bullet had whizzed past, taking a small chunk of his side with it.

Victor snapped on some latex gloves. "Lie down," he said. "Let's take a look." Tanner complied and Victor splashed brown disinfectant over the wound then probed and prodded until his side burned with fresh pain.

"Chino's worried about you," Victor muttered as he cleaned out the wound.

"That's his problem," Tanner hissed through gritted teeth. Hot pain lanced his side. "Fuck. Take it easy, man."

"Why? You can take it. You're a tough guy. Don't need anybody or anything as long as you get your revenge. You finally get out of that pit just to do something that's going to put you back? Stupid *pendejo*," he muttered.

Another arc of pain pierced Tanner's side and he hissed out a breath. "Chino's got a big mouth. I didn't need his lecture and I don't want one from you."

Victor smiled grimly and lifted thick dark eyebrows. "He knew you'd get yourself into fast trouble and he was right." He pulled out a hooked needle and some suture line. "Do yourself a favor and stop now. Go back to your family and fix your life."

As if that was even possible. He wouldn't be able to face his family even if he wanted to. He'd hurt his mother and his sisters and the damage was irreparable. He'd shut them out to the point of no return. He might have had a shot with them before his father died, but now... "It's too late for that. I don't have a family."

"Bullshit," Victor said. "You're just too fucking stubborn to open your eyes and see the truth."

JESS MADE HERSELF AS still and small as possible while she listened to the hushed conversation between Tanner and the medic. Though she didn't pride herself on eavesdropping, it seemed to be the only time she got any useful information about the man who'd suddenly fallen into her life.

The conversation came to a halt when Victor started stitching the wound. At least she thought that's what he was doing. Thankfully, his body blocked her view. One certificate on the wall verified that Victor Gonzalez was for real, a medic in the United States Army. Or maybe a former medic. The certificate was dated eight years ago. But this setup looked well used. Whether he still worked for Uncle Sam or a local hospital, he clearly helped people here in Inglewood who wouldn't normally get help. Like gangbangers. Or Tanner.

Tanner wasn't what he wanted her to believe. He intimidated through his bulk, his attitude, but underneath lurked someone very different. One sign of his vulnerability came when he'd seen the blood on his side. The surprise in his eyes showed a picture of a man not so full of confidence. He may have thought himself invincible, but obviously he'd learned how wrong he'd been. The more she replayed the night's events the more convinced she became. His expression when she'd opened her eyes in his room. His consideration of her injury...and the guilt she'd seen in his eyes, when she mentioned it. He'd taken her not because she'd seen him, but because he felt obliged to make sure she was all right. He hadn't tied her or gagged her. Instead, he'd made a deal with her.

Fact of the matter was that she *would* need him when it came to Maurice. Maurice didn't think she'd do anything further to get the money she needed. He'd blown her off as usual. He didn't realize how desperate she was. Idiot. But Tanner might be able to scare the money out of him. A gun should make a man do about anything to stay alive and from the way Tanner spoke, he had no qualms about killing Maurice. Which seemed fair since Maurice didn't show any remorse when it came to "taking care of" Tanner or not helping her family. She wouldn't have believed it if she hadn't heard it for herself. Maurice was Mr. Slick. Had he always been so heartless and she'd just never seen it before? How could a man just order another man's death?

How could Facinetti threaten her entire family? Jess wanted to scream thinking about her parents and brothers bound and gagged, waiting to die. It made her angry enough to kill. A shiver raced down her back. Being a party to murder didn't sit well with her no matter what the circumstances.

But if they really did trade Maurice for her family, then Tanner wouldn't have to murder him and what Facinetti did was his problem. At least Tanner would be clear of Maurice's death and wouldn't have to go back to prison. Would Tanner care who killed Maurice as long as he died?

Was she really arguing with herself about *who* would kill Maurice as opposed to finding a way to keep the man alive?

Either way, the trick was getting to Maurice. She—they—should do it tonight in case his guys woke up, escaped the wine cellar and gave him the news that Tanner had escaped. Of course, Maurice had no reason to think she and Tanner were allies. Even though she'd quit her job, she still had access to everything. Maurice wouldn't start changing things until tomorrow at the earliest. No, the trick wasn't how she'd get into Maurice's penthouse on Wilshire Boulevard, the trick was getting him out, and she didn't have much time to work with.

After a few minutes, Jess peeked over her shoulder and watched Victor work. His body still blocked the wound, but her gaze roamed to Tanner's very impressive chest and shoulders. She'd never seen a man as cut. Absolutely ripped. His biceps curved impressively as he clenched his fists against the pain. A handful of scars marred his chest and arms. Long slices and round puckered nicks. The man had seen pain before tonight. A layer of sweat coated his skin and he gleamed under the bright light.

"Can't you give him a local or something?" Jess asked. She hated pain. Hated seeing other people in pain even worse. Maurice had broken his collarbone two months ago and had been in serious pain for weeks because of an infection after surgery. Every grimace had gone straight to her heart and she'd done everything in her power to make him more comfortable. Now she wished she hadn't been so sympathetic.

Victor glanced over his shoulder. "I could give him some lidocaine, but I try to discourage action that lands my patients on this gurney. They tend to stay clear of stupid activity if the visit here hurts as bad or worse than the actual injury."

"Spoken like a man who's never had stitches without painkillers," Tanner muttered.

The medic finished stitching Tanner's side and gave him antibiotics. Showed him how to clean the wound, change the bandages and included her as he spoke. "I used catgut, so your body will absorb the sutures." Maybe he thought she'd be helping. He didn't know the sight of blood was one of the triggers for her passing out.

"When was your last tetanus shot?" Victor asked.

Tanner shook his head. "I don't know."

Victor opened a cabinet and took out a huge needle. With his back to her, he worked at the counter and when he turned around, he took Tanner's arm and gave him a shot.

"Fuck!" Tanner clenched his jaw hard.

"Did I forget to say this might hurt?" Victor asked. He smiled grimly. "Where are you going after this?"

Tanner's dark gaze captured hers. Where were they going? It seemed crazy to try for Maurice again now. He'd probably be taking extra precautions after everything that happened tonight. There was always Tanner's place in Hollywood, if he'd deign to tell her the address. Did he expect her to stay glued to him until this got resolved? Didn't he understand the time bomb hanging over her family's heads?

She wasn't scared of him anymore. Not the way she had been initially. Clearly there was more to Tanner than he let on and whether she liked it or not, she'd made a deal with him. He said he'd help get her family back and she needed help.

"Let me ask a different question since that one stumped both of you," Victor said. "How far away is the bed he'll be sleeping in tonight?"

Again she locked eyes with Tanner. His were dark, intense.

Her parent's Hancock Park house was twenty minutes away. A little closer than his hotel.

"Twenty minutes," she said at the same time he said, "thirty minutes."

"Perfect." The medic wielded another needle and pumped it into Tanner's arm.

"What the hell was that?" Tanner snapped.

"Sedative. With your size and the amount I gave you, you've got about twenty minutes before you'll be out on your ass. I suggest you hurry home."

"Goddammit, Victor, I didn't want a fucking sedative." Tanner sat up and swayed. Victor steadied him with a grip on his arm.

"I know and I don't usually give 'em." He smiled again, his eyes gleaming. "It's just my little way of slowing down your stupidity. You can thank me later and you can consider this *my* thank you for watching Chino's back."

Victor helped Jess get Tanner into the car, and she drove fast and furious toward the home she grew up in. Tanner looked dazed, out of his element. Now was as good a time as any to ask the question that had been burning in her head for a while.

"What did Maurice have to do with you going to prison?"

Tanner rested his head against the back of the seat. "He hired me a real good lawyer. A lawyer so good he made absolutely certain I'd go to prison instead of Alex."

"Alex is—was Maurice's son, right? He died about a year before Maurice hired me." Jess had only seen pictures of the man. He'd been in his early twenties when he died. From what Jess had discovered, he'd overdosed and it had devastated Maurice.

"Bingo," Tanner said. "He was also my best friend. My best friend who robbed a convenience store and let me drive away without saying a word. I had no idea when the cops stopped us that I was going away for the next seven years. Juneau made sure Alex got off and pinned the whole thing on me."

"Oh my God," Jess whispered. The idea appalled her. Having seven years of his life taken from him...hard to comprehend. "I'm sorry."

"Yeah...me too." His chuckle surprised her and Jess looked over to see him shake his head. "Alex was fucking nuts. He lived life on the edge. Was always looking for the next high. I'd never met anyone like him." Tanner's words slowed as the drug settled in. The hard edge in his eyes disappeared as a smile curved his lips and softened the hard planes of his face. "I remember one time, Alex got us into a bar downtown. He just slipped the bouncer some bills and we cruised in like we owned the place. God, what a night we had..." His smile dimmed. "He almost always got what he wanted."

"Almost?" Jess took advantage of the sedative working in his bloodstream.

"He never got his daddy's attention." Tanner leaned his head against the seat. "Not until the trial." Tanner didn't say anything else. What was the point? His best friend had let him take the fall. No wonder the man was filled with rage.

Jess pulled up to her house just in time. Tanner could barely keep his eyes open. She tucked the car into the garage and helped him out, slinging his arm around her neck and wedging her shoulder under his armpit. The man was a bona fide tank, made of solid muscle. He weighed a ton.

Opening the side door brought back the terror. The sheer panic of walking in yesterday—except now it was officially two days ago—and finding the house bloody and demolished. She'd cleaned what she could, but the destruction was evident in the red spots on the carpet and the dents in the walls.

Jess barely got Tanner into her brother's room before he passed out. Eric had a double bed, but Tanner filled it with his huge body. He didn't look any less dangerous with his eyes closed and body prone in sleep. She covered him with a quilted blanket her mom had made, ran her hand over the soft fabric.

Her mom had been miserable making this quilt. "My first and last," Terry St. John had vowed six years ago. Terry never let a challenge go by and that included a dare of quilting a blanket. Her mom had done almost everything once. From mountain climbing and sky diving to water skiing and tennis. If she hadn't participated in a sport, then it hadn't been invented yet.

She had more energy than ten people put together, which she'd needed to raise five kids, four of whom were rambunctious boys.

Exhaustion crept up on Jess as she wandered the house, fixing things she'd missed the other day. The clock on the wall said two-thirty a.m. She hadn't slept in two days and her lids felt weighted with bricks. Obviously, finding Maurice tonight wasn't going to happen, so maybe she needed to recharge. With a clear mind, she'd be able to figure out how to get Maurice away from his "guys" long enough to get him into Tanner's hands. Long enough to either get the money she needed or trade her lying boss.

CHAPTER 7

TANNER HEARD THEM COMING, felt his pulse rev. He canted his head, saw four of them this time. All big, bald, ugly and tattooed within an inch of their lives. He wouldn't come away unscathed. But he wouldn't die. Not today. At least he hoped not.

Dark clouds covered the sun and made the dry desert scenery stark. Barren. Dirt, cactus and tumbleweeds didn't compare to the lush green Colorado mountains where he'd grown up. The prison fence closed around him, afforded no way out. But how many times had this happened in the past four years? How many times would it happen until they left him alone? Or killed him. The answers really didn't matter. The one important thing that kept him focused was survival. He had to survive to even the score.

The first one attacked. Tanner ducked and all but threw him over his head. A second one grabbed his arms from behind and Tanner used him as leverage to kick another in the chest. He did the same with a different guy, but this time the force took him backward into the man behind him and they tumbled to hard-packed earth. Tanner turned and shoved his forearm under the man's throat, cut off his air.

Sweat popped out on Tanner's forehead, slicked his arms as he gasped for breath. With a little more pressure he could make sure this guy never bothered him again.

Someone beat on his back, a feeble attempt to get his attention considering how he'd taken all these men down. Pain lanced his side and he groaned, but kept the man pinned. A second blow to the same area had him rolling over in agony. He fell. The ground disappeared and his body slammed against hard surface, jolting him.

Tanner's eyes snapped open. He was on a wood floor, breathing hard. Early dawn barely lit the room. His side throbbed like hell and pain rumbled across his body. A ceiling fan hummed softy and circulated cool air over his sweat-coated skin. Tangled sheets draped off the bed. A tall oak bookshelf sat next to a similar desk along the wall in front of him. On his right, a mirrored closet door reflected the beating he'd taken last night at the hands of Juneau's men. He didn't recognize the room as he sat up on his elbows.

But he recognized the woman huddled in the far corner, her eyes wide, glassy with tears and a hand over her throat.

"Jess..." He whispered her name, barely got it out as the entire picture cleared in his brain. He'd been dreaming. Dreaming of a fight...of choking a man. But shit. Instead of strangling a man in his dreams, he'd almost killed Jess. "Jesus, Holy fuck, Jess?" He made a move toward her on his hands and knees and she held up a wobbly hand, warning him back, shaking her head. The terror in her eyes decimated him. He sat, took a deep breath. "Goddammit, I didn't mean to hurt you. I don't want t—" He dropped his head in his hands, shame swamping him the way it usually did when he fucked up. Just as quickly he forced another look at her.

She nodded as one slow tear streaked down her face. She pointed to his side. "I opened up your wound." Her gravelly voice whispered over the quiet room. Blood stained the fingers she pointed with and Tanner looked at his side. She'd grabbed him or punched him to get him off her. Smart girl. "You were dreaming," she whispered. "I tried to wake you up and you...you..."

Attacked her. He'd attacked her in her own home. She'd saved his life last night and he'd repaid her by nearly choking her to death.

Tanner fell back against the floor. He should never have touched her, or taken her out of that soundstage. The day he got his gun, he should have used it on himself. But he'd wanted to use it on Juneau first.

"I'm sorry," Tanner murmured. He covered his eyes with an arm, couldn't look at her. "I'm sorry." Sorry he'd shot her. Sorry he'd made her part of his twisted scheme to get Juneau. Sorry he'd barged into her life like a runaway train. It took a minute, but he finally faced the music and sat up. She hadn't moved from her spot in the corner, but her eyes were clear. A thick red line the size of his arm marked her neck and fresh guilt ate him up.

"Does that happen a lot?" Her brows quirked up in a leery arch.

"The dreams?" Or nearly killing an innocent woman? She nodded and he owed her the truth. "Yeah. The dreams happen a lot. But I've never attacked anyone because of them before. I'd like to say this was a first and a last."

Her eyes widened a fraction before she swallowed and slowly stood. "Next time I'll poke you with a broom stick or something,"

Tanner almost grinned. She hadn't asked him to leave or made him feel worse. She'd made a joke. A minute ago, he doubted anything would make him feel better, but she'd managed to take the edge off. "That might be a good idea," he said.

"Or maybe I'll throw a bucket of water over you."

That single sentence took him back more than ten years. To the time he and his sisters were washing the family cars for extra money. The girls had ganged up on him and dumped a bucket of cold, soapy water over his back. He'd retaliated by spraying them with the hose. His dad had stormed out of the house, yelling for them stop. He'd confiscated the hose and lined them all up on the driveway. They'd all been sure they were going to be grounded for a month, but with a wicked grin, Dad stated. "He who controls the hose is master." Then he'd doused them all senseless. The ensuing water fight had lasted a solid hour with massive bouts of squawking, squealing and yelping. Tanner couldn't remember a time he'd laughed harder.

Pushing the memory from his mind, he nodded. He might've smiled at Jess's wry statement, but felt like too much of a scumbag. "Are you okay?"

"I think so. I'm sorry I hurt your side. We should check the stitches."

Tanner saw the blood on his shirt. Not a lot, but it had seeped through the bandages. They'd need to be changed and he'd need Jess to help him. The minute she put her soft little hands on him, his cock would jump, grow rock hard and he'd be in a different kind of pain the rest of the day.

Fuck that.

"I can do it. I need to get used to changing them myself anyway. I'll let you know how it looks."

She eyed him suspiciously and slowly shook her head. "No, you won't." He started to protest and she cut him off. "Oh, you'll change the bandages, but you won't tell me if you need more stitches. I have a feeling Victor was right. None of his patients want to go back to him anytime soon." Jess eased by him. "He gave me extra bandages last night. I'll get them for you."

She'd nearly moved past him when Tanner snagged her ankle with his hand. She froze.

He looked up, caught her gaze. That same energy that bounced between them yesterday sizzled up again now. Even through her jeans he felt the tensile strength of her leg. She was tough. Tougher than he'd pegged her for when he'd first seen her arguing with Juneau. The longer he spent with her, the more she impressed him. His sisters would've approved and they'd always been tough critics when it came to the girls he'd brought home. Not that he ever planned to bring someone home again.

But she stared down at him now and he said, "I'm really sorry."

Jess nodded. "I know." She eased her leg from his grasp and left him on the floor.

AN HOUR LATER, THE doorbell chimed. Tanner had refused Jess's help and cleaned his wound himself. He assured her she hadn't pulled out any stitches, but it didn't make her feel better. It was crazy but she felt guilty that she'd hurt him. Grabbing his side had been the only thing she could think of to get him off her. He'd taken her down so fast...pulled her beneath him on the bed with lightning speed. She fought back a shudder remembering his strength, the way he could've snapped her like a twig. That was one lesson hard learned, but she wouldn't make the same mistake twice. She rarely did.

They'd been discussing her plan to snag Maurice. It seemed too simple to work, but Jess figured that's what made it a possibility.

Now, Jess went to the door, leery because of the early hour.

Who'd be at the door at six in the morning? Tanner followed her, staying low and out of sight from the front windows. She checked the peephole but didn't see anybody and after opening the door a fraction, she spotted a small brown box on the doorstep. Clear tape kept it closed and her name was printed neatly across the top. A wave of dread cycled through her stomach. Small boxes delivered by invisible people? Not good.

With a trembling hand, she took the package and locked the door, showing Tanner as she headed into the kitchen for a knife. "No return address," she told him.

"I didn't think there would be," he said. "Here, let me." He set the box on the table, took the knife and sliced open the top, careful not to upset the contents. He peeled back the cardboard and a note lay on the brown tissue paper.

Tanner picked it up by the corner and read. "A token to remind you of what's at stake." He swallowed and looked at her before pulling back the tissue paper.

Jess tried to make sense of what she saw. Three familiar earrings, but something else... Oh God. Her stomach heaved. They were Brendan's earrings. Along with flesh and blood. Part of an earlobe was still attached to the jewelry. *Brendan's* earlobe. Jess ran for the kitchen sink, her gut churning with nausea, bile thick in her throat. Despair hit so hard she couldn't breathe, couldn't think.

How could this be happening? Why did such sick people exist in the world?

Anger flared and pushed over despair. She hated Maurice for putting her and her family in this position. But she hated Facinetti more. He was an animal. She'd do anything to see him go down. Jess got control of her nerves and the dry heaves stopped. She wiped tears fiercely from her cheeks before turning to Tanner.

He hadn't moved from his spot. His dark eyes watched her intently, focused, ready for anything. Well, he'd damn well better be because she wasn't backing down. All her life she'd been "the good girl." She'd helped raise her little brothers and as a role model, she'd taught them right from wrong. She'd almost always taken the high road instead of face confrontation. She'd begged her brothers to turn the other cheek. But sometimes a person couldn't look away. Sometimes a person needed to take action.

The thought of Brendan bleeding, of his pain...

Jess took a deep breath. She had no qualms about what she needed to do.

"Let's get started. You need something to wear. I want Maurice now. That SOB is going to pay for this. Then Facinetti is going to pay." They'd already discussed how to get into Maurice's penthouse and get him to her car. It was the only viable plan. Jess straightened her shoulders. She grabbed the breath mints on the table and popped two into her mouth. Maurice didn't have a clue as to her capabilities. She couldn't wait to show him.

Tanner stopped in front of her on the way out of the room. "You sure you're okay?"

His size, his strength, fed her hope. She had a real chance at making this work with his help.

He had to drive her to the studio to pick up her car, but once they'd done that, everything would start. Jess had her job and Tanner had his. Maurice had his chance to make things right. Now his ass belonged to her.

Jess brushed by as she passed him. "No." Not even close. "I'm mad."

If her mother had taught her one thing it was this: Never piss off a St. John.

JAY LEANED HIS FOREHEAD against the bathroom door, struggled to keep his emotions in check. He didn't want Terry to see him lose control, so he'd been holding onto it, dearly, with both hands. None of them had gotten much sleep last night and that only put more strain on all their emotions.

"Your turn," she said, flushing the toilet and moving to the sink.

Three men had been taking them in pairs to use the half bathroom outside the basement. The no frills bathroom had a toilet, pedestal sink and two racks with towels. Each pair got five minutes before the door opened and they got yanked out. It was the only reprieve from the handcuffs.

They probably wouldn't have gone in pairs if two of the boys hadn't been so badly hurt. Brendan and Danny had a tough time moving, most likely courtesy of a couple broken ribs, and it took Blake and Eric to help their brothers to the bathroom. Terry, who fancied herself an actress, played more hurt than she was to make sure they let Jay go with her. Although Jay didn't buy her dizzy routine, the goons with guns had.

Terry washed her hands, splashed water on her face and neck before checking out her eye in the mirror. "Damn. I look like a zombie," she muttered. All the blood vessels had popped and the whites of her left eye had gone blood red. The opposite jaw had a black and blue mark from the backhand she'd received last night after talking to Jess.

"It'll heal," Jay assured her softly. He'd love her even if she looked like the bride of Frankenstein. "As long as you can see out of it, you're doing okay." He zipped up his pants, flushed and took the spot next to Terry at the sink. He didn't look too hot himself. He had a cut along his cheek and one over his eyebrow. He washed his hands and face, noticing the blood on the towels already hanging over the rack as he reached for the cleanest. All four boys had been in here first and all had suffered after last night's call. Especially Brendan.

Jay's stomach lurched remembering last night. They'd all been helpless as one of the goons ripped out Brendan's earrings taking half of his earlobe with it. They'd all lunged, screamed and cursed. None of it had done anything but amuse the men watching. Brendan—wild thing that he was, a trait he clearly inherited from his mother—with blood running down his neck and dripping onto his shoulder, had spit at the man who'd hurt him. That stupid move only got him a kick to the ribs. Jay wanted to throttle him, but he couldn't help but be proud at the smile Brendan gave his attacker. The "fuck you" could not have been clearer if the words had spewed from his son's mouth.

It had taken time for Jay to get used to the idea of his son getting an ear pierced, but when Brendan had come home with three earrings in one ear, Jay nearly had a coronary. Now he wished he'd taken Brendan up on the offer to get his ear pierced as well because at least then, they might've hurt him and not his son.

He'd be able to make a joke about it now instead of consoling his distraught wife. *Hey honey, I went a couple of rounds with Tyson. Evander and Me...we're like* this. But he couldn't joke.

Jay suspected the earrings, and that piece of Brendan, were headed directly to Jess. God willing, she had listened to the clues they'd given her. Then maybe she had a chance of finding them.

Jay straightened, saw Terry leaning her head against the door as he'd done a few minutes ago. Only her shoulders were shaking as she silently wept. Jay's chest constricted and he wanted to howl. No one made his wife cry.

No one.

He turned her around, pulled her close. Terry never cried. Yeah, okay, maybe because of a death or a sad movie, but in tough situations, she didn't break down. She acted. But not this time. He knew his wife. The helplessness was eating her up inside.

Terry wrapped her arms around his waist as she cried into his shirt. This many years later, he could still be surprised at how small she was against him. How much he towered over her. She was always so strong, so ready to take on anything that he always considered her more of a giant.

Jay kissed the top of her head, stroked her back. "We're going to get out of here. I promise," he told her. He checked his watch. He had two more minutes of alone time with his wife. He hefted her onto the sink's edge and cupped her face in his hands. "Do you believe me?"

She tried to break free of his grasp, but he held her still. Finally she met his gaze, her blue eyes desolate. "Don't make promises you can't keep," she whispered.

Jay shook his head. "I wouldn't do that." He leaned close, brushed his lips against hers. She tilted her head a fraction, made it easier for him to take more of her mouth and he did without hesitation. Maybe she thought this was the last time they'd kiss because she wrapped her legs around his hips, pulled him close and sucked the living hell out of him. She'd always been a little wild, a little wicked, as evidenced by getting pregnant and having their first baby at sixteen. Sure, he'd been just as responsible... or irresponsible. Terry had a sex drive that would keep two men happy much less one. But this kiss wasn't about sex. It was about love. Survival. It was about vows they'd spoken twenty-four years ago when Terry had finally agreed to marry him after two years of him begging. For better or worse, richer or poorer, sickness and health. There'd been no mention of kidnapping, but that clearly fell into the "worse" category.

Jay pulled away, looked into the blue eyes he loved so well. The blue eyes she'd given to all their sons. "I'm going to get us out of here. We're not going to die."

Tears shimmered in her eyes. "You heard him last night." Yes, Jay had. They still didn't know his name. He said he'd start killing them one by one if he didn't get what he wanted. Something Jess could get him. "Who is this guy? What does he want?"

"I wish I knew." Maybe that's what Jay needed to do. Find out what this guy wanted and see if he could get it for him. It beat not trying anything at all.

Jay leaned forward and kissed her again, more softly this time. The kind of kiss he gave her when he planned for seduction at night. The slow this-is-just-a-taste-of-what's-coming-later kiss.

Someone banged on the door three seconds before it burst open. Two men with guns waited in the hall. One of them dangled the cuffs in his hand. "Time's up," he said.

Back to the basement they went.

AFTER JESS PULLED HERSELF together, she and Tanner rummaged through her brother's closet and found a uniform for him. Apparently, Danny worked summers as a valet for private parties. The white dress shirt could've been a touch bigger, but considering it even came close to stretching over his shoulders, Tanner didn't balk. The snug shirt rubbed against his bandages, but he didn't bitch about that either.

While Jess had scrounged for the vest, Tanner had eyed the family photos on Danny's shelves. Her father wasn't a tiny man either. Actually, Tanner had thought her father was an older brother until Jess had told him differently, but they'd all had on sunglasses and baseball caps and there'd been no distinguishing between them.

She'd been quiet as she rifled through her brother's things.

71

Angrily so. He didn't blame her. If anyone fucked with one of his sisters, he'd be likely to kill them, and she obviously had a soft spot for her brothers. All of whom were younger. That tidbit almost made him smile considering they were all monsters like himself.

Now, in his Volvo, Tanner followed Jess's tiny Smart car to a high rise building on Wilshire Boulevard. He didn't see how a human fit in that tin can of a car, but she clearly loved the thing and it was exactly the kind of vehicle they needed to make this con work. They both realized how tricky the situation was. The fact that Jess had paperwork Juneau needed for his meeting this morning was luck on her part. Asking for her paycheck just added to the reasons to be here. Once Juneau's car wouldn't start, the con was on.

Jess pulled toward the garage, spoke with one of the two men on duty and pointed back to Tanner's Volvo where he forced himself to smile benignly.

The building itself had to be twenty stories. Large balconies decorated with potted plants or wrought iron furniture dotted the exterior. Behind a glass revolving door, a giant lobby with marble floors reeked of wealth.

Whatever Jess said worked because the gate opened and the men signaled him to follow her. Tanner waved as he drove past. Friendly, friendly. Once in the garage he parked in a visitor spot and quickly caught up with Jess where she'd parked in the back near Juneau's black Town Car. More than a dozen cars still littered the garage so there was still a chance that someone might see him. Jess looked around as she opened the door and then popped the hood of the sleek car.

"Merry Christmas," she said quietly. "It's all yours. Do your worst. I told the guys up front that you're a new hire and this is your first day. They'll leave you alone. You've only got fifteen minutes, max, before we'll be down. Maurice doesn't like to be late and he's got a business breakfast this morning at eight."

"You're sure he won't throw you out on your ass and call for a cab when he gets down here?"

Jess held up the large folder in her hand. "He needs this research for his meeting, so he can't throw me out until he has it. I told him I'd get it to him this morning plus it's going to take him a few extra minutes to make out my check. A cab will take too long to get here and he wouldn't get in Hector's beat up Chevy if you paid him money. He'll beg me to take him, and for the nominal fee of the cash in his wallet, I'll do him a huge favor and drive him to his meeting. My car is a two-seater. His guys will be stuck here waiting for the auto club. Just make sure whatever you do is something they can't fix fast."

Tanner lifted his eyebrows. "You doubt me?"

She shook her head, her big brown eyes luminous. Tanner read her fear, but mostly he saw determination. He wanted to tell her that everything was going to work out, but he honestly didn't know if it would.

Jess popped two little breath mints in her mouth and headed to the elevator at a jog. Her tight little ass called to Tanner in a big way. Yeah, he'd keep his distance, but he didn't know for how long. Getting back to business, he lifted the hood on the car. With a last glance over his shoulder, he went to work, loosening wires and discreetly slicing hoses. This was just plain fun.

He finished with plenty of time to spare, got back in his car and waited for Jess to come down. He was supposed to leave the building, but wanted to make sure everything went off as planned. Juneau had no idea what car Tanner drove and he wouldn't be expecting him after last night anyway. Tanner wanted to be close in case Jess needed him. He owed her that much and more.

Twelve minutes later, just the way she planned, Jess came out of the elevator with Juneau and two of his henchmen. Juneau and his men got into the Town Car. Jess pretended to answer the phone as Juneau's driver tried to start the car. The engine didn't turn over. That usually happened when the battery wasn't connected properly. The guy tried the engine again, and this time Juneau's door opened a crack. Jess turned toward him, checked her watch and shrugged. She might be a fluff ball, but at the moment, she was a highly competent one: an actor of the highest caliber showing no fear. He wished he could hear her. Her body language practically revealed every word. *"Car trouble? You want me to take you to the meeting? Are you kidding me? Yeah, I know you don't have much time. A cab is going to take at least twenty minutes and that's if you're lucky. Okay, then, if you really want me to take you, it's going to cost you.*" She held her palm out looking for cash.

For the first time in a long time, a genuine smile curved Tanner's lips. This girl was outstanding.

Juneau got out of the Town Car, slapped some bills into her hand, spoke to his goon and followed Jess. Watching him fold himself into the tin can made Tanner's day. Seeing the look on Juneau's face later when he'd realize he'd been had would make Tanner's month. But Tanner didn't want to get ahead of himself. He pulled out of the garage before Jess started her car. Wanted a jump on the situation. It wasn't over yet.

CHAPTER 8

"CLICK IT OR TICKET," Jess growled as she buckled her seat belt. She popped a breath mint before starting the car.

Maurice glared at her as he strapped into her sardine can of a car. He couldn't understand how she drove this tiny piece of shit she called an automobile. Never dreamed in a million years that when she bought it a few months ago, he'd actually have to sit in it. Especially now, when she didn't work for him anymore. Had she really expected him to fork over eight million dollars last night? Was she delusional? Of course, he had just handed over the hundred cash in his wallet for the ride, but this meeting was too damn important to miss. Robert McBride was about to fork over millions of dollars for the next film and those kinds of investors didn't come along that often.

Hell, if Jess hadn't quit, he would've fired her.

But he had a lot going on and she *was*—or *had been*—the best assistant he'd ever hired, bar none. She'd kept him organized, did his research, ran his errands, made his phone calls and kept the hounds at a distance. Replacing her was going to be a bitch.

Yeah, he understood her family was in deep shit. He knew deep shit. He'd been threatened before and dealt with angry investors, but this was the first time someone had tried to kill him. People usually took legal action, not lethal action. That's why he'd hired extra security. None of which he had around him at the moment. Glancing over his shoulder, he checked his surroundings in the darkened garage.

Every few years a patsy came along with a bucket load of money and no clue as to how Hollywood worked. Maurice took it as his responsibility to educate those people, and help relieve them of their monetary surplus. It was no secret that Hollywood was a crapshoot. Some of his movies did okay, and others not so much, but Maurice saw no harm in squeezing a few dollars from the wealthy. He worked hard and he deserved it. With Jess's unknowing help, he had paperwork to back up the figures in his books.

"You might want to duck if you're worried about someone seeing you," Jess said as the security gate opened.

The idea appalled Maurice, but his survival instinct kicked in and he leaned forward as Jess eased out into traffic. Fury swept through him at the cowardly act, but without his bodyguards, his confidence sputtered.

"Relax," Jess said. "No one would look for you in my car. But just in case, stay low for another block or two."

She had a point. That's why he liked her...used to like her...because of her smarts. Of course getting involved with him hadn't been too smart where her family was concerned, but that wasn't his problem. Jess was a big girl, made her own decisions. She had to live with them like everyone else.

"Where're we going?" Maurice asked when he lifted his head. Jess wasn't headed toward the restaurant he needed to be at in— he checked his watch—thirty minutes.

"There was an accident over on Beverly Glen and traffic's backed up. I thought I'd take a detour."

"In the wrong direction?"

She glared at him. "I'll get you where you need to be. Have I let you down in three years?"

No, she hadn't, which is why he'd kept her so long. Maurice sighed and settled back in the seat. Like that was even fucking possible. "This is your car?" he asked, knowing he hadn't managed to keep any skepticism from his tone. "You drive this on a regular basis?" The open-mouthed look of incredulousness answered his question. Yes. So he had to ask. "Why?"

"Because the gas mileage is good and the price was right. I don't make a ton of money." She shot him another glare as if it was his fault. Which technically speaking it was. He got away with murder when it came to paying Jess. She worked way more hours than he paid her for. But he'd always been good at finding young women who wanted to work in the movie business, eager to give, some with their bodies, most with their time and energy. Usually the ones that gave their bodies wanted to be in front of the camera. They thought putting out meant he'd put them in one of his films. Two of them had been right.

Part of him had been disappointed that Jess didn't want to act. The camera would love her. Her short brown hair had streaks of red and her pale skin glowed fresh and clean. The smattering of freckles across her nose could've been covered with makeup. Her clear light brown eyes would come across on movie screens like a beacon. That's where her true innocence glared bright. Sweet, little Jess gave everything up with her eyes. She was an open book. A do-gooder. A simple fact she proved by showing up this morning with the research he needed even though she'd quit. Any other assistant would've burned the file, but not sweet, stupid Jess. Actually, the backbone she'd shown so far surprised him. He thought she would've fallen apart after last night.

She missed another opportunity to go over another canyon. "Jess, where the hell are you going? I'm not going to make this meeting," Maurice fumed.

"I just realized I left my organizer at home. I need to stop and pick it up and we're right here, so I can't miss the chance. I'll call your eight a.m. appointment and tell him we're running a little late."

Maurice clenched his jaw. That was it. If she hadn't already quit, he'd have fired her. Again. He'd rent a car for the rest of the day. After Jess dropped him at the restaurant, he'd probably never see her again. Just as well.

A few minutes later, she pulled up to a monster house in Hancock Park. The peach stucco and Spanish tiled roof screamed ultra-chic Los Angeles. Two big willow trees shaded the neatly manicured front lawn. A large bay window jutted out near the front door, but the curtains were closed and Maurice had no view of the interior. Jess rolled down a long driveway toward two detached double car garages in back.

"This is your house?" Even as he said the words, the answer

popped into his head. She lived in a small apartment in West Hollywood, which meant this place belonged to someone else.

"It's the house I grew up in. I still think of it as mine."

Of course. He should have realized this house belonged to her father. He vaguely remembered the background check he'd had done of her father over seven years ago. Not just any man could represent his son. Maurice had searched for the best and Jay St. John had been it. He'd paid St. John a fortune to keep Alex out of prison and the man had been worth it. But later, he'd discovered St. John's firm had disappeared. Maurice just figured he'd retired early. He hadn't had a reason to keep tabs on the man.

Jess pulled the car all the way up into the first detached garage. Tall, gray cabinets lined three walls floor-to-ceiling and circled the space, making it look like an ad for a home show. "Be right back. Won't take but a minute." She cut the engine, scrambled out of the car, and took the keys with her. If it was only going to take a minute, she should've left the damn car running in the driveway. Maybe Jess was losing her touch.

Something rumbled. The garage door stared closing behind him. What the fuck? He got out of the car and followed Jess out the side door into another two-car garage. Clearly the one they just parked in had been an addition. This second garage had thick padding on the walls, a drum set on one end with speakers, microphones, amps and recording equipment. A music studio. Odd guitars and basses adorned the walls and hung from the ceiling as art pieces. On closer inspection they weren't real, but made of some kind of iron or metal. Someone in the family considered themselves an artist.

A bad artist maybe.

Maurice headed for the door on the opposite side.

A click stopped him. He felt someone's presence behind him, knew the sound he'd just heard. Slowly, Maurice turned, glanced at the gun trained on him then stared into the eyes of Tanner Bryant. He just couldn't get rid of the bastard.

Sweet little Jess had an ex-con in her garage. Wouldn't she be surprised to find that out when she came back to the car? Another click, but this one happened in Maurice's head. Anger filled him, fast and furious. The little bitch had set him up. He'd hired more than a thousand pounds of extra muscle and a little hundred pound piece of ass had cornered him.

Maurice smiled and spread his hands out wide. The bruises on Bryant's face gave him a certain amount of satisfaction. "Bryant. What a surprise. I didn't think I'd be seeing you again after last night."

"That's right," Bryant agreed easily enough. "You thought I'd be dead by now." He shrugged a shoulder. "After you left, your guys had an impromptu meeting with a baseball bat."

Maurice clenched his jaw. He hated inane muscle, not that he had time to think about that now. Now he needed to get out of here. He edged toward the door, but Bryant only smiled and lifted his brows.

"You don't honestly think you're going anywhere, do you?"

Stopping, Maurice again spread his hands wide. "Look, you've got me. I'm willing to make a deal. I can get you more money than you'll see in a lifetime and all you have to do is let me go."

"Really?" Bryant nodded, considering. "Last night you gave the order to have me killed and today you're ready to pay me off. Funny how the universe changes, huh, Juneau?" Bryant advanced on him, the gun steady in his hand. "Karma is the only thing that kept me going the last seven years, Juneau. Karma...and knowing that as soon as I got out, I'd hunt you down and hurt you the way you deserve. I've been looking forward to breaking you apart."

Maurice didn't see this going well. He'd instructed two of his guys to grab a taxi and meet him at the restaurant, but even if they figured out where he was, they'd be way too late to help him. He put his hands up next to his head. Complete surrender. "Bryant, you don't want to kill me," he said. "I can do more for you alive than I can dead."

"I don't think so." Bryant's dark brown eyes glittered with motive. "With you dead, I not only get peace of mind, but I won't have look over my back, waiting for one of your guys to finish what they started last night." His voice was so low, Maurice barely heard him.

Sweat popped out on Maurice's forehead, ran down his temple. "You know my guys are going to find Jess when they come to the restaurant and discover I never made it there. You and that little bitch are going to be in a world of hurt."

The gun connected with his head. The door opened next to him, but Bryant didn't flinch.

"I've got the flex cuffs," Jess said as she entered. "Tanner!" She paled, watching the gun that Bryant had wedged against his skull. "Put it down."

Bryant didn't budge, his jaw ticked. "Cuff him. Keep it tight," he ordered.

The little bitch obeyed, pulling his hands down one at a time and wrapping the tough plastic around his wrists, tightening it so he had no chance in hell of getting loose. Bryant patted down his waist and chest, checking for a weapon.

Maurice hid his panic. "Jess, honey, you don't want to do this," he told her. "Let me go and we can work something out." Was this because of her family? How had Tanner and she even hooked up? Last night? Before last night? Shit, did it matter? The fact that Bryant ended his pat down gave Maurice breathing room. "Jess, really, let's talk. I'm sure we can negotiate a way out of this."

The gun pressed harder against his head. "You'd like that wouldn't you," Bryant said softly in his ear. "You'd like nothing more than to walk out of here a free man."

A free man. The words hit Maurice like a stone. They shouldn't have, but they did. Bryant was all about vengeance. Retribution.

"Tanner, put the gun down. We made a deal," Jess said, her voice shaky. She sounded very worried that Bryant was about to go back on a deal, which clearly involved his life.

Tanner's harsh breath rasped near his ear, "You'll be lucky to last out the week, Juneau. I guarantee it."

"Jess," Maurice implored, "don't listen to this guy, he's a lunatic, can't you see that? He's a killer. He just got out of prison for nearly killing a man, he has no qualms when—"

"Shut up!" Bryant yelled. "Shut the hell up."

He glanced down at the tug on his jacket pocket as Jess snagged his cell phone. She yanked him to the far corner of the garage where she pulled a bike chain from a drawer. "Sit down, Maurice," she told him.

"Seriously, Jess, for a smart girl, this is the fucking stupidest thing you've ever tried. Let me go. I won't go to the cops," Maurice said, but she pushed him toward the old carpeted floor.

Bryant snorted. "Perfect. Sweet talking will get you what you want," he mumbled sarcastically as Jess threaded the thick chain in the small space between his wrists. "By the way, he told his guys to meet him at the restaurant for pick-up so we need to circumvent that."

Jess connected the two ends and padlocked him to a metal shelf unit that was screwed into the floor. "Not a problem. I'll send Hector a text from Maurice's phone and cancel." She stood up and brushed her hands together. "How does a spur of the moment vacation to Santa Barbara sound, Maurice? That should give me some time before your guys get suspicious."

Maurice shook his head, stunned that Jess could think like this.

"He sent me my brother's earlobe this morning." Her narrowed gaze shot daggers.

"What?" It took Maurice a second to understand. The shit was flying too fast. "Facinetti?"

"Yes, Maurice. Facinetti sent a package this morning."

Holy shit. No wonder she'd flipped out. But there had to be a—

"So you need to figure out the fastest way for us to do this," Jess continued. "Personally, *I* think you deserve a say in your future, unlike other people in this room." She glanced at Bryant who stood close by, his gun still pointed at him as if he might fire any minute. Her face flushed as she snatched Bryant's arm and hauled him to the door with her. "Can I speak to you for one minute," she said.

"You don't want to do this, Jess," Maurice yelled at her back.

Jess turned. "You need to keep your mouth shut and I need to talk this man out of killing you." She hit the lights and left him in the dark. "You've got five minutes, Maurice. This is your chance to make the right choice." She pushed Bryant in front of her and turned back. "Just so you know, we sound-proofed the room when Dad started playing drums. No one will hear you if you decide to scream or shout." She shut the door behind her. A click of the lock and Maurice found himself just as trapped as her family.

JESS GOT AS FAR as the kitchen door before the shaking started. Her insides and her outsides wobbled like a big bowl of Jell-O.

Anger mixed with her nerves. Blood roared in her veins. "Dammit, Tanner!" Jess turned on him. "We had a deal. I can't get my family back if Maurice is dead."

Tanner shrugged his huge shoulders, the gun still in his hand. "He's alive. You didn't say I couldn't scare the shit out of him."

"My God, don't do that to me. You about gave me a heart attack." She stalked up to him, poked her finger in his chest. "I thought you were going to kill him in there."

"That was the best part. He thought so too. That's what sold it. Your eyes, your face. It was perfect. He thought he was dead." Tanner actually smiled and the expression softened his features. Straight white teeth flashed in the brightness of her mother's kitchen and Jess caught a glimpse of a man she had yet to meet. She'd had a hint in the car when the sedative had taken effect, but not for very long. Heat flared beneath her skin, spread from her chest up her neck and to her cheeks. Smiling like that made him look like a normal man, despite his bruises, not a gun-wielding ex-con bent on killing. Baring a smile that brightened his eyes, he'd turned into a man she wanted to know.

This was the kind of guy she could like.

The room suddenly heated up. Maybe she needed to turn on the AC. Apparently kidnapping screwed with her radar.

Tanner's brows knit together. "Something wrong?"

Jess took a step back, cleared her head. "Yes, something's wrong! I'm holding my boss hostage in the garage, of course something's wrong." She paced the long kitchen, not caring that Tanner watched her every move.

Okay, that was a lie. She hated him watching her this way. He probably thought she'd crack any minute and back out of their plan. She wasn't a wimp.

She'd prove it.

She marched back into his space, hoping to intimidate him as he'd done to her last night. Granted, she wasn't his size, but now she had the attitude. Besides, things had changed. They were partners of sorts and she had the right to get in his face. "Don't go playing good cop, bad cop and keep me out of the loop. I'm not playing games. This is too important."

"I agree. We want him to give up his money. Or himself. I don't care which, but I doubt he's going to happily agree to walk freely into Facinetti's hands. So, let's give him a minute to think about how he's going to get all that money where it needs to go. Hell, we should make him wait five hours, instead of five minutes, b—"

"But we—"

"I know." He put a finger against her lips and shushed her. "We don't have that much time." He said the words, but his gaze lingered on her lips. Her stomach somersaulted as his eyes darkened. Heat exploded in her center and blossomed upward to her chest and face. She'd have to remember the next time she invaded someone's space that the person should be smaller than herself.

Now, she should step back. Step away from the large man with the gun. A man who nearly killed her last night and choked her this morning. An unstable man...with the darkest, most intense chocolate brown eyes she'd ever seen and the most amazing body...she wanted to touch.

Uh, oh. Not a good thought. Not good the way he stared down at her either. His gaze sizzled, stoked the heat that crept up her body and flushed her cheeks a second time.

She should move her head down instead of craning to look at him. Standing this way gave him a target and he clearly had a target since his gaze was still fastened on her mouth as his finger gently traced her lips.

"Uh..." She went dumb. Had nothing to say and forgot what she'd been about to say. "I, uh..."

Tanner bent his head a fraction and Jess's heart thumped so hard it was bound to register on the Richter scale. He kept moving closer, his lips closing the gap between them and Jess didn't pull away. Couldn't. He gave her nothing but time to change her mind. Slow, slow, slow.

Back away, leave, *don't let him kiss you.* But she didn't budge.

Her eyes fluttered closed, his lips brushed hers and time stopped. He grazed her mouth, back and forth, barely a touch, as if were he to do more, everything would stop and the illusion would shatter. This *had* to be an illusion. Jess didn't kiss ex-cons. She hardly kissed at all, couldn't even remember the last time she'd been on a date.

The kiss beat any date-ender by miles and Jess didn't pull away. She moved closer, nearly brought their bodies into contact, but not quite. He leaned down, put more pressure against her lips and Jess reciprocated, lifted onto her toes to fit better. They did fit. Perfectly. His lips molded to hers, firm but soft at the same time. She didn't expect him to be tentative, she'd expected—

Boom.

He grabbed her, pulled her tightly against him and took her mouth hard. Drove his tongue past her teeth and filled her with himself. He tasted like the coffee they'd shared that morning. He tasted dangerous. With his arms wrapped around her so tight she couldn't budge, didn't try. She took his kiss, stunned at the ferocity, at his strength. At the obscene way he owned her.

She should be scared. She should be fighting to get free, struggling to get out of his bear-like grasp. Instead, heat spread through her body. Chills streaked down her back. She wanted to feel the muscles of his arms, his back, wanted to touch any part of him, but he'd grabbed her, wrapped his arms around her and pinned *her*, holding her tight as if she might run otherwise. His mouth continued to take hers. His tongue stroked roughly around hers, deeply into her mouth as if he couldn't control the motion, as if he had never experienced it.

At least not in seven years.

The shockingly hard ridge of his erection burned against her stomach. A flare of panic spiked in Jess's chest. Just as quickly as it did, Tanner let go. She stumbled backwards and gasped for air, her whole body awash in tingles.

His eyes were wild, stunned, so dark she couldn't tell where the pupil ended and the iris began. He stepped back, leaned his head against the door and shut his eyes. "Jesus." Wiping a hand down his face, he shook his head. "I'm...I didn't mean..." He opened his eyes, watched her. "I won't do that again. I'm sor—I won't do it again." He opened the door and left her alone, with her lips throbbing, stinging from his kiss, and her body overheated from his touch.

TANNER COULDN'T GET OUT of the house fast enough. Every cell of his body wanted Jess and he'd barely controlled the urge to take her on the kitchen floor. What scared him most wasn't the fact that he wanted her—that was a no-brainer after being celibate for seven years. No, what freaked him out was the way she'd stood on her toes to get more of him. Didn't she get it? He was an ex-con. They were leagues apart in every aspect of life.

He should never have touched her. Holding a finger to her mouth had been worse than stupid. Getting a feel of her soft lips had pushed him over the edge. Yeah, he thought he could take a little and back off. *Idiot. Dumbshit.* He'd even given her time to come to her senses. He'd been slow, sure she'd back away or slap him, put him in his place. But the little fluff ball had wanted more and in the blink of an eye he'd lost control.

She got way more than she bargained for. But she'd think twice before getting in his space again, so he had to be grateful for that. He hated people in his space, especially her. She smelled too good, looked too good. He'd almost apologized too. Wasn't that an ass-kicker? Yeah, he was sorry he couldn't relieve the hard-on, but not sorry he'd tasted her. Her mouth was a sensation of hot and cold. She tasted like the tiny mint breath fresheners she chewed all the time, but her mouth was warm, dark and so damn inviting.

Tanner shook his head, finding himself in a shaded corner of the backyard, near a slider bench. His parents had one just like it. When was the last time he'd been on one? Ten years ago? More? He refused to go back to that time when he had family and friends, a life.

He couldn't go back and who knew what his future held. All he had was now.

Blood still pounded through his veins, settling in his rigid cock. He needed to lose the hard-on in a big way. He dropped to the cool grass, set the gun on the wood chips under the nearby hedge, stripped off his T-shirt and did the only thing he could do.

Push-ups. He did them in the morning and at night. He did them in prison anytime a hard-on got too extreme to ignore. He punished his body with exercise since sex wasn't an option and having an audience to any solo relief hadn't appealed to him.

But maybe little Miss Fluff Ball was an option. She'd invited him, hadn't she? Stood on her toes and asked for more, not having any idea what *more* really meant. She'd learned quickly enough though. She'd been shocked as hell. She'd frozen like a possum in headlights. Every muscle in her body had tensed and told Tanner what he already knew. Jess didn't want him. Would never want him. She knew by now what a loose cannon he was.

Breathing steadily, Tanner kept going, up and down, nose and stomach to the grass. He'd do as many as he could in the few minutes he had remaining. The stitches on his side pulled as he pumped, but the pain only helped his body focus on something else. It also helped bring the peace of mind he needed to face Jess again.

Finally, he heard her behind him, felt how her tension changed the air.

"It's time," she said. "We should talk to him."

Tanner hopped to his feet. Jess didn't back away as he expected, but she watched him warily. Was she going to pretend like it never happened? Did she think he was going to forget it happened? He almost laughed out loud at that idea. He went to the nearby water hose and bent over to douse his head and neck with cold water. Then he splashed it over his chest and under his arms.

He had control back.

But for how long?

CHAPTER 9

"**HEY, PAULIE, YOU UP** yet?" Frank Grubb asked from the other side of the bedroom door.

Paul Facinetti closed his newspaper with a snap. Foreclosures, murder, suicides... The world was going to hell. What happened to honor and living by a man's word? He pushed the breakfast tray aside and tightened the belt on his black, silk robe as he got out of bed. He let the grand simplicity of the open room soothe his nerves. He hadn't been in Los Angeles since his sister's death, but he was glad he hadn't sold her house. Though he liked Vegas and the money he made there, he understood his sister's love for the water and appreciated her style. This master suite on the top level of the house gave him a spectacular view of the Pacific and with the walls painted an ocean green, it was almost as if the water flowed right from the sea and into the room. Beige drapes billowed from the breeze coming through the French doors and matched thick carpeting under his bare feet.

"Yeah, I'm up," he answered.

Frank walked into the room, announcing his presence with enough cologne to kill a moose. "I just wanted to let you know that everyone's behaving. No stupid moves or nothing like that."

"*Anything* like that," Paul corrected as he shoved his feet into comfortable slippers.

Frank just stared at him, his head cocked as he tried to figure out what he'd just been told. It was not a look uncommon to this man. Paul sighed.

Frank spoke like a punk with no education. Of course, he *was* a

87

punk with no education, but Paul had always hoped he'd quit talking like a man with no brain and too much muscle.

"How long before we hear from the assistant bitch?" Frank asked.

"How many times have I told you not to categorize someone before you've met them? From what I can tell, Jess St. John is a very nice person. Her boss put her in a bad spot. The fact is we have her parents and brothers, and that would make anyone unhappy. If we'd met her under normal circumstances, I'm sure she'd be very friendly."

Paul had spoken to Jess on the phone a few times before he'd met with Maurice Juneau, and she'd been very accommodating. Very nice. He could practically see her smile over the telephone. He regretted what he had to do, but Juneau had cost him too much time and money. Jess St. John had been the next easiest option. She ran Juneau's life and the man had been stupid enough to brag about it.

"Friendly?" Frank latched onto Paul's last word and took it out of context the way he usually did. He swaggered, a bull sniffing for a mate. "Like, uh...just how friendly?" He lifted bushy brows and smiled crookedly.

Paul wouldn't have kept Frank employed if they hadn't been together so long. Frank had saved his ass in high school more times than Paul could remember. What he lacked in brain-power he made up for in loyalty. Frank would never betray him, he'd never try to take over the business. He knew where his place was and he never bitched or moaned. He made more than a decent living and took plenty of vacation time. Paul knew enough women so that Frank always had a good fuck when he needed. Life was good for Frank. He'd never screw it up. In this world, that meant something.

Take Maurice Juneau for instance. The man had promised a movie. He'd laid out a plan, shown Paul where his money was going, who the stars were and where the film would shoot. Paul had always wanted a taste of the film industry and he knew a few guys who'd invested and made some money. One film had gone on to be nominated for an Oscar. What a frickin' ride that would be.

Not that Paul expected that type of success out of the box.

Films were hit-or-miss. He understood that. That's why he'd demanded to read Juneau's film. It was gritty. Real life. Maybe that's what spoke to Paul so strongly, why he connected so much. It was about a kid working his way from a bad neighborhood to rise up and become a man of substance, someone to be reckoned with, someone who deserved respect. Paul felt like it was his story. So he'd forked over eight million dollars. Eight fucking million dollars had got him jack-shit. There was no movie, no nothing.

The more digging Paul did, the more he found out about Maurice Juneau. The man was a scum-sucking magpie. But he'd been smart enough to hire more security after Paul called him. Paul sighed at his mistake. He should've just picked Juneau up and gotten it over with. Either get the money or exterminate the man. But Paul still liked to think that business relationships could remain friendly when all parties played fair. He should've known better by this stage in his life.

"Hey, Paulie, you done with this melon?" Frank asked, pulling him out of his thoughts.

Paul used words Frank understood. "Knock yourself out."

Frank popped the honeydew melon in his mouth and smacked appreciatively. "While we're talking about friendly," he said. "That St. John woman in the basement, she ain't friendly at all."

Paul cringed at the reminder. "How is Lou feeling? He still have a headache?"

"It's going to be another week before he's active again. His head aches, his balls ache. She whacked them all the way into his throat." Frank gave him a pointed look. "It ain't right that she get away with that. Give me the word and I'll make sure she don't do it ever again."

"I don't think that'll be necessary," Paul said. "We're not going to hurt these people." Well that wasn't true, since he'd ordered the younger brother's earrings be sent to Jess as incentive...along with most of his earlobe. "At least not more than we have to," he amended.

"You think I can have a crack at her before this is all over?" Frank asked. "C'mon, Paulie, I never ask for nothin'. I'd just like to give her one good hard fuck before this thing ends. It'll be a little going away party." Frank laughed at his own joke. "You gotta admit, she is one piece of ass. I can't believe she gave birth to all those guys. She must have some expensive-assed plastic surgeon."

Paul doubted Terry St. John had any surgery at all. She was one of those women who didn't age. But did she deserve to be mauled by Frank just because her time was up? Not in Paul's book, she didn't. He'd just have to make it up to Frank with another girl. A different redhead so Frank could pretend he was fucking Terry St. John. If anyone deserved the woman, it was Lou, the one she'd taken down.

"I don't need an answer now. Just think about it." Frank popped another piece of melon in his mouth and headed toward the door. "Anyway, just wanted to give you the morning report like you asked. I'm heading down to relieve Kwami. See ya later."

Paul watched his friend leave the room. The world owed him a favor for keeping Frank off the streets.

He checked his watch. Jess only had a few more days before her deadline. Would she come up with the money, or the man? Either one suited Paul. He admired her phone call last night, even if it *had* been late. He'd been about to go to sleep and had to get dressed to face her family. Clearly he couldn't intimidate anyone in his pajamas. Then he'd had to show her there was a price for going against his rules. Had to make sure she understood the consequences.

He really didn't want to have to kill all those people in the basement.

But he would if he had to.

MAURICE SAT UP STRAIGHTER as the door opened and Jess walked in with Bryant on her heels. That little bitch had left him tied up like a goddamn steer at a rodeo. An obnoxiously big clock had ticked the minutes away on the wall over the drum set. But he wouldn't let his temper guide him. Right now, he needed to be the negotiator. The producer. He had to get results because he wasn't going to be handed to Paul Facinetti like a side of beef. If Facinetti took the earlobe of an innocent kid, then what the hell would he to *him?*

"Did you make a decision?" Jess asked.

Making eye contact, Maurice nodded. He'd done some thinking the last few minutes. If Jess wanted to fuck around, she'd picked the wrong man to play with. "I was wrong before when I wouldn't help you. It's my fault this happened. I take full responsibility." Maurice shook his head, filled his voice with contrition. "Jesus. What was I thinking? Look, I've got an account in the Cayman Islands. I can transfer the funds as soon as you let me out of here."

Little bitch Jess narrowed her eyes, suspicion clear in her gaze. She'd been around him long enough to know his bullshit, but he looked her straight in the eyes as if he meant every word. Finally, she headed toward him, but Bryant stopped her with a hand on her arm.

"How much is in the account?" he asked.

Maurice wanted to throttle him. He took a measured breath, reigned in his anger. "Three million dollars. It was earmarked for the next film, but I'm giving it to you, Jess."

Her bunny rabbit eyes grew wide. "I need eight million. You know that, Maurice. He gave you the money. You have the money."

Yeah he had most of the money, but he sure as hell wasn't forking it over to her. "I told you, Jess, most of it's gone. I have that account and two more that come to just over four million total and you're welcome to it. Just take these cuffs off and let's do this. Please, Jess, my shoulder is killing me. I can't be in this position. I'm dying here." He adjusted his sore shoulder for effect. Jess hated to see people in pain. One of her many weaknesses.

Jess moved toward him at the same time something slammed against the square glass in the door. A second later glass shattered outside. Bryant looked over his shoulder, then backtracked toward the noise. He looked out the window. Maurice doubted it was one of his guys, but hope had his pulse racing.

"Wait for me," Bryant instructed Jess, before going outside. The door shut behind him.

"Since when do you take orders from cavemen, Jess?" Maurice asked. He needed her in his corner, not Bryant's.

"About three years now," she said, leveling him with a flat stare.

Funny.

Maurice smiled. It was either that or fly into a rage and he couldn't afford to lose the ground he was making. He didn't have much time with Bryant gone. "C'mon, Jess, unlock these." He flinched as he adjusted his shoulder. "You don't need them." Maurice tugged his wrists behind him, ignored his sweaty palms and forced another grin. "It's me, remember? You're like a daughter to me, Jess." He took a deep breath and sighed. "Look, I'll get you the money. I swear. I didn't think Facinetti would go this far. I admit, I was stupid. Let's just take it one step at a time." He used his soft voice, the one that coaxed money out of wallets. The same voice he used on actresses when he needed them to strip...and it wasn't in the script.

She glanced toward the door, clearly considering the consequences, and Maurice pushed a little harder.

"Where's the Jess I've known the past three years," he cajoled. "This isn't you." He grimaced and tried to roll his shoulder. He never thought his broken collarbone would come in handy. "You're letting Bryant's agenda cloud your thinking. This isn't about him. It's about you and me doing the right thing. C'mon, unlock these. We can go straight to the bank. Let's go help your family."

When she finally nodded, Maurice felt a wave of relief rush through him. Jess wanted to believe the best in people. She wanted the fairy tale, and he was more than happy to give it to her. She was too easy. She bent behind him and Maurice heard the lock unsnap, felt the chain slide across his wrists. The plastic tightened briefly, pinched his wrists then became slack. He loosened his hands.

Free.

The door opened as Bryant came back. Blood revved in Maurice's veins. No time to waste if he wanted out of this damn garage. He lunged and grabbed Jess as Bryant stepped inside. She gasped as he wrapped his arm around her skinny little neck and held on tight.

"Change in plans, shitheads."

Bryant planted his feet and straight-armed his gun. He didn't have a shot with Jess blocking his way. Tension in the room cycled higher as they warmed to their Mexican standoff.

Getting out wouldn't be easy, but it was doable as long as he kept Jess as a shield. Maurice smiled as he eased toward the door nearest the adjacent garage. "We're walking out of here," he said quietly.

Bryant shook his head and headed them off. "No, you're not."

Anger erupted in Maurice's veins. "Don't fuck with me, asshole. I'll snap her neck quicker than you can blink."

"Do I look like I care," Bryant shot back. His face was set and he hadn't glanced at Jess once. Hadn't looked at her eyes or shown any sign that she meant anything to him.

What if he'd miscalculated their little partnership? What if Jess was just a pawn?

"Maurice, I'm no help to you," Jess said, futilely tugging at his arm. "He already shot me once, he'll do it again. Just cooperate and everything will be fine."

What? The girl had lost her fucking mind. "You're delusional, Jess. If he shot you, you wouldn't be here, and we both know nothing's going to be fine for me if I stay here."

"Didn't you wonder how we came to meet," she insisted as she squirmed in his arms. "He took me after you drove off. I've got the bandage on my shoulder to prove it. This isn't going to help because he doesn't care if I live or die. I was just a way to you. You'd better—"

Maurice clamped his hand over her mouth, didn't want to hear her babble, but no sooner had he shut her up then he felt pain slice through his hand and up his arm. The bitch had sunk her teeth into his palm. Maurice stepped to the side and delivered a hard blow to her midsection. Jess doubled over—with an audible whoosh of air from her lungs—which hadn't been his intention. He'd just wanted his damn hand back. But Bryant was on him too fast. Maurice saw the giant fist before it made contact with his face. A crushing round of pain exploded in his cheek quickly followed by another. The second sent him crashing against the filing cabinet before he hit the ground, dazed. Fuck that hurt.

He should've planned this better. Waited when he had Jess to himself longer. But he'd blown it. Anger quickly took the edge off his pain. That miserable little bitch had no right to his money.

With his face buried in the old, dirty carpet, he found himself chained faster than he could spit out the blood pooling in his mouth. Dammit, if he'd just been a little quicker, he could've reached the gun in his ankle holster and taken them both out. Gladly.

Bryant grabbed the collar of Maurice's best white dress shirt and yanked him up, but Maurice couldn't really see him from his left eye, which throbbed like a son of a bitch. "Tell her how to access that money," he gritted out.

"When did you become such a violent asshole?" Maurice muttered.

"When you sent me to the pen, asshole," Bryant hissed back.

Behind him, Jess staggered to her feet, a hand over her side, surprise on her face. She really had no idea the kind of trouble she'd made for herself. If she thought Facinetti was trouble, then she had no clue what Maurice would do to her.

"You okay?" Bryant asked, but he never loosened his grip or looked her way.

"Yeah," she said, but she lacked her earlier confidence. Maurice was happy to have stripped that from her. He grinned because he saw that Bryant understood the subtle change. She wouldn't last in this game. She couldn't win against Facinetti so what was the point in playing.

"You need to let me go," he called after her as she stumbled to the door. Poor baby, needed to regroup. "You can't get the money without me and if Facinetti doesn't get it soon, he'll kill them."

The door closed behind her and Maurice smiled up at Bryant. Bryant growled then threw another fist. Pain exploded in his head right before everything went black.

JESS HOBBLED TO THE kitchen, fighting back tears. Her ribs hurt, but not as bad as her pride. She hadn't seen it coming. Hadn't suspected Maurice of using her as a hostage. Not that Tanner seemed thrown off by it. Jeez, he'd looked ready to shoot through her. Again! It was the surprise on Maurice's face when she told him about Brendan's earlobe. The absolute certainty in his voice that he'd help her. She hadn't even considered his shoulder and the pain he might be in. All of it overrode her better judgment.

She wasn't cut out for this.

She snatched an ice pack from the freezer and placed it against her sore ribs. Maybe if she got the money from his account and delivered Maurice with it, it would be enough to save her family. Maybe once she got into Maurice's files, she could find other accounts with more money. He'd already mentioned three accounts that had half the amount she needed.

She eased herself onto a seat at the huge country table. A mountain of despair took residence in her chest. Her throat thickened with a giant knot. Jess dropped her head in her hands and held back her tears with iron will.

That's how Tanner found her a few minutes later. He set the gun on the counter, washed his hands in the sink and Jess felt his eyes on her the whole time.

"What?" she muttered. "You've never seen a girl get her ass handed to her by a former boss?" She wiped at her wet eyes, anger and frustration beating at her insides.

Tanner didn't say anything as he took the seat next to her. He turned the chair, faced her. "Let me take a look," he said softly. "He whaled on you pretty good."

What, no lecture? She eyed him suspiciously. None of it would've happened if he'd been in the room. Not that she blamed him. She was the one who'd set Maurice free. Tanner had told her to wait for him. *Real good listening, Jess.* "What was the noise outside?" she asked.

"A frickin' giant crow slammed into the glass then knocked over a vase. I found it in the side yard, dazed. Look," Tanner said, clearly needing to get something off his chest, "I figure we're both learning as we go, right? I'm learning not to kill the man at the first opportunity and you're learning how dangerous he is." He tipped his chin toward her middle. "Let me make sure he didn't break a rib." He crouched next to her.

Jess's heart thumped harder and she swallowed a knot of nervous tension. Tanner wouldn't hurt her. He'd told her that. A part of her needed the attention. Needed someone to lean on, so she set the ice pack on the table and lifted her T-shirt, exposing her midriff.

When he grimaced, she looked down, shocked to see a fist-sized mark already forming. They locked gazes and the concern and helplessness on his face knocked her off balance.

Ridiculous. She had to be imagining the odd feelings racing in her system. The sense of camaraderie she felt with this man she barely knew. Her sudden case of dry mouth was very real. Her skyrocketing heart rate was very real. So was the wave of goose bumps washing over her arms. All of it stemmed from the very real heat blazing from his eyes.

"Back in the garage," he said softly. "When he had you in front of him..." He hesitated, but his focus never wavered. His dark gaze burned into hers. "I wouldn't have taken a shot. I wouldn't risk hurting you again." A small grin curved his lips and those eyes sparkled. "But I appreciate you telling him that I would."

A flush warmed her cheeks. He made it sound like they were a team. Partners. Whereas the idea would've seemed ridiculous to her last night, today it held some appeal. He was a force she'd rather have working with her than against her.

Tanner's gaze shifted back to her bare skin. He gently glided calloused fingers over the area and Jess sucked in a rush of air at the new chills racing along her skin. He lifted his hand, the size of it dwarfing the mark, dwarfing her stomach. "Hurt?" he asked.

"I'm okay," she whispered.

He studied her. The fire in his eyes banked and something else took over. He took a stray tear from her cheek with his thumb. The touch went straight to her heart. A half smile curved his lips. "You're one tough little fluff ball," he told her.

She could've taken offense. Would have, if one of her brothers had said the same thing, but she didn't. She'd never been as tough as her mom, but she'd always had confidence and always believed in herself. Her parents had given her that. But Tanner didn't know her, didn't understand the role model her mother was and continued to be. Maybe Jess was as strong as her mother and she'd just never had the need to prove it before now.

"Fluff ball," she scoffed, pulling down her shirt and sorry at the same time that she wouldn't be feeling Tanner's hands on her again. How could his touch send her body into such a flush? Why did she have to be so attracted to him?

He was not a man she pictured herself liking. An ex-con? Jess squeezed her eyes shut, had to remember that he hadn't done the crime that put him away. He was an innocent man. At least he had been until he broke the law. Which he'd done when he'd shot at Maurice and hit her instead, and which they'd done together when they'd kidnapped Maurice.

"If my mom heard you call me a fluff ball, she'd knock your lights out."

Tanner gave her the big grin that turned her upside down. The one that crinkled the edges of his gorgeous, dark eyes and deepened the lines around his mouth. He was too hard to be pretty, but he was a dangerously sexy man. "She's tough too, huh?" he asked, turning the chair and straddling the seat. A very macho thing to do and she smiled.

"She's superwoman," Jess admitted. "I've always wanted to be like her, but never quite measured up."

Tanner scowled. "She said that to you? That you never measured up?"

"No!" Jess squawked. "Of course not. She's the best mom a kid could have. She's just really strong. Really independent."

"Why do you think you never measured up?" He held her gaze, softly, sweetly, giving her the feeling this was the pre-prison Tanner, a man who could have a conversation without bitterness or regret or revenge on his mind. A man who could listen, be a shoulder for someone who needed it. A friend.

"I'm not the fighter she is. I'm not into confrontation. I let the world happen around me and I don't impact it the way she's done. She attacks life. I let life go by."

"I think that's bullshit." Tanner leaned toward her, but not in any sexual way. His eyes glittered as he commanded her attention. "From the moment I first saw you, you were fighting." He smiled again and this close up, it knocked her socks off. "Hell, I didn't take a shot for the longest time because you kept dancing, getting in my way, back and forth, arms flailing all over the place, giving Juneau a piece of your mind. The last thing I wanted to do was hit you."

"And yet..." She smiled to downplay her words and he grinned back at her.

He lifted a hand, almost as if he might touch her shoulder, but he pulled back. "How's the shoulder doing, by the way?"

"The jab to my ribs pretty much took my mind off it. Thanks for asking."

He nodded, his smile softening. Their eyes stayed locked.

Trouble. Red alert. She couldn't start something with this man. Not with her life the way it was now…with her family in the hands of a lunatic and her lying, cheating, crazy bastard of a boss tied up in her garage.

Oh no. Maurice was still in the garage.

Jess straightened and got some distance from Tanner. "Maurice. We should go back and talk to him. Find out how to access his accounts."

"Don't bother." Tanner sat up, crossed his arms over the back of the chair. "He won't be talking for a while. I pretty much made sure of it."

She shouldn't have felt a thrill at that news. Shouldn't have been happy that Maurice had paid a price for hurting her. But she did. Tanner had stood up for her. Of course, he didn't need much to set him off. Hitting Maurice had probably felt really good.

She couldn't blame him.

But the clock was still ticking and she didn't have time to waste. Jess got a bucket from the pantry and filled it with cold water from the sink.

"What are you doing?" Tanner asked.

"Waking up Maurice. I need those accounts and I need that money." Chaining Maurice in the garage was bad enough, but dumping cold water on him was going to make him ballistic.

Tanner gave her the grin that melted her insides. "He's not going to like that."

"No, he won't." She smiled back. "But it looks like you will."

He nodded, but his smile faded as he assessed her the way he'd done in the car. "I haven't met your mom, but I think you're more like her than you give yourself credit for."

Emotion clogged her throat, and Jess swallowed the thick lump. "Like you said, you haven't met her," she murmured as water filled the bucket. She heard the scrap of the chair legs on the hardwood floor, felt Tanner close the distance and stand behind her. The heat of his body radiated the length of her. Another round of chills chased up her spine.

He leaned close to her ear, his cheek brushing the short strands of her hair. "Doesn't matter," he whispered. "I'll bet you're just as tough, just as smart. I'll bet she'd be damn proud of you right now."

Her chest tightened and her vision blurred. How could her mother be proud of her when she lived in a ratty studio apartment, did her laundry at home and barely made ends meet? She'd taken a job against her father's wishes and now they all were paying for it. No, Jess didn't think *pride* was a word her mother would use when describing her feelings about her only daughter.

Jess didn't have words to answer Tanner. The water reached the gallon mark and Jess turned off the faucet. She hefted the bucket out of the sink and headed toward the garage.

Show time.

CHAPTER 10

TANNER FOLLOWED JESS, WATCHED her tight little ass as she opened the kitchen door and went outside. She was as tough as she was sensitive. Jess hadn't recognized that tough part of herself, but he had. Her bruised ribs had to hurt like hell, but aside from a brief retreat, she was returning to do battle.

He shouldn't have let the distraction take him away earlier, but for all he knew, one of Juneau's thugs had followed them. Seeing Juneau's arm wrapped around her neck had sent fury blazing to the surface. A quick calculation of the odds had told him Juneau wouldn't kill her. Not then anyway. Not when he needed a shield...the coward. The pride Tanner had felt when she'd bit Juneau's hand had been short-lived once the scumbag hit her so viciously. He could've killed Juneau right then. Would've done it in a second if Jess didn't need him alive so badly.

Jess was growing on him. He couldn't deny it. The longer he spent with her, the more he wanted to help her. As each new card was dealt, the deck stacked in her favor.

Of course, the idea of Juneau getting a different kind of retribution held appeal too. Facinetti didn't sound like a man Tanner wanted to tangle with, but if he wanted Juneau, he could have him.

Knowing Juneau, a man who clearly loved his fortune above all else, Tanner liked the idea of him suffering the loss of millions of dollars before he died. Any way to stick it to him more was fine with Tanner. Regardless, Tanner didn't mind this part of the process. He liked seeing Juneau at his mercy. Wanted to see the man suffer, even if it wouldn't be a fraction of the amount deserved.

In the garage, Jess didn't get close enough to be in Juneau's range. She said his name once. Twice. When he didn't respond, she hefted the bucket of water and doused him, square in the face.

He sputtered and coughed, turning to sit up. He muttered a few foul curses and leveled her with hard eyes. Well, one hard eye since the other happened to be swollen shut. "You're going to die just like your family, Jess. I'm going to see to it," he gritted out.

If the threat registered on Jess, she didn't show it. Instead, she tossed the empty bucket, snagged her phone from her pocket, and with a pointed look at Juneau, started punching numbers.

"What are you doing?" A healthy dose of paranoia lived in Juneau's question.

"Calling Facinetti. He can get the money out of you. I'm done."

Juneau's eyes bugged out wide. "No! Jess, hang up the fucking phone. I'll give you the account numbers, whatever you need. Just don't call."

She glared at him, let the screen go black. Her sweet brown eyes were all business. No sensitivity in the vicinity. More pride at her fortitude edged its way into Tanner's gut.

"I need my laptop," Juneau said. "Take me to my laptop and I'll get you the money."

Jess rolled her eyes. "Yeah, sure. I'll just take you to where your guys are. I might be a slow learner when it comes to human nature, but I'm not the idiot you think I am, Maurice. I've been trying to tell you—oh, forget it." She headed to the door. "You can use my laptop."

"I need mine," Maurice said. "I change the passwords regularly and they're on my laptop."

Shaking her head, Jess faced him. "Paranoid, Maurice? What a surprise." Tanner hid a smile at her dry comeback. "Where's your laptop. I'll get it myself," she said.

"It's at the penthouse."

She narrowed her eyes, advanced a fraction but still stayed clear of Maurice's range, and Tanner felt another spark of pride for her. "Are you sure about that?" she asked. "The last time I saw it was last night at the Malibu house. If you're leading me on a wild goose chase, Maurice, so help me, God, I'll call Facinetti the second I realize you lied to me an—"

"I'm telling the truth!" he said, seething. "I took it with me when I left last night. It's at the penthouse."

Quickly and silently, Jess headed to the side door attached to the other garage.

"Hey!" Tanner said, jogging to catch up. "What are you doing?"

"You heard him," she said, reaching her car and opening the driver's door. "The laptop is at the penthouse. I'm going back to the Wilshire condo. I'll be back in an hour or so. Hold the fort." She sat down and stood up again. Got in Tanner's face—at least as much as she could, being as short as she was. "Do not kill him." She said the words distinctly. Her gaze never wavered.

Tanner bit back a smile. Her fierceness amazed him. Attracted him. He was beginning to think of her as the fluff ball that wasn't. "We made a deal," he told her. "I won't renege on my end."

Her eyes softened, her cheeks brightened and she looked rightly chastised. "I'm sorry. I was just thinking about earlier and..." She met his gaze. "We have to trust each other and that's hard because we don't know each other. But I promise to keep my word and I have faith that you'll do the same."

She trusted him? Had faith in him? The words *trust* and *faith* hadn't been in his vocabulary for most of the last decade. But she was right. For all she knew he'd kill Juneau the second she pulled away. He'd get what he wanted and she'd lose everything. Why should he care what happened to her?

Turned out there were several reasons. The first being she saved his life last night. Then the fact that he'd shot her. Oh, and choked her. Yeah, he owed her this.

Tanner stuck his hand out. A stupid thing to do, but apparently the more time he spent with this woman, the less brain cells he made use of. She narrowed her eyes, but laid her hand in his. He closed his grip around her hand, felt her strength as they slowly shook.

"I give you my word that I won't kill him." He said the words quietly and her eyes went soft. She had the prettiest light brown eyes, the color of smooth whiskey. A tiny freckle peeped out at the top of her cheekbone, and several more smattered across her nose. She was the picture of innocence.

The exact opposite of him.

Tanner quickly released her and stepped back. Too late. His cock was already rising to the occasion. The smell of her, the sight of her, the heat of her body had him aching all over.

Once again her eyes widened as if she knew. But Tanner didn't see fear. Surprise, yes. Heat? Maybe. As well as he read her, she still kept him on his toes. Kept him guessing at what really went on under that innocent exterior.

Her cheeks flamed and she lowered her gaze as she settled in the driver's seat and closed the door. "I'll be back soon," she said, cranking the engine. She hit the remote, which lifted the garage door.

The closer she came to leaving the more Tanner worried about her. What if something went wrong and he wasn't there to help her? He crouched at her open window. "Hey, how the hell are you going to get it?" She didn't seem to be much of a planner.

"I'm going to walk in and take it. I have free reign of all his houses and offices. The guys won't think anything of it."

"What if Juneau told them about last night? What if they have orders to keep you out?"

She bit her bottom lip, considering the questions. "Even if Maurice told them I quit, he wouldn't explain why. They heard me say I was driving him this morning as a last favor, so if anyone asks, I'll say he begged me to come back. Plus, I have his cell phone." She lifted it for emphasis. "If anyone calls, I can return the call on his behalf. No problem." She put the car in gear.

He should tell her to be careful. Tell her to call when it was over, but the words didn't form in his dry mouth, and she backed out of the garage. Besides, saying those things out loud showed he cared and he didn't. He didn't want an attachment to her. Didn't want to think about her or worry while she was gone. He had his own agenda with Juneau and if Jess couldn't take care of herself, it wasn't his fault.

So why did he feel like crap, as if he'd left something undone? Why did apprehension continue to gnaw its way in his gut? He might not want to care about her, but he did, and just because she'd proved she could handle tough situations didn't mean he felt good about her going out on her own. The car rolled away and none of the words Tanner wanted to say came out of his mouth.

The wrongness of it hit him in the chest, but Tanner forced the uneasiness aside. He had a dead man to babysit.

Well, almost. Because Juneau's days were numbered.

At least now Tanner had time to face the man who'd ruined his life. What did he want from him after all this time? An apology? That would never happen. Remorse? Fat chance. Guilt? Didn't Tanner already know those emotions didn't apply to Juneau? Didn't really matter. He'd waited seven long years to have Juneau to himself and he wouldn't waste the opportunity.

He wanted some type of penance. The only thing he had to do was avoid killing the man. He owed Jess that much.

JESS ONLY GOT AS far as the driveway before she hit the brakes and checked her watch. She couldn't go yet. *Damn.* After slamming her palm on the steering wheel, she cut the engine.

"What's wrong?" Tanner asked, jogging toward her.

"I have to wait before going back to Maurice's. If the guys are still there, they'll know something's wrong. It would take me at least an hour to get from the condo to the restaurant and back again. Probably more in morning traffic."

Tanner lifted dark eyebrows. "Good thing you thought of that."

Jess checked her watch again, rolled her neck and leaned her head against the seat back. Emotion clogged her throat, made her chest heavy. She wanted to do something *now*. The waiting killed her.

Tanner opened the car door. "Come with me," he said, dragging her out. He took her to the back yard and eased her down next to him on the bench. It seemed completely ridiculous to be sitting when her family's life hung in the balance. But at the moment she had nothing else to do. Showing up at Maurice's place would only alert his guys that something was wrong.

Something was wrong. There was something she needed to do… "Oh, my God." She hopped off the bench, pulled out her cell phone and called Maurice's potential investor, an oilman from Houston, waiting at the restaurant. With a very genuine apology, she cancelled the meeting with Robert McBride, giving Maurice's regrets and promising a phone call in the near future to reschedule. No reason to give the idea that a meeting would probably never happen. Not if she ended up trading Maurice for her family, which she might have to do.

Her stomach churned at the thought.

Bobby, as he insisted she call him, took the news in stride and didn't seem too worried. He simply thanked her for passing on the message and hung up.

Jess made another call before it got too late. She told Hector, Maurice's long time muscle, that the meeting was canceled and Maurice wanted to go location hunting for the next film. Deciding it was best to plant the seed now, she mentioned that since Maurice had groveled so effectively and begged her not to quit, she'd reconsidered. After assuring the man they'd meet up later, she stuffed her phone in her pocket and dropped her chin to her chest. What happened if she messed up? What happened if a detail got by and someone found out she had Maurice handcuffed in her garage?

"Jess." Tanner's low voice sent an instant wash of goose bumps along her arms. It was crazy. She turned when he tugged softly on her T-shirt. "You doin' okay?" he asked.

She could fall apart any minute or she could be more like her mom. Get determined, get the job done. She faced him. He didn't seem the least bit frazzled by all this. His relaxed strength only made her more jittery. More on edge.

"Am I doing okay?" she repeated. She sat next to him and shook her head. "No. I don't think so. I've had better days."

"I hear that," he muttered. He shifted and grimaced.

"Your stitches hurt?" she asked. Had he pulled them out when he hit Maurice? "Should we check?"

"Naw. I'm good. Every once in a while I get a little twinge. Nothing major."

Her shoulder still twinged, but it probably didn't hurt half as much as Tanner's side. Jess remembered last night. Pictured Victor stitching up Tanner and thanking him afterward. Her curiosity got the best of her. "How did you help Chino in prison? Why did Victor thank you?"

Tanner shrugged a shoulder. "Chino had been in a gang and when a rival gang-banger landed in our cell block, the punk thought Chino had ratted him out. He came after him, set him up, and I happened to be there."

"You mean you saved his life." Jess didn't ask. She knew it. The more she learned about Tanner the more she liked him. That was very dangerous. Because he was very dangerous. He hadn't done the crime that put him in prison, but prison life had made him a hard man. She'd gotten a glimpse of the man he was before his incarceration, but the dominant, ex-con prevailed most of the time.

"Five-to-one odds pissed me off," Tanner admitted. "Chino's not a big dude. Don't get me wrong, he can fight, but he couldn't have handled all five guys alone."

Five guys? Tanner was either very brave or very stupid. She picked brave. He couldn't have gotten onto a secure lot last night and gotten them both out of there if he was stupid. "And that's where you came in?" It was crazy, but Jess found herself smiling.

Tanner grinned back. "I just wanted to even the odds for him. He didn't rat out anybody and he didn't deserve what was going down." The smile faded. "Besides, I'd been there before. Faced lousy odds and it sucks."

No wonder the man had nightmares. Anybody would. Jess swallowed as a wave of compassion rolled through her chest. What broke her heart most was that Tanner might land back in prison if they kept going on their current path.

"I don't want you to go back there," she said.

Tanner cocked his head and faced her. "I don't plan to." He searched her eyes. "Why would you say that?"

She gestured to the garage before she stood and paced away from him. "You should go home or go somewhere, but you shouldn't be caught here with Maurice tied up in my garage. This is crazy." She turned and saw him standing too. An ominous figure with a scowl on his face. "Look, I know you want revenge or retribution or whatever, but don't you see? You finally have your freedom. Don't risk it for someone like him. You deserve better, Tanner. You deserve your own life."

"You don't get it, Jess. I don't have a life." Tanner took three giant steps and got in her space, but she didn't move. He didn't scare her anymore. "He took that from me and I plan to make sure that what's left of his life is as miserable as mine was for the last seven years."

"But is it worth the *rest* of your life?" Jess stared up at him, hoping to break through his anger. She'd have a tough time doing this whole thing without him, but she'd manage.

Tanner looked up to the sky and let out a frustrated laugh. "Unbelievable," he muttered.

Jess didn't understand. "What?"

"You sound just like..." He bit off whatever he was about to say and turned away from her.

"Who? I sound like who?"

"Never mind." He checked his watch. "Are you sure you can do this by yourself. I don't like you going there alone."

The change of subject threw her off, but Jess went along with it. She should've known better than to try to convince him to leave. He'd made his intentions more than clear. He didn't care what happened to himself as long as he got even, and she couldn't begin to control him. Why bother trying.

"I'll be fine," she assured him as she checked her watch. "You tagging along will only cause problems and besides, we need you here to make sure Maurice doesn't try to escape." She went back to the bench and sat down despite her frustration. She still had time to kill.

Tanner took the spot next to her again. The bench creaked under their combined weight. His shoulder grazed hers. Birds chirped in nearby trees. A cool breeze lifted her hair. Seconds ticked by and neither of them said anything. She kept her focus on the hedges on the far side of the driveway and didn't dare look at him. They were too close. She couldn't take the chance of another kiss. One had been more than enough and she didn't have time to kiss him anyway. Thank God, he'd pinned her arms because if he had any clue how much she'd wanted to touch him, he'd be all over her now.

Why was she thinking about that stupid kiss?

"Can I ask you a question?"

It beat sitting around thinking about kissing him. "I guess," she said.

"Why did you start working for Maurice in the first place?"

Jess leaned her head back and stared up at the sky. "I wanted to learn about filmmaking and I knew his name from my dad. I'd interviewed with a dozen different companies by the time I met Maurice and I was desperate to get my foot in the door." Maurice must have been laughing inside when he found her. So eager and willing to work her ass off just to learn about the business.

"So your dad told you about him?"

"To an extent, yes. I mean my dad didn't want me working for him, but he never gave me a specific reason why. I don't think he was a big fan of Maurice's. I just needed an in. I wanted to meet people, make connections. Without connections it's impossible to get a project off the ground. If I want to make films, I need to know the players."

"What is it you want to do specifically?"

"Write, produce and direct."

Tanner arched a brow. "That all?"

Jess huffed a laugh. "I gave Maurice a screenplay I wrote a few years ago and he keeps telling me that it needs work. That he'll consider shopping it when it's ready, but not before, and that even if he finds a backer, I probably won't be able to direct because no one's going to give a first time screenwriter the chance to direct her own film."

"Why not?" Tanner asked.

Jess snorted. "Because it rarely happens. The people who invest big money want to know they'll have a veteran directing their film or at least someone with a track record."

Tanner nodded. "So basically, Maurice has been dangling the carrot for three years to keep you towing the line."

Oh God. She was the biggest idiot on the planet. How long would she have continued to work for Maurice before realizing he was never going to help her? He used her any way possible as long it benefitted him, including let her take over Caitlin's position the past couple of weeks. Jess had only wanted to prove herself and instead she'd just made herself a bigger doormat.

Tanner shoved his knee into hers. "Hey, the good news is you only lost three years. The better news is it wasn't behind bars."

Meeting Tanner's gaze, Jess felt a fresh surge of compassion for the man. "What about you? What were you planning before..."

She couldn't finish the sentence, afraid to bring up the chunk of life that Tanner lost.

"Before Maurice put me away?" Tanner finished her question and she nodded. "I'd only been in college a few months. I wasn't sure what I wanted. I figured I'd go into business. It seemed pretty general and I could—" He cut himself off. "No sense in talking about it now."

"You could go back to school, you know. It's not too late."

He laughed. "Uh, yeah. I think it is too late. Can you imagine me sitting in a class with a bunch of eighteen year olds?" He shook his head. "I sure as hell can't see it."

"If you walked out of here right now. Where would you go? What would you do?"

The question seemed to stump him. He looked up at the trees and pressed his brows together. Finally, he looked at her, his gaze soft. "I don't know, Jess. I have no idea."

Jess ran her hands through her hair. It was crazy to talk about the future when the present was so screwed up. She couldn't think about tomorrow when she had to get through today first. "If it's any consolation, at the moment, I have no idea about anything either. I know more than I did three years ago about filmmaking. I've learned a ton." Jess sighed, sick at the way things had turned out. "I'd give it all up to have my family back here and safe."

Jess jumped up to pace in front of him. "I hate this waiting. I feel so trapped." It took another two steps before her words caught up to her brain and she shot a look at Tanner. He'd waited for seven years and he'd definitely been trapped. She ran her hands through her hair again. "I am so sorry." Sitting next to him, she inhaled and exhaled, long and slow. "That was stupid of me."

He shrugged. "Trapped is trapped. Yours is different than mine, that's all."

Because he'd spent it locked in a cell.

Every conversation came back to the same place. To Tanner's prison stay. Jess couldn't take any more. The conversation or the waiting.

"I have to go," she said, heading to the car.

"Jess."

She turned and found him right behind her.

"Be careful, okay." He looked worried. It was an odd feeling having him concerned for her. "Call me when you get out of there. If I don't hear from you within the hour, I'm coming over."

Nodding, Jess opened the car door. She still had more time to kill, but she'd rather drive around than stay in Tanner's reach. She needed alone time. Needed to think without the distraction of his presence.

She waited another twenty minutes, sitting in the lot of a nearby park and using the time to text Hector from Maurice's phone. Thoughts of her family, of Tanner and Maurice swirled in her brain and jumbled together until her head threatened to explode. She couldn't afford to make any more bad decisions. Too many lives depended on her. Her partnership with Tanner could only go so far. His help was a means to an end. Her main concerns centered around Maurice, his computer and his bank accounts. Without those things, she had nothing to bargain with. Losing her family wasn't an option. How could she live a life knowing she'd cost them theirs?

With new determination, Jess headed to Maurice's penthouse. Her stomach flipped as she took the plush elevator to the top. Her mouth went bone dry as she opened the penthouse door. The place was silent, not a bodyguard in sight. Her pulse revved when she walked into his office, her footsteps echoing on the Italian marble. With shaking hands, she scooped the laptop into her arms and shoved it in its case. She shouldn't be worrying, since she'd told Hector she hadn't quit. She felt as if the lie had been marked across her face in a black sharpie and anyone looking at her would know.

Almost done. Almost out. Sweat popped out on her temple and she swiped her forehead with her arm as she moved out of the office. Her strides got longer as she neared the door. The knob turned, the door opened before she reached it. Panic arrowed deep in her chest.

Run! Hide! The words screamed in her brain, but she stood completely still.

Hector walked in.

Jess didn't falter, didn't let panic guide her. "Hey, Hector. Maurice forgot his laptop. I swear if he doesn't pay me more for gas money, I'm quitting for real." She heard his grunt and nearly reached the door when his beefy hand on her arm stopped her.

"I thought you were scouting locations," he said.

Jess's stomach knotted. "We are. He's talking to some guy in the valley about using his house for the next film. I have to pick him up right now, then he said there was someplace else we have to go." This backed up the text she'd sent from the park—from "Maurice"—about his sudden decision to go to Santa Barbara for some R&R. It would be just like Maurice to ask her to take him without telling her beforehand and Hector would love knowing something she didn't. She tried easing her arm out of Hector's grasp, but he didn't let go.

He gave her a feral grin. "You've got him, don't you?"

Jess felt her whole body flush. Her mouth dried up again. "Got him?" she eked out.

"Yeah. Wrapped around your little finger. He must have done some real ass-kissing to get you back on the payroll. Last night he made it sound like you weren't coming back ever. "

A sigh nearly escaped, but Jess kept it in check and forced a grin. "You know Maurice. A real smooth talker." This time, Jess got her arm free from Hector's giant fist. "See you later." She continued toward the elevator, her heart pumping rivers of adrenaline, making every cell alive and screaming the need to run. But she didn't.

Her mother would be proud.

CHAPTER 11

THE BIG GUY THEY'D dubbed "No Neck" uncuffed Jay's right hand so he could eat the egg sandwich that had been dumped in front of him. Systematically, No Neck freed one hand each on the whole family before slipping the key into the lower pocket of his cargo vest. They hadn't eaten since yesterday's lunch and everyone dug into the food.

There was probably only one way to break through to the muscle heads taking turns watching them. Jay saw no point in wasting any more time, and No Neck seemed like a good candidate. "What's he paying you?" he asked.

The man sat in a folding chair by the door and holstered his gun. The chair groaned under his two-hundred-plus pounds. "Enough," he growled.

"I'll double it if you let us go."

Terry glanced at him, her jaws suddenly still before she looked at No Neck. "Yeah. We'll double it. Triple it," she offered, getting into the spirit. "You can disappear. No harm, no foul." Her gaze went straight to the pocket of his vest. She'd seen where he'd put the key too.

No Neck shook his head, his face a monument of zero emotion. If his eyes were any flatter, he'd be dead. Getting anything from this guy would take some work.

A cell phone buzzed and No Neck reached into his pocket to answer the call. "What?" He listened, stood up and opened the door. "Mr. Facinetti didn't mention that to me," he said as he closed the door behind him. His words disappeared into the hallway.

Facinetti? The name rang a bell. Jay had heard it at work on more than one occasion, but could it be the same man? As in Paul Facinetti?

"What?" Terry asked him. "You look like you thought of something."

"That name. Facinetti."

"You know him?" Eric asked before taking a bite of his sandwich.

"I know of him," Jay said. "If it's the man I'm thinking of, he's being investigated for money laundering, racketeering, tax evasion. The list is long. He owns a casino on the outskirts of Vegas."

"So what's he doing in L.A.?" Danny asked around a mouthful of food.

"That's what we need to find out."

No Neck came back into the room, pocketing his phone. He eyed everyone suspiciously, as though one or all of them had managed to get out of their cuffs in the last few seconds. Too bad no one here was named Copperfield.

"When do we find out what the hell is going on?" Jay asked.

"Shut up."

Eloquent.

Terry lifted a brow. The same look she'd give one of the boys if they said something disrespectful. A gesture that said more than words. No Neck didn't notice. He rested both chins on his chest and kept his gaze traveling the room while everyone finished eating.

Within five minutes they'd all demolished the food and cold coffee brought to them. No Neck cuffed them again before clearing the trash.

Another man came in and strolled around the room. They'd seen him a couple of times. Jay didn't like him or the obvious interest he took in Terry. He didn't look any smarter than the other men who'd been assigned to watch them, but he had a confidence about him that scared Jay. This man was no regular flunkie. Or maybe he was the top flunkie. That might've been where his attitude came from. He stopped in front of Terry and stared down at her with a leer. His gaze roamed from her chest to her feet and back again. Though she was wearing jeans and a loose, flowing green shirt, he looked at her as if she were naked. A geyser of possessiveness erupted in Jay's chest and he bit back the urge to lunge.

Terry had her legs in front of her. She looked relaxed enough, but Jay felt her tension, knew the hard expression in her eyes and on her face. He'd seen his wife when her patience was all used up. If this guy did one thing to piss her off, she'd lose her cool and they weren't in a position for her to do that.

"Terry. Don't." Jay said the words as softly as he could, barely moved his lips. But the guy standing over them heard anyway.

And he smiled. Maybe he recognized the defiance in her eyes. Maybe he didn't care and just wanted to see what she'd do. He kicked her foot and she lashed out fast, nailed him hard in the shin with the heel of her boot. Jay launched his body in front of her as the guy recovered and grabbed her shirt collar.

"Let her go," Jay growled, his blood pumping hot and violent. With his hands bound there was nothing he could do if this man chose to cart Terry out of here. Terry's chest rose and fell as Jay kept her pinned against the wall, his body the only thing between her and the jerk standing over them.

"Before this is over," the man said, staring into Terry's eyes, "you and me are going to go a few rounds. The nicer you are to me, the better it'll be for you later."

"Oh, we'll go a few rounds," Terry gritted out. "But it's not going to be what you're looking for. You'll be very sorry you messed with me and my family."

"Big talk from a little thing like you." He seemed genuinely amused by her. Maybe he hadn't heard what she'd done to his pal at the house. They hadn't seen any sign of him since.

"Why don't you take off these cuffs and we'll go now."

"Dammit, Terry, don't," Jay hissed. She wanted to get free, wanted to take this guy on. Clearly along with the tears in the bathroom, she'd leaked some common sense.

The guy released her shirt and stood up. He grinned at her. "Oh, we'll be going, sweet-thing. You can count on it."

Fury blinded Jay. He lashed out and kicked the guy high and hard on this upper thigh. It was reflexive. He couldn't let the guy threaten Terry and not do something about it. The man quickly recovered and grabbed a chunk of Jay's hair, holding him steady before pounding him with a hard left in the jaw. Pain exploded in his face, as the force threw him away from Terry.

Terry screamed and kicked out again, the boys raised hell too, and the man backed away.

He pulled out his gun and pointed it at Jay's head. "You want to fuck with me?" he asked.

"Leave him alone," Terry screamed. "You want me, come and get me."

The boys started shouting, probably to drown out their mother's words. Jay struggled to sit up, blinked to clear the stars circling in his head. He understood his family trying to protect each other, but the job belonged to him first. If he could distract this sleazeball from Terry, then he'd do it. Even if it meant getting his ass kicked. Or worse.

Across the room the door opened and the leader—Facinetti— walked in, still wearing that stupid mask. Of course, that mask was the only thing keeping them alive. As long as Facinetti thought his identity was safe, then Jay believed they had a shot at survival. He hoped the rest of the family realized it, because if someone said his name, their chances for a future went down the pipe.

Facinetti quickly assessed the situation. "Frank, step outside," he said.

Frank still had his gun pointed at Jay's head, but he slowly tucked it in his shoulder holster. He gave one last leer at Terry before heading out of the room. "She's mine," Frank muttered as he passed Facinetti. "She just sealed that deal."

Jay's gut churned and he took a deep breath to quell the nausea. Terry scooted closer, taking her place by his side. She looked as fierce as ever, refusing to let anyone see how scared she was. But Jay knew. He knew because he was scared shitless too.

The door closed and Facinetti surveyed all of them. "I wouldn't get Frank angry if I was you. He's not such a nice guy."

That was pretty fucking ironic coming from Facinetti. A man who had not only kidnapped a family of six, but had watched with no visible emotion as some goon had maimed Brendan last night.

"Then keep him out of my face," Terry snapped. "Better yet,

we'll be happy to skip on out of here if you take these cuffs off."
She jangled her wrists against the pipe.

"No can do." Facinetti shrugged.

"Tell me what you want," Jay said, straightening up against the
wall. The movement had his head and eye throbbing. He should've
come up with this earlier. He had a ton of contacts, including a
good, discreet private investigator. "I'll help you get whatever you
need, anything at all. Just release everyone else."

"Hmm." Facinetti seemed to consider it. "No. I don't think so. I
have a feeling your daughter can do the job just fine on her own."

Another shot of fury erupted in Jay's chest. He'd known since
the phone call that they were leverage, but hearing Facinetti talk
about it so casually made his blood roar. That this man was using
his daughter ate him up inside. "What the hell does Jess have to do
with this?"

"It's very simple. She has access to a man who owes me money.
She can either get me the money or give me the man. When she
delivers either, she gets you in return."

It all made sense. "You want Juneau, don't you?" Jay asked. A
part of him had hoped that Jess wouldn't run into trouble working
for him, but the lawyer part of him had suspected otherwise.
There'd been something about the man that had put Jay on edge
years ago, but with nothing to back up his feeling, he'd ignored it.
What a mistake. When Juneau's son, Alex, had been up on charges
of armed robbery and assault, Jay had done his job and gotten
Alex off with only some probation time, but the same couldn't be
said for Alex's buddy. Jay had believed Alex when the kid told him
that his best friend had put him up to the job. He'd been sincere,
desperate. It had been Jay's job to make sure Alex stayed free and
he'd succeeded. Only to have the sinking feeling when it was all
over that he'd made a terrible error. That maybe the wrong man
had been sent to jail.

Facinetti studied Jay. "As I said, he owes me money."

"So kidnap *his* fucking family," Blake muttered from across the
room.

"Nice mouth," Facinetti said, glancing at him. "I would have, but
his only son died a few years ago and he doesn't have any other
relatives. At least none that I could find. I took an alternate route."

"Kidnapping. Blackmail. You don't really want to face those charges." Terry said the words Jay had on his mind. He wished she hadn't. They only added to the list already there and maybe the longer the list got, the less the man cared.

Facinetti smiled. "I don't plan to."

Did that mean he planned to kill them regardless of whether he got his money or not? Jay didn't particularly want the answer. He tried again. "Look, let them go. I give you my word they'll stay clear of the cops. Keep me. Let my wife help Jess get your money."

Shaking his head, Facinetti grimaced. "I don't think so." He let his gaze roam the whole family. "It's nothing personal."

"Just business," Blake piped in.

"Exactly." Facinetti ignored the sarcasm and seemed pleased that at least one of them understood. The guy was out of his mind. He seriously considered this a business arrangement.

"What happens when Jess delivers?" Danny asked. The whole family watched Facinetti intently and he took his time answering.

"I guess that depends on what she delivers and when." Facinetti checked his watch and headed to the door. He shot one last look at Terry. "I'd be careful about getting Frank riled up. He likes you." He winked and let himself out the door, leaving Jay to worry that much more about something different altogether.

MAURICE LOOKED AROUND THE converted garage, frustration eating at him. His eye throbbed and the need for revenge raced in his blood. He leaned his head against the paneling along the wall and his gaze slid to the filing cabinet three feet away on his left. It sat askew, which didn't surprise him since he'd slammed into it after Bryant's punch, but the carpeting bulged abnormally behind the cabinet. Maurice took a closer look. He shifted a fraction and saw a flash of metal. Straining with one good eye, he struggled to make out the object lodged under the carpet. Maurice angled his body along the wall, wedged his foot behind the metal and pushed the cabinet. It moved without much muscle. Relief had his pulse racing faster. Once he'd cleared a few more inches, he used his heel and peeled back the carpet.

A screwdriver. Someone had dropped a screwdriver and left it, or lost it. It was short with a thick handle. Perfect. If he could get to it. That wouldn't happen with his shoes on. Maurice toed off his left shoe, glad he'd worn the slip-on kind instead of something with laces.

Sweat beaded his forehead, collected along his spine and under his arms. Using his right foot, he kept the carpet pulled back and with the left he edged the screwdriver along the wall and closer to his reach. He inched back, slowly making progress. After a few minutes, when he finally got his hands on the tool, elation bubbled in his chest. Maybe he could sharpen the edge of the flathead with the cement under the carpet and slice through the plastic cuffs. It was worth the try.

A noise outside made him freeze. Bryant? Or Jess? He didn't know. His pulse soared as he quickly let the carpet fall back, used his feet to push the cabinet in place then shoved his foot into his shoe. He faced front just as the door opened and Bryant came in.

Maurice didn't see the gun. Most likely Bryant had it tucked in the back of his jeans. The man sure as hell wouldn't come in here without one. Why would he come in here at all? Without a computer to access his account, they could only wait for Jess to return, which meant Bryant was here for another reason.

"What the hell do you want?" Maurice had lost all patience. He was hot and cramped and had no reason to put on an act. He was also pissed that he'd fallen into this situation to begin with. As soon as he sawed through these plastic cuffs, he was going to show Bryant exactly what kind of mistake he'd made. He'd show Jess too.

Bryant stood over him, his giant arms crossed over his chest. Considering the guy had spent seven years in prison, he looked damn good. He'd been a skinny kid when he'd been escorted from the courthouse, but he'd filled out. The man was enormous. He'd used his time well. He was strong. But did his strength match his mental health? Maurice doubted it.

"You never gave a second thought to putting me away, did you?"

Maurice rolled his eyes. "You're kidding me with this shit, right? What, am I supposed to feel guilty for saving my son? Go waste someone else's time, punk."

"But you couldn't save him, could you, Juneau? Alex went ahead and killed himself anyway. Ever think that if I'd stayed his buddy, I'd have kept him clean? Ever wonder about that? Maybe putting away your son's best friend contributed to his overdose?"

No, Maurice hadn't thought about it. Anger rumbled to the surface. Nausea swirled in his gut. "You have no idea what you're saying, Bryant. You're just a punk like all the other punks my son kept as friends. I told him to stay clear of all of you."

"Ever consider that your son was the punk and anyone who associated with him landed in trouble? And maybe it was his friends who helped him realize he needed more than the things his dad could buy him? Maybe he needed someone to listen to him instead of throw money at him to keep him quiet?"

Maurice yanked on the flex-cuffs, itched to wrap his hands around Bryant's neck and squeeze the life out of him. He'd given Alex everything. Yes, he'd worked his ass off and maybe he wasn't around a ton, but he had to make a living. Had to afford to give his son the best. "You have no idea what you're talking about," he growled.

"I know that even while I was in prison, Alex was up to his neck in trouble and drugs. Putting me away didn't change anything. You fucked up with your own son. You may as well have killed him yourself."

Maurice thought he might puke. Bryant hadn't spent near enough time in jail. Maurice couldn't wait to destroy him personally. "You're fucking insane, Bryant. You have no clue what you're talking about. You're grasping."

"I don't think so."

"No, you just don't think," Maurice shot back. Bryant thought he could make him squirm, but Maurice had learned to turn the tables on his opponents. He knew Jess's weakness, now he wanted to find Bryant's. "You never did think for yourself. I saw that much with my own eyes. You latched onto Alex because you didn't have anyone else. My son did you a favor hanging out with you."

Tanner simply shook his head so Maurice pushed him.

"I know what this is all about. You need someone to fuck with since you don't have your prison buddies to fuck anymore? Is that it? You're missing your boyfriends in Leavenworth."

Aside from the darkening of his already dark eyes, Bryant didn't budge. "Southern New Mexico Correctional Facility."

Maurice hadn't known where Bryant served his time. Hadn't cared. "You went in there pretty scrawny. Bet you got used to being somebody's bitch."

"You'd have liked that, wouldn't you, Juneau?" Bryant's gaze didn't waver as he stepped closer. The urge to check if he'd replaced the carpet burned in Maurice. He fisted the small screwdriver, kept eye contact and made sure Bryant's gaze didn't stray as he continued to speak. "I'm thinking I should call a few of the guys that were into that. Let 'em know I have a world class chump just waiting for a little action."

Bryant was full of shit. Maurice hadn't paid too much attention to him when he'd hung around Alex all those years ago. Teenagers were usually full of crap, but it was interesting that Bryant thought he could use scare tactics.

"What are you getting out of all this?" Maurice finally asked. Jess didn't have money to pay him. Bryant could get his revenge right now by unloading a bullet in his head. "Are you fucking Jess? Is that it? She leading you around by your crusty cock?"

"What makes you think I won't beat the hell out of you right now?" Bryant asked. He spread his legs, got more comfortable in his spot. "Whether she delivers you or the money doesn't mean you have to look good when it happens. If she does deliver the money, then you're all mine. Either way, you might want to drop that smile."

Maurice didn't. He wanted to stick it to Bryant any way he could. "Yeah, I'll bet Jess is a great fuck." What would it take to ruffle Bryant's feathers? Maurice wanted his weak spot more than ever. What hurt the man? "But it's hard to tell with those innocent ones. She does have a nice ass. Great tits too. I thought about doing her myself, but…" He shrugged. "Never got around to it."

Bryant's jaw clenched. Direct hit. "You haven't changed at all, Juneau. You're still the same sleazy creep you were all those years ago."

"But I was free, wasn't I? No prison cells for me. Nobody making me bend over and take it every day." Baiting this asshole was too easy. Bryant hadn't budged, but the tension in his body vibrated through the room. He pulled out the gun from the waistband of his jeans, but kept it at his side.

Maurice laughed. "You won't kill me or you would have already. Jess must have you by the balls just like your buddies in prison. I wouldn't be surprised if—"

Bryant lifted the gun and an explosion of sound reverberated in the room. The hiss of a bullet whizzed past Maurice's ear and he ducked to the left. Fuck! His adrenaline skyrocketed. He looked at the wall where a bullet lodged a few inches from where his head had been.

"You really have a fixation with my sex life," Bryant muttered dryly. "If I was you, I'd be more worried about when and how I was going to die. You know, I thought you might possess a fraction of remorse, but that would require you to have a conscience and clearly that isn't the case." Bryant kept the gun leveled at Maurice's eyes and the intense look on his face had Maurice sweating.

"You'd better thank Jess when she gets back," Bryant growled. "She's the only reason I'm walking out of here right now, because if I stay, I'm going to kill you. But this conversation isn't over, Juneau. Not by a long shot." Bryant tucked the gun into the back of his jeans and strode out the door.

Maurice exhaled and clenched the screwdriver in his hand. Time to get the hell out of here.

CHAPTER 12

A SENSE OF ACCOMPLISHMENT filled Jess as she jumped out of the car and sprinted into the house. She'd called Tanner after leaving the condo, so he knew she was on her way. "Tanner?" She set the computer on the kitchen counter and checked the den and living room. "Are you in here?"

Silence. Which meant he had to be in the studio. With Maurice. A seed of worry blossomed in her gut, but she fought the feeling before backtracking into the kitchen and rushing outside. Tanner had promised he wouldn't go back on his word. He'd told her he'd left Maurice alone to stew but planned to check on him before she returned. So why was her stomach turning summersaults?

Jess opened the studio door and the hinge creaked.

Tanner turned as she stepped inside. Behind him, a flash of movement widened Jess's eyes. Her pulse skyrocketed as Maurice launched himself at Tanner. Jess couldn't get a warning out. Didn't have the air in her lungs or words on her tongue. Tanner must have sensed the danger because he tried to dodge Maurice's body as he reached in his waistband for his gun. Too late. Maurice slammed into him hard. The gun bounced out of Tanner's reach. Maurice landed on top of him, pinning Tanner's right arm beneath him as he lifted his fist high in the air, ready to strike. Something flashed, and paralyzed, Jess could only stare, horrified, as Maurice viciously came down with a weapon in his hand. Tanner caught his wrist before the weapon imbedded in his head. A screwdriver? Maurice had a screwdriver in his hand!

Maurice's face was a mask of determination as he bared his teeth and fought like an animal. She never would've given him

122

credit for half the strength she saw, but adrenaline did amazing things for the blood stream.

Jess screamed. She had no idea what came out of her mouth, she was only aware of the pounding in her head, the violence and danger happening in front of her. She searched for something, anything that might help and spotted Tanner's gun on the floor.

Oh, God, she'd never held a gun. Hated guns with all her heart. But with shaking hands she picked it up and shouted one more time. "Stop!"

Both men continued to struggle. Sweat beaded Maurice's forehead as he adjusted and delivered several hard punches with his left fist, landing square in Tanner's face. The movement threw Maurice off balance and Tanner shifted enough to get his arm free. He returned the punch, knocked Maurice off him.

Jess almost breathed a sigh of relief. Until Maurice reached under his pant leg. Tanner lunged, but stopped short as he stared down the barrel of the gun and a satisfied smile on Maurice's face.

"You're such a stupid fuck," Maurice growled. "You were stupid then, and seven years in prison never changed you. You couldn't even hold me for a fucking day."

Jess lifted the gun. It was heavier than she expected, cool in her damp palms. She pointed it at her boss. "Maurice, p-put the gun d-down," she said. Her voice shook, her raw nerves rattled in desperation.

Maurice didn't bother looking at her and Tanner didn't either. They kept their eyes on each other as Maurice sneered. "You pat me down for a gun, but you're too stupid to find it."

When had Maurice ever carried a gun? How come she hadn't known about this?

Panic rose and made Jess sick to her stomach. She couldn't shoot him, but she couldn't let him shoot Tanner. "Maurice, I won't say it again, put the g-gun d-down." She put her finger more securely on the trigger.

"What are you going to do, Jess?" Maurice taunted, never letting his gaze move from Tanner's. "Stutter me to death?" The barb barely registered and he went on. "*I'm* going to do what I should've done years ago, Bryant. I'm going to put you out of your misery. How's that? No prison. No life. Just death. Maybe I'll make Jess here dig your grave. She seems to like you. Doesn't seem to faze her that you took it up the ass in prison." Standing a few feet from Tanner, Maurice wouldn't miss if he fired.

Tanner's nostrils flared. His fists clenched with unleashed fury.

Nausea roiled in Jess's stomach. She adjusted her aim, toward the ceiling. She wanted to scare Maurice, not shoot him. He hadn't even glanced at her, still had no idea she had a gun. She added a bit more pressure to the trigger.

"Adios, asshole." Maurice grinned, lifted the gun a fraction and took a step forward.

The gun exploded in Jess's hand, shocked her. The kick vibrated in her palms. Everyone flinched as a spark flashed overhead

Deadly silence descended over the room. Maurice swayed and the gun fell from his hand. He dropped to his knees then keeled over on his side.

What the... What happened?

Her gut clenched. The possibilities swirled in her head. "No," she whispered. The room tunneled, until Maurice was the only thing she saw. She waited for him to get up, trained the gun on him in case he tried to shoot Tanner.

Maurice, get up. But the words wouldn't come. She didn't have an ounce of spit in her mouth. The gun felt heavy in her hand, a thousand pounds of steel bogging down her whole soul. She willed him to move anything at all.

"Oh, Jesus," Tanner muttered. Funny, how she heard his words so clearly when the gun blast still reverberated in her head, in her whole body. He knelt next to Maurice, put two fingers to his throat. A few seconds later he looked at her, his eyes wide, filled with a mixture of panic and surprise. He saw the gun and edged toward her. "Jess, drop it." Yes, she wanted to. She wanted to give him the gun, but she couldn't move her fingers. They stayed locked tight around the butt. Tanner put his hand over the muzzle, lowered the weapon as he eased it from her grasp. "I've got it. Let go," he whispered.

She swallowed hard and shook her head. "Maurice?" she asked. She moved toward him. "He took a step," she blurted. "I wasn't aiming for him. I purposely raised the gun high." She knelt next to him, shook his shoulders. "No, no, no. Maurice! Get up! I didn't even hit you!" She turned back, looked at Tanner as desperation strangled her chest. "Help me," she wailed. "We need to get him help."

Tanner just stood there, watching her, his eyes dark, unreadable. But Maurice's eyes…they were sightless. Open and staring at nothing. How could that be?

The flash from overhead. Jess looked up at the dozen or so sculpted steel guitars hanging down. Blake had been making them for two years. One had a ding in the bottom. A ricochet?

Then she spotted it….the trickle of blood that ran next to Maurice's ear. She followed it to the neat hole in his head, hardly any blood except that little trail next to his thin sideburn. Her stomach clenched, bile backed up in her throat.

Dead? He was dead?

No, no. This couldn't be happening. "I told him to drop it," Jess cried. Maurice was her only hope. Without him, she didn't get her family back. "I t-told him."

"I know," Tanner said, taking her shoulders and helping her to her feet. Her legs barely held her and he picked her up, cradled her in his arms as he stalked out of the room.

"Tanner!" She fought his hold, looked back to Maurice. "What are you doing? We need to do something." The last word drowned in a sob as Jess's world crashed in around her. *This* wasn't an option. She couldn't lose Maurice. She needed him. Without him, she had no leverage, nothing to bargain with. She buried her head against Tanner's neck as the full realization set in. "Oh, my God. What did I do? What did I do?" She chanted the words over and over.

She'd sealed her family's death.

SHE'D SAVED HIS LIFE, but that hadn't registered with her yet. Tanner wondered if it ever would. All she knew was that Juneau was dead and she'd killed him. Didn't matter how inadvertent or accidental it was.

It was his fault. Tanner shouldn't have left him alone. He should've watched the scumball like a hawk. But if he'd stayed in that room, he would've killed Juneau. Remembering all the vile comments Juneau made about Jess still had Tanner's blood hot. Pulling the trigger and seeing the fear in Juneau's eyes had only satisfied him a little. If he'd listened to him another minute, he'd have a put a bullet between the man's eyes, but he'd given Jess his word so he'd stuck to it. He'd left Maurice alone for the better part of forty minutes. Forty minutes for Tanner to cool off. Forty minutes that had changed everything.

Now it was all over. He'd lost his chance. Sure, he got the result he'd come for, but even if he took the blame, which he planned to, Jess was the one who'd pulled the trigger. She was the one who had to live with it.

Tanner held Jess close against his chest as she fell apart. How the hell were they going to get out of this? He opened the back door and set her in a chair at the kitchen table. He crouched in front of her, held her face in his hands. "Jess, we'll figure something out."

She yanked away from him. "How?" she roared. "How am I going to get the money if he's dead? I can't even deliver Maurice now." Her flushed face twisted in horror as she shot out of the chair, forcing it over, nearly toppling Tanner too. "I've killed them. I killed Maurice and I may as well have killed my whole family."

He saw Juneau's laptop on the counter. "We still have the computer. Maybe we can—"

"Don't you get it?" she screamed, turning on him, her eyes wide and wild. "I killed him. There's no negotiating. No way to get my family back." She dropped her head in her hands. "I didn't mean to. Oh, God, I didn't mean to." She sank to the floor and Tanner's heart bled as her sobs echoed in the big room. "I just wanted to scare him. He never looked at me! He didn't see I had a gun."

Hell, Tanner hadn't known she'd had his gun. They'd both dismissed her, hadn't even glanced at her. Who'd have thought Jess would pick up a gun, much less pull the trigger?

She lifted her head, her face tear-streaked and swollen. "What did you do?" she asked, accusation in her tone. "Did you purposely let him go? Did you *want* to fight him?"

What? "No!" Tanner bit out. "You saw him. He jumped me

when you opened the door. He sawed those fucking cuffs off on his own." Speaking of sawing, for the first time, Tanner acknowledged the wetness dampening his shirt. He tugged at the collar of his ripped T-shirt to see the bloody line from the screwdriver. Juneau had sliced across his shoulder on his first attack. Fuck. He stripped off his shirt, grabbed the nearest dishcloth, and wiped up most of the blood.

"Oh, God," Jess said, already in another panic. "You're bleeding." Her face went another shade paler as she got to her feet. "I didn't know you were bleeding." She reached for the wall for support.

Tanner grabbed her shoulders, shook her a little. "I'm okay, Jess. Take a deep breath. I promise, I'm okay."

"You need stitches," she murmured. All color drained from her face just as it had when she'd spotted the bullet hole in Maurice's head. He'd seen it immediately. Had known in a second the man was dead. He'd been surprised, but his concern belonged to Jess.

She swayed.

Uh, oh. Tanner caught her and moved her into the den, onto the giant brown leather sofa in the middle of the room. Four ottomans tucked into the U-shaped sofa and made a huge bed. He laid her down, stuck a couple of pillows under her knees. "Stay here a sec. Don't move."

Now was his chance to go back to the studio. Jess was too out of it to follow or ask questions and he didn't want her going in there again. He needed to see what the police were going to see when they found the scene. There was too much DNA in there to cover this up. It was only a matter of time before the truth came out.

Tanner surveyed the room. Juneau was just how they'd left him, staring blindly ahead. The bullet had entered neatly and left a hole, but only a little blood trailed near the wound. The damage inside had to be pretty massive for the outside to be so neat. Tanner had heard that once. A bloody wound sometimes meant the damage inside wasn't as critical. On the other hand, very little blood on the outside, didn't bode well for the injured party.

Not that Juneau was injured. He was just very dead.

Tanner found a rolled up blanket and spread it over Juneau. He spotted the screwdriver, but didn't pick it up. He studied the flat end, as deadly as any knife blade. Juneau must have found it on the floor. There was no other explanation. Tanner didn't want to disturb the scene. Yeah, they may have brought Juneau here against his will and Tanner may have wanted him dead, but it wouldn't have happened if Juneau hadn't attacked him. It had been self-defense and Juneau's handprints on the screwdriver and his gun would prove it. So would the slice on Tanner's shoulder and so would the ding in the guitar where the bullet ricocheted. Tanner wouldn't have cared, but the fact that Jess had pulled the trigger changed everything. On his way out the door, Tanner turned up the AC to keep Juneau's body from decomposing quicker than necessary.

Tanner leaned against the closed door. Let the sun shine down on him. He hadn't gotten any answers. He'd wanted information from Juneau and now he had nothing. He'd wanted confirmation that Juneau had paid his lawyer to see him go to prison. He'd wanted a little regret from Juneau. Yeah, so that wouldn't have happened, but Tanner had still wanted to make Juneau sweat just as he had every day in that rotten prison.

He had no feelings for Juneau. At the moment, his concern lay fully with Jess. She'd done something he'd wanted to do with all his heart and she hurt for it. She'd agonize over it. Tanner wouldn't be able to tell her that it was no great loss, because killing Juneau meant the loss of her family.

Unless they came up with another plan.

Tanner entered the house and found Jess where he'd left her. She stared up at him, her eyes wet. "I f-fucked up," she whispered.

He hadn't heard her swear until now. Obviously it wasn't something she did often. If ever.

This was bad. He got that. She looked desolate. Destroyed. Her eyes glowed amber in her pale face and the familiar feeling of helplessness washed through Tanner. A feeling he'd lived with for years when it came to himself, but one he had harder time reconciling when it came to this woman.

Her gaze shifted to his shoulder and she sat up. "C'mon, we need to fix you."

"Just hang tight a minute and get yourself together. It's not bad," he said, swiping at the cut with the dishcloth.

"Don't treat me like a child." The steely look she shot him blazed anger. "I can see what's in front of my eyes and you need help." She moved off the sofa and left him to follow her. She disappeared inside the walk in kitchen pantry.

With the dishcloth soaked in blood, Tanner opened drawers and looked for something else to place on his shoulder. He found something better. Krazy Glue.

Chino had told him how his brother used it in emergency situations. That it was originally intended to put the skin back together but found wider use for everything else. No reason not to test the theory. After a last wipe with the dishcloth, Tanner pieced the skin together and spread the glue along the seam.

Jess came back from the pantry with a red first aid kit. "What are you doing?" She took a closer look at his shoulder then at the glue on the table. "You didn't do what I think you did, did you?" Anger laced her voice and Tanner held back his smile. There was something so fresh and innocent about Jess that even now, when they should've been shitting bricks and figuring out what to do with Juneau's body, she was making him grin.

Fishing in the kit, Tanner found some bandages in case the Krazy Glue didn't work.

Jess slapped his hand away. "Let me do it. You're all thumbs. Sit here," she ordered, pulling up a nearby stool from the center island. She adjusted the bandages and Tanner struggled not to breathe her in. She smelled like flowers, like spring. Like something he didn't deserve. Her fingers fluttered over his skin, heated him up. He looked away from her, over her, anywhere but at her, because if he gazed into her eyes, all bets were off. It didn't matter that a dead man lay in her converted studio, if she kept touching him so tenderly, kept wafting her soft breath near his ear while she worked, he was going to explode.

Adrenaline already had him hard as a post. Having her so close didn't help one damn bit. She made his condition worse, made him hunger with uncontrollable need. Just when Tanner reached his limit, when he meant to take her in his arms, she pulled back, slammed the top of the kit down and stalked away.

"I have to think of something." She paced the big kitchen. *"Think."* She kicked the big stainless steel garbage can. Her denial had turned to anger. About time. She should've been this angry from the beginning, but fear had been her driving force.

Tanner had been angry so long he hardly knew any other emotion. Except lust maybe. The last day had him very much thinking about lust. And sex. Hard driving, sweat inducing, lusty sex. He turned his back to her, faced the open part of the spacious kitchen, because if he watched her much longer, he wouldn't be able to keep his hands or certain other body parts to himself.

A definite silence stilled the air and Tanner looked over his shoulder. Jess watched him with narrow eyes and hands on her hips. "You're leaving, aren't you?"

"I hadn't thought about it." Which was the truth. But he sure as hell could walk right out her door and leave everything behind him. He got what he wanted even if it wasn't the way he wanted it. Juneau was dead and Tanner could move on.

Except leaving Jess didn't seem like an option. Not one he wanted anyway.

"I told you I'd help you and I intend to."

"Why?" Quick and to the point. The girl didn't fuck around. "What's in it for you?"

He shrugged. "I don't know." Maybe it was time he did something proactive instead of destructive. Hadn't he been sabotaging himself the last eight years of his life? First by hanging out with Alex, then putting his future in Juneau's hands by letting him hire his lawyer, and lastly by alienating his whole family by ignoring them while he sat in prison.

Maybe he just liked being around a woman. Maybe he liked watching the way she walked, the way her ass swayed. Or maybe it was her smell, or the whiskey color of her eyes. Hell, no maybes about it. Everything about her turned him on.

"Well you might want to figure it out, because I'm up shit's creek without a paddle and I need somebody I can count on. If that's not you, then get out." Did she intend to cut him loose and start fresh by herself?

Tanner rose and stood in her path as she glared up at him.

"Why the hell are you so mad at me? I didn't free Juneau and I didn't kill him." A low blow. One he instantly regretted.

Her chin quivered and that's all it took for the slime ball feeling to swamp Tanner's chest. The pain in her eyes cut him soul deep.

"You son of a bitch," she cried. She was hurting and he had no clue how to help. She hit him, slammed her palm against his chest and didn't stop. Tears streamed down her face as she let loose with her small fists. Tanner let her pound him. He deserved it. She wanted a fight and he wanted to die. He hadn't meant to hurt her physically or emotionally and he'd done both. He took every blow she delivered. A few of them packed more punch than he'd have given her credit for, but he didn't stop her.

Finally, breathing hard, she wore herself out. The violence didn't faze him, but when she sank against him, when she buried her face in his chest and cried... That knocked him out. Broke through every barrier he'd ever erected.

His arms went around her. He didn't intend to do it, but there they stood in her parents' kitchen, holding onto each other as if the world might end any second. Her crying slowed and eventually stopped. She pulled back and looked up at him.

Tanner's mistake was looking into her eyes. Seeing all that pain and not caring how he might hurt her again. Jess's mistake was looking at his lips, inviting something that would ignite and blow out of control with very little prompting. She gazed into his eyes again, offered a clear invitation when she rose on her toes, slanted her head to the side and spread her warm hands on his chest. Tanner met her halfway, brushed his lips against hers, tasted the salt of her tears and the desperation of the day.

Desperate.

That word described them both. She was desperate for help and he was desperate for relief. Desperate for the warmth of her skin and the comfort of her hot body.

His control broke.

Tanner pulled her close, trapped her lips beneath his and took what he wanted. She didn't fight him. Goddammit, she should be fighting him. She should be scrambling to get away, because if she didn't, she was going to be in way over her head. Instead she was clawing to get closer. He palmed her head, drove his tongue into her mouth and tasted the mints she chewed like an addiction. He ran his hands along the sides of her body, felt the hot little curves that had been driving him wild.

She moaned and the sound vibrated into his body, made him hotter. He lifted her against his erection, pushed the small of her back so she felt exactly what was coming her way if she didn't fucking fight him.

But no, she moaned again and Tanner felt his insides snap. He couldn't do this to her. Not after she'd saved his life. He would hurt her and she didn't deserve that. Tanner released her and stepped back, breathing hard, fighting to maintain his distance.

Her lips were red, already swollen from his kiss. Her whiskey eyes glowed bright, not with tears, but with desire. "What? What's wrong?" She was breathing hard too. The sheen in her gaze faded as she watched him. Her eyes narrowed and her anger inched its way back. Tanner would've seen it coming a mile away. She advanced on him and he steadily backed up until he hit the wall and could go no farther. "You're going to kiss me like that then stop as if nothing happened," she blasted. "Maybe I wasn't done. Maybe I need more."

Who the hell was this girl? How had she taken control from him? Didn't matter. Time to take it back. This little slip of a girl was not in charge. Tanner stood taller and loomed over her. "You have no idea what you're getting into with me, Jess. You're damn lucky I stopped when I did."

"Don't tell me I'm lucky," she railed back. "I'm the most unlucky person on the planet. Maybe for a few minutes I didn't want to think about it. I thought you might be willing to help me out with that, but I guess I was wrong."

"What did you think was going to happen? That I'd say shit you needed to hear, tell you lies like 'everything's going to be fine'? You think it's going to be one thing and I can guarantee you it's going to be the opposite." He advanced on her and this time she had the common sense to move back. "It's not going to be gentle. Or tender. Or romantic. Are you ready for the truth, Jess? If I touch you again, it's going to be hard. It's going to hurt. I won't be able to stop and you won't be able to stop me. You'll cry, scream. You'll fight to get away from me and I won't let that stop me from taking you. Is that what you want?"

She punched his chest again. "Is this your tough guy act?" She mocked him, stood tall and close as if she matched him. Stupid girl. "Who said I wanted gentle? Or tender. Or romantic." She threw his words back at him, with the same volume, same force. "Maybe I need something more than that. I need to forget how totally fucked up this whole—"

Tanner kissed her. He didn't need or want to hear more.

CHAPTER 13

TANNER SOAKED HER IN. From her hot mouth and voracious tongue to her tight little body and curvy ass. He couldn't keep his hands off her. Couldn't keep his tongue from exploring her mouth. He planned on tasting every inch of her. He backed her up against the kitchen wall, rubbing against her as if just the motion might ease his desire.

Not a chance in hell.

He should slow down. He had her, she'd all but demanded it of him, so he should back off and go slower, but he'd told her he wouldn't be able to stop and he'd been right. He wanted to drive himself so deeply inside her that it wiped out the last seven years of his miserable life. He wanted salvation in her body. He wanted to feel alive.

He couldn't wait to touch all of her skin. He wanted to feel her with his hands, his mouth, his tongue. He wanted to hear all the sounds that went with taking a woman. He wanted her moans, her gasps, wanted her screaming his name and digging her nails into his skin.

He wasted no time in stripping off her T-shirt. The bandage was a reminder of the night they met, but it was the sight of her full, pert breasts hidden under a white lace bra that stopped him for a second. He moved his palms up her sides, pulled the cups down and touched her, thumbed her tight nipples and groaned.

Tanner unhooked the back of her bra as he sucked one hard peak into his mouth. She gasped, arched into him and sent him further out of control. He wasn't going to last. He needed her now, needed her hard and fast. But he had to touch her, had to explore all the places he'd been dreaming about.

Dropping to his knees, he made quick work of the button and zipper on her jeans. He stripped them over her hips, down to the floor. "Step out," he ordered, his voice guttural, not his own. He shoved the discarded jeans and her shoes aside and held her hips. Her bikini underwear molded her body. She was so fucking tiny.

It wasn't going to stop him.

He eased the white lace slowly down, giving himself Christmas in the middle of May, forcing himself to enjoy the anticipation instead of driving into her so hard that she'd never forgive him. That was bound to happen, but the longer he could hold off, the better they'd both be. The elastic band stretched in his thumbs, her breath hitched as he removed the thin barrier. Tanner glanced up at her, saw the sheen of desire in her eyes…and the innocence. The combination revved his pulse faster.

The lace fell to her ankles and she stepped out of those too.

Tanner breathed her in as his hands traveled up her thighs and over her hips, committing this moment to memory. Auburn curls glistened with moisture. He smelled her excitement. His cock hurt so bad and he stifled another groan as he leaned in and took her with his mouth.

Candy. She was the best candy he'd ever tasted. Sweet and tart at the same time. Her fingers tunneled through his hair and drove him on. No problem there. He liked this spot just fine. He hadn't had a woman like this in so long he'd nearly forgotten the pleasure. But he burned for her and he wasn't going to last, so he started slow, but soon worked her hard, used his tongue over her clit and pushed two fingers into her slick heat until he brought her to a fast climax, felt her clench and shatter as she called his name and trembled in his arms.

He needed her. Now.

Tanner stood and took her mouth, kissed her hard and long, drove his tongue deep inside her as his shaking hands fumbled with his zipper. And, goddammit, she helped him. Blindly, they both fumbled to get his jeans over his hips, to pull his erection free. Her hot little hands circled his cock and another harsh moan croaked in his throat. Tension cycled tighter in his gut as he lifted her, pinned her against the wall with the bulk of his body and guided himself to her wet entrance.

Tight. So tight. He'd made her as ready as he could, given her a hard orgasm and loosened her up, but she was still so tight, the feeling ramped up his need. He wedged the head of his penis inside her, shoving hard and retreating in increments. Mind numbing pleasure ate away his thoughts. Everything faded but the incredible tightness of her surrounding him. He buried his head in her neck as he continued to thrust, working his hips, driving inside her until he was deep. He would've stopped, just to soak her in, to feel the sensation of total penetration, but he couldn't. He kept driving, barely aware of her heels digging into his ass, her arms wrapped around his neck.

Her muffled gasps drove him nuts, her fingernails dug into his shoulder blades. Harder and harder he pounded her, his heart slamming against his ribs, sweat coating his skin. Two more hard thrusts and he came, shooting his come into her welcoming body, continuing to drive up inside her as he gave every last drop of himself.

Oh, God, it wasn't enough, he needed more. Still hard, he kept moving, kept her pinned until her cry penetrated his slogged brain cells. Tanner stilled long enough to look at her, to see the tears in her eyes. He'd hurt her. He told her he would. Contrition swept through him in a massive wave.

"The wainscoting," she said.

"Huh?" His mind wasn't working.

"The molding on the wall," she said. "It's right against my lower back."

"Shit!" That was bound to leave a mark. Every hard thrust had slammed her against the molding and she hadn't said a thing.

Tanner held her close and moved into the den, still deep inside her, still hard and hurting with his jeans hung low over his ass and the urge to drive into her harder and faster. Panting, he lay back against the giant leather couch, keeping her on top of him, holding her hips tightly to his.

Though there was something stirringly erotic about having a naked woman covering him when he was partially dressed, next time they did this he'd have to lose the jeans. Right now, he didn't care. He wanted more.

"Ride me. Hard," he grated. He palmed the back of her head again and took her lips in a fiery kiss.

JESS TOOK HIS HARD, erotic kiss and gave back as good as she got. She wanted him this way. Hard. Uncompromising. In some perverted way, she'd wanted the pain. It was penance for screwing everything up. For working for Maurice in the first place. For killing him and probably killing the chances of getting her family back. What she hadn't expected was Tanner's intensity. It overwhelmed her. Shook her. Granted, she'd been limited in her sack time with men, but she sure as hell wasn't a virgin. Yet that was how Tanner made her feel. He kept her off balance, made her burn. No man had ever wanted her so badly that he couldn't wait for a bed. Her need had never been so powerful that she hadn't cared.

The power he radiated, the sheer force of his sexuality made her dizzy. His sculpted chest, dusted with dark hair, rippled under her fingertips. Veins bulged in his arms.

The sensations buffeting her body sent her flying. Tanner couldn't seem to stop touching her. If his hands weren't on her hips, they were on her breasts, or cupping her head or stroking her skin. He was everywhere. His tongue filled her mouth, licked inside her with wild desperation. She'd never felt so needed, as if her body alone held some type of redemption.

"Do it, Jess," he rasped. "Ride me hard."

A flush heated her cheeks. No man had ever talked to her this way either, or taken her so fiercely. His fingers bit into her hips as he adjusted her on top of him.

She hadn't had sex in so long she doubted her ability to give him what he wanted. And she'd hardly ever been on top. Her old boyfriends had been happy to keep her underneath, happy to keep control. Not that she had any control now. Tanner thrust up and took her off her knees, holding her steady as he moved, driving her down on top of him. The friction was too good. The burn made her cry out.

Tanner's jaw clenched tight, his eyes shone bright, watching her, owning her. "Jess." He hissed her name, the same plea unspoken. *Ride me hard.*

Balancing her palms on his chest, Jess snapped her hips, riding Tanner in rhythm with his powerful thrusts. She felt him deep, deep inside her, driving her toward another orgasm, whipping her body into a whirlwind of sensation, making her feel more than she ever had before.

God, she was so close, so close to coming, when he pulled her down, crushed her chest against his and took her mouth.

"Harder," he grated against her lips. "Grind down on me." He palmed her tailbone, one hand stretched across both butt cheeks, pressing her against him. She gasped into his mouth as the motion put pressure on her clit and sensation exploded inside her.

"That's it." His voice was low, strained. "Like that."

Jess ground herself on him. Electric streaks tore through her with every rub of her clit against him. His palm stayed on her ass, one finger pressing in the cleft between her cheeks, driving her harder. Sensory overload. Feeling him move inside her, along with the rasping of her already sensitive clit, Jess barely found air to breath. Sweat coated her skin as she slid over Tanner's chest.

"Come on me, Jess," he whispered in her ear. "I want to feel you rain that hot cream all over me." He thrust up and pressed her down at the same time, sending her hurtling into the abyss. Time stopped. Everything stopped. Her heart thundered behind her ribs, in her head. Pleasure like she'd never known exploded from the inside out, blew her brain cells into tiny fragments of nothing. She lost touch with everything but the waves cresting under her skin, raining through every part of her like the perfect storm. Unimaginable satisfaction spread within her, stealing her breath, her sanity. Her lips parted on a silent cry and Tanner's face blurred in front of her.

Baring his teeth, Tanner's grip tightened on her hips, his shout echoed in her ears. His second climax shot inside her with more intensity than the first. His invasion tore through her heightened senses and she clenched around him, milking him, taking everything he gave.

After every last ripple washed through her, Jess collapsed on

Tanner's damp chest. Gasping for breath, she closed her eyes, would've pulled away the wet strands of hair off her cheek, but she couldn't move.

Breathing hard beneath her, Tanner still had his arms around her, kept them connected tightly together. Slowly, his hands roamed her slick skin. His rough fingertips sent tiny currents racing through her exhausted body, brought chills to the surface.

This touch felt different. More than sexual. As if he wanted to imprint her form into his head. As if he might never get the chance to hold her, or any woman, ever again. His palms roamed over her butt, up her back, along her sides, his touch firm, but tender.

The real world crashed in when he stopped stroking her. When he lifted her off him. His withdrawal from her body had them both taking a sharp breath. Emptiness swamped her, flooded her senses as he sat up, his legs over the couch, elbows on his knees, head in his hands.

With the silence came a wave of regret so massive Jess got nauseas.

What had she done? How could she have done it? What did she do now? Her eyes burned with the threat of tears. She couldn't seem to stop making everything worse.

The phone rang and saved Jess from falling apart with an instant nervous breakdown. She grabbed the chenille blanket on the sofa and wrapped herself up before answering the phone on the corner table.

"Jess? That you? It's David. Is Bren around? He's not answering his cell and I can't find him anywhere. We're supposed to meet up tonight." David Meyer had been Brendan's best friend since third grade. They were almost as close as Brendan was with his twin, Blake. David and Brendan suffered from egghead syndrome with their fascination of anything computer or video related. Though the twins had come out at the same time and were eerily close, their personalities were completely opposite. Blake's knowledge of computers stopped after Google and email.

"Hi, Dave."

Tanner's gaze locked on her. She turned her back on him, self-conscious in the blanket, her face flaming with embarrassment and her thighs uncomfortably sticky from sex. Unprotected sex. Oh, God, what had she done?

"Bren's not here," she said, finding her voice. But she had a dead guy in the studio and a virtual stranger nearby who'd just screwed her brains out. Jess swallowed and subtly used the blanket to clean the wetness from her thighs.

"Have you seen him? We're supposed to go to the Mac store to check out the new laptops."

"No. I haven't s-seen him," Jess murmured. But she did have a laptop here. Maurice's laptop. With information she needed. "Mom told me the boys took a quick r-road trip to Vegas. Bren must have forgotten about your computer date. He should be back in a day or two." *If only*... Her face heated at the blatant lie.

"I can't believe that shithead didn't call me. He knows I'm looking to upgrade."

Guilt swiftly reared its ugly head and Jess scrambled to change the subject. "Hey, Dave, can you hack into a computer?"

He laughed, and some of her tension eased out in a breath. "What's Bren been telling you? Look, I only wanted to get into Chloe's address book. I had no idea she—"

"No, Dave. Listen to me." God, what if someone else was listening to her right now. What if the phones had been tapped? What if Facinetti had that kind of power? "Better yet, can you come by here?"

"When?"

Jess glanced over her shoulder. Tanner still watched her, but he'd pulled up his jeans and covered himself. "Now."

"I can't right this minute. I'm still at work, but I'll be off in another few hours. I can come by when I'm done. Everything okay?"

"Yeah, sure." She couldn't tell him the truth. Didn't want to involve him more than she had to. He didn't have to know why she needed his hacking skills, and he'd either find what she needed or he wouldn't. "Everything's fine. I just need your help with a computer issue....Thanks." Jess said goodbye and hung up the phone.

"Who's Dave?" Tanner asked.

She felt his solid presence behind her, smelled the sex that still lingered on his body and in the air. "He's my brother Brendan's best friend. They're both computer geeks." Jess found her courage and faced Tanner. Just because she felt like crap, didn't mean Tanner had to know it. "I thought he might be able to hack into Maurice's computer and find those accounts."

"Even if he does, we don't have the bank passwords."

"Maurice said they're on the computer. It's just a matter of finding them. If we can't, I'll go back to his office. Maybe there's a master list somewhere or a flash drive he used as backup. I don't know. It's worth a try." Emotion clogged her throat. "I can't stay here and do nothing." She definitely couldn't stay here and have more sex with Tanner either.

Tanner's dark eyes watched her as if he knew what she was thinking. He set his palms on her shoulders and rubbed along her arms, sending chills across her skin.

"You shouldn't go back to his place," he told her quietly. "It's too dangerous. Once was bad enough, but you can't risk it again."

There was only one thing she couldn't risk again and it had nothing to do with going to any of Maurice's places.

Jess stared up at him. "You don't understand. I'll do whatever I have to, whether it's going to all of Maurice's stupid houses or offering myself in place of him. I lost all my bargaining power when I k-killed Maurice so nothing matters as long as I get the information I need." Just saying the words aloud made her dizzy.

"Bullshit." Tanner's grip tightened on her arms. "It matters. You need to stay alive to help your family so being stupid isn't part of the plan."

Stupid? Wasn't that the magic word? She'd been stupid to work for Maurice in the first place. Stupid to hold a gun in her hand, stupid to kill the only man who could get her family back alive. The word lingered inside her like a bomb and the explosion erupted with little warning.

"Get your hands off me!" Jess stepped back, out of Tanner's immediate range. "I've already proved the stupid part by killing Maurice, so spare me the lecture. I fucked up. Are those words you understand?" Jess turned before he saw the emotion in her eyes. She couldn't, didn't want to break down in front of him.

Once again his presence loomed behind her. "Maurice fucked

up when he wouldn't help you in the first place," he said quietly. "Maurice fucked up when he didn't give Facinetti his money back." One strong arm came around her waist and pulled her snuggly against him. "*You* did *not* fuck up. You saved my life, Jess. I won't ever forget it and I won't take it for granted. I owe you in this and I'll do whatever you want." His warm palm smoothed down her arm. "But I can't help you if you're dead, get it?" He moved his hand over her throat until her head rested against his chest. A totally dominant position. He could snap her neck like a twig and be done with her, Maurice and the whole situation if he wanted. Instead, his lips nuzzled beneath her ear. "Drop the blanket," he told her.

A zing of sexual electricity sparked in her blood, tore through her veins. Her mind might have decided to avoid sex, but it hadn't told her body.

His voice stayed calm in her ear. "I didn't realize the molding was hurting you. You should've told me. Let me see the damage I did."

A flash of disappointment hit hard. "I'm okay. Just a bruise." But she felt him tugging at the material.

"Drop it, Jess." The command was quiet, but steely.

Jess kept the material gathered around her front, but let it fall in the back, exposing the sore spot at the base of her spine.

"Ah, damn," Tanner muttered. His thumb brushed over the spot and she jerked. Not because it hurt, but because his touch affected her on a molecular level. He drew her back against him, more gently this time. "I'm sorry," he whispered in her ear. "I didn't want to hurt you. I *don't* want to hurt you." He turned her in his arms, cupped her face in his hands. "How about some ice for your back."

Not the words she expected to hear.

But Tanner had yet to do something she expected. He looked big and mean. Sometimes he even acted mean, but deep down he had a soft side. He'd threatened her, but he'd never followed through. Well, aside from shooting her and choking her, but nothing had been done with malice or premeditation.

"Why are you smiling?" he asked, his lips curving in a rare grin.

"Because, I'm adding this to the list of your transgressions."

"Transgressions?"

She ticked off the list with her fingers. "Shooting me, choking me and now slamming me into the wainscoting."

His face darkened and his eyes narrowed. "None of those things happened intentionally."

"I know. Can you imagine if you meant to hurt to me?" She arched a brow. "I feel sorry for the people you don't like." Maurice for instance. Maurice, who was dead in her garage because she'd shot him. Maurice, who was the key to getting her family back safe.

"Hey, don't," Tanner scolded, almost as if he knew what she was thinking. His hands moved to her neck, his thumbs under her chin, keeping her head up and her gaze on him.

Jess pulled out of his grip, anger and frustration clawing its way up her chest. "Don't?" she mocked. "Don't think about it? Not possible. I killed a man, then I promptly slept with you. I must be nuts? I've lost my mind. My whole family is being held hostage and I'm standing here in a blanket because my clothes are on the kitchen floor because I let you take them off me." She stalked past Tanner, toward the kitchen and the clothes she needed to put back on.

But Tanner was right behind her. "You started the whole thing, Jess, so don't go blaming me. I told you from the beginning what was going to happen if you pushed me so don't start—"

"I know!" She turned on him. Made him stop short as he loomed in front of her. "It was my fault. This whole situation is my fault. My dad told me not to work for Maurice and did I listen? No, of course not." She scooped up her jeans and underwear from the floor. "I had to make my own way. I had to take the first job that came along that would get me into films. I had to be on my own, prove I could be independent." Jess turned so Tanner couldn't see the emotion on her face. She couldn't blame him for anything. This whole situation was her fault for working for Maurice in the first place.

"When are you going to get it through your thick head that you didn't do this?" Tanner asked softly. "When are you going to quit beating yourself up for something Maurice created?"

"When I get my family back."

Jess dropped the blanket and yanked her underwear on. Her jeans came next, but she flinched when the waistband hit the bruise on her back.

"Dammit, Jess." Tanner banged around in the freezer and came back with an ice bag. "C'mere." When she didn't, he stalked toward her, his face set, his jaw clenched. "Don't make me put you over my knee," he said.

She flipped her shirt on and turned to him, furious that he'd even suggest it. "Don't you dare threaten me."

"That's not a threat, baby, that's a promise. Pull the jeans down." When she glared at him, he continued, "Not all the way down. Far enough so we can put some ice on you." He wiped his hand down his face and when he opened his eyes, he looked exhausted. "I don't want to fight you, Jess. I just want to help."

That did it. Tears welled up in her eyes. He did want to help. He'd been proving it since the minute he absconded with her at the studio. Tanner tugged her into his arms, held her close. "We'll figure it out," he said. "We just have to stay together on this." His chest radiated heat. "When does this Dave guy get here?"

"He's a barista and he works the morning shift. He won't get here for another few hours."

"So we've got time."

"Time for what?" Jess asked. She couldn't just fall back into his arms. She had to stay clear, stay focused on what mattered.

Tanner set the ice bag on her back and Jess gasped. "Time for some ice." When she looked up at him, he gave her a half grin, then slowly leaned down and kissed her. This kiss differed from the others. This one was soft, tender. This one unraveled her senses in a different way. His tongue licked at her lips, enticed her to open for him. Even as the ice cooled her back, his kiss heated her up. His tongue danced with hers, slick and hungry. His big hand stroked through her hair and sent her senses flying. "I want to be inside you again," he whispered at her lips. The words prompted a full body flush. "But I can wait until tonight."

"I don't know." She had no idea what the rest of the day would bring. Could Dave hack into Maurice's computer? Could they access the accounts? And if they did, could she get her family back tonight? Jess backed away from Tanner and he let her. He could push her if he wanted. They both knew it. She'd melt under his touch because she needed the contact, the reassurance. But she needed her independence more. Needed to be strong, when she really wanted to forget everything and fall into Tanner's strong arms. She picked up his T-shirt from the back of the chair and tossed it to him. He caught it one-handed. The less skin she saw the less tempted she'd be. That and staring at the bandages and all those scars made her ache for him.

He eyed her before whipping the T-shirt over his head. "You want to tell me what's got you all tongue tied now?"

She was on the edge. Way too emotional as she blinked back the sting in her eyes. "I was…I'm sorry about all your scars. You went through hell and…" She didn't know what to say. Maybe it was one fight in seven years that had given him all those marks. Maybe it wasn't as bad as she feared. "Are all those scars from one fight?"

He shook his head. No. "More like a dozen. When you stand up for yourself and fight, you become a target. Every man wants to be the one who brings you down."

She couldn't imagine being on guard all the time. Always having to watch her back or risk being attacked. "I'm sorry," she whispered. "Sorry you went through it. Sorry Maurice did what he did to you." Even though he was free of prison, the attacks stayed with him in his dreams. How long would he have to live with that? Was he scared to go to sleep at night because of what his mind might conjure up?

She ran her hands through her hair. "Look, I can't explain why this happened." She gestured between them, indicating the physical relationship. "But I don't promise that it's going to happen again. I need to stay focused on what matters. I need to think this through."

Tanner nodded. "I hear you. But I'm not letting the situation get in the way of *this*." He stressed her same word as he motioned between them with her identical gesture.

Life just got more and more complicated.

CHAPTER 14

TERRY HAD A PLAN but Jay must have misunderstood it.

"What?" he asked. He knew the question made her suggestion sound idiotic, but honestly...that's what it was.

"I'll get the guy outside to unlock my cuffs." Clearly his tone hadn't fazed her because she launched into the idea again. "I'll tell him I have cramps and need to use the bathroom. I'll trip on the way out and fall against him then I'll pickpocket the key. When he leaves, I'll get all our cuffs off. Then we'll lure him back in here and you can smash him over the head with something." She sounded so hopeful. Looked it too, with her wide blue eyes.

Just because they knew which pocket the key was in didn't mean she could get it unnoticed. "No, Terry." Jay said it quietly, but the there was no mistaking the unequivocal order. They were in enough trouble without her doing something so risky.

"It's worth a try," she whispered, shooting a glance toward Eric. Neither one of them wanted the boys to know what they were talking about, but Eric was watching, probably trying to lip-read. He'd always had the biggest ears of the all the kids.

Jay struggled to keep his voice down. He had to make her see how crazy this sounded. "You don't even know how to pick a pocket."

Terry's brows lifted, excitement brightened her eyes. "Yes, I do. Remember when I was in that production of Oliver at the community center?"

Was she serious? "A play? You think because you acted in a play that you can do the real thing?" Had she gone off the deep end? Did she really think playing a street urchin pickpocket gave her the ability to do it in real life?

146

"I got good at it, remember?" she insisted.

He did, but that didn't make this plan any more enticing. "This isn't a play, Ter. These guys are big and they have guns. Did you forget what they did to Bren and Danny?" Both boys had a couple of cracked ribs and extra bruises on their faces, not to mention Bren's lack of an earlobe.

Terry glanced at the boys and anger lit her eyes. "No. I didn't and I'm not going to sit here like a helpless victim when I can try and do something to get us out of here." She took a steadying breath. "I can do this, Jay. Remember all that time I spent with the guy Joshua hooked me up with?" Joshua was their neighbor and fellow lawyer. When Terry was preparing for her role in the play, he'd introduced her to a reformed street thug whose specialty was picking pockets. Terry had been a quick study. For weeks, she'd enjoyed swiping keys, watches and wallets from every unsuspecting family member. Her ability had been frighteningly natural. But still, from doing a play eight years ago, to doing the real thing now... That was a stretch for anybody much less someone out of practice.

"I hate it."

"I don't love it either, but we're desperate and it's worth a shot."

Jay shook his head. If he wanted to be honest, his wife might be able to pull it off. She was small and constantly underestimated. Very few people understood her strength—of body or mind. They overlooked her as inconsequential. But Jay had learned in high school what kind of woman he'd fallen in love with. She fought for the underdog and stood up for what she believed in and most of all, she protected her family. None of the guards watching now had been at the house when she'd taken out the first guy who'd attacked her. By now they'd heard the story, but since they hadn't seen her in action, chances were they didn't understand the scope of her abilities.

He sure as hell never learned how to pick a pocket. His boys didn't know how. He hated where his mind was going.

"I see it on your face, Jay," Terry said, watching him closely. "It's better than doing nothing. We have to try." She purposely used *we* because they were a team. Always had been.

The silence between them stretched for a long time. Terry's pleading eyes drilled into his. She wouldn't do it unless they agreed on it. That's how they based their marriage and this wasn't any different. "Don't you dare get caught," he said. His insides twisted just thinking about it. "If anything happens to you..." He couldn't even finish the sentence. They were supposed to have sixty, seventy, maybe eighty years together. Losing her didn't compute.

Her eyes lit up in triumph. "I won't. I promise. I'll make you proud." She didn't waste any time calling for the guard outside as she doubled over, feigning pain.

The guard barely got the door open before Terry started begging. "Please, please, I need to use the bathroom. My stomach is killing me." She looked up at the guy...and damn if she didn't have tears in her eyes. When had she become such a good actress? Hell, her pick-pocketing skills had been tremendously superior to her community theater acting skills. Had she ever played him with tears like this over the years? He'd have to ask her when they got out of here. And they *were* getting out of here.

"Mom? You okay?" Blake sat up and the other boys piped in as well. It worked that they didn't know she was faking. They made it all the more real.

The guard unlocked her cuffs, but slipped the key into a different pocket in his cargo vest as he helped her up. Had Terry seen where he'd stashed it? She stayed doubled over and the door closed behind them, leaving Jay to go out of his mind with worry.

"What's she doing?" Eric asked softly.

His oldest son knew something was up. Jay and Terry both thought of their sons as "the boys," but that was no longer the case. They were men, and Eric especially had learned his mother's strengths over the years. Nothing she couldn't handle. Nothing she was afraid to tackle.

Jay shook his head, unwilling to say anything out loud for fear of jinxing it. "Just cross your fingers," he told his sons.

Long, long minutes later, the door opened and the guard basically threw Terry across the room before shackling her back to the pipe next to Jay.

"I told you I didn't do it on purpose," she said to the man. "I just tripped. I'm only human."

The thug grunted then stalked out of the room and Jay breathed a sigh of relief that Terry was back in one piece. By virtue of her entrance, she must not have been successful. Why else would the guy have tossed her so roughly if he hadn't caught her doing something?

"You okay," he felt compelled to ask. Clearly she was fine. The door snapped shut after the thug.

"Oh, yeah." She sounded chipper. As if nothing had happened. As if maybe...

Jay slowly looked her way, heard the rattling of her cuffs against the pipe. No way. She couldn't have...

Her smile bewitched him, just as it had when he was fifteen and dying to get in her pants. When she lifted both hands from behind her back, one holding a small key, and raised her brows innocently, he wanted to shout. To laugh. He wanted to pull her into his arms and never let her go.

"I'll be damned," Eric muttered from across the room. "How'd you...?" The answer might have dawned on him because a grin curved his lips, but he never got a chance to verify it.

"I have many talents," Terry whispered as she quickly released Jay's wrists. Damn, it felt good to have his arms in front of him. Terry quickly released all the boys, moving efficiently and without a sound.

"Hey, Mom, ever thought of becoming a secret agent for the government?" Blake asked quietly.

"Who says I'm not?" she joked with a wink.

Once she had them all released they gathered in the middle of the room. "I'll call this guy back," she said softly. Everybody get in your spots. When he comes to me, one of you needs to bonk him on the head. Hard."

"I'll do it," Blake said. "I'm the farthest in the corner. He won't see me when he comes in, he'll be watching you. I just need something to smack him with."

They all looked around and Jay spotted a rickety old wood chair in the corner. Without much trouble, he loosened one of the legs and snapped it from under the seat. "This ought to do it." He handed the piece off to Blake. "Let's just give it a few minutes. He's not going to let you take another break so soon. He didn't seem too happy with you when you came back in."

"He wasn't." Her cocky smile spoke volumes. Her confidence attracted him now as much as it had on the first day they'd met.

After so many years together, he read between the lines. "Oh, and why's that?"

"I had to distract him," she said, all innocence. "I grabbed his family jewels while I picked his pocket. He was too busy protecting his privates to notice I had my hand in the candy jar."

"Jeez, Mom," Blake said, suppressing a grin. "You're not supposed to cop a feel on a stranger when you're husband's in the other room."

"If copping a feel is going to get us out of here, then I'll do it with a smile on my face. Now get back to your spots in case someone comes in," she whispered.

The longest five minutes in the history of mankind passed before Terry let out a yell for help. Jay didn't want to wait longer than that in case the guy realized he didn't have the key. The big guy opened the door, his gun in hand. "What now," he grunted.

"My stomach again," Terry groaned. "I think you poisoned me with the food this morning." She doubled over and moaned in agony, making sure to clank the cuffs against the pipe behind her. It didn't seem possible, but Jay fell in love with her even more.

"No one else is complaining," the guy said, but he moved toward her, taking measured steps as if he hadn't decided yet if he meant to help her.

"Please, they're animals. They all have cast iron stomachs." She bent over again. "Oh, God, please, I need the bathroom. Please." She moaned louder as Blake crept up behind him. Three feet, two feet... He readied the chair leg over his shoulder and let loose as the guy reached into his pocket.

Wham! A homerun if Jay had ever seen one. Their newest guard hit the ground hard. One down and who knew how many to go. But this was a start.

Terry grinned at him, then at her son. "I knew all that batting practice would pay off." She rose to her feet. "Let's get the hell out of here."

PAUL FACINETTI CHECKED HIS watch. Why should he be so antsy when Jess St. John still had three days to come up with his money, or Juneau? But something didn't feel right and Paul always followed his hunches. They'd gotten him this far. Too bad he'd avoided his hunch about Maurice Juneau. Could've saved a lot of time, trouble and a truckload of money.

He picked up the cell phone and called Frank. "What's going on?"

"With what?" Frank answered in his heavy Bronx accent. They hadn't lived in New York in twenty years, but Frank hadn't lost a bit of the flavor.

"With our guests. Who's watching them?"

"Dennis."

They'd hired a couple of new guys on this trip, and Terry St. John had taken out one of them with her purse in her kitchen. His man had taken a shot near his temple and had just gotten out of the hospital. He was still seeing double. Dennis was the other newbie. So far he'd been pulling his weight, but Paul reserved his opinion until the job was finished.

"Where'd you find this guy?" Paul asked, looking for Dennis's resume.

"He's Buster's cousin."

Buster? Who the hell named that guy? "Has he done this kind of work before? He's someone you trust?" Paul asked.

"You bet. Why not?"

Frank lived in a fantasy world. He had very few of his own problems. He mainly dealt with Paul's. Because he took orders so flawlessly, he considered himself invincible. He lived a comfortable life, liked his job and his freedom. But things had gone his way for so long that Paul worried about his complacency. The man didn't want for anything. But he'd expected Frank to snap into the real world at some point. He'd been waiting a long time.

"Meet me downstairs. I want to check in with the family." Paul slid into his black suit coat and buttoned it as he walked out of his office. Appearances were important. He checked for the slim black mask in his pocket, hating that he had to wear it. But if the mask meant he might not have to kill six people, then he could live with it. Because if the St. Johns identified him, their lives ended.

He met Frank on the first level and together they took the stairs to the basement room. In the hallway, Paul looked around, the hair on the back of his neck standing up straight.

"Where's your man, Frank?" Paul had given Frank carte blanche to hire the muscle and he'd done a great job for years. He might have finally fucked up.

"Maybe he's in the room," Frank said. No sign of worry, but Paul new better. He felt it in his bones.

"Open the door," he ordered. He stood back and waited as Frank unlocked the heavy door. Frank's "Oh, shit," sealed what Paul already knew in his gut. He surveyed the room.

Empty.

Except for Dennis, bound and gagged, unconscious in the corner.

Paul went into fix-it mode. "Get everyone we have." That was only four guys, but everyone had a gun so the odds were in their favor. "Have one of them check inside and put three in the front yard. You and I will take the back. Tell them to case the perimeter and spread out. I want every St. John back in this room within the next five minutes, got it?" Paul didn't wait for an answer. He took the stairs two at a time to retrieve his gun from his desk. He wasn't one of those bosses who let his guys do all the work. He couldn't sit around especially now when he wanted that family back where he needed them. As his leverage.

Moving back downstairs, Paul's mind raced. Where would he go if he were Jay St. John? None of the St. Johns knew where they were so they'd probably take the nearest exit outside and attempt to escape that way. From the basement, they had to climb a short flight of steps to the laundry room and that would lead them to the door of the back yard, where they'd find a terraced yard, a spectacular view of the Santa Monica Pier, the Pacific Ocean and a steep drop down a rocky cliff.

Frank caught up to him as he slipped out the back door. "I got guys in the front. We'll get 'em," he muttered, gun in hand.

Paul stood on the steps, scanned the yard. His sister had built a Jacuzzi tub encased in a large gazebo. Tall palms kept the lawn shaded, and large hedges cut out intimate spots where furniture sat in secluded clusters.

Each side of the yard had a gate, so Paul had a fifty-fifty shot at guessing the right one. He was about to send Frank to the right when he heard something to his left. Motioning Frank to follow him, he moved toward the south entrance. Crept along the wall, with Frank at his six. Relief rushed in his veins when he heard more noise. There was no easy way for six people to move quietly.

Peeking around the corner, Paul nearly ran right into Terry St. John's back. He took her arm at the same time he held the gun to her head.

She froze like a good girl should. "Jay." She hadn't whispered and her husband turned around, no doubt to chastise her for the error, but he paled instead. Two of the boys were just dropping to the other side of the wall, but Paul counted on his guys up front to snag them.

The look on St. John's face was priceless as he checked if any of his sons had made it out. Then his gaze landed back on his wife. Paul appreciated the man's despair. No doubt about it, life was a real bitch sometimes.

"This was not a very good idea," Paul told him calmly. He looked behind St. John to the two boys remaining. "Come back this way. This is something you need to hear." When they hesitated, Paul stuck the gun harder against Terry's head and the boys jumped to join them. He heard more commotion in the front and knew the other two had just been caught.

Relief rushed through him in a gratifying wave.

He kept his tone neutral. "I can totally understand the urge to leave," he said reasonably. "Sometimes in life, things spin..." He paused until the right words came. "Things spin out of our control. I'm afraid this is one of those times for you. You do what I say when I say it." Paul tugged Terry closer just to watch the anger surface in her husband's eyes. He slipped his arm around her waist and pulled her tightly against him, using the best leverage in the world. "I'll bet you'd hate it if something happened to your pretty wife, wouldn't you, St. John?" Paul spread his palm against her stomach, his thumb resting just below the center of her breasts, where he rubbed it against her silky shirt. "See, now I can respect the vows of marriage," Paul went on. "But my friend here..." He gestured to Frank who stood next to him, his gun pointed in the general direction of all the St. John men. "My friend doesn't really care about that. When he sees a woman he likes, he tends to just go for it." Frank had an evil-ass grin on his face, confirming the words.

"So because of this little stunt..." Paul eased Terry toward Frank. "I'm going to give Frank a little present." Frank took Terry roughly and brought her up against him, her back to his front. He'd want St. John to see the panic on his wife's face. Frank gloated with a lecherous leer and lust in his eyes.

Paul had always overlooked Frank's deviant behavior. Owning a casino meant a lot of women came in and out of their lives on a regular basis and many were as depraved as Frank so it seemed an easy problem to ignore.

He truly felt sorry for Terry St. John. But at least she still had her life. And it wasn't like she was a virgin. Frank would use her hard, but that didn't make her dead. Not yet anyway.

Dead came later. For two reasons. One, the St. Johns had a general idea where they were and two... Paul hadn't put on his mask. No way he'd let them live now.

Too bad.

Frank picked that moment to turn Terry and lay a kiss on her. Terry shocked them both when she grabbed onto Frank's shirt almost as if she wanted him, or needed him...for support? She canted her head like a woman might if she wanted a kiss. Oh, shit. Paul took a breath to warn Frank, who was too dazed to realize her motive. Too late. Her knee shot up hard into his groin. A tortured groan and rush of air exploded from Frank's mouth as he doubled over.

"Shit," Paul muttered, yanking Terry away from Frank and motioning for the St. John men to move in front of him. "Hang tight, Frankie. Be right back."

Five minutes later, all the St. Johns were back in the basement and Frank had a bag of frozen peas on his aching sac.

CHAPTER 15

TANNER RUBBED HIS EYES and listened as the grandfather clock ticked away the afternoon. Every few minutes Jess pulled back the sheer drapes and looked up and down the street. They'd spent the last four hours hunting through Juneau's documents trying with no luck to find his master list of passwords. Tanner hadn't wanted to be the voice of doom, but the odds seemed pretty slim of finding what they needed. Juneau could've hidden them anywhere. Long minutes had passed as they searched the hard drive for files with keywords like *account, password, username,* and then opened and scoured every document that came up and waited for her brother's friend. They hadn't said too much to each other in that time.

They had showered, solo, before sitting at the computer. What a shame to waste water like that, but Tanner had patience. If nothing else, prison had taught him that. He'd have Jess again and when the time came, he'd go slower. He'd be able to. Probably. Most likely. At least he hoped. With his initial sexual urge slaked, he could watch her now with a critical eye. His thoughts weren't sexual. Well, not *as* sexual.

He hadn't seen a soft side to her. She'd been scared, angry, frustrated, nervous, pissed and a few other adjectives that didn't pop into his mind at the moment, but she hadn't been soft. What would sex be like if she really wanted him? Yeah, sure, she'd been on board with everything he'd done, but it had been raw. Sex at its most basic level. They'd both just wanted relief. A distraction. Something to keep the nightmares from becoming real. But the nightmare was still lying in her garage with a hole in his head. It seemed Jess had pushed their encounter out of her mind. She had barely looked at him since she'd yanked her clothes on in the kitchen.

What a sight that had been. Damn, she had a nice body. Petite and firm. The right curves in all the right places. Not to mention those sexy sounds she'd made.

Tanner shifted in his seat, pissed at his train of thought. So much for being sexually slaked. Apparently all he had to do was think about her to get hard. Maybe that was natural after getting something he hadn't had in more than seven years.

Okay, so he needed to concentrate on the problem instead of her great ass and the gentle bounce of her breasts as she paced in front of him. He averted his gaze.

This house was amazing, huge, but not in an uncomfortable or pretentious way. Big furniture decorated every room, hardwood floors mixed with luxurious carpet. Tanner focused on the framed pictures sitting on the mantel of the giant mahogany fireplace. He'd seen some pictures in her brother's room, but hadn't taken the opportunity to really look around.

Jess watched him as he moved closer to the pictures. She took a few steps back as if she needed the distance from him, but then resumed her pacing.

Tanner scanned the photos. These were better. He got to see their faces. Their eyes. The ones upstairs were all action shots taken when the family had on caps or sunglasses, but these were posed family portraits.

All her brothers had dark hair with streaks of red. Same as Jess. They got their blue eyes from their mother, whereas Jess got her whiskey colored eyes from...

Tanner quit breathing. His heart raced. He recognized her father. It had been seven years since he'd seen the man. He'd only heard the name of Alex's lawyer a couple of times, but now Tanner connected the dots. St. John. It took a full minute to find his voice. "This is your dad? Your last name is St. John?"

Jess nodded absently.

"He's a lawyer?"

This time she turned toward him. "Yes. How did you know?"

Swallowing back the shock, Tanner scanned the rest of the photos. Jess's parents on their wedding day, pictures of the family celebrating Christmas and graduations. In all the shots, her father's face remained the same, and Tanner had seen his face almost every day in court for two months.

"How'd you know he was a lawyer?" Jess demanded again.

"He represented Alex in our trial," Tanner said, turning to watch her face.

"What?" she whispered. A hint of denial laced her tone.

She didn't know? "Your dad got Alex off with probation while I did seven years." Tanner advanced on Jess. He had no reason to hold anything against her, but resentment sparked in him regardless. "Alex said I put him up to the robbery and that was their defense."

"Was he your lawyer t-too?" Her wide eyes filled with despair.

Tanner shook his head. "No. No, Juneau hired someone else for me. Someone who let me get railroaded into doing Alex's time. Juneau planned it that way, I'm sure. It's why he said he'd take care of my lawyer fees. He told me not to worry. But all he wanted was Alex's freedom. He didn't care how much it cost him." Tanner lifted his arms wide. "Well, he got what he paid for."

"My dad folded his firm about seven years ago," Jess murmured.

"That's interesting. Maybe he was paid to do that."

"No!" Jess shot back. "He would never take a bribe."

"So you remember all this?" Tanner asked. "The trial?"

"No. I never kept up with Dad's trials. I was in college. I lived in the dorms. I wasn't even here most of the time. But I know he worked on a case that changed him." Jess ran her hands through her short hair. "He closed the firm and took a job in the public defender's office. He wanted to help people who just needed a second chance."

Tanner had to laugh at that. "Guess he grew a conscience too late."

"That's not true!" Jess yelled. She advanced on him, her fury emanating from her like white, hot energy. "In all the years I've seen my parents together, those were the toughest months they ever went through. I didn't know why, but Dad was miserable. Mom told me he dreaded getting up every day and when he got home, he just shut down."

"Like I said. Sounds like he had a problem with his conscience."

Jess's eyes looked tortured. "Maybe he had a problem with the whole trial."

"He wouldn't be the only one," Tanner muttered.

"It was his job to defend Alex Juneau. It wasn't his fault that Maurice sabotaged you."

Maybe. But maybe not. Tanner hadn't decided yet. If St. John knew Tanner was being railroaded then he held as much culpability as anyone.

Tanner intended to find out.

As long as the guy didn't die before he spoke to him. Which just made one more reason he needed to help Jess find her family. He had business with her father.

Tanner continued to study the pictures. Jess was the image of her mother with the exception of her father's eyes. If he'd ever actually taken notice of St. John's eyes, he might have recognized the similarity to Jess, but he'd been too preoccupied, and rightly so, with his own lawyer and dismal representation.

Exhaling hard, Tanner leaned his head back and stared at the recessed lighting in the ceiling. He had one question in particular to ask Jess's dad:

Did you know Juneau set me up?

Because if St. John did know…Tanner was better off where he was right now.

As much as he thought his anger would die with Juneau, he'd been wrong. Now it was directed at someone else.

A car pulled up in front of the house and Jess ran to the door. This must be Dave. The guy looked like the average egghead. Unlike Jess's brother—or all her brothers—who was big and strong, this kid was short, skinny, and wore glasses with dark, heavy frames.

Jess had the door open and he strolled in.

"Hey," he said, giving her a quick hug. "I was surprised to hear your voice when I called. I was expecting your mom or one of the boys."

Boys? Glancing at the pictures, Tanner had a hard time thinking of these giants as boys.

Dave finally glanced his way then back to Jess. "Everything

okay?" he asked. The question made Tanner feel like a menace. As if the words ex-con had been tattooed on his forehead for the world to see. A familiar shot of shame arrowed through his gut.

"Yes. Fine." Jess made quick introductions and ushered Dave into the dining room where Juneau's laptop waited on the table. She pulled out the chair and gestured for Dave to sit. "I need you to find something for me on this thing."

Dave looked between the two of them, suspicion in his brown eyes. "Is this legal?"

A hell of a first question. But since the owner of the computer was dead, did it matter?

"Don't ask." Jess leaned over Dave and accessed a particular file titled *Finances*. She leaned back and looked at Dave. "Can you find and access financial accounts on this thing?"

After studying them both for a minute, Dave sighed. He punched a few keys and different pages came up on the screen. "I don't know," he said, drawing out the words. "Let's see." Silently he went to work, then hit a page and stopped. "I need a password," he said.

"We've been trying to find a master list of passwords. Do you think you can find that instead?" Jess asked.

Dave shrugged. "I can try." His fingers flew over the keyboard again, but the look on his face didn't bode well.

"Isn't there anyway to get around passwords?" Jess asked.

"If there is, no one told me." He sat back in the chair and looked up at her. "Look, I don't know what Bren told you, but I'm not a hacker. I might spend a lot of time on my computer and mess around a little, and I can usually get rid of a virus or fix something wrong, but I'm not so sure about nosing around in someone else's computer. I usually have someone with me who knows the computer and can help me get in."

Jess nodded, her eyes wide, her hands fidgety. "Okay, then, thanks for coming by." She walked toward the door, surprising Tanner.

That was it? She was giving up?

Dave followed her to the door. "You going to tell me what's wrong?" he asked.

She shook her head. "Can't. And I'm asking that you say

nothing to anyone about this visit. It's important, Dave. Not a word to anyone."

"This sounds way intense, Jess. First, I can't find Bren. Then you're freaking me out with this computer shit and telling me not to say anything to anybody. If you guys are in trouble then you should get help." Dave glanced at Tanner, suspicion apparent in his eyes, before he looked at her. "How about you come with me and we talk."

Jess caught the insinuation. He didn't trust Tanner. "I'm okay with him." She held Dave's gaze. "I promise. It's okay." She opened the door and Dave slowly backed out.

"Call me if you need anything, Jess. I don't like what I'm seeing."

Nodding, Jess forced a smile and closed the door. She rested her head against the wood, her shoulders sagging.

Tanner's anger evaporated at her body language. She was tapped out. Jess moved away from the door. She looked pale. Hallowed out and empty. The circles under her eyes seemed darker, as if the last few minutes had stolen all her hope and now nothing remained but despair.

She reached the laptop and shut the lid. "You should go."

What the hell was she thinking now? "Why?"

She faced him, and the fire that usually burned in her eyes had dimmed. "Because Maurice is dead and I..." She swallowed hard. "You've been through enough and there's no reason for you to risk your life further." She turned away and pulled her cell phone from her pocket.

"What are you doing?" Tanner made it across the room in three strides and snatched the phone from her hand.

"I'm calling Facinetti. I'm going to offer the computer and myself for my family. You should go." Calmly, too calmly, she took her phone and walked to the door.

Tanner didn't move. He couldn't let her do this. "You're not thinking straight."

"I don't have any options here." She shrugged and her resignation nearly killed him.

"When was the last time you slept?" Just because he'd passed out last night after that damn sedative didn't mean she'd slept.

Tipping her head sideways, she gave him a look that said it all. She didn't know and didn't care. Sleep hadn't been one of her priorities in the last couple of days.

Tanner strode toward her, took her hand and started up stairs.

"What are you doing?" she said, trying to jerk from his grasp. But he was ready for that and didn't let go. Instead he reached the top of the stairs and headed for the only room that didn't clearly belong to one of her brothers. It might have been her old room, but now it looked more like a guest room. One double bed occupied the center with a dresser across from it on the opposite wall. The green, peach and gray color scheme might have been relaxing, but not under these circumstances.

He pulled back the pale peach spread. "You need to sleep. Once you rest your brain, we can start over and figure out what's next." Tanner turned and the image of Jess, her shoulders stooped, her eyes lost, sent another shot of pain into his gut. He didn't like her like this. Hopeless and sad. He liked the tough chick who fought for herself and for her family.

He scooped her up and before she got her yelp all the way out, he laid her on the bed. "Go to sleep," he ordered. "I'll have something for you to eat when you get up."

"I'm not hungry."

Tanner sat on the bed's edge. Jess didn't flinch. She didn't do anything but stare at the ceiling. "I'll help you find your family, Jess," he told her softly. "But you have to help me by getting some sleep and eating something when I put it in front of you. We need to come up with a plan and you need to be strong."

Her gaze snapped to his eyes. She studied him and nodded. Something had registered with her, but damned if he knew what it was.

She looked tiny in the big bed and joining her would've been too easy, except that defeated the purpose of her getting some sleep and clearing her head. So before he changed his mind and stripped off their clothes, Tanner left the room.

CHAPTER 16

JESS WOKE UP. HER gritty eyes hurt as if she'd been crying. Maybe she had been. Her dreams had been scary, filled with visions of her family bloody and beaten. She'd seen them from a distance, but no matter how far or fast she ran, they stayed out of her reach. Her chest felt constricted and air wheezed in and out of her lungs with painful gasps.

The setting sun glowed orange and pink along the thin horizon outside the window. Another day almost gone and Jess was no closer to getting her family back. Or finding them.

Heaving herself out of bed, she splashed water on her face in the bathroom and changed into a pair of her mom's loose drawstring sweats. She studied her pale reflection in the mirror. Physically, she felt sluggish, as if every move she made went against the tide. Mentally, she felt inconsequential. Helpless. Without the financial information or Maurice, she couldn't save her family. She only had the computer and/or herself to offer, and what the hell would Facinetti want with her? Her only hope was to trade the computer for her family, and Facinetti might just laugh at that idea. Panic edged its way past helplessness.

The smell of pizza wafted into the room, but Jess wasn't hungry. She went downstairs anyway, each step jarring her back into real life, only to find a truckload of food scattered across the countertops. Pizza boxes, a bucket of chicken, a huge salad, and a six pack of soda.

Tanner looked up after tossing a plastic bag in the garbage. "I called the number for the pizza place on the fridge," he said. "The guy on the other end asked if I wanted the usual and I figured, sure, why the hell not. I was expecting a ten-dollar pizza and I got dinner for ten for forty-five bucks."

A reluctant smile crept across Jess's face. "It's the usual order when they call Dr. Pizza." She chuckled at his wide-eyed survey of all the food. "Don't forget, there's five men and my mom."

"Let me guess. The salad is your mom's?"

"You're partially right. Mom and Dad split the salad. She told him he needs to watch his weight so she's making him eat better." Jess set a couple of plates on the counter. "Have at it. You paid for it."

Tanner lifted the top of the first pizza box. "Half cheese, half green pepper." He wrinkled his nose. "Who eats green peppers on their pizza?"

"That would be me." Jess faced him. "Problem?"

"No, no. No problem," he said, quickly back peddling as he opened the second box. "Ah…meat lovers. Now we're talking."

Jess hid a smile. Tanner sounded like her brother Eric. "The other pizza has everything on it." Either Tanner hadn't heard her or didn't care. He took a huge bite out of his slice, closed his eyes and chewed. The absolute pleasure on his face made her warm inside. That a simple bite of pizza could make him so happy only drove home how much he'd missed the last seven years. He'd had a similar look on his face when he'd had her pinned against the wall earlier and when she'd been on top of him on the sofa.

A blush heated her cheeks and Jess turned back to the counter, keeping her embarrassment private. She'd had sex with this man.

Unprotected sex.

A giant wave of heat exploded in her middle, resulting in a full body panic flush. He'd been in prison for a long time. Who the hell knew what had happened to him or if he carried any diseases. How the hell did she ask?

"Aren't you going to eat?" he asked. He'd settled at the big kitchen table and added a second slice of pizza to his plate along with two pieces of chicken.

More than ever, her stomach felt a little queasy and she couldn't seem to move or make eye contact. The chair scraped as Tanner grabbed her plate and set a pizza slice on the middle. He poured a soda into a cup and placed everything next to him at the table. Then he guided her into the chair.

"Eat," he told her. "You need to keep strong."

He was right. Her mother would be brainstorming how to fix the situation, not shutting down. So Jess forced pizza into her mouth. She ate and drank and concentrated on keeping the food down. With a little more sleep, she might even be able to come up with a plan. A way to rescue her family, a way to salvage the current horror flick her life had become.

Of course, she had to add the possibility of a sexually transmitted disease because life wasn't bad enough without it. God…she was so stupid.

"You're thinking way too hard over there," Tanner said before sipping his cola. "What's going on inside that brain of yours?"

Probably nothing he'd want to talk about, but she'd have to ask eventually unless she wanted to live what was left of her life in fear. "We had sex earlier."

He lifted one eyebrow. "We had fucking *amazing* sex earlier. So?"

She swallowed. "So…we didn't use a condom." There. She couldn't get more to the point than that.

Tanner nodded, wiped his hands on a napkin. "You're not on any kind of birth control?" he asked carefully.

"I'm on the pill, but…"

He waited and when she didn't say anything else, he tilted his head sideways. "I get it. You're worried about what Juneau said earlier. You're afraid you're going to catch whatever disease I got in prison."

Jess couldn't deny it, but she couldn't affirm it either.

Tanner looked her straight in the eyes. "Contrary to what that asshole said, I never 'took it' anywhere in prison. Before this afternoon, I haven't had sex in over seven years. So if you're asking if I've given you an STD, I haven't. I went into prison clean and I came out clean." He squeezed his empty soda can like tissue. "*And* I'm not apologizing for this afternoon either," he said, facing her. "It was the best damn twenty minutes of my fucking life." His eyes were hard and angry, but he tipped his head back and stared at the ceiling. Shame swamped Jess. His anger came from hurt.

She'd hurt him. A full minute ticked by as they sat, silent. When he looked at her again, the anger was gone. "Is that it?" His tone softened. "Anything else you need to know?" He spread his arms wide, but not in a threatening way, ready to take whatever she dished out.

"No," she said stoically. "That was about it. I was just...thinking. I was worried..." Nothing came out the way she wanted. "I didn't mean to imply that..."

He sighed, ran a hand through his hair, faced his plate, but didn't eat. "I know. It was a fair question. Forget it."

But she couldn't. She'd made him feel as small as Maurice must have. She owed him the same honesty. STD's worked both ways. "I'm clean too," she said quietly.

His head turned a fraction. She felt his eyes watching her, assessing her.

"I haven't had sex in a long time either." Maybe that was why she'd come like a rocket earlier. Not only had she forgotten the pleasure of sex, but she was pretty sure she'd never had *that* kind of sex ever in her life. Nothing had ever been as explosive, or erotic. No man had ever made her feel as absolutely necessary as Tanner had. She could just blurt out how many times she'd had sex in the last half a dozen years, but there was only so much a girl could embarrass herself in one day.

"How long?" Of course Tanner had to ask. She'd opened the door wide.

"Since before I started working for Maurice. I had a boyfriend, but we were drifting apart, had different schedules. Working for Maurice basically took over my life." Jess shrugged. "It seemed worth it at the time. I wanted to be a filmmaker and what better way to get my foot in the door than to work for one. Through Maurice, I could make contacts and meet investors." She just hadn't known she'd be selling her soul to the devil.

"You haven't had sex in over three years?" That *would* be the topic at the top of his list. He sounded more than skeptical, which would've normally made her laugh, but life just wasn't funny anymore.

"That makes an even ten between us." Jess took a bite of her pizza, hoping to deflect his question.

But Tanner didn't smile or grin, much less give any indication that she'd said anything. Finally, he shook his head as if he didn't really grasp the concept. An awkward silence filled the room and Jess ate her pizza. Tanner grabbed a piece of chicken from the bucket and plopped it on her plate. His narrowed eyes dared her to fight him.

It was easier to eat than to argue, so Jess did. Surreptitiously watching Tanner as he inhaled food, Jess finished her dinner and cleaned up the kitchen. There'd never been this much food left over and it only drove home the fact that she had to come through for her family.

Jess rinsed her glass, stuck it in the drain board and stared at her reflection in the window. She looked like crap. Her hair spiked out in every direction and half-moons darkened her eyes. Obviously the only kind of guy who'd want to have sex with her was a man who *hadn't* had sex for most of a decade.

Tanner stepped up behind her, caught her gaze in the reflection. His warmth radiated along her back, sent a hot little chill down her spine. He set his hands on her collarbone, used his thumbs to rub her neck. Gently, he kneaded tense muscles until she relaxed in his grip. Her eyelids drooped like weighted bricks as his warm, calloused hands stroked her.

"C'mon," he said, softly. "Get back in bed. We'll come up with something first thing in the morning." His palms eased down her arms in a delicious caress and a sweet shiver rumbled through her body. Tanner took her hand, linked their fingers, and a strange sense of belonging skittered in her head. It was crazy. Ludicrous. But the way Tanner led her through the house, up the stairs...the way he took control as if it was the most natural thing in the world.

"Lie down," he told her. "On your stomach."

"What?" She narrowed skeptical eyes. "Why?"

His lips curved into a grin. "I thought you might want me to finish that back rub."

"You just want to get laid again."

"Do you want a backrub or not?" He lifted his hands and wiggled his fingers and Jess tiredly matched his smile.

Why deny herself this one night? She still had a little time to think of something other than trading the computer. Maybe she could find some money another way. Her brain was too fried to come up with anything at the moment. Her future was practically out of her hands. She had nothing to lose. If Tanner wanted her body, he could have it. Jess stretched out on the bed and closed her eyes, not at all naïve to what this would lead to.

The bed dipped when Tanner sat on the edge. He stroked his palms over her back, across her shoulders, careful of the bandage she'd replaced after her shower. Then he was kneading, rubbing sore muscles and making her a big ball of Jell-O.

His fingers edged along her sides, stroking her curves while his hands pressed into her back. An involuntary moan rumbled in her throat. He had magical hands. Warm—even through her shirt— and strong and so damn sure. After working his way down, he eased up underneath her shirt, the contact hot, electric. Another sound vibrated in Jess and she pressed her back against his hands, seeking more contact.

"Lift up," he whispered. He glided the shirt up and over her head, then went back to work. A few seconds later, he unhooked her bra and peeled the edges back, leaving a trail of goose bumps. His hands emitted heat along her back and rough calluses scraped across her skin like a cat's tongue. From her shoulders down to her hips, he worked his magic. His fingers digging deep, his palms caressing. Methodically, he pressed along her spine and cracked her back in a few places.

It had been a tough couple of days.

He rubbed her so long, her body actually loosened until she felt like a wet noodle. Then his fingers edged into the low waistband of her sweats and all her senses shot back to alertness.

"Easy," he whispered. Lowering the cotton, he took her underwear down with it until cool room air kissed her bare butt. Tanner glided warm palms over her ass. She jumped at the shock of his lips on her lower spine. A swipe of his tongue between her shoulder blades.

He let loose an all-out assault on her senses.

His palms played over her skin, his fingers tickled, his lips nipped and sucked. He used her back as his playground. Her sweats and underwear disappeared and he kept her off balance with his hands, his mouth, constantly stroking, kissing, and licking until he ruled her with every touch.

He rolled to the side and the soft rustle of cotton whispered in the quiet room. Then all his weight rested along her back, skin on skin. His erection settled between her butt cheeks, so thick and hard, and his lips caressed her neck, sucked on her ear lobe. Jess barely got air in her lungs. Every new place Tanner explored had her gasping, squirming beneath him.

"You feel so good," he murmured in her ear, his breath warm. "I want to be inside you again, Jess." He rubbed against her and Jess squeezed her ass cheeks together, cupping him firmly. He groaned and she reveled in the low rumble against her back.

"You have to finish my massage first." Where her moxie came from, she couldn't imagine, but Jess turned beneath him, stroked her palms over his sides as he moved between her thighs. His dark eyes gleamed with heat, desire. Sweat beaded on his forehead as if he'd exerted a ton of energy the last half hour. He probably had. He'd been holding back for her sake. Warm emotion constricted her chest.

Instead of diving in for the sure thing, Tanner sat up, straddling her thighs, his penis, fiercely erect, jutting proudly between them. Still battered and bruised, he looked delicious. He gripped her waist, gently kneading her front, before easing up, cupping her breasts. Jess closed her eyes, the pleasure intense as he plucked at her hard nipples. But he deserted them and rubbed her arms and her good shoulder, leaving her panting for more of his touch.

"Tanner." She hadn't planned to say his name, but it came out in a plea anyway. She looked at him, at his intense dark gaze and hot, hot eyes. His hands came back to her breasts and he lowered his head, took a tight nipple into his mouth. Jess nearly exploded on the spot. Pleasure streaked its way through her body to her groin. As Tanner stretched over her, his heavy weight pressing her into the mattress, Jess stroked her hands over his back, reveling in the sleek, corded muscles.

His soft lips trailed up to her neck and Jess adjusted to take his kiss. He hovered a fraction above her lips until Jess opened her eyes. He looked so serious, as if this moment meant something to him. Something more than sex between two virtual strangers. His fingers eased into her hair, then palmed her head, trapping her. Holding her down with the strength of his body, he sucked her into a web of seduction. When his mouth came down on hers, Jess gave herself over to the pleasure, to the mastery of his lips, his tongue, the way he slipped inside and explored, claimed. He did it all so gently. So differently than before. He alternated, teased her with his lips, barely grazing her mouth and then taking her fully, mating his tongue with hers in a sinful dance. Little nips of his teeth followed by soft strokes of his tongue. He held himself up with the arm beneath her and the other touched her, ran along her side, cupped and stroked. For a man who hadn't done this in so long—with the obvious exception of this morning—he was damn good. He kissed her until she couldn't think about anything but having him inside her.

Jess lifted her legs, rubbed them against Tanner's hips as he settled more firmly between her thighs. A groan rumbled from his chest when he pumped his hips two long strokes, rubbing his erection along her clit, forcing a gasp from her lips.

"You're so hot and slick, Jess." His lips hovered near her ear before he tongued inside the shell and sent sparks zinging under her skin. "I have to taste you again." Before she said no, he was moving down her body, licking and nipping, sending her into a frenzy. She wanted him now, inside her, filling her. Instead, he set her legs over his shoulders and licked her, a long slow swipe that separated her before he flicked over her clit with devastating effect.

Okay...this wasn't so bad either.

Unlike earlier, he took his time. He teased her with long licks and quick lashes of his tongue. He used his thick fingers, stroking into her as he sucked on her clit. A firestorm of sensation swamped her, destroyed her. She gasped for air as she fisted the sheets and arched into his mouth. So close. So ready.

She'd never been this way in bed before. She'd always been reserved, shy. She'd let her partner lead the way and it had never involved any of the things that Tanner did to her or made her feel. When had she ever felt so utterly needed or wanted?

The answer was easy. Never.

Her thoughts fizzled into nothing as Tanner redoubled his efforts between her thighs. His teasing had her on the edge. Her insides hummed at the same time she coiled tighter.

"Tell me what you want," he murmured, his voice low, sexy. Oh, God. She felt another full body flush creep over her skin. "Do you want to come?" He circled her clit with his tongue, tortured her with the possibilities. "Tell me."

"Yes," she panted. "Make me come. Oh, God, please make me come."

"Oh, yeah." Satisfaction filled his tone. As if he wanted her begging, pleading for him. "Here ya go, sweetheart. Just what you want."

Pressure built on her clit, hard and fast. She had no idea what he was doing, how he was touching her, but she zoomed freight train fast into the most intense orgasm of her life. She detonated. No other word for it. She exploded and the resulting ricochets bounced through her body with such intense pleasure she couldn't breathe. Still he kept going, kept his fingers moving and his tongue stroking until another orgasm followed and decimated her.

When she came down, came back to herself, she couldn't move a muscle. Her legs felt weak and Tanner was steadily working his way up her body using his lips and that devilish tongue, tasting all of her until he reached her mouth and took that too.

He owned her.

Without any further hesitation, he pushed inside her, moving deep, deeper until he was fully buried. He stretched her, filled her. Instead of moving he stayed still. Except for his mouth which continued to take her lips so brilliantly. He made her oblivious to everything but the heat and strength of his body. He seemed content to take his time, to make every second count.

A shock of realization had her body flushing again, but he was too preoccupied to notice. Earlier they'd had wall-banging sex, but this was Tanner making love. There was a clear difference. The demarcation only pointed out how little she knew this man and how much she wanted to change that fact. Beneath the hardened ex-con with intense eyes was a gentle man who had a sense of justice and innate sense of goodness. She felt it with every kiss, with every slow stroke of his hand on her skin.

Slowly, he started moving, barely rocking against her, but making her ultra aware of his size and strength. The minutes ticked by and his movements became more focused. The new friction forced a moan from her throat. Tanner's too. Slowly, he increased his pace, worked her over with his hard body and killer lips, taking her up when she didn't think she could go again.

"So good, Jess," he whispered in her ear. He had her pinned, one hand behind her head and the other below her spine as he pistoned inside of her. Taking her mouth in a rough kiss, he stole what little breath she had, but it felt perfect. He felt perfect. Sweat poured off both of them, made their bodies slick. She did the only thing she could and held on tight.

This was something she'd never known, this kind of passion or pleasure. She'd never participated in anything so carnal. Sex had always been relatively neat in her experience and this was anything but neat. It was hot and dirty. Shockingly primal.

Tanner adjusted his grip near her ass and ground down on her. The move raked over her clit and made her cry out. "One more time, Jess. I want to feel you one more time." He did it again and Jess nearly lost her mind. The third time was the charm as he hammered into her. Tears leaked from her eyes as Jess came undone, calling his name and digging her nails into his back, trying to hold on, to keep her sanity. But it didn't happen.

With one final thrust, Tanner erupted inside her. The heat of his come bathed her internally and her orgasm milked him of everything he had to give.

Breathing hard, he collapsed on top of her and Jess took stock of the moment, reveled in the wonder of the act. Tanner rolled to his side, but took her with him. The move separated where they'd been joined, but he kept his arms tightly around her. The security she felt wasn't permanent, she knew that, but she accepted it for now and let herself relax as his hand stroked along her skin.

Jess knew so little about him and the more time she spent with him, the more questions she had. Especially now that they'd been so intimate. The way he treated her today alone spoke volumes about the man.

"What's your favorite color?" she asked.

His hand stilled on her hip. "That's your first question after mind-blowing sex?" He chuckled and shrugged. "I don't know. I don't have a favorite color."

"No way," she said, tilting her head to look up at him. "Everybody has a favorite color. There has to be something you like. A color that reminds you of something fun or a good memory," she prompted.

"If I had one, I don't remember. I haven't been around too much color the last seven years. Just a lot of gray."

"You've been out for a few weeks, right? What colors have you seen that you like?"

Tanner shifted and ran his palm through her hair. His dark gaze raked over her face. "Red," he said. "I like the red streaks in your hair. That's my favorite." His voice was low, sexy. He followed up with a long soft kiss. When he pulled away, Jess was breathing hard. "If you don't stop talking, in the next few minutes we won't be doing *any* talking, if you get my drift. You should go to sleep."

She understood his meaning. If she wasn't asleep in the next few minutes he'd be ready for another round of sex. Quite honestly, she was tired, and more than a little sore. But a few minutes gave her time for one last inconsequential question.

"When's your birthday?"

He huffed a quick sigh. "November thirtieth."

Eric's birthday was the twenty-ninth. Tanner was a Sagittarius, just like her brother. They had the same qualities. Strong, protective, loyal and independent. Not to mention macho. Jess listened to the steady beat of Tanner's heart and went down the list of qualities that made Tanner a standout. He had a sense of fairness, of honor. Not to mention the gentleness under his rough exterior. Her list faded as she fell into oblivion.

WHEN JESS OPENED HER eyes, darkness still penetrated the room. She didn't look at the clock, didn't want to know the time. Her head rested on Tanner's chest and his arm draped possessively around her shoulder.

Sleep softened the hard lines of his face, made him almost look his age, but not quite. He was hard bodied, hard minded, but in sleep she saw a different man. Maybe it was the man he'd been before prison.

What had happened to her? Jess St. John didn't sleep around. She didn't hook up with virtual strangers much less ex-cons. She tread carefully when it came to men and most especially sex. But here she was in the arms of a man who had stormed into her life unannounced and unwanted. The scariest thing of all was that she wanted him. She should be getting out of bed, creating distance, and instead she stroked his chest lightly, brushed her thumb across his flat nipple.

She was a changed woman. Her life was a dead end. After tonight she had very little hope of going back to who and what she was. There was so much she hadn't done, hadn't lived. She'd never been bold, never explored or been strong like her mother.

Maybe tonight was her last chance for something like that.

Jess had watched her parents for years. As a kid she'd grimaced at their kissing and hugging, but as she got older, she'd admired their closeness. None of her friends had parents who constantly touched or showed each other physically how they felt. Her parents were all about touching. More often than not her dad had his hand on her mom's ass and her mom wasn't shy about it. "Not in front of the kids," she'd admonish, but she always smiled or grinned wickedly.

They kept each other happy...had been for more than twenty-four years of marriage.

Had what she experienced with Tanner been something close to what they shared physically? Was that part of the bond that kept them so connected? Jess always hoped to find someone the way her parents had found each other, but it seemed unlikely. Love like that didn't come along that often.

Not that good sex created love. Hardly. But she finally understood this aspect of her parents' relationship in a visceral way.

She also understood the fragility of life and her odds of survival in the next one or two days. What about Tanner's survival if he continued to stick with her? He had to know that staying with her meant risking his future in one way or another. With what they'd done so far, he faced another prison term or worse, death.

She owed him. Tonight would be her last chance not only to say thank you, but to break out of her cocoon and venture into the unknown. Jess grazed her palm across his chest and the muscles that stood out even in sleep. He was gorgeous.

He'd pulled a sheet over them while she slept, but his growing erection tented the soft cotton as Jess continued to touch him. She'd never gone down on a guy. Had always been too shy, too scared to take that step. But now she wanted to more than ever. She wanted to know the taste of him, the texture of him. She wanted to give him the same pleasure he'd given her.

Jess eased over Tanner and kissed his chest, sliding her palms down his stomach and following with her mouth. She wanted this opportunity, this experience.

If by some miracle, Tanner survived this mess she'd gotten him into, she wanted him to remember her.

CHAPTER 17

TANNER SLOWLY CAME AWAKE. Everywhere but his cock. His cock was *already* wide-awake and erect, anticipating the mouth moving south. The erotic dream he'd been having had been way better than his usual fight-or-flight dreams and now it was reality. He didn't open his eyes, didn't move. He let the sensation of Jess's lips ripple through him. Let her warm breath wash over his abs as she methodically inched down his body.

Damn. She was amazing. He ran his fingers through the softness of her hair and encouraged her to keep going, to take him to heaven. Still, he didn't open his eyes, he just experienced her as she touched him, kissed him, her soft lips, sucking, taking little nips of his skin.

Goddamn. So good.

When she circled his navel with her tongue, his stomach contracted, he sucked in air. The lower she went, the faster his heart pounded, the more his cock stiffened. She was going to blow him away. Literally, he hoped.

Her warm hands slid down his groin on either side of his cock and pressed his thighs apart as she eased between his legs. He hadn't been this vulnerable in years. Hadn't felt so much anticipation ever. The way Jess had gone about this so far had every cell alive and screaming for more. She hadn't even touched his cock and he was happier than he'd been in years.

Tanner finally opened his eyes. Saw her contemplating his erection. He couldn't help but smile, couldn't keep the spark of elation from shooting through his body. When she smoothed her thumb up the length of him, he stiffened and immediately lost the smile.

She was going to kill him. This wasn't going to be quick. It was going to be torture.

Taking her time, she smoothed the drop of pre-cum around his cock head and he groaned. She took him fully into her hand, or tried to anyway. A little sound, almost like a hum, vibrated in her throat and he wanted her to make that same noise while he was in her mouth. Wanted to know what it felt like.

Her tongue snaked out and tasted the tip and Tanner about came off the bed. He wanted to hold her head steady and guide her over him, but he didn't. Her tentativeness gave him a clue, so did the way she explored him. She might have been on the other side of twenty-five, but that didn't make her sexually experienced. She hadn't been a virgin, but she was no slut either and the longer she took to take him into her mouth, the more he wanted to be there.

"Jess." The word was strangled. A plea if he'd ever made one. "Go ahead. Please sweetheart. Take it." God, he was already panting like a fucking dog. Waiting, wanting.

She met his gaze with glittering eyes, and a silent promise, before covering the tip with her lips. Every muscle in Tanner's body went rigid. He lifted his arms over his head, dug his hands under the pillow to keep from holding her steady and driving deep into her mouth. She was in dangerous territory and didn't realize it. But Tanner did. He struggled with himself, struggled to let her go at her own pace no matter how much it killed him.

Her tongue circled and swiped at the top before she took him deeper in her mouth.

Ah, God. "That's it." He moved his hips, forced her to take a little more. "So good, Jess. It's so damn good."

She made that sound in her throat and it vibrated through his cock and straight up his spine. *Fuck.* Sensation swirled up his center, coiled his body tighter. When she pulled off, he silently swore for pushing her too far.

Moonlight shone down from the high window over the bed and lit her face. "Tell me if I do something wrong," she said. "I'm probably not very good at this." Then she licked him from base to tip and the wet heat of her tongue made his eyes roll back in his head. Jesus, was she wrong about that. She adjusted over him for a better angle and wrapped her hand around his shaft before going down again.

Holy fucking God.

He'd become some sort of science project, a guinea pig for her use and she used him so well. Minute by minute, she worked him over, alternating with her tongue and going deep, taking him until he felt the back of her throat. Just when she hit a rhythm one way, she changed to something else, driving him crazy with inconsistency and hurtling him to the finish.

Second by second she brought him closer to heaven and he held on by a thread, loving her mouth on him, her hands on him, the way she moaned and licked him. A firestorm of heat built at the base of his cock, in his balls. She was five seconds from pushing him over the edge.

"Jess…" God, he could barely speak. "I'm not going to last." He felt obligated to warn her. She hadn't struck him as a girl who went this far, but she didn't stop. "I'm serious. I won't be able to…" Ah, God, he couldn't hold back. "This is it," he rasped as she took him all the way. Instead of pulling off, she grabbed his hips and held on, gripped him with nails digging into his skin and her mouth covering his cock.

Watching her sent him over as much as her actions did and Tanner gave into the release. He pumped his hips as his come jetted into her mouth, down her throat. She took everything. Pleasure roared through him, bursting from the middle and rippling to the edges in unparalleled waves. Gritting his teeth, he forced his hips still and concentrated on complete satisfaction. On the way her hands stroked his skin after his orgasm crested. On the tight sheath of her mouth.

The moment when she slowly and carefully pulled off and looked at him branded in his brain. A glimmer of pride lurked in her sparkling eyes. The tiniest of smiles curved her swollen lips. She was the sexiest woman he'd ever known. When she glanced away, Tanner saw the sudden blush creep into her cheeks and he refused to lose the bold woman who'd taken control. He pulled her up and rolled her beneath him, taking her mouth in a warm kiss. He tasted his tangy essence on her lips, drove his tongue deeply into her mouth. He could kiss her all night. All day. Her soft lips conformed to his, her warm breath mingled with his. Her hands stroked along his nape and kept him close.

She made him feel valuable. Not because of the great sex, but along with it. Like he might actually be worth something and when was the last time he'd ever felt that?

"That was the best wake-up call I've ever had," he whispered, brushing his mouth across hers. She was one hundred percent pure sweet, hot woman and she needed to know it. "That was amazing." He kissed her again. "Outrageous." He held her face in his hands and stared into her bright eyes. "Thank you for that."

She smiled shyly. "You're welcome."

He slid his hand down her side, across her stomach and down to the soft patch of curls between her legs. She was slick, more than ready for him. In another five minutes he'd be able to go again, but he didn't want her to wait. Her eyes widened when he slipped two fingers inside. "Look how wet you are," he murmured, watching her. Her gaze skittered away and Tanner didn't have to see her blush to know she had. "Look in my eyes, Jess." Moving slowly, he stroked his fingers inside her. When her gaze locked onto his, he circled her clit with his thumb and pressed down. Tanner took her gasp into his mouth. He'd wanted to watch her, to see her eyes when she came, but also wanted to be in her everywhere at the same time, his tongue in her mouth, his fingers in her body. Her hips moved in time with his thrusts and Tanner kissed her deeper, harder. Her cream covered his fingers, slicked up his palm as he teased her. When he finally hit the spot she needed, it only took another minute before she came hard, clenching around his fingers with spasms that rocked her the same way his had rocked him.

Breathing hard, she stared up at him with sated eyes, stroking her thumb across his cheekbone. It was a look he'd never forget. "You're pretty good at that," she whispered.

"Yeah, go figure. I'm pretty damn rusty too. Imagine the possibilities with a little practice." He meant it as a joke, but her smile faded. So did the glow in her eyes. Yeah, he shouldn't have brought up the possibilities because clearly she wasn't thinking along those lines. Whatever her life had in store, it didn't involve him. At least not in the long run. Not that he wanted any type of long run, but he wouldn't have minded a few months of having her all to himself. She had too much going to think about the next time she'd be having sex with him. But he got that.

It didn't change the fact that he wanted her. A lot. He could spend the next month in her bed and not think about anything else. That was probably normal for a guy who'd been celibate as long as he had. He'd managed to deal with it, but now that the drought was over, he couldn't imagine going without.

Tanner shifted Jess onto her side and brought her up close against his chest, spooning her body and keeping his palm on that sweet, wet heat between her legs. He smoothed his lips across the soft skin of her shoulder, gently kissing and nipping, content to touch her because he suspected she wouldn't give him the opportunity once this night ended.

She was in a state of flux. He understood it since the same could be said about him. He didn't know where he was going or where he'd end up. One thing he did know… Jess was a damn fine detour. He couldn't stop touching her, didn't want to. That was normal. Right? Because he hadn't been with a woman in so long, it was natural that he couldn't keep his hands off her…or his mind from thinking about her. This was only temporary. Didn't matter that it felt great having her in his arms. Didn't matter that their time was limited. He'd lived in the "now" for a lot of years. He'd had to stay focused on each day, each minute and he wouldn't change because his circumstances had.

But damn if he wasn't going to enjoy Jess for as long as he could. She was incredible softness and tinsel strength all meshed up in one small package. She was shy and bold, innocent and wicked. She was a contradiction in every term.

"Where are you from?" she asked softly.

The question came from out of nowhere. But maybe she was feeling a little self-conscious, a little uneasy. Maybe she just needed some reassurance that he wasn't from Mars.

"I grew up in a little town south of Denver." Lush green country he missed more than he wanted to admit.

"Are you going back there when you leave here?"

Shit. Apparently answering one question meant that an

avalanche of more followed. He could cut her off, but that would probably send her out of his arms and he didn't want to lose this time with her.

It seemed inevitable that he would leave *here*, but he hadn't figured out where to go. "No. I don't know." He was lying because he knew damn well he wouldn't—couldn't—go home. Not after what he'd put his family through. "I doubt it."

Jess turned in his arms. Her face gleamed in the moonlight, silky smooth. "How come?"

She had no idea she was swimming into rough waters, landing on a topic he didn't want to discuss. For years he'd put his family in the back of his mind. Doing his best to forget they existed, only to have their memories rise up and bite him in the ass when he least expected it.

Jess squeezed his arm. "Tanner...tell me. How come you won't go home?"

Tanner probably owed her some answers, if only to say thank you for the incredible sex. "I hurt my family when I landed in prison. I don't want to hurt them anymore. They don't need me showing up now after all this time."

"What makes you think that?" Her eyebrows quirked up in question.

"Davis is a small town. A lot of gossip. I embarrassed my parents when I got convicted. My mom doesn't need me coming back now and starting up all the gossips again. I wouldn't do that to her or my sisters."

"What about your father? You haven't mentioned him. How does he feel?" The girl was a pit bull when it came to wanting information.

He remembered his dad going through his first bout of cancer, telling him how Tanner would be the man of the house, how he'd have to take care of his mother and sisters if he died. His dad had survived that go-round, but not the next. Instead of graduating college with a degree, Tanner had gotten himself arrested and thrown in jail, so that when his father had died, he hadn't been any good to his mother and sisters. He'd been stuck in the pen.

"He died while I was in prison."

Jess lifted up on her elbow and stared down at him. "Oh, Tanner. I'm sorry." Her face had a look of horror mixed with concern. "That must have been so hard."

The hardest news he'd ever heard. Worse than the judge's sentencing at his trial.

"But that's even more of a reason to go home. Your family needs you."

Tanner shook his head. "They don't need me. They've been living without me for this long, they don't need me."

"That's ridiculous. Of course they need—"

"Jess!" She flinched, but didn't move away from him. Damn, he hadn't meant to do that. "Look," he said, after taking a deep breath. "I haven't had contact with them since I went in, okay? They don't want me around, I can guarantee it."

Her eyes narrowed. "No contact?" She shook her head. "Didn't they write to you? Or visit you?" She didn't give him a chance to answer as she sat up. "How could they do that to you? I can't believe they'd just—"

"Slow down." Tanner pulled her back down next to him where he had her soft skin at his fingertips. "They didn't do anything. In the beginning they tried to visit, but I wouldn't see them. I didn't open their letters either."

"Why? Why would you do that?" she asked softly, searching his eyes.

Did it matter if he told her? He'd kept his feelings buried so deep for so long he wasn't sure he could even talk about this. "I was ashamed, all right. Embarrassed. No one in the family tree had ever been arrested, much less be convicted of a felony and do time. I couldn't face them. I didn't deserve them. I blew it."

"Oh, Tanner. I'm sorry. But you didn't blow it. You got railroaded. You can't ignore your family because of something that happened to you. Because of something you had no control over."

Tanner forced a smile. "I blew it by hanging with the wrong crowd. Alex Juneau was not your average college student." Instead of living on ramen noodles and peanut butter like the rest of their buddies, Alex ate steak and drove a convertible. Thinking about Alex only brought up the anger and resentment, and those two emotions had kicked Tanner's ass enough already.

He eased Jess beneath him and trailed his lips to her ear. "I don't want to talk about it anymore."

"But—"

He silenced her with a kiss. "Shh." Then he made her forget about everything but him.

JESS WOKE WITH A start, her eyes opened wide as her heart thundered in her chest.

A dream. She'd been having a dream. More like a nightmare. She'd seen her family bloody and bruised and she'd been running, trying to get to them, but no matter how hard she'd tried, her legs had felt like bricks. No matter how close she'd gotten, they'd stayed out of her range. Blake had been calling her names from their childhood. Screaming at her. Teasing her.

She took a steadying breath, became of aware of Tanner holding her closely, their bodies skin to skin, her back to his front. She'd never met a guy who touched as much as he did. Her past boyfriends had been happy to sleep in their own zip code after sex, whether it be on the other side of bed or literally a different zip code.

Not Tanner. He touched, kept her close. He made her feel protected when her life seemed to be crumbling around her.

He'd opened up to her too. Let her see a little into his world, into his family. She wanted to know more. Wanted to know about his mother and sisters. Wanted to know if he was the oldest, youngest or in between. She wanted to know the man he was before prison.

"You okay?" His husky voice whispered in her ear. She'd woken him up.

She nodded. "Bad dream." It was still dark out and Jess avoided the clock again. She'd rather not know how little sleep she'd had all night.

"Want to talk about it?" he asked.

"No." She shook her head. Didn't want to think about her family bloody or bruised, or dead. She could barely remember the last time she spoke to them with the exception of that horrible phone call from the other night. Her memory seemed fuzzy since this whole thing started. Her time frame had gone to hell. Minutes had turned into hours and into days but she didn't how many had passed. She'd barely slept, barely eaten...

"What are you thinking about?" Tanner gave her a small squeeze, his warm hand on her bare hip. When she didn't immediately answer, he lifted on his elbow and pressed her shoulder back so she had to look up at him.

"I keep hearing their voices from that phone call." He nodded as if he understood who she meant. "The way they sounded..." She couldn't describe it.

"What?" Tanner asked. "You've got a funny look in your eye."

"I'm just thinking about what Blake called me." Tanner lifted curious brows and she clarified. "He called me Smelly Feet. He hasn't called me that since we were tiny." He hadn't been the only one to call her a name from her distant past. "Eric called me Junior. That was weird too."

Tanner smiled, the gesture softened his face, put lines around his mouth. "Junior? Is there a story behind that?"

"Mom still hadn't married Dad when I was born, but they were seeing each other. He'd been proposing for months, but Mom kept saying no. She didn't want him to marry her for a baby, she wanted him to marry her because he loved her. Which he did. Mom was just too stubborn to see it. Anyway, Dad wanted the baby to keep the first name tradition in his family and said the least Mom could do if she wouldn't marry him was to give him that courtesy. So they named me after Dad. Well, kind of," she explained. "His name is Jessie, but everyone calls him Jay for short. Everyone's always called me Jess.

"Anyway, Eric used to tease me and call me Junior because I was named after Dad and he wasn't."

"Junior sounds better than Smelly Feet. Where'd that one come from?" Tanner stroked his fingers through her hair and the sensation zipped along her nerves with devastating effect. It seemed incongruous for him to be so gentle when everything about him screamed hard, tough and knocked around.

"Mom had taken us all out one day and when we got back in the car, I took my shoes off. I hadn't worn socks and the stink hit fast and hard." Jess grimaced at the memory. "The boys were all little and kids are so damn honest…there is and was no diplomacy when it comes to little boys telling their sister she has stinky feet."

Tanner chuckled. "How old were you? I'd think it wouldn't bother you."

Jess had to think back. "The boys were really little and I had to help Mom a lot to keep them all corralled. "I was eleven. Fifteen years ago."

"Fifteen years ago," Tanner repeated. His face changed. His smile disappeared. "Didn't your mother say something about fifteen years?"

Queasiness blossomed in Jess's stomach and she sat up. "Yes. She did." Jess recalled her mom's words specifically. "She said it felt like she hadn't seen me in fifteen years."

"Did your brother call you Junior when he was that young?" Tanner asked, sitting up next to her.

"He did. He was six and he was a pain in the ass. His best friend was named after his father so he understood the concept. He was mad for a long time that he wasn't named Jessie, since he was the boy."

"Okay…so let's think back to the whole phone call," Tanner said. "Did anything else stand out as weird?"

Her queasiness turned into full-blown nausea and her family's words jumbled together in a raging symphony in her head.

Tanner squeezed her hand. "Your dad came on first, right?"

Taking a deep breath, Jess willed herself to focus. "Right. Dad came on and told me to listen carefully to everything I was told." She looked at Tanner as panic rose from her center and quickly spread through her veins. "I thought he meant everything Facinetti said."

"Maybe he was trying to tell you something."

Oh, God. She'd wasted all this time not trying to figure it out. Her stomach roiled.

Tanner grabbed her arms, shook her a little until she met his gaze. "Don't lose it now, Jess. They're counting on you. Let's think back to what everyone said. One at a time. Your dad said to listen and your mom said she felt like she hadn't seen you in fifteen years. That puts you at eleven, which is the same age when one brother called you Smelly Feet and the other called you Junior. Now what else did they say?"

Jess shut her eyes and went back to that moment in the car when she'd been so terrified and sick to her stomach that she thought she'd puke. Taking a deep breath, she pushed back the same nauseous feeling. "Eric said, something about being miserable. 'Good thing that I wasn't there because I'd be miserable.'"

"Good. What else?"

"Danny..." She flipped the covers off, yanked on the T-shirt at the bottom of the bed and started pacing, thinking back to her brother's words. "Danny told me not to let Facinetti run me around like a fucking merry-go-round." She ran her hands through her hair and glanced up, searching for the next part of the phone call. "Blake said something about a snow cone and Brendan told me that they'd done all they could and it was my turn now." Jess put her hand to her mouth, devastated that she'd missed the clues.

"What do the merry-go-round and snow cone refer to?" Tanner asked.

"Mom took us to the Santa Monica Pier. That's when I took my shoes off and Blake called me Smelly Feet. I was miserable that day because I had to help Mom more than I got to be eleven and do what I wanted to do."

"Everything points to that day at the Santa Monica Pier."

"Are they trying to tell me they're at the pier?" Jess shook her head. That seemed so obscure.

"Maybe they're near the pier," Tanner said.

Jess stepped into her sweat bottoms before running to the computer in her dad's office. Tanner strode in a few seconds later wearing only his jeans. Looking away, she concentrated on the computer screen instead of his chest.

If Paul Facinetti owned real estate in Santa Monica, Jess vowed to find it.

CHAPTER 18

TANNER WATCHED JESS'S FINGERS fly over the keyboard. Outside, streaks of early morning sunlight broke the horizon and started a new day. At least this one seemed off to a better start than the last few. Clearly Jess had a plan and Tanner let her work in peace. Bending low over her shoulder accomplished two things. First, he could watch what she was doing, and second, he could smell her. Yeah, he'd spent the night with her, but he wasn't nearly satisfied. If anything he wanted her more. Something told him he'd just tapped into her sexuality and he wanted to keep exploring. See exactly what they could do together with a little more practice, a little more time.

A small gasp sounded in her throat and Tanner blinked his focus onto the screen instead of her exposed collarbone. "What?" he asked.

"Facinetti had a sister and she had a house in Santa Monica," Jess said. She'd pulled up an obituary on the screen. "Sarah Facinetti, thirty-eight, of Santa Monica, died of cancer. This is from 2007. Her only surviving family member was her brother Paul from Las Vegas."

Jess glanced at Tanner with hope widening her eyes.

"You think Facinetti's making his home base at his sister's house," Tanner said.

"It's a place to start. I just need to find the address."

Tanner spun the chair around and crouched in front of her. "Slow down. Let's say you find the house? What then? Are you going to go to the police?"

She shook her head and Tanner kept going. "Or do you plan to go in on your own? You need to think this through, Jess."

186

"I can't go to the police. If Facinetti finds out, then he'll kill them. I have to go. I have a plan. Mostly."

He hated the *mostly* part. "What's your plan?"

"Facinetti has a lot of pull. A lot of money. Enough money to hire someone who can either find Maurice's passwords or hack into his accounts. Chances are he can access Maurice's money as long as he has his computer. I'll offer to trade my family for the computer. And me."

No, he couldn't have heard that right. "What did you just say?"

"You heard me." Her steely gaze turned desperate. "I don't have a choice, Tanner. I have to do something. I'm the one that got them into this and I'm the one that has to get them out."

"What makes you think he'll even go for this?" Tanner asked.

"Because, it's all about the money." Jess pushed the chair back and stood up, putting distance between them as she crossed to the window. "Honestly, I don't know that he will go for it. I just know he wants his money and if he wants any chance to retrieve it, he'll do what I say."

She sounded so damn unsure and Tanner felt for her. Moving closer, he pulled her against his chest and wrapped her in his arms. She didn't resist. She sunk into his body as if she belonged there. As if they'd been made for each other. It seemed odd how such a simple gesture could mean so much, how the feel of her could settle him the way nothing ever had.

Suddenly, Jess launched herself away from him. "I've got an idea!" Back at her father's desk, she flipped through the Rolodex, picked up the phone and punched some numbers.

"Is this Troy Mills?" she asked. She blushed and looked at the wall clock across the room. "Sorry. I didn't realize how early it is. My name is Jess St. John. I'm—" She listened and nodded. "Yes, Jay's daughter. I know my timing is bad, but I really need your help. Could you find an address in Santa Monica for a Sarah or Paul Facinetti?" She explained how Sarah had died and Paul may have sold the house. She asked him to look into it as quickly and quietly as possible. Jess hung up the phone and met Tanner's gaze triumphantly.

"Want to tell me who that was?" Tanner asked before Jess got a word out.

"Troy Mills. He's a private investigator. My dad uses him when he needs information. He said he'd get back to me with an address this morning." She bolted out of the room and Tanner followed.

"Where're you going, now?" he said, jogging up the stairs behind her.

"Shower. I want to be ready to go when he calls back."

"Sounds good to me." Seemed like the perfect time to conserve water.

"WHAT WAS I SUPPOSED to do?" Anger laced Terry's question as she stared at Jay. Lack of sleep and fried nerves made them all testy. "Let him just kiss me in front of you and the boys and not fight back? You know me better than that, Jay."

How many times had they gone back and forth on this subject since yesterday? "You didn't have to maim the guy, Ter. He's going to be out for blood the next time he sees you."

"Let him try."

Jay rolled his eyes. Terry's attitude had always been twice her size. "Just be smart is all I'm saying. To get out of this we have to be smart and stay alive."

The boys all sat in their spots, pretending not to listen when they obviously heard every word. Jay and Terry never fought in front of the kids. Well, almost never. They'd made a pact at the very beginning to be a united front as parents and to avoid arguments when the kids were around. But they were no longer kids and Jay refused to keep his opinion to himself with something this important.

"I doubt he's going to walk in here and shoot me," Terry insisted. "Or he would've done it already."

Jay caught her blue-eyed gaze and held it. That's what worried him. Frank would take his revenge with a pound of flesh. Terry's flesh.

"I'll be okay," she assured him quietly. "I can handle myself."

The vision in Jay's head of Terry against two or more of these guys made his skin crawl. Sometimes her confidence went beyond the realistic. She just seldom realized it.

He'd been waiting for the other shoe to drop since Facinetti's goons had shoved them back to this basement yesterday and locked them down.

"Do you think Jess figured out what we told her?" Terry asked softly. She leaned her head against his shoulder and all the anger rushed out of him. He could never stay mad at her and God knew he loved her because she was a fighter. It wasn't like he wanted to see her get mauled in front of his eyes and he had to admit the sweet satisfaction he felt at watching Frank double over when she'd kneed his groin.

"I don't know," he said, rubbing his stubbled cheek against her hair. Damn he needed a shave. All of them did. He'd never seen the boys with so much facial hair. They looked more like men than ever before. "I hope she did," he said, trying his best to be optimistic.

The door opened and slammed against the wall with a bang. All of them jumped and the sick feeling in Jay's stomach multiplied ten-fold.

Frank stood in the doorway, one angry man. More than angry. His gaze didn't waver. He fixated on Terry with the darkest eyes Jay had ever seen. He pointed at her. "You. You're coming with me."

"No thanks," Terry shot back. "I'm good right here."

"Terry," Jay hissed. This is just what he'd been talking about. Don't escalate the conversation or aggravate the situation.

Frank strode toward Terry and the boys started smack talking, trying to deter him. He didn't pay them any attention. Terry tensed, bent her legs. She wouldn't hesitate to kick Frank and maybe the guy realized it because he kicked Terry's leg aside, hard. Hard enough that she grunted and if Terry made a sound, it meant it hurt. The move put her off balance and Frank unlocked her cuffs and yanked her to her feet as she struggled. "Don't fucking move," he told her.

Instead of listening, Terry elbowed his ribs and half turned to slam her palm in his face, but Frank expected it and wrapped his arms around her body, holding her tightly against him, keeping her back to his front. The noise escalated as the boys got louder.

Frank turned so they saw the grip he had on their mother.

"You fucking shut up, or I snap her neck right now." That got the desired response. They all looked on just as helplessly as Jay, and just as panicked.

Turning back to Jay, Frank went on. "Here's the deal, babe," he said softly in her ear. He looked at Jay as he spoke to Terry, knowing full well he was talking loud enough for him to hear. "You and me are going into another room." She struggled in his arms and he adjusted his hold, tightening the arm around her neck until she couldn't breathe. Jay nearly went out of mind as he struggled against the cuffs holding him to the pipe. When she quit fighting, Frank loosened his grip and Jay took a steadying breath. "Like I was saying... You and me are going into another room and you're going to be real nice to me." She struggled again and Frank put his arm behind his back and returned with the biggest knife Jay had ever seen. Terry's eyes widened. "And if you're not nice to me, I'm going to fuck you right here, right now."

Terry stilled and Jay's stomach dropped to the floor. Bile collected at the back of his throat.

"You fight me at any point and the party moves center stage. Your boys, your husband..." Frank glanced at the boys then looked right at Jay, his smile evil, "... they're going to watch me fuck you every which way but loose. You're going to take it in your pussy, in your mouth and I can't wait to try that sweet little ass. Any resistance adds a kiss of my blade."

Jay wasn't looking at Frank anymore. He watched Terry. Watched the fight go right out of her. She'd do anything to protect the boys, anything. That included submission if it meant sparing them seeing something as vile as their mother being raped or cut.

Jay felt Frank's eyes on him, but he wouldn't give him the satisfaction of knowing how absolutely piss-in-his-pants scared he was for his wife. Terry, goddammit, Terry wouldn't, or couldn't, look him in the eye. She saw the writing on the wall and Jay did too. He needed her to know that as long as she stayed alive, nothing mattered. As long as she survived he'd love her 'til the end of time. Recovering from something so devastating wouldn't be easy, but he'd be there every step of the way. As long as she survived.

He willed her to look at him and finally, right before Frank turned his grip across her middle into something else, something more sexual as he palmed her stomach, she met Jay's gaze. He saw her struggle to stay still, her terror. She knew how to fight, how to defend herself, but the repercussions of fighting right now were too immense, so she didn't move.

The boys were wide-eyed, breathing hard and pale, their fear and panic, palpable.

Jay wanted to howl. He wanted to lose it, but doing that might only insight Frank more.

I'm sorry. He didn't have to hear Terry say it. It was in her eyes. In the tears that didn't fall. Submitting was against every cell in her body and that was what she was apologizing for.

"Don't," Jay said, forcing his gaze from Terry and looking at Frank. "I've got money. A lot of money." He had what he'd saved for all the college tuitions, and his parents had plenty of money. "Whatever you want, just let her go. Leave her alone. You want to pound out your frustration, take me out and work me over. Go ahead, keep the cuffs on and go to town, but leave her alone."

Frank gave another evil grin. "I got money," he said and Jay heard the blade slip into its sheath at Frank's back. "It's been a long time since I fucked a redhead." He shoved Terry out the door and Jay closed his eyes and swallowed back bile.

They needed a miracle.

Jay had never really believed in miracles.

JESS FELT THE HAIR on her nape and arms stand on end as she moved closer to the house at the end of the block. Three levels stacked high on the mountain that looked out to the Pacific Ocean. Tanner and she had driven by only once, not wanting to call attention to themselves as they passed.

A cool breeze blew off the water, but Jess didn't care about the view. This close to the house, she felt urgency, a need to get there. They'd gone to the studio office first. It was the safest place for Maurice's computer since security guarded every entrance. No one got in without a pass, with the obvious exception of Tanner the other night, but that had been an anomaly. Tanner had convinced her to fill out the paperwork and have his photo taken for a lot badge. That had eaten up twenty minutes, but now he had access to the studio and the office if he needed to get the computer for any reason. Jess agreed it was a good idea in case something happened to her.

Which she highly expected.

She was no dummy. She realized the trouble she was in. No illusions here. She was giving herself up. Of course something was going to happen to her. That was a foregone conclusion. Tanner had wanted to do this at night, but Jess couldn't wait that long. Really, what was the point?

The house looked suspiciously quiet as she moved closer, using the neighbor's large hedges to shield her. This house had a for-lease sign in front and looked completely deserted. That worked for her. Tanner was approaching from the other end and if her phone vibrated it meant he'd found a better way onto the property. He'd told her not to get too close without him, but a ferocious feeling in her gut told her to keep moving.

Jess quickly moved into the backyard and jumped up the wall. Grasping the top with her palms, she ignored the pain as rough brick bit into her palms. She heaved herself up until she could peek over the top. Facinetti's terraced yard wasn't large, but it had a lot of sections to it. Enough that might keep her hidden as she cased the place.

The longer she waited, the more that feeling in her gut multiplied. Jess took a deep breath, levered herself over the wall and dropped into the yard behind a gazebo. Scanning the back of the house, she didn't see any cameras. The house itself seemed a little shabby. It needed new paint and the lawn furniture had seen better days. Toward the left side of the cemented porch, opened Venetian blinds covered French doors. To the right were two sets of large windows with big glass panes.

Jess edged her way closer to the house until she flattened herself along the back wall. She peeked through the window just as the door inside opened and two people came in. She froze, completely unable to move when she spotted her mother getting tossed inside. Her heart nearly pounded out of her chest at the relief of seeing her mom alive. But just as soon as the feeling swamped her, it ended when the man backhanded Terry across the face. The force spun Terry into the wall before she hit the floor.

The man shut the door, locked it and turned. He wasn't a giant, but he had mammoth shoulders, a nine-month-pregnant gut and dark slicked-back hair. He wore tan slacks and a black button down shirt with a stain on the front. He smiled at Terry with an evilness that made Jess's skin prickle.

Fear like she'd never known crawled through her veins in ice cold waves and made her sick.

She waited for her mother to get up. Terry had taken several self-defense courses. She was not someone to mess with, but instead of getting up, she looked dazed as she lifted her head and watched him get closer.

Fight, Mom, fight! The words screamed in Jess's head, in her heart. What was wrong? He'd hit her, but Jess had seen her mother take worse on the stupid roller derby team.

The man towered over Terry as he circled her. Jess couldn't hear what he said. There was too much roaring in her ears, too much static blazing in her head. Why wasn't her mother fighting? The man ended up with his back toward the window. The giant knife sheathed at his back answered her question. He grabbed Terry's hair and forcibly moved her, still on her knees, in front of him. Jess's stomach roiled. She didn't need to watch anymore to know what would happen next.

A rusted wrought iron chair sat five feet away and Jess didn't think. Grabbing the chair, she hefted it over her shoulder, baseball bat style, and took a few sideways steps to get the most bang for her buck. Then she slammed the chair into the window. Glass sprayed into the room and the man turned, his pants partially over his hips, her mother still in front of him.

Jess roared, or made some type of inhuman sound. At least she thought it was her. She wasn't sure. Her pulse raced frantically as she threw herself at the guy at the same time her mother lunged for his back. He was bigger than her so she pushed extra hard. Her momentum knocked him toward her mother. She expected him to attack after she bounced off his chest. Instead he gasped, wide-eyed, before his gaze turned glassy. He didn't even try to attack her. Just stood there, swaying…until he fell forward.

What the hell...

Terry looked down at her hands. Bloody hands. Jess looked at the man's body. The giant knife wedged into his lower back. She saw two inches of steel and the hilt.

Jess watched her mom, realized what had happened.

"I—I didn't mean to do that," Terry stammered, surprise clear in her eyes. "I just wanted the knife. I didn't intend..."

Jess stepped over the man, pulled her mom into a rough hug. "It's okay, it's okay." God, what did she do now? Run? Or keep going? Try to get everyone out? No, she needed to get her mom out of here. Her dad would expect that of her. "Go through the window, Mom," Jess implored, urging her toward the shattered window. "Get out of here."

Her mother picked that moment to snap back into her real personality. "No. I can't." She reached for the prone man on the floor. Blood spilled from the wound on his back. Terry searched through his pockets for something. "I'm not leaving without your father and your brothers." The doorknob jiggled and a second later, a gunshot blasted the knob off. Terry stood and they turned in unison as two men busted down the door. They had huge shoulders and bigger guns.

CHAPTER 19

PAUL HAD HEARD THE commotion, grabbed his gun and ran for the lower level. He elbowed his way into the room between the two hulks Frank had hired, and stopped short. The sight of Frank lying face down on the floor momentarily paralyzed him. The curtains billowed from the ocean breeze and a giant hole in the window marked where a lawn chair had broken through. Glass littered the floor. Two of the new hires had guns trained on Terry St. John and another younger woman. They stood next to each other in the corner of the room, wide-eyed and waiting.

Paul didn't take the time to make sense of anything. "Frank," he said softly. He moved toward his friend, a man he'd known for thirty years, and knelt next to him, setting his gun on the floor. "Frankie..." Paul took his shoulders and turned him on his side, careful of the knife still lodged in his back.

Frank stared at him with panicked eyes. "Paulie...can't feel my legs," he rasped.

Oh, shit. Paul kept his panic under wraps and ignored the staggering amount of blood on the floor. He'd always joked that Frank's knife was more like a machete and knowing that most of the eight inch blade was buried deep didn't give him much hope. "It's okay, Frankie. We'll get you help. It's gonna be okay."

"Don't be an idiot, Paulie. We can't." Frank shook his head. "Too many questions."

"Fuck the questions." Yeah, they both knew an ambulance was out of the question, but getting help wasn't. "We'll take you to a hospital right now, Frankie." Paul looked over his shoulder. "Get a God-damn car ready to roll now," he told the men behind him.

"And get them the fuck outta here," he added of the two women. He'd deal with them later.

Both men left the room. One with his gun on the women and the other down the hallway toward the garage.

The pool of blood steadily grew under Paul's knees. He gave Frank a grim smile. "Frankie...what am I going to do with you?" he joked. "Here I thought you were only going to fuck the one girl and you end up with two."

Frank's lips lifted in an attempt at a grin. "I wish," he said before losing the smile. "They fucked me good." He shook his head. "It's bad, Paulie. I can tell it's bad."

"We'll get you the best doc—"

"No." Frank shook his head. "Not doing the hospital thing. I won't be a helpless bastard getting a sponge bath from some two hundred pound nurse with a mustache."

The image made Paul smile despite the seriousness of the situation. It was just like Frank to think the worst. "C'mon Frank, you might get a hot blonde you can finger while she's rubbing you down. Nothing bad about that."

"Car's ready." The second guy appeared in the doorway with a blanket in his hand. His gun holstered at his shoulder. "I'll help you move him. We can get him on the blanket and carry him out like a stretcher."

At least this guy had a brain in his head. "Good. Careful of his back," Paul said, shifting to arrange the blanket so they could shift Frank onto it.

But Frank moved too fast. Paul should've seen it coming. He should've known better. In the split second it took to see Frank reaching for his gun, he knew he was too late. Maybe Frank's legs didn't work, but his arms and hands worked fine.

Paul took a breath to scream, *"No!"* as Frank aimed the gun, but the shot went off like a canon and took most of Frank's head with it. Blood and brain matter splattered everywhere.

Falling back, Paul landed on his ass and stared in shock at what was left of his friend. They'd been through everything together. Elementary school, junior high, high school. Frank had protected him for thirty years. He'd done all the dirty work and kept Paul clean. He'd always been an ear to listen and a rock to depend on.

He'd mentored the new hires and kept them in line. He was an important part of the machine and just like that he offed himself.

Frank had watched his father crumble bit by bit in a nursing home for fifteen years and had always said he wouldn't die a slow death. Compounding his father's situation had been Paul's sister's fight with cancer. Sarah had whittled away to nothing after seven years. Frank wouldn't live in a hospital or nursing home. He'd promised to take matters into his own hands before ever living out that fate.

He'd kept that promise.

But Jesus…it shouldn't have happened this way. Frank was too young. At forty, he was just hitting his prime. Sure, he didn't take great care of himself, but he enjoyed life.

Reality set in and Paul's chest constricted. He glanced at the man staring dumbfounded at Frank's body. Dark hair, dark skin… He didn't even know the guy's name. The smell of death permeated the air.

Slowly and surely, anger built from his center and Paul wanted revenge for his friend. A lot of revenge. A family's worth of revenge. He picked himself up from the floor. "Bring those bitches to my office in ten minutes." He'd have to make arrangements for Frank. He'd give him a burial fit for a king. Until then, he'd have to do something with Frank's body. "Call a local mortuary. Buy a coffin. A nice one." He looked around the room, at the blood and gore. "Clean this up."

Paul climbed the stairs to the main level. He'd planned to change, but decided that having bits of Frank splattered on his clothes might actually make a more gruesome sight. He splashed some water on his face and washed his bloodied hands.

A few minutes later, two of his men hauled in Terry St. John and the younger woman. Paul walked around the front of the desk and faced both women as his men stepped back. Terry had blood on her hands, on her clothes. She'd killed Frank with a knife to his back. It didn't get much lower than that. The lady next to her was too close in looks to be any other than her daughter.

Simmering anger boiled hotter.

"You killed my best friend," Paul bit out the words to Terry. Unlike Frank, Paul had never hit a woman. But there was a first time for everything. Lightning fast, he backhanded her to the floor. When Jess screamed and lunged for her mother, Paul slapped her next. Breathing hard, he looked down at both women. "That was for Frank." He yanked Jess to her feet and held her by the collar. "I don't know how you found us, and honestly, I don't give a fuck. But if you bring the cops down on me, I'll kill every member of your family before I go down. You understand me?"

She shook her head. "No cops. I swear. I found your sister's obituary and thought I'd check. I didn't think you'd be here. I swear." Her eyes glittered with fear. A red mark already blazed on her jaw. Good. He wanted her to hurt. He wanted both of these bitches to hurt. "It was my fault that he died," Jess went on to say. "I pushed him—"

"Jess, no!" Her mother said, rising from the floor. "Frank killed himself." She eyed Paul fearlessly, a pretty stupid thing to do considering the circumstances. "The knife did damage but by the looks of your suit, he took his own life. Can't blame me for that."

Paul released Jess and took a step toward Terry. He'd have hit her again if the door hadn't swung open.

"Someone at the front door," Hollister said. "He says he knows you have the St. Johns. I coulda shot him, but in case he told someone else as a back up, I figured you want to talk to him. He says he wants to make a deal."

Paul eyed Jess, his anger spilling over once again. He didn't know which St. John female to kill first. But he had an order of business. "Take them back downstairs, keep the new guy in the living room. I'll be down in five minutes after I change. Too bad his timing sucks. He's going to die like the rest of them." He could kill all eight people and be out of this place in no time flat.

It only took Paul four minutes to put on a new suit. It was one thing to show the St. John women what they'd caused, but it was another to meet a man, wearing someone else's blood and brains. Even if he planned on killing the guy in a matter of minutes.

Entering the living room, Paul sized up the man across from him. Big, serious and not very happy. Paul could relate. He was two out of three of those things. "You are?" he asked.

"Tanner Bryant. And you're Paul Facinetti."

Paul wasn't in the mood to be nice. "Mr. Bryant, you've got one minute, so make it good."

"Jess St. John owes me money and I want it before you kill her."

Not something Paul expected to hear. But this seemed like a conversation he wanted to have while Jess St. John occupied the same room. He wanted to see her face. "Follow me," Paul said, leading the way downstairs to the lower level of the stacked house. They walked down a short hallway. One of his men stood at the end, his large gun prominent in his shoulder holster, and opened the door as they neared. Two men shoved Paul's newest guest inside and followed him in.

Paul looked at the scene through Tanner Bryant's eyes. The whole St. John family sat along two walls with their hands behind their backs. Two of the brothers looked pretty messed up. So did the mom. Jess had a bruise forming on her jaw and Paul felt the tingle in his hand where he'd hit her. No sense in waiting any longer. Paul forged ahead and looked at Jess.

"You owe this guy money?"

"Yeah, she does," Bryant piped in before she said anything. "Like I told you upstairs…" he pointed to Jess, but kept his eyes on Paul. "She owes me for a job. It's real simple. I need work and from what I've seen of your operation, you need some muscle."

"Funny. I don't remember a help wanted sign on my front window," Paul said.

Bryant was all business. "You didn't need one. Maybe I'm a mind reader." He gestured outside. "You didn't have anybody watching the outside of this place. A sure sign that you're short-handed. Maybe you can't trust hiring new guys. I don't know. What I do know is you want money from Maurice Juneau and I know how to help you get it. Without her." Bryant pointed to Jess.

"What are you doing?" Jess screamed, her face turning red.

"You seem to know a lot about me, Mr. Bryant."

"I know what Jess told me. You invested in Juneau's movie scam and he stole from you. You're from Nevada and you're only here to collect. Basically, I know everything Jess knows."

Son of a fucking bitch. He hated people nosing into his business. "Go on," he pulled a small Berretta from his pocket and gestured with it. Every damn person in this room should be worrying about dying in the next two minutes.

Bryant glanced at Jess again. "Did she tell you Juneau's dead?"

"You son of a bitch, bastard," Jess hissed.

More anger bubbled from Paul's gut. "Juneau's *dead?*"

"Very. She shot him in the head." At those words, every member of her family looked at her.

"Tanner!" The shock in her voice was as real as the surprise on her face. "Shut up!" Jess's words were clear, concise and full of unadulterated malice.

Paul changed the direction of his gun. Instead of pointing at Bryant, he aimed at Jess. "So I have no reason to keep any of the St. Johns alive."

"Wait!" Jess shouted. "I have his computer. I'm the only one that can get it and I won't do it if you touch any of them." She tipped her chin gesturing to her whole family. "You can get all Maurice's information if you find someone to hack into his computer. It's not impossible. People do it all the time."

Paul gritted his teeth. Now he had to bring someone else into the operation. Someone who'd end up costing him a fortune. But it'd be worth it if he got his money back. "Where's the fucking computer?" He spit out each word succinctly. This job had turned into a major goatfuck.

"I told you. I'm the only one who can get it. But you have to let them go, first."

"This is bullshit," Bryant said. "I can get the computer too."

Jess's eyes hardened. "Tanner." The word itself was a warning, her narrowed gaze filled with venom. "He's lying," she said. "He can't get it."

"Sweetheart," Bryant said, his voice soft. "Just because you had my cock in your mouth doesn't mean you own me."

Okay then. More information than Paul needed to hear. But it was a good shot as far as low blows went. Jess turned a color so red Paul couldn't even describe it. Bryant had hit hard and in front of her whole family no less. That comment was going to cost him. Every one of her family members shot him a glare that could've put him six feet under. Paul guessed if he released even one family member, it'd be Bryant they'd go after and not him.

Paul laughed humorlessly and turned to Bryant. "Where's the computer?"

"Not so fast." Bryant turned his back on the family and faced him. "In return for the computer, I want the two grand she promised me and a job."

Not likely that would happen. "What was the two grand for?" Paul asked.

"Helping her snag Juneau and getting her family back."

Paul grinned. "Looks like you fucked up on both accounts."

"I wasn't the one who shot Juneau or the one who told her to bust into the house. That was her fault. She still owes me for helping her with Juneau."

"You've got a case there." Paul stretched his neck, contemplated the deal. This guy had an agenda and Paul respected that. Plus, he'd been right about the need for more muscle. Reliable muscle. Especially now with Frank gone. Not that this guy could take over for Frank. He'd have to prove himself before he got hired to do anything. "So you want me to give you a job?" He waved the gun around. "Why should I do that? You don't seem to be very loyal." He pointedly looked at Jess who was about ready to blow her top. Her reaction more than anything convinced Paul that Bryant was a free agent and might actually be able to help him.

"I'm loyal if you pay," Bryant said. "You want the truth? I got out of prison a month ago. Want to know who put me there?" He locked gazes with Jay St. John and smiled grimly. "This bastard. He made sure I went away for a long time and there's nothing I'd like better than to even the score."

This just got more and more interesting. At least the kid had serious motive.

"No one will hire me," Bryant continued, still watching St. John. He finally turned his back on the man. "Your kind of operation is exactly the kind of place for a guy like me. I'll make this a no-brainer for you," he continued. "You bring me on and I'll make all the St. Johns disappear."

CHAPTER 20

JAY DIDN'T DOUBT A word Bryant uttered. The way Bryant stared him down a second time made his blood run cold. The man had serious motive and not much chance of getting caught if he stayed with Facinetti.

There was so much information to process, Jay hardly knew where to start. His mind reeled from the minute Facinetti walked in with Tanner Bryant until both men left the room. Jess had not only walked into a time bomb by working for Maurice Juneau, but apparently she'd compounded it by teaming up with a convicted felon.

Jesus... Tanner Bryant. Although he'd recognized the man's face, it wasn't until Facinetti had said the name that everything registered. The man had changed. He'd grown in prison, up and out. He was a good four inches taller and that many wider. It was easy to see how he'd spent his time behind bars. Though he had to be about Jess's age, he looked older.

A swift wave of contrition hit Jay. He'd inadvertently helped put Bryant behind bars. When he rethought the trial and the other attorney's lack of defense, he suspected Juneau had paid the lawyer representing Bryant to railroad his client. There were attorneys in the world who didn't care about the outcome of a trial as long as the paychecks cleared. Jay shoved the guilt and memories to the back of his brain. He had too much to think about now to dwell on the past.

Processing everything he heard, Jay studied his oldest child. She had her head down, eyes closed. His relief at seeing her alive battled with the wish that she wasn't here at all. Good thing he had a strong heart, or he'd have had several massive coronaries by now.

He had a million questions, so he started at the top. "Jess, honey, are you okay?"

She nodded, glanced up at him and quickly looked away. Maybe because he looked as if someone had used him for a punching bag or maybe because she felt responsible. Jay didn't know. Right now, he wanted some answers.

"You finally figured out what we were trying to tell you?" Eric asked.

"Took you long enough," Danny kidded. The boys usually resorted to humor in tough situations. Even now, when it was clear that Jess was devastated by all that had happened.

Jess eyed him but her gaze softened at Danny's teasing smile. She looked at her brothers and misery shone bright in her eyes.

"How'd you end up with Tanner Bryant?" Jay asked.

Glancing skyward, Jess sighed before meeting his gaze. "It's a weird story. I was with Maurice on stage at the studio and Tanner...uh..." She either didn't want to tell him or didn't know how to tell him and Jay just nodded, encouraging her to continue. "Tanner...was shooting at Maurice and..."

"Shooting?" The question lurched out of Jay's mouth before he clenched his jaw and waited for the rest. He already hated it. *Shooting?* Not the word he wanted to hear. Terry's eyes were as wide as his. "And," he prodded.

"And he missed. Kind of got me instead."

"Kind of? There are no 'kind ofs' when it comes to bullet wounds. You either get hit or you don't," Terry said.

Jess's brows quirked together in that little slant that usually preceded an apology. "I'm fine. Really, he barely nicked me and he didn't mean to do it. He apologized."

Apologized? Jay briefly dropped his chin to his chest before looking back at Jess. "An apology is supposed to make up for you taking a bullet?" Jess leveled him with upset eyes, so he moved on. "So he shot you and you became...pals?" Jay couldn't even let his mind wander to the other thing Bryant had said. No way, no how. Yeah, sure, Jess was an adult, but she was still his little girl and little girls didn't... He pushed it out of his head.

"Tanner thought I was hurt worse than I was and he…well, he took me. Kind of."

There she went with the *kind ofs* again. "Took you? As in, kidnapped you? Instead of taking you to a hospital!" Jay growled. If he survived this, he was going to make sure Tanner Bryant spent every last day of his life behind bars. Or six feet under.

Jess seemed sufficiently torn. "Well, maybe at first, but then we made a deal and he's been helping me."

"Helping you? You think this is help?" How could he have raised a daughter so naïve? He'd always loved that Jess was so sensitive and caring, but now he wanted to shake a little sense into her. But, too late to go back now.

"I never expected him to do this." Jess's eyes widened, the betrayal clear in her tone. "He helped me with Maurice. He helped me…" She shook her head. "He just seemed like he wanted to help and I trusted him." Two tears leaked down her face and Jay looked away. Couldn't stand to see her pain.

"It's okay, honey," Terry said. "Is what he said true?" Her voice carried the compassion of a mother. "Did you kill Maurice?"

Jess pressed her lips together, but never opened her eyes as she nodded. "I didn't mean to," she whispered. "It was an accident."

Jay leaned his head against the wall. The pain in his chest hurt like nothing else. His little girl had killed a man. An act she'd have to live with the rest of her life.

"He had a gun on Tanner," Jess continued. "He was going to kill him and I just wanted to scare him. I wasn't aiming for him when I pulled the trigger, but the bullet hit one of Blake's guitars hanging in the garage and it ricocheted and…" She shook her head, couldn't finish. But she didn't have to.

Bryant had wanted Maurice dead and Jess had accomplished it for him. Obviously Bryant knew what he had when it came to Jess. Retribution on a large scale. Robert Briscoe had defended Bryant in the trial and he'd done a piss-poor job. The man had died from complications of diabetes several years ago, so Bryant couldn't mete out his own justice when it came to his lawyer, but he sure as hell could when it came to Jay. If he wanted, Bryant could wipe out all the St. Johns while Jay watched. That was a hell of a lot of retribution. Jay's stomach knotted.

Bryant couldn't have known who Jess was when he'd originally hurt her. Or had he?

"Jess…" How should he ask this? "Is it possible that Bryant was after you and not Juneau?"

Jess shook her head. "No way. He wanted Maurice. I heard them talking when we got into Maurice's house. Tanner wanted him to suffer. He wanted justice."

Justice. The word stuck in Jay's throat. Bryant sure hadn't gotten any seven years ago.

"Did you know who Bryant was?" Jay asked.

"No. Not until he saw your picture at the house and brought it up," Jess said. "Then I realized it was your case and both of us connected the dots."

"Isn't it possible, honey, that once he connected those dots, he changed his initial plan?"

The forlorn expression in his daughter's eyes answered the question. She'd been had and they were all as good as dead.

GETTING ONTO THE LOT and into the office wasn't a problem. Tanner had taken Jess's keys and walked in like he owned the place. Grabbing Juneau's computer was also not a problem. It sat in the top drawer of Jess's desk. Figuring out how to get Jess and her family out of Facinetti's hands was definitely a problem. Tanner had gambled with the only thing he had and that was knowledge and Juneau's computer. Informing Facinetti of Juneau's death did two things. It gave the man valuable info, and set Tanner up as the guy to help him with his problem. Jess's reaction had been perfect, because it was real. Tanner had stolen her bargaining chip and made it his own. About the only thing keeping Facinetti from killing Jess and her family was the fact that if Tanner somehow failed to retrieve the computer, Jess remained the only other option. Therefore Facinetti shouldn't be hasty in any actions regarding her family.

Tanner just hoped the man stuck to his word.

Even so, once he went back to the house with the computer and once Facinetti retrieved the information he wanted, the St. Johns were history. Not to mention the possibility of Facinetti taking

Tanner out as well. If Tanner didn't prove he was useful to have around, he'd be next on the hit list.

So where the hell did he go from here? Tanner sat forward in Jess's chair and dragged his hands over his head. He was so fucked.

The door opened and a man walked in carrying a large box. The sun streaked in and lit his blond hair as a breeze blew it forward. He wore blue jeans and a green T-shirt advertising The Prop House. The box nearly dwarfed him, but he deftly set it in the corner of the room.

"Hey, there," he said. "You must be new. I'm Ron. Props. Be right back." He came back a minute later with another box and set it on top of the first one. "Is Jess around?"

"Ah…no. She's not. Can I help you with something?" Tanner asked, walking around the desk and facing the man.

"Can you just tell her I brought the blanks and blood packs that Maurice wanted? I kept the blanks he liked, but these are the ones he really hated. I think he's unloading them to another production in exchange for something else, but…" he shrugged. "I have no clue what that man does." He rolled his eyes.

He doesn't do anything *anymore*, Tanner wanted to say.

"Are you a new production assistant?" Ron asked. "It's about time Maurice hired someone to help Jess. She's been running this office by herself for years. I think she does more than Maurice."

"I'm sure you're right." Tanner studied the boxes in the corner and the word blanks clicked in his head like a light bulb. "So what's wrong with these blanks?"

"Nothing. Except they're full of wadding, not crimping. The wadding makes them sound really fake. Maurice won't use them. I had them because you never know what a producer might want on the set. These make it possible to use at closer range without needing a squib and with little risk to the actor. But Maurice would rather the theatrics so these have been banned."

"Could you use a suppressor on the gun to hide the sound?" Tanner asked.

"I guess so. Since it wasn't in the last script we never considered it, but I don't know why it wouldn't work. Why? Will I need to get a suppressor for the next film?" Ron asked.

"I don't know. Just curious," Tanner said. "I'm new to the film industry."

"You'll love Jess. She'll teach you everything. It's only a matter of time before she's producing her own stuff. She's that smart."

Tanner nodded. "Yeah, that was my first impression." Actually his first impression was that she was a fluff ball, but she'd dispelled that pretty quickly. Tanner glanced at the boxes again then back at Ron. "You got a minute? Could you show me how these things work? I was thinking about getting into props one day, but..." Tanner shrugged. "I haven't made up my mind. I'm just lucky that Jess is giving me a chance to get my foot in the door."

"Sure." Ron opened up the box on top. "I can show you, but you can't touch this stuff. Don't even breathe on it. You wouldn't believe the training you have to go through to do this shit."

Tanner didn't care, and he got a crash course in blanks, guns and blood packs.

CHAPTER 21

JESS STARED AT THE floor. She'd screwed up big time. The kind of screwing up that cost a person their life. Or in this case seven lives.

She still couldn't believe Tanner had betrayed her. Couldn't believe that he'd sold her out so quickly. Maybe her dad was right…Tanner had just been waiting for an opportunity to even the score. Maurice might have been the top of his list, but he wasn't the only one on the list.

Jess twisted her wrists against the rope binding them. Her raw skin burned as she continued to pull at the middle knot. Every movement sent hot shards of agony through her arms, but she wouldn't stop. She was their only chance. A trickle of something wet slid into her palms and she gritted her teeth. Blood or sweat? She didn't want to know. Her shoulders and back ached and none of it mattered because as soon as Tanner got back with Maurice's computer her whole family was dead.

She'd trusted Tanner. Somehow he'd wormed his way into her heart. Had it been the sex? Had she actually let good sex equal trust? Apparently the answer was a resounding *yes*. More like *yes, stupid*.

She'd not only led him straight to her dad, she'd patched him up, made him stronger so he could kill her whole family. Anger washed through her and she twisted her wrists viciously, deserving of all the pain the movement cost.

How could she have missed this part of Tanner? How had he fooled her so easily? He'd seemed so honorable. He'd warned her, been up front with her. He'd seemed so sincere. But he'd been just as sincere when talking about making her family disappear. She'd seen that same look in his eyes when he'd confronted Maurice in her garage. That same cold, calculated gaze that made a chill run down her spine. Those cold dark eyes belonged to a man who wanted not only justice, but revenge. Retribution.

She'd practically handed it to him on a silver platter.

A tiny part of her held out hope that he'd been lying to Facinetti. Maybe he intended to help her and was only buying time by offering his help to the enemy. But even thinking that made her sound more naïve than she already felt, so she kept quiet.

Jess glanced at her parents. Emotion clogged her throat. Disappointment made her chest heavy. For years she'd struggled to be as successful as her parents. She'd worked hard in school and at her job. She'd been convinced that by following the rules and doing the right thing, she'd get ahead in life. Now look where she was. Look how she'd brought her whole family down with her.

Jess yanked again on the rope and felt a tiny bit of give. Her pulse picked up as she worked the strands with cramped fingers. This had been the longest three hours of her life, but if she could get out of this damn rope, she could do something to help.

More rope slipped through the knot and for the first time in her life, Jess thanked God her little brothers used to tie her up. There hadn't been a knot she'd been unable to escape and her talent, although rusty, remained intact.

Just as she pulled her wrists out of the rope the door swung open and Tanner walked in with another goon. Jess recognized the satchel over his shoulder. It belonged to her and it had been in the office. The giant bag was stuffed. Tanner set it in the middle of the floor.

He pulled out a gun.

Jess's adrenaline soared. Her parents and brothers had the same panicked look that must have been on her face as well. Had she been so wrong about Tanner? Was he just going to kill them all without hesitation? That tiny seed of hope got smaller.

"I'll take care of this," Tanner told the other guy. "Why don't you wait outside. I'd like a little privacy with the family."

The goon shook his head and pulled out his own gun. "Not on your life. We don't do anything until the boss gets here."

Tanner took a few steps, the gun held carelessly in his palm, and circled the man. "So what's the deal? All of you are paranoid? I thought it was just the man in charge." He stopped with his back to the door, but Jess didn't have a clear view because the goon stood in front of her.

Had Tanner done this on purpose? He had no idea she'd freed herself, so that couldn't be it. Still, she had an opportunity and if she had any trust in Tanner, now was the time to find out who he stood with. All she had to do was distract the goon and let Tanner do the rest.

Tanner lifted the computer out of its case and Jess's mouth went dry. "Here." He stood, held the computer in front of him like a shield. "You can take this to your boss now and he can start looking for the information he needs. You can leave me here to do the rest. No problems."

Ohgodohgod. This didn't sound good. But what if he just wanted to get them alone without the goon? Or what if he really planned on killing them when the guy left?

She glanced at her parents, whose complete focus centered on Tanner. Confusion made her pulse triple and Jess reacted. She launched to her feet and jumped the goon from behind. With one precise right fist she knocked him in the temple. Roaring in her head made her deaf as she hit the deck, sprawled on top of the big guy. He didn't move a muscle and her sudden elation vanished as she stood and saw Tanner coming at her. The shouts from her family didn't help. His body language was all business as he set the computer on the floor and tackled her. It was like getting hit by a two ton wall. They hit the ground hard, but Tanner took the brunt of the fall.

Disoriented, Jess tried to get to her feet, but Tanner rolled and trapped her with his body. What the hell was he doing? She struggled harder, kicking and twisting.

"Easy, Jess," he hissed.

Her family's shouting stopped abruptly as Facinetti appeared with his gun drawn.

"Trouble?" He didn't look the least bit amused, but then neither was she. Their one shot at freedom had gone to hell quicker than a snake can strike. Her trust in Tanner all but disappeared completely.

Tanner shifted on top of her. "Nothing I can't handle." Sweat beaded his forehead. Breathing hard, he leered at her, but spoke to Facinetti. "Your guys can't tie a fucking knot to hold a hundred pound female for more than a few hours? You need to hire better help. But then I think you just did." He smiled down at her.

"I haven't hired you yet," Facinetti said.

Tanner stood up and brought Jess with him, his grip like a steel band around her arm. "I brought the computer." He pointed to the Mac on the floor. "You'll get your money back."

Facinetti shook his head, a look of amazement on his face. "Who the hell died and put you in charge of deciding what I do? What makes you think you can walk into my house and start giving orders to my guys?" He looked down at his man on the floor and shook his head.

"Get him out of here," he said to another man at the door. It took a minute to haul the prone body out of the room.

Tanner pulled Jess in front him and wrapped his arms around her. His heat seeped along her back and the sensation brought back too many memories. He wasn't the man she thought he was. Jess squirmed to get some distance, but Tanner only held her tighter, nearly squeezed the air out of her lungs.

"You wanted that computer so I brought it. In return for a job, I take care of the St. Johns. I'm just trying to expedite the situation. What's the problem?"

"The problem is I don't know you, asshole." Facinetti's gun leveled at Jess. Tanner purposely used her as a shield. The giant coward. He was no better than Maurice. If Jess hadn't been so angry she might have been freaked-out terrified.

"Look," Tanner said. "I meant what I said before about proving myself."

"That doesn't give you the right to walk around my house like you own the place. My guy told you to stay in the front room. That means you stay in the damn front room until I get there."

"What's your problem, man?" Tanner asked. "I got no beef with you. I'm here to do you a favor." Behind her, Tanner shifted and a gun appeared in his hand.

Jess glanced at her parents, caught the mix of defeat and fear in their eyes. Blood rushed from her head as panic seized her. A few feet away, Facinetti aimed his gun higher, right at Tanner's chest, right at her eye level. It was too close to call who he wanted dead most.

"I told you I'd take care of her family and I meant it. There's just one part of the agreement I want to change." When Facinetti didn't answer, Tanner met his gaze. He looked as if the gun didn't faze him, but his heart slammed against his ribs and she felt every beat against her back. "Instead of the two grand she owes me, I want something else."

Facinetti's dark eyes narrowed. "What would that be?"

"Just a little more time with her." Tanner bent his head and nuzzled her neck. A shock of sensation whistled through her blood. Jess hated her body's betrayal. She struggled to be free, but he only held her closer and whispered something in her ear. Her pulse pounded too hard to hear him. His lips brushed her lobe, and she fought harder for her freedom, but he only chuckled as his lips grazed her neck. "See," he said, raising his head and talking to Facinetti. "She can't wait to be with me again."

The creep had to add *again*. She sure knew how to rack up the disappointment points. Not to mention the humiliation ones. She didn't have the courage to look at any family members.

"Look," Tanner continued, "I'm still going to take care of all of them. I just want some extra time with Jess so I can give her a proper goodbye." He bent his head near her ear. "You'd like that, wouldn't you sweetheart? One last screw before you die?"

"You scum sucking maggot." Jess threw her weight forward and back, tried to dislodge herself, but Tanner only chuckled again.

"Hold still," he told her. "I wouldn't want you to get hurt." He waved the gun in front of her face and she froze. "Atta girl." He glanced up at Facinetti. "She's real good at taking orders.

"Look, you're right," Tanner told Facinetti, still waving the gun around. "You don't know me and you don't trust me." He squeezed her during the last two words. Was that supposed to be a message? *Trust me.* Was she crazy? "But I have no problem showing good faith." In one quick move, Tanner turned, aimed at her dad and fired the gun.

Jess screamed along with her mother, and her dad jolted as

pain seared his face. A red spot on his thigh grew as the blood ate up his khaki pants. Her brothers all went ballistic and Jess fought like a demon to get out of Tanner's grasp.

"No, no," he told her very carefully. "Don't move unless you want me to do that to your mother too."

Jess froze. Her eyes stung as she watched the agony on her dad's face. "Daddy," she whispered. "Daddy, I'm sorry." He couldn't have heard her with her brothers making so much noise and her mother talking to him. Noise, there was so much noise and the room started spinning.

Another man showed up and Facinetti said something but Jess didn't hear it. He nodded, put his gun away and left the room. Then Tanner told the goon about her puking at the sight of blood which wasn't true, she just passed out, but the next thing she knew, Tanner had pushed her forward and the guy took her down the hall to the bathroom. He closed the door on her and Jess sank to the floor in a heap of defeat and misery.

He'd shot her father at close range. Without a second's hesitation, and right after he'd told her to trust him, Tanner had shot her dad. The bastard had used her just as her father had guessed. Once he'd realized who she was, he'd helped her so he could follow his own agenda. She'd been too naïve to see it. What if he intended to torture her dad? What if he tortured her whole family for revenge against her dad? A sick wave of nausea rolled through her stomach and to her utter horror, Jess puked into the toilet. A few minutes later, she splashed cold water on her face and took a deep breath.

Tanner wanted her alive, but no way in hell was she going down without a fight. She'd fight to her death because that was in the cards either way she looked at it.

JAY CONCENTRATED ON DEEP, focused breaths. If his hands had been free he would've put pressure on the wound, but that wasn't an option. The hole in his leg wasn't giant, but it was still a gunshot and burned like hell. His leg was on fire and blood continued to slowly eat away at his pants.

After the other guy had taken Jess out of the room, Bryant

crouched next to his bag and removed half a dozen blue plastic tarps. Next came two handfuls of packets of some kind. To say that Bryant wasn't going to get away with this would've been stupid, so Jay kept the comment to himself. Clearly the man knew he could.

"Sorry about your leg," Bryant said over his shoulder as he moved to Brendan who was furthest away from Jay. "I had to do something to make Facinetti trust me." Bryant bent next to Brendan and lifted his shirt. Brendan wasn't strong enough to fight him.

Jay couldn't see what was happening. "What the hell are you doing?" If this son of a bitch hurt his boys he was going to haunt him from the grave.

"I don't have much time for this," Bryant said, crouching next to Blake. He did the same thing, lifted his shirt and placed something on his chest. Blake let him. "These are blood packs," he explained quietly, moving onto Danny. "I've got another gun filled with blanks. When I shoot, you all play dead." He moved to Eric and placed a pack under his shirt. "It's the only way I can get you out of here." He talked fast and worked faster.

Bryant glanced at Jay with serious eyes as he moved toward Terry. "I don't know if this is going to work. Sorry, ma'am," he said as he lifted her shirt and placed a pack over her heart. "There's double stick tape on this. It should hold, but don't move around too much in case I'm wrong." He adjusted Terry's shirt in place. "I need to get close enough for the blank to break open the pack, but if I'm too close I'll break open a chest."

Terry paled.

Jay was still processing Bryant's words. *Sorry about your leg* and *play dead.* "So shooting me was an *act?*"

"Yeah. Mostly." Bryant crouched next to him, looked him in the eye. "Did you know what Juneau had planned at the trial?"

The moment of truth. Jay knew it was coming. It was real possible that Bryant would kill him if he told the truth, but the man deserved it. It explained the hesitation on Bryant's part. Every other family member got the pack in place without a word, yet now, Bryant waited for an answer. Jay could lie and tell him he didn't know, but that seemed like the coward's way out.

"Not at the beginning. I suspected toward the end, but I didn't know for sure until after the trial when I heard Alex talking to Maurice. They either didn't know that I was close by or didn't care."

"You didn't say anything?" Bryant asked.

Shame reared up and bit Jay in the ass. "No. I didn't. Breaking client confidentiality would get me disbarred. I couldn't afford it. I had too many people relying on me." Jay looked around the room at his boys, his wife, and met Bryant's gaze.

Bryant looked around the room too. He nodded, lifted Jay's shirt and placed a pack on his chest. Holding back his sigh, Jay silently took back every bad thought he had about Tanner Bryant. More than that, he regretted the pain the man had gone through for so many years. The tape pulled at Jay's chest hair, but the annoyance didn't compare to the fire in his leg or the heaviness in his chest.

Bryant went back to his bag and retrieved another gun. This one was much bigger than the first. He twisted a suppressor on the end and Jay's pulse revved higher. None of this looked fake. That was one big honkin' gun.

"Does Jess know about this?" Jay asked.

Bryant shook his head. "Not yet. No way to tell her, but I will if I get a chance."

"Why'd you send her out of here?" Terry asked.

"I needed the other guy to leave so I could set the packs and make sure you went along with the plan. If they think I'm keeping her alive for my own reasons, I can do this and leave here with all of you in my car."

"Sure hope you have one big ass car," Eric muttered.

"It's big enough to carry six corpses," Bryant said dryly. That comment sobered the whole family.

"We have to find a way to tell Jess," Terry said. "If she thinks we're dead, when she sees us…" She shook her head, her eyes shone with tears. "We can't do that to her."

"If I can, I will," Bryant said. "But I won't blow the chance to get you all out of here if warning Jess means getting caught."

"He's right." Jay looked at Terry. The last thing Jay wanted was to give his daughter more grief, but he didn't see any way around it. "I hate it as much as you do, but we don't have another option."

JESS WIPED HER EYES and took one last deep breath. She had to do something. She tested the knob, surprised to find it open. In a flash, she yanked it wide, caught the goon off guard and slammed him against the wall as she ran toward her family. A muted pop sounded as she rushed in the room. Just as quickly as she took in the site of Brendan with blood streaming from his chest and his body lying lifeless on the floor, the goon caught up to her and yanked her back.

"No!" She screamed as Tanner grabbed Blake by the hair and shot him at close range. Tanner's body blocked the action, but the jolt of Blake's body said it all. "No!" She screamed the word over and over, pain searing through her as if *she'd* been shot, her voice wailing in the freakishly quiet room.

Ignoring her, Tanner moved to Danny and did the same thing. Grabbed his hair to hold him still and shot his chest. The suppressor whispered in the room and Jess only heard the roaring in her ears as she screamed.

Blood splattered everywhere, seeped from her brothers' bodies onto the cold floor.

She screamed his name, her brothers' names. She screamed for him to stop. Begged for him to stop. Anguish, fear and desperation ruptured in her chest and with every shot that took the life of a family member, Tanner killed a part of her. Tears cascaded down her cheeks. The unbearable pain of loss tore her apart. Guilt, desperation and panic collided and made her dizzy, but still she struggled for freedom.

After methodically killing her siblings one by one, Tanner moved on to her parents.

The goon behind her held her by the waist, kept her back while Tanner stopped in front of her mother. The horrific scene made her nauseous.

"Just do it," Terry told him, her eyes bright with tears.

"Mom! No! Tanner, no!" She screamed the words, but almost nothing came out of her wrecked voice.

The shot whispered out and Terry jolted and drooped against the wall. Blood was everywhere, covering her chest, splattered behind her on the wall. Rage swelled and the room spun as dizziness swamped Jess. She held on long enough to see Tanner stand in front of her father and extend his gun.

She knew at that moment she had nothing to live for. No reason to exist. Without her family she had nothing. Tanner would kill her too, but she wouldn't give him what he wanted beforehand. She'd fight him so hard he'd have to kill her.

Tanner and her father shared a look and her dad nodded.

Tanner shot him in the chest.

That was the last thing Jess saw before blackness swallowed her whole.

CHAPTER 22

"KILLING" THE ST. JOHNS had been easier once Jess passed out. The room had grown deathly quiet as Tanner wrapped each body in a blue tarp. One by one, he released the cuffs and eased their arms forward, knowing how painful it would feel after being stuck in the same position for so long. They all looked pretty damn lifeless. What if he *had* killed them? What if he'd missed the blood packs or the blanks had been too close and he'd actually shot them?

A sick wave tightened Tanner's gut and he tamped down the urge to vomit.

He tossed the last pair of cuffs to the mammoth, Kwami, standing next to Jess. With his broad forehead and bushy beard he definitely gave off a don't-fuck-with-me attitude. "Put these on her," Tanner said. "I don't want her doing another Houdini before we get our alone time."

Kwami eyed him, his thick brows nearly met. "You're one cold motherfucker."

Tanner forced a grin. "You have no idea." His older sister had once told him the bigger the lie, the more people were inclined to believe. Tanner sure as hell hoped so.

Facinetti insisted they use Kwami's truck for the job. Tanner wondered if the man trusted him after all. Maybe the truck had some kind of GPS so Facinetti could follow him at a distance. The idea didn't sit well with Tanner, but he didn't see a way out. Kwami backed into the two-car garage. It took time to load all the St. Johns. Tanner worked up a healthy sweat as he stacked the family three across and two high. He put the healthiest ones on the bottom and the most injured on top. Twice, he heard a groan and a gasp and he huffed and puffed to cover the sound. The noise told him that at least two of the St. John's were alive, but what about the others? Once everyone was loaded, he carried an unconscious—and handcuffed—Jess to the passenger seat and buckled her in. His heart pounded harder with each step he took to the driver's side.

Almost there. Almost there.

All he had to do was start the truck and go.

Tanner stuck the key in the ignition and someone rapped on the window. He nearly jumped out of his skin and turned to see Facinetti. He cranked the engine and rolled down the window.

"I wasn't sure about you," Facinetti said. "But Kwami told me you really took care of everything. No hassle." It was true. Kwami had watched him wrap up every member of the family in the tarps. Tanner hadn't said a word as he'd done the job and Kwami hadn't seemed intent on helping.

"That's me. No hassle. You want something done, I'll do it, but I expect compensation. The next time won't be free."

"I wouldn't dream of it." Facinetti gestured toward Jess. "Your girlfriend is waking up." He smiled. "I'm guessing she's not going to be as cooperative as she was the first time."

Tanner shrugged. "Not a problem. I don't need cooperation."

"Come back when you're finished. We'll talk about something permanent." Facinetti's eyes held a chilling sincerity. As if this were a routine business matter he dealt with on a regular basis. He punched a remote control and backed away from the truck as the garage door slowly opened.

"Stop him!" A voice called. "It was a set up! It's not real blood! He's—"

Tanner didn't wait for the rest. Neither did he wait for the garage door to finish going up. Bright sunlight streamed in front of him screaming freedom, and Tanner slammed his foot on the gas as the garage door stopped and started going down again. Tires squealing, Tanner busted through the door, the sound of ripping metal and aluminum roaring in his ears along with gunshots behind him.

Jess came fully awake with a start just as a bullet zipped between them, ripping a hole in the front windshield.

"Get down!" Tanner shouted, yanking her down out of the line of fire. Shit, what if one of those bullets penetrated the truck and hit someone in back? Adrenaline zipped through his blood stream and his palms sweat fiercely.

"Don't touch me!" she railed back. She struggled against him and Tanner couldn't really blame her. She had no clue what had happened or what was currently happening.

"Jess, take it easy," Tanner said, trying to control the truck and her at the same time, but she squirmed beneath him and turned, lashing out with her legs and nailing him hard in the thigh. "I didn't—"

"I hate you. Go to hell, you heartless bastard!" Jess nearly spit the words, her voice a hoarse whisper after all the screaming she'd already done. "You're a scum sucking maggot and you deserve to die a horrible death and live in hell the rest of your life." She continued to lay into him with every vile word in her vocabulary, calling him every name she could come up with as she continued to literally kick the hell out of him.

"Dammit, Jess, listen to me. I didn't—" Another bullet went through the windshield. "Get down before you get shot!"

"I don't care!" she screamed. "It doesn't matter! Nothing matters anymore!"

Bullets still riddled the truck as Tanner pushed it faster. He looked in the rearview mirror as he continued down the street. Two cars loaded with Facinetti's men gave chase. He glanced forward again. "What the hell?" he muttered. Two police cruisers headed toward him. Their lights and sirens came on as he watched. Facinetti's men or the real thing? Tanner didn't know.

Jess wasn't paying attention to anything but kicking his ass. "I'd rather die from one of their bullets than—"

"Don't you wonder why they're shooting at us?" he roared.

Under a hailstorm of bullets, a tire exploded. Tanner white knuckled the steering wheel as the police passed him. The truck spun, slamming Jess into her door as they skidded to a halt. They had front row seats as more police cars came out of the woodwork and surrounded Facinetti's men in the first car. The second car pulled a U-turn and the police began pursuit.

Tanner moved to pounce on Jess in case more bullets started

flying, but Facinetti's men dropped their guns out of the windows as a dozen officers swarmed both cars with weapons drawn.

Jess looked on, confusion in her eyes as she tried to get out of the truck, screaming for help with her hoarse voice.

"Jess, they're okay," Tanner said, opening his door. He'd spun out at the edge of the residential neighborhood. Another block or two would've put them in the heart of Santa Monica. "They're okay. Let me do this." Tanner didn't waste time when three of the St. Johns were being crushed by three other family members. Not to mention the spinning halt he'd come to after the tire had been shot out. Jesus, what if one of those bullets had ricocheted in the bed of the truck. He bolted toward the back, opened the tailgate and raised the tarp covering the bodies as Jess watched him from inside the cab.

He lifted the lightest tarp on the edge—Jess's mom—and unwrapped her. He looked over Terry's shoulder and caught Jess's wide-eyed unbelieving stare.

Two ambulances pulled up with lights and sirens blazing. Tanner reached for another tarp and unveiled Jess's youngest brother.

Terry squirmed out of her plastic wrap, her shirt wet with fake blood, and ran around to the passenger seat. "Jess, honey, it's okay. We're okay." She opened the door and threw her arms around Jess.

Tanner couldn't look. Seeing that family bond, knowing he'd severed his own relationship with his family, he forced his gaze away. Hearing them cry was hard enough as it was. One by one, with help from paramedics, he unrolled tarps and released St. Johns.

"Can I get the keys to these cuffs?" Terry called.

Tanner tossed them then sliced the plastic covering the last man.

Jay St. John sat up. Tears brightened his light brown eyes. Jess's eyes. "Thanks," he said. "You didn't have to do that, but I...I thank you for getting my family out of there. I owe you."

Tanner knew what he wanted, but Jay couldn't give it to him. Only Jess could. After what he'd put her through, the chances of her talking to him again were pretty fucking slim.

Tanner faded back as more paramedics stepped in. Another

ambulance pulled up followed by more police cars. The eerie silence as police and EMTs worked to sort out the situation set Tanner on edge. It seemed like another calm before the storm. Jess reunited with every family member. The tears on her face were happy ones as she gave them her smile.

Leaning against the hood of a cruiser, Tanner turned his back on the scene and lifted his face to the warm sun. Once upon a time, he had a family. People who loved him, whom he loved back. But he'd disappointed them and he couldn't undo history. He'd thought he'd found something with Jess, a connection. She hadn't run from him or judged him. After a while, she'd trusted him. He liked that feeling. Liked knowing that someone counted on him. He'd forgotten what that felt like.

But his past showed that he was a fuck up. How could he have let his guard down with Jess? How could he let someone break down his walls without him even realizing it? Not that it mattered.

It was over. The whole fucking thing was over.

Maurice was dead. Tanner didn't mourn him. But he hated that Jess would have to face the music. Unless he took the fall. God, the thought of prison made him sick. He'd wanted out of there so badly and he'd vowed to never go back. But Jess didn't deserve to be there. Hell no. Just thinking about her being locked behind bars made his stomach turn. She deserved to be with her family. Happy. Look at the hell she'd gone through the past few days. She'd saved his life, so wasn't it up to him to return the favor? Didn't he owe her that much? His gut cramped just thinking about what he had to do. But he only saw one option. The least he could do was take the fall for Maurice. He hadn't wanted to go back to prison, but for Jess… For Jess, he would.

A hard blow smacked into his bicep and Tanner turned. Jess stood beside him, her eyes red-rimmed.

"You bastard," she croaked. Her bottom lip quivered and Tanner readied himself for the rest of her onslaught. He deserved it. Her tears ripped him apart and the fact that he'd made her feel this way chewed up his insides. Instead, she threw herself into his arms, held him tightly, squeezing the hell out of him.

Relief nearly knocked him to his knees. His breath stopped as he wrapped his arms around her. Holding her set him free. He pulled her closer, buried his face in her neck and took in her scent. Emotion long suppressed geysered up his chest and his eyes stung knowing how much pain he'd caused her. "I'm sorry. I'm so sorry. I had no way to tell you. I wanted to."

She didn't say anything, just held him tighter. Her silent forgiveness meant everything to him. So did the woman herself. He could stay like this, holding her, for a very, very long time. The longer they held each other, the easier Tanner's decision seemed. Jess had been through too much to face any more heartache in the future. He'd do whatever was necessary to make her happy.

Maybe this wasn't the reaction he expected, but the whole thing *was* over. Facinetti was probably in custody by now and Jess had her family back and would go on with her life. A life he didn't fit into. At all.

"I'm sorry," she whispered in his ear. "I should've trusted you. I should've—"

"Shh. Stop. Don't." God, how could she be apologizing when he'd just shot her father?

Holding her only made life harder. She was everything he wanted and he had to let her go, so Tanner gently set her from him. Jess studied his face, held his gaze. He loved the soft brown caramel of her eyes. No doubt about it, he could fall for a slip of a girl like Jess. Hell, he already had. Everything about her attracted him and she was everything he'd ever fantasized about. Besides the great body, she had a brain. She also had spirit and unrelenting will. In just a few days, she'd slipped under his skin in a way he'd never expected.

"I realize what you did back there, but I don't know how you did it." She folded her arms across her chest. "You got to the office, got the computer and..."

"I ran into your prop man, Ron, from the last film. He brought in two boxes filled with squibs, blood packs, blanks and a couple of guns that Maurice planned to unload somewhere. He was nice enough to give me a lesson on the use of it all."

"When that creep took me into the bathroom, you used that time to place the blood packs?"

Tanner nodded. "I didn't want to waste time once Facinetti had his hands on the computer. I didn't know if he'd get one of his own guys to do the job. I didn't want to take the chance."

"So you worked fast."

"Real fast," Tanner agreed.

"When did you call the police?" she asked.

"I didn't. I wasn't sure they were going to show up. I called your friend Troy Mills, but he didn't answer. I left a message. I wasn't sure he'd help me or not. When I saw the cruisers, I wasn't sure if they were the good guys. Facinetti could've been setting me up, by having his cops arrest me. When they went after the guys with the guns, I realized they were reinforcements." He spotted two officers talking and pointing in their direction. If he wanted to save Jess, she had to play along. Tanner pulled her close again, looked right into her eyes. "When the cops start asking questions, we tell them that I killed Maurice."

Her brows pulled together in a soft pucker and she shook her head. "No...no." She backed up a step. "We'll tell them the truth. I did it."

Tanner stood, loomed over her. "Let me do this, Jess. I don't want you to take the fall. The guy is dead. Let me handle it."

"You're nuts! You've already served seven years in prison for a crime you didn't commit. Why the hell would you go through that again?"

"Because..." Tanner stroked her soft cheek with his thumb. "Because I don't want you to have go through it. I've been there. I can handle it."

"Well handle this, tough guy." Jess put her hands on her hips. "We're telling the truth."

To hell with that. The truth had never gotten him anywhere. "My word against yours. I'll tell them you're protecting me."

Jess shot a look to the ambulances surrounding the truck. "My whole family heard you say that I killed him."

"I'll tell them I was lying. Just like I lied to Facinetti about killing them. It was just a plan to get them out. I wiped down my gun. Only my prints are on it."

"No." Jess shook her head. "Get it out of your mind right now. I killed Maurice and I'll face the music. It was an accident. You've done nothing wrong." She smacked his arm hard. "Do you really think I could live with myself knowing you were in prison for something I did? Especially after everything you've already gone through?" Her eyes darkened, stormy and bright at the same time. "Let me answer that for you." She barely took a breath. "No! Not for a second. I think you're an honorable man. A man who deserves a break. You deserve a family and a life and all the things that were taken away from you seven years ago."

Tanner felt an ache in his heart. He couldn't remember a time when someone had stood up for him so fiercely. Jess had been there for him since the night at Juneau's house. She'd saved his life more than once and the way she stood looking up at him with fire in her eyes made him want to hold onto her forever.

Yeah, he could see forever with this girl. She was that kind of girl. Dependable, smart and sexy as hell.

Do I deserve you? The question was on his tongue, but he didn't ask. He knew better.

She deserved a guy who didn't have a record. A guy who could get a well-paying job and keep her in a safe, comfortable environment. He didn't have a college education and was seriously behind the curve when it came to finding a decent job. In short, he couldn't give her what she deserved. Even if he managed to pull his life together and make something of himself, it would take years of struggle.

His thoughts took a different route when two men in suits approached with another man behind them. Every instinct Tanner possessed screamed, "Cop!"

"Are you Tanner Bryant?" The closest asked. He was a tall son of a bitch. And wide. He flashed a badge. "Detective Patrick. This is my partner, Detective O'Kelly. We'd like to ask you a few questions."

Even if he didn't take the fall for Juneau, he and Jess were guilty of kidnapping. A federal offense, if he wasn't mistaken. With his record, he'd definitely be seeing jail time. It was crazy to think he could have any future much less one with Jess. Since when did he live in a dream world?

The third man tapped Jess on the shoulder. "Miss St. John,

your mom asked me to tell you that your brother's ambulance is leaving. She'd like you to go with him to the hospital."

Jess's gaze shifted from the waiting ambulance to Tanner and the cops.

"Go," he told her. "I'm fine." He glanced at the detectives. "You know where I'll be." Another jail cell, no doubt. How the hell had he gotten himself into this? He'd sworn not to go back. But if it kept Jess out...he'd do it in a heartbeat.

"We need to speak with you too, Miss St. John," the smaller detective said.

"Can you talk to her at the hospital?" Tanner asked. "C'mon, let her be with her family. She's been through hell the past few days."

The detectives shared a glance before O'Kelly nodded. "Okay. Go ahead. We'll talk at the hospital."

"Look," Jess said, backing up toward the ambulance. "We'll both cooperate, but not before we talk to our lawyer." She saw Tanner's raised brows and pointed to the departing ambulance carrying her father. "Our lawyer just left and we'll both talk to you after we've talked to him at the hospital." She disappeared inside her brother's ambulance and it moved down the street with sirens blaring.

Tanner was right back where he started, with someone telling him who his lawyer would be. The circumstances hadn't changed much either. He didn't doubt Jay St. John would do everything in his power to make sure his daughter stayed out of prison. Tanner didn't blame him. At least they felt the same way. But Jess wasn't the type to let either one of them run the show. She was honest to the core. So did Tanner start talking now and take the fall or did he wait until he talked to Jess's father and play the game his way? He faced the three men, still deciding what the hell he was going to tell them.

"Who are you," he asked the third guy, hoping to stall another few minutes. The truth really had never done him any good. Chances were good that no one would believe him anyway.

The man put his hand out. "Troy Mills." They shook hands. "I called for reinforcements after I got your message. You can trust these guys," he said, gesturing to the detectives. "The more information I uncovered on Facinetti, the more I thought you could use some extra help."

"You were right about that. Thanks." Tanner studied the two detectives watching him. "Jess didn't know who to trust. Facinetti had a couple of cops keeping an eye on her. They did a good job of scaring the crap out of her. Jess should go through a list of LAPD officers so she can ID the creeps working for Facinetti. I'm pretty sure she'll be more than willing." It didn't get past Tanner that had they not scared her, he never would've had the time to get to know her.

But Tanner had already wasted too many years and now he wanted this over with. "You might want to check out the St. John's garage. Aside from that, unless you want to offer immunity to Jess, I think I need to wait for my lawyer."

The beginning of the end.

CHAPTER 23

SO MUCH HAD HAPPENED in the three months since Tanner had rescued her family that Jess felt as if she'd fallen into a Robert Altman film. Most of the time, she'd been so busy that the weeks had flown by but other times, like now, the seconds ticked along so slowly they almost hurt.

Tanner and she had both been arrested and released on bail posted by her father. She'd nursed her family back to health, which had given her something to do since she no longer had a job.

Only as she spoke to the dozens of crew members from past films and some of Maurice's investors who'd called after the news went public did she realize that she was much more than just his assistant. Maurice had done such a good job of keeping her down that it hadn't dawned on her she was practically doing his job.

Jess toed the skin under the ankle monitor that had become her mandatory jewelry the last several months. Despite the comfort of house arrest on manslaughter charges, she still hated the implication of the monitor. She'd never run. Especially since her dad had put the house up as collateral for her bond.

Alone, sitting at the large round table in the new solarium of her parent's home, Jess stared unseeing at the flashing icon on her computer screen and took a deep breath. There was no more to add. She'd gone over it multiple times and she was officially done. Typing *the end* should've given her a sense of pride or fulfillment, but it hadn't. Because finishing the screenplay was only a fraction of her battle. The screenplay wouldn't mean anything if she went to prison. Her cell phone rang, but she didn't recognize the number so she let it roll over to voice mail. It felt as if everyone who'd ever done business with Maurice had learned of his death. Rumors and conjecture ran rampant, and the publicity surrounding the trial was nearly harder to bear than the actual crime.

She'd come to grips with what she'd done. The fact remained that she hadn't killed Maurice on purpose and it didn't matter how many times she replayed the scene in her head because the outcome would never change. For the thousandth time, the question ran through her brain, "Would I have shot Maurice if he'd fired at Tanner?" Although she thought the answer would be yes, she wasn't a hundred percent sure that she'd have been in the state of mind to pull the trigger. Knowing the way she froze in panic situations, Maurice might have just as easily gunned her down after Tanner. Of course none of it mattered. What mattered was that she had three months before the trial. Thanks to her father's reputation—and a few pulled strings, she didn't have to wait a year or longer to know her fate. She'd had twelve weeks to enjoy home cooked meals or take out from her favorite restaurants. Ninety days to soak up the love from her family. She swallowed back the knot in her throat and shook out of her stupor.

The house was quiet for the first time that Jess could remember since her house arrest began. She looked around the new room that had been added on to the back of the house. Her parents had been talking about an addition for years, and after the whole Facinetti incident they'd decided to go for it. "Life was too short to put off living," they'd said. The side and back walls were made of tinted glass that kept out the California summer sun, but gave the room a feeling of being outside. A comfortable sofa and two extra wide chairs filled the main space. Though the room had only been finished for two days, Jess had moved her computer and files in here and made it her unofficial office.

She should've been happy to have the place to herself, but the silence was unnerving after the all the noise she'd lived with for the past two months while the room was being built. Up until now, it was as if her family had made a point of someone being home with her. Not because they were afraid of her running, but because they were afraid of her being alone. Alone with her thoughts? Or alone to consider what being in a cell might be like?

Either way, there'd always been someone at the house with her.

The kitchen door squeaked. "'Lo?" *Tanner.* Her parents had given him a key a few weeks ago.

Her heartbeat picked up the way it usually did when she heard his voice. He'd become a regular fixture in the house, part of the family. At first she didn't think he'd stick around once her dad managed to get the charges dropped against him. Why hang around a town that had only caused him misery? But Tanner had promised to testify on her behalf and do whatever they needed. Still, the trial was another three months away and he could've moved somewhere else. He hadn't. He'd chosen to stay. Jess wasn't sure if it made her happy or sad. Happy, because she got to spend time with him and sad because she worried that her life was a dead end and he was simply wasting time being around her.

"In here," she called. Jess saved the final draft on her laptop and closed the lid as Tanner entered. He looked gorgeous in a ribbed, black, long sleeved shirt that couldn't hide the definition of his muscled chest. Dark jeans and black boots completed the picture. He was the ultimate male. Strong, confident and full of sex appeal.

"Where is everybody?" he asked, looking around the room.

"Out." Avoiding eye contact, she methodically stuffed her notes into a file. She had a ton of calls to make tomorrow regarding a location, but it was too late to do any more work tonight.

It was hard to look at him and not want him. Despite the intense physical relationship they shared months ago, they'd hardly touched since. When they did, the contact was electric. At least it was on her part. Maybe he didn't feel the same. Granted they hadn't been alone together, but he'd shown very little interest other than friendship.

"Out?" The surprise in his voice made her smile.

"Yep. Dad's buried under paper work at the office. Mom volunteered to serve dinner at the local women's shelter, but they had some kind of power outage so she's waiting there. Eric and Danny are unpacking the last of the boxes in their new place. Mom can't believe they really moved out—she's not taking it too well." Jess grinned sympathetically. "And the twins went to a Seger Hughes concert in Anaheim. Aside from some leftovers in the fridge, you're stuck with me. But don't feel obligated to stay."

She got the feeling he sided with her family when it came to her being alone. Everyone worried about her. It should've made her mad, but it only made her realize how much her family loved her.

"I know you worked your butt off today. You can take off. Have a night to yourself," she prodded. He'd started working for her father almost since the day Jay had bailed them both out of jail because Tanner insisted on repaying his bond. Then he'd joined the construction crew that built this new room. She understood his need for money and loved her dad for giving Tanner the chance, but now the room was done and Tanner had no reason to hang around. He'd have to find a job, which he could do in another city since he didn't have to be back until the trial. Of course that meant finally giving up her apartment since she'd sublet to him when the house arrest began. That would mark the beginning of her actual loss of freedom and the thought made her stomach cramp.

"Today wasn't so bad," he said, moving farther into the room. "Just returned some of the materials."

"Yeah, but they weighed a ton."

He shrugged it off then turned and faced her. Working outside had given him a healthy tan and he looked better than ever. His hair had grown out and she itched to run her fingers through its thick softness. It was hard to believe they hadn't touched each other in three months. The first month, the whole family had focused on recovering from the trauma. Then the construction on the house had started and what was supposed to be a four week job had doubled because of one thing or another. In all that time, Tanner had melded into the family. He'd stayed for meals and her family had treated him like gold.

"How's the screenplay going?" he asked, gesturing to her computer as she zipped her files in a case. She'd been working on it since the room construction started. Two months of intensive hours at her computer, trying to come up with a screenplay good enough to make Bobby McBride want to invest his money with her. It was surreal to think that Maurice's potential partner, the oilman from Texas, considered doing business with her. Bobby told her he'd noticed her problem solving abilities and her attention to detail. It was his appointment she'd canceled the morning she'd abducted and shot her boss.

Like several of Maurice's other investors, Jess had called to tell him there would be no meeting. That Maurice had been killed in a freak accident and if he still wanted to invest in a Hollywood film, then he needed to find a producer looking for money. In the course of a half dozen calls, he'd asked tons of questions about show business and movies, and he'd decided that she was the producer he wanted to work with. Bobby had told her if she brought him a project he liked, he'd fund it. She'd been upfront with him during their phone calls. Told him she'd never produced a movie before, but he hadn't seemed bothered by the fact. He insisted he was prepared to write her a check whenever she was ready.

Instead of involving a scriptwriter, instead of unnecessarily getting someone else's hopes up, Jess had another idea. It was Tanner who convinced her to run with it. So in the span of two months, she'd written a screenplay. It hadn't been hard. The story was fresh in her head. She called it Payback. It was certainly the kind of thing that moviegoers wanted. Action, intrigue, romance. It had a little of everything. Including violence, which Jess had hated writing.

The pride she hadn't felt at typing the end suddenly washed through her, but only because she knew how Tanner would react.

"It's done. For real."

His eyes widened and a giant smile lit his face. "Finally!" In two strides, he reached her and pulled her out of her chair, crushing his arms around her in a massive bear hug. "That's great! God! That's so great!"

Jess closed her eyes and focused on the warmth of his body, the strength of his big arms wrapped around her. She hugged him tight, reveling in the moment before it ended. In all these months, Tanner hadn't made a move on her. Hadn't given any sign that he wanted her, and even though her conscience argued that the guy hadn't had a chance to do anything with a houseful of people and considering that he'd worked from sun up to sun down most days—she still didn't know what to make of it.

But now, as Tanner eased back and stared down at her, she saw something else in his eyes. She saw the man who'd snuck into her heart three months ago. One hand eased through her hair and his gaze smoldered.

"Your hair is growing out," he said softly. He'd barely glanced at her hair. He focused on her eyes, then her mouth.

A sharp thrill zinged beneath her skin, down her back. She loved when he looked at her like he might eat her up in one bite. It made her feel valued. Desired. Jess pushed aside the unfamiliar feelings. "So is yours." She had to touch him and stroked her thumb across his jaw.

He slowly leaned down and Jess braced herself for contact. But nothing could ready her for the electric sensation when his lips touched hers. He didn't kiss her hard, but he kissed her well. Jess ran her hand up his muscled chest as his tongue explored her mouth. She'd forgotten how good it was to kiss him. How safe she felt in his arms. How the intimacy always made her forget everything around her. His erection grew against her lower belly and Jess rubbed against him, loving the fact that she made him this way. That she had that kind of power over this man. His hands trailed down her sides then roamed lower and cupped her ass until he'd brought her more firmly against the hard ridge in his jeans.

Desire flared hot and hungry, and Jess lost the will to take her time. She stood on her toes, yanked Tanner closer and took control of the kiss. A second later, he jumped on board, and what had been sweet and soulful turned rough and raunchy. Their kiss exploded into a ferocious taking of lips and mouths. Their hands searched out soft skin and hard muscle. Jess wanted him more than anything else in the world, every part of her focused on the way his fingers moved along her body and the way his tongue danced with hers, so when he pulled back, breathing hard, she didn't understand his problem.

"The phone," he panted. When she looked at him blankly, he said it again at the same time she heard her cell phone ring. "You'd better answer it. Don't want anyone worrying about you if they think something's wrong."

Taking a deep breath, Jess reached for her phone on the table. The distraction was probably a good thing. What would be the point of hooking up with Tanner? She couldn't risk starting something with him on the chance she ended up in prison. The man deserved a full life with a woman at his side and her odds at remaining free were fifty-fifty at best.

TANNER RAN A HAND through his hair and reined in his libido. He'd been about two seconds from tossing Jess onto the new sofa and making her his. He wanted her so bad he could barely think straight. He was so damn proud of her he wanted to burst with it.

"This is Jess," she said, answering her phone. She listened and looked up at him. "Yes, hi, Bobby. How are you?"

Bobby McBride. The man who could make her dreams come true. Tanner held his breath, waiting for Jess's side of the conversation. McBride was just the kind of patsy that Juneau always targeted, a man with a ton of money and no experience in show business. It was Tanner's idea that Jess write something herself. He figured it would take her mind off the trial and kick-start a career she wanted more than anything. Her family had agreed. Instead of trying to rewrite an old screenplay, Jess had started fresh with a new idea. The past two months, she'd spent as many hours at her computer as he'd worked on the new room.

"Actually, I was going to call you tomorrow," Jess said. "I have a project you might be interested in." She listened and her eyes went wide. "Tonight? Oh, I don't know about to—" She listened again and looked a little panicked before finally nodding her head. "Yes, I can, it's just that I—" She waited again, darting a glance at him. "Okay. Sure. I'll email it to you as soon as we hang up." Another brief pause and she went on, "Okay. Thank you, Bobby. You too. Goodnight." She hung up the phone, sat down and scrubbed her hands through her hair. "He wants it now. Tonight." Then, as if Tanner might not understand her words, she looked at him with wide eyes and repeated them very succinctly. "He wants the screenplay now! Tonight!"

Tanner grinned. "Yeah, so? You finished it. Your exact words were *for real.* Send it to him. What's the problem?"

"The problem? The problem?" She jumped to her feet and started pacing. "The problem is I just typed *the end* ten minutes ago and I'm not sure it's good enough. I mean, am I really done or do I need to change the ending? Maybe I should read through it again and see if it's really good enough. I should—"

Tanner snagged her by the shoulders as she passed him. He kissed her hard, just once, and set her back. "It's good enough. Send it."

"How do you know? You didn't even read the whole thing."

"I read most of it. I would've read it all if you'd let me. Besides, you didn't *just* finish. You finished it weeks ago and you've been obsessing over it since. I know it's good." It was better than good. It was their story. She'd called it his story, but it was about them. He was dying to know the ending, but she'd struggled over it and he didn't want to press her. "It's ready. Send it." He watched her worried eyes. "Look. What's the worst thing that can happen? He'll say no to this project and ask you to find another one."

"Or he'll take his money somewhere else," she said.

"Or that. But you risk that with any project you send him. You're the one who told me it's subjective. Not everyone is going to like the same things. You have to take the risk." He rubbed her shoulders and tried to ease some of the tension out of her tired muscles. "Go on," he told her. "Send it." He gave her a little shove toward her computer and lifted the lid. Jess waited for it to boot up, then typed a quick email, attached the screenplay and, after a few seconds of hesitation, hit Send. The ensuing silence hovered like a fog filled with mind-numbing possibilities. Would McBride like it enough to offer the money Jess needed? If he did, would Jess retain her freedom and make her dreams come true?

Tanner closed the lid on her computer and put an end to the stilted quiet. He helped Jess to her feet and turned her toward him. "You have to risk to win," he told her. "Life's too short to put off living."

Jess arched her brows. "Since when did you start quoting my parents?"

"Since I decided they know what they're talking about." He hadn't planned on liking Jay and Terry so much, but some things couldn't be helped. They were fair, decent people who looked out for their kids and their community. Since the day he'd gotten them out of Facinetti's house, they'd looked out for him as well. He could've refused the offer to work on the construction crew, but Tanner hadn't seen the logic in that. Taking the job accomplished a few things. It gave him the income he needed to survive, it kept him in Los Angeles before the trial and most importantly, it gave him close proximity to Jess. Even though he hadn't been this close to her—and man, how he'd missed it—he'd been able to see her and talk to her practically every day. But having her in his arms...that was something he'd fantasized about for months. He'd been waiting for a sign, any kind of sign that might indicate she wanted him, but he hadn't had one until now. Maybe she was afraid of what her family might think of them being together. Maybe she didn't want a relationship with an ex-con. He'd been so close to calling it quits, packing up his belongings and taking off. But the thought of leaving Jess made him empty. Emptier than when he sat in a cold prison cell. As crazy as it seemed, the St. Johns were all he had. They'd circled the wagons to protect both of them from the media and anyone that might do them any harm. He wasn't sure where he fit in. He just knew he wanted to.

Now, sticking with her parents' new motto, Tanner seized the moment. Staring into Jess's whiskey eyes, he traced her bottom lip with his thumb. Her eyes glazed over and a wave of emotion struck Tanner head-on. He didn't take the fact that she wanted him lightly. Most women wouldn't want a man with a prison record. But the desire in her eyes shone bright and it matched exactly what he felt for her. With a hint of pressure, he pressed her lip down and bent his head, taking her mouth with a hunger he'd been suppressing for too long.

Jess gave into his kiss with a soft moan, her mouth open and welcoming as he tasted her. It was when she pulled back and shook her head that Tanner sensed trouble.

"We shouldn't," she said. But her eyes said she wanted to.

Tanner moved toward her and she stepped back. "Why?" Why put on the brakes when they clearly wanted each other so badly. "Are you worried about someone coming in or—"

"No, no." She shook her head. "That isn't it." She ran her hands through her hair the way she always did when she was torn, but now that it was longer, it settled against her scalp in messy, sexy layers. "I'm just thinking about the future. About the trial. I shouldn't do this when I don't know what my future is going be." She paced away from him. "You especially, you should be going out and meeting people. You aren't chained to my family just because my dad got you a job. You should be doing all the things you didn't get to do when you were in prison." Facing him, she looked as innocent as she always did, concern in her eyes and in her voice.

Was this her way of trying to get rid of him? Considering she was the one who'd lost control before the phone rang, he doubted it. "Be straight, Jess. If you want me gone, then say so, but don't deny what's between us because you're worried about the future. That's only another reason why we should live for now." He moved toward her. "I want you more than I want to breathe. I want to feel what it's like to be inside you again. I want your taste in my mouth. What happens at the trial isn't something we can control, but we have control over right now."

"Fine. Let's say we do it your way. What happens three months from now if I go to prison? Are you going to move on with your life? If I get fifteen years, will you find a woman, fall in love and have a family?"

"I don't know what the hell I'm going to do in two days, much less three months from now. I think your parents have the right idea, Jess. You have to live in the now, because you don't know what's going to happen in the future." Tanner stalked her until Jess had the wall at her back. It was very similar to their first encounter in the kitchen and his blood revved hotter just thinking about taking her here. "Your call, Jess. Are you really going to give up the time you know you have left?"

"It's not about me, it's about you." she insisted. "I want you to be happy. What's the point of being with me when you can be out meeting someone who might not be spending the next ten-to-twenty years behind bars?"

"You're wasting your breath, sweetheart," Tanner whispered as he cupped her neck and brought his mouth closer to hers. "There's nowhere else I'd rather be than right here with you." He sealed his words with a kiss, molding his mouth against hers in a connection so hot it would've set the drapes on fire had there been any.

He felt her cave. Knew he had her when she wrapped her arms around his neck and kissed him back just as hungrily as he kissed her.

"This is just for now," she breathed. "No ties, nothing serious."

Tanner grunted his answer as he took her mouth in another soul shattering kiss. She could call it anything she wanted, but he'd already learned she was the kind of woman he wanted for the long haul and the last three months had only solidified that fact. He didn't expect the feeling to go away any time soon, but damn if he planned on telling her and scaring her off even more.

When her cool palms reached under his shirt and slid under the waistband of his jeans, all thoughts of saying anything fled completely. The only thing on his mind was making her come.

Tanner hefted her against the thick archway that opened into the room. All the other walls were made of glass and he didn't trust their strength. He would've checked for wainscoting on the wall, but he'd helped build the thing and knew it was smooth.

"Ohgodohgod," she breathed, rubbing against him with a long slide.

Tanner growled a response before taking her mouth in a deep, wet kiss.

"Upstairs," she huffed the next time they came up for air.

Probably a smart thing to do. One of the St. Johns could walk in at any time. Jess had her legs wrapped around his hips as he carried her through the house, their tongues still tangling as he bumped his way through the den across the living room. He hit the stairs, blindly taking them as fast as he could. Big mistake. He got half way up, distracted by Jess's hand on his erection and her tongue in his mouth, when he misjudged. Jess yelped as they went down. Tanner managed to land sideways and keep her safe in his arms, but they still hit like a wheelbarrow full of bricks.

"Shit!" he breathed, looking down at her. "You okay?" Her answer didn't come immediately. But a smile spread across her face before she laughed. Then just as quickly she wrapped her arm around his neck and pulled him down for a searing, hungry kiss. "I'll take that as a yes." God, he'd missed her mouth, her kiss and the way her tongue dueled with his. He missed the minty taste of her. That wasn't the only taste he wanted.

Tanner moved his kisses to her ear then down her neck as he lifted her shirt. He wanted to lick every part of her. Quickly he unhooked her bra and shoved the cups aside, holding her breast as he took her nipple in his mouth. Her hot little whimper made him harder. He wanted her here. Right now. He worked his way down her stomach, unbuttoning and unzipping her skinny jeans. Goddammit…they didn't want to come off. He had to sit up and peel them off her. She inched up the stairs, still on her back, her elbows supporting her as she climbed, helping him strip her of her clothes. She pulled her legs in, as he got her jeans and underwear off, but he grabbed an ankle and began tugging her back down. He saw shock on her face, the sudden understanding that he planned on finishing this right here.

"Don't even think about it," she warned. Her voice cracked on the last word. She must have seen it in his eyes, because she laughed. She also yanked out of his grip, flipped over and started up the stairs. The smooth white globes of her ass tempted him like nothing else ever had. He caught her before she got to her feet, but her position couldn't have been more perfect. He moved to his back, laid his head on a step and continued to pull her down. And down and down until he had her right where he wanted her. When his mouth connected with her warm, wet center, she quit fighting him. "Ohgodohgodohgod. Tanner, you can't." But even as she said it, she pushed against his mouth, begging him to take her. He gripped her ass and drove his tongue deeply inside her. She tasted even better than he remembered. And her scent, God almighty there was nothing like it. Tanner tongued her clit as he pushed two fingers inside of her. In seconds she spasmed around his fingers, her climax fast and hard. That was about all he could take. His rigid cock hurt so bad, he didn't think he'd make it inside her. Keeping his mouth on her skin, he continued to pull her down over his body, kissing her stomach and breasts and fumbling with the button and zipper on his jeans as she squirmed on top of him. The farther down she got, the farther up her shirt went until it was completely off and she straddled him totally naked. Damn, it was so much like the first time. The heat, the intensity, the speed in which they took each other. Tanner couldn't stop it. Didn't want to. Just like that first time, she adjusted herself on top of him and guided him into her body. Tanner gritted his teeth against the sensation of her surrounding him, of the heated clench of her soft flesh. Without a word she rode him. Hard. Just the way he liked it.

She ground over him, hitting the right spot for her and sending him headlong into his own climax. The stairs digging into his back and thighs did nothing to hinder the rush of excitement. A few good thrusts was all it took for him to lose control. He tried to hold off, tried to wait for her to come again, but his release rocketed into her, hot and violent. Jess cried out against his neck and shuddered, her own release milking him dry. A sheen of sweat slicked her skin as Tanner ran his palms over her bare back and down to her silky smooth ass.

He still wanted her. Just like the last time. He was still inside her, still hard. His need for her went beyond anything he'd ever known. She'd mentioned him going out and meeting other people. Women. That was out of the question. Not even a consideration. She was it for him. The one and only. He figured he had about an hour to show her.

It took him a minute to find his breath and when he did, he could only think of one thing to say.

"Let's go find a bed."

CHAPTER 24

TANNER PULLED UP IN front of the St. Johns' house and killed the wipers, headlights and engine. Three months had flown by like three days. November rain hit the windshield in a deluge, and palm trees swayed in strong wind gusts. Instead of taking an immediate soaking, he psyched himself up for another "family" dinner. It wasn't that he didn't like the St. Johns—all of them—because he did. It was dealing with them now that they were in the middle of the trial that made things more difficult. They had banded together, surrounding Jess with their love and support, which just made Tanner more aware of what he'd given up with his own family. That's what stuck in his chest and twisted.

But he had nowhere to go and ultimately nowhere else he'd rather be. After the construction job ended, he worked for her father in a series of odd jobs around the house, then Jess had hired him to help her with the movie's business plan. They'd worked together so well the past couple months, budgeting the picture and pricing the crew. Every day he learned more and more about producing, and Jess was ready if McBride gave her a green light.

The rain tapered off and Tanner got out of the car. He waved to the bodyguard parked out front. Jay had hired a guy to watch the house to ensure Jess's safety, but he usually only came when Jess was alone. They all worried about Facinetti striking from prison.

Tonight shouldn't be different than any of the others, but it was. The more time that went by without a verdict, the more tense everyone got. Four days had dragged on. Jay had hoped for a quick deliberation, but the longer it took, the more somber he became and the bleaker Jess's future looked. A rare boom of thunder punctuated Tanner's thoughts. He took a deep breath, didn't want to think the storm was any indication of Jess's future. The weather was actually a nice change from the stuffy room they'd been confined in while waiting for the jury to decide.

"Hello?" His voice echoed in the large kitchen. He heard Jess coming from the solarium as he shook off the rain and hung his leather jacket on the coat rack. She stood in the doorframe and about took his breath away. Wearing an oversized sweater and leggings, she looked like a kid. But Tanner knew better. She wore her hair in a bob that barely hit her shoulders. It looked thick and silky and made his palms itch to touch it. Despite her thick, cream sweater, she had her arms crossed over her chest.

"Hi," she said. "I wasn't sure you'd come by. The weather's horrible."

Her comment shouldn't have surprised him. She'd been dropping those little bombs for weeks now, looking for an excuse for him not to be there. Jess had insisted, "No ties, nothing serious" three months ago and he hadn't pushed her. At times he wondered if she really meant it, but then they'd kiss and she'd urge him on faster and harder and… How could she not know by now the way he felt about her? True, he hadn't told her his feelings and he'd purposely kept their conversations light, but he sure as hell had *shown* her how he felt. The last three months had been chock-full of quickies. They'd grabbed any and every spare minute alone, on each other like bees on honey. Anywhere in the house was fair game. Tanner had hoisted her on the bathroom counter, the washing machine and against a wall in nearly half the closets in the house. They were pros at vertical sex. Nothing could keep him away from her.

Except maybe prison. Shit. Stupid thought.

"Me? Miss out on food? You think a little rain will get in my way?" He grinned and she smiled back. "Where is everybody?" He'd seen her father's car in the driveway, so that killed a chance for a quickie.

She shrugged. "Not sure. Mom and Dad went upstairs to change. Eric and Danny aren't here yet. I don't know where the twins are. They had a stop to make. We ordered Dr. Pizza so it should be here any minute." The mention of Dr. Pizza always reminded Tanner of that one and only time six months ago when they'd spent the entire night together. Jess watched him and he knew she was thinking about the same thing. Hot, incredible sex. Burn up the sheets, carnal sex. He'd taken it slow that night. Real slow. He'd kissed, licked and sucked nearly every inch of skin. God, what he wouldn't give to do that again. To be able to take his time with her. That night had been about enjoying the sensations of a woman, about hearing the sounds and reveling in the feel and texture of her. But if he got the chance again...it would be about loving her. It would be showing her exactly how he felt. Not something easily accomplished with a quickie.

Part of Tanner didn't care that her parents were in the house. He wanted to pull her close and kiss the shit out of her. He wanted to yank down those leggings and push inside her. They'd been so careful and he couldn't take a chance they'd kick him out now. Not when they potentially had so little time together.

A sick feeling rolled in his gut. What if she didn't reciprocate his feelings? What if she'd been serious about 'just for now'? She'd never acted as if she didn't want him around, but she'd also never confessed any emotional ties either. Neither had he, but only because he'd been afraid she'd pull away from him.

A car pulled up next to the kitchen door and the twins raced into the house still dressed in their suits. Blake pocketed his phone as he jogged by her with Brendan on his heels. "Hey," Brendan said. "Hope it's cool, Jess, but we got invited to David's sister's gallery opening. We'll probably crash at his place tonight, so don't wait up."

"Just need to change and pack my jammies," Blake called from the hallway.

"Yeah, sure," she said at her brothers' backs. But they were already gone, their footsteps pounding up the stairway.

The phone rang and Jess picked it up. She listened, glancing at him again before looking away. "Oh, that sucks. Sorry. Hope you get it fixed." She nodded and kept the phone to her ear another minute, mumbling quick responses before hanging up. She took out four plates and set them on the kitchen table. "Looks like none of the boys will be here tonight. Eric and Danny have a leak in the roof and they're trying to find the manager. They're afraid to leave in case it gets worse. They said they'd be at the courthouse in the morning."

Wow. Four people out of the way in under a minute, but Tanner didn't think he'd get a shot. The odds were against them having a whole night together.

They heard commotion in the upstairs hallway as Jess set out glasses and silverware for four. Her brothers raced out of the kitchen as quickly as they'd come in, only this time they had on jeans, boots and jackets. They each carried suits covered in plastic and had athletic bags over their shoulders. An awkward moment passed when they took turns hugging her. Then they quickly called out their good-byes and said they'd see her at the courthouse tomorrow.

Her parents came in next. They each also had a bag packed. Something was up.

"All right, what's going on?" Jess asked.

Jay set his bag on the table and looked at Jess. "I got a call a little while ago."

Tanner's stomach knotted and the idea of food didn't appeal any more. Jay must have heard something and wanted to break the news without her brothers around. On second thought, maybe her brothers already knew and that's why they'd become scarce. Maybe he should give them privacy too, but he had as much a right to know what was happening as anyone here.

Jess straightened her back and got ready for the worst.

"Looks like we'll get the verdict first thing in the morning," Jay said. He pulled her into a tight hug and squeezed his eyes shut. The emotion on his face and the implication put a knot in Tanner's gut.

Swallowing, Jess nodded as she stepped back. She'd been waiting for this, they all had. Tanner hadn't expected it would happen this way. With so much time—a whole night for everyone to consider the consequences.

Another car pulled up by the kitchen door with the Dr. Pizza logo on the roof.

"I've got that." Her dad reached for his wallet and took out a few twenties. The delivery guy handed over the usual three pizzas, chicken, salad and soda and took his money. He scampered back to the haven of his dry car. Jess and Terry helped Jay with all the food, but the room was eerily quiet.

"Just put the leftovers in the fridge," her mom said as they set everything on the counter. "We'll get to it tomorrow. Or whenever."

Her mother froze, her back to the room. She took a deep breath then reached for Jess and wrapped her in her arms. Jess held her tight and that knot in Tanner's gut lodged in his throat. Finally, Terry let go and grabbed her bag. The whole thing got weirder and weirder. Her parents were leaving too?

"So wait," Jess said, clearly not yet understanding the situation. "Where are you going?"

"Out," her mother said. "You know how your father and I like to keep things interesting. We're staying downtown at the Biltmore for the night."

"Terry…" Jay gave her a look loaded with meaning.

"Okay," she said, facing Jess again. "We thought—" Jay cleared his throat and Terry rolled her eyes. "*I* thought the two of you deserved a night alone, so I'm making your father leave. For the record, he's not thrilled with the idea." She paused. "But this isn't about him, it's about you." She looked at Jess before her focus landed on him. "You won't mind bringing her to the courthouse in the morning, will you, Tanner?"

Mind? That was like asking a dolphin if he minded swimming in the ocean. "No, ma'am."

"Great." Her eyes shone bright, as she hugged Jess again then headed for the door. "We'll see you in the morning, honey." Terry passed him, but paused. She faced him, smiled and wrapped her arms around his shoulders in a motherly hug before stepping back. "Goodnight." She dragged Jay out with her, but not before he looked at Jess and then him. The eye contact was fleeting…a father wanting the best for his daughter.

Was this for real? After months of quickies, they were leaving Jess alone with him for the whole night? Did they think this would be her last free night for the next eight to ten years? Was this their way of giving her a night to do whatever she wanted?

The smell of pizza and chicken filled the room as Jess stared at him. The silence in the kitchen felt as uncomfortable as the silence in the stuffy room at the courthouse. Usually when they had a few minutes they were in each other's arms in a heartbeat, but Jess busied herself by putting away two of the place settings, leaving two on the table.

She didn't look at him. Whether she wouldn't or couldn't, he didn't know. She opened the fridge and shoved the salad and drinks inside. Something had her spooked and he wanted to know what it was. She closed the fridge and turned. Right into his chest. She didn't look into his eyes, just stared off to the side, out the kitchen window. He placed his hands on the fridge, blocking her in. The air charged with their combined heat and energy.

"What's up?" he asked quietly. "Why are you avoiding me?"

She still didn't make eye contact.

He finally had a chance to tell her how he felt without interruption. At least now he'd know whether he'd made a dent in her boundaries these last few months. Did she want him to stick around or not? Tonight was his last chance to find out. He wasn't even sure where to start.

Jess finally looked into his eyes and hers filled with emotion. For the first time in months he got the feeling that maybe she'd been fighting the same sentiment.

"Do you know how many times I wanted to hold you no matter who was in the room?" He paused, let his words sink in. "But I was afraid if I did, your dad or mom or one of your brothers might toss me out and I couldn't stand not being around you." Her eyes filled with tears and Tanner felt a knot constrict his throat. "I want to be around for the long haul. I want to be in your life—"

"No!" she blurted, her eyes opened wide. She ducked and slid past him, only turning when she got to the edge of the kitchen. She pointed an unsteady finger at him. "If I..." *go to prison tomorrow.* She didn't say the words, but Tanner heard them anyway. "If I'm not around after tomorrow, then you have to live your life. Go home. Go back to your family. But you may not wait for me," she ordered. "You've already lost too many years." Tears leaked from her eyes and Jess swiped at them fiercely. Tanner slowly walked toward her and she backed up the last two steps that brought her against the wall.

"You can't tell me what to do," he told her softly.

"Yes, I can," she shot back. "I refuse to be the reason you put your life on hold. You have choices. You're a free man." She gestured out the kitchen window. "Go live your life, find s-someone and be happy." She choked back a sob.

"Don't you see, Jess..." Tanner looked down at her, knew the emotion he felt radiated from his eyes. *I did find someone.* He took another step closer. "And I'll do whatever it takes to be with her. Even if that means waiting."

Jess shook her head as two tears streaked down her face. "I couldn't live with myself if I thought you were waiting." She was a broken record stuck on the same line. Nothing had changed her mind all these months.

"Let's just worry about tonight, okay? There's no waiting tonight." He looked at her, didn't know what part of her to touch first. "Can you do that for me?" Stroking his thumb softly along her jaw, he willed her to give in.

Jess studied him for a long time, her eyes tortured, before glancing behind him to the table. "What about dinner? Don't you want...?" She let the sentence dangle. Maybe it was the hunger in his eyes that stopped her. He knew everything he felt was in his gaze.

He shook his head, relieved that she wanted to give them at least this one last night together. "I'm not hungry for food." His voice was low, rough, as guttural as he'd ever sounded. He tipped her chin up at the same time he lowered his head.

He couldn't help himself, his lips took hers. Firmly. Fiercely. Hungrily.

THE KISS CURLED HER toes.

She'd been fighting the feeling for months, knowing he'd leave at some point, or that her confinement would keep them separate. She'd fought the attraction from day one, but now it all came crashing down on her. She loved him. And loving him meant setting him free.

Tomorrow.

Instead of letting guilt and depression swamp her, Jess chose to live this night as a free woman. She wanted all the things Tanner made her feel. She wanted the passion and the heat. She wanted his heart too, but it wasn't fair to ask for that.

Just like the last time he kissed her in this kitchen, it got out of control in a matter of seconds. Hot, short seconds.

When he lifted and pressed her against the wall, she expected the wainscoting to slam into her back like before, but that didn't happen. Tanner protected her with an arm wrapped securely around her. His body was hard and strong and just what she needed. But not the only thing she needed. She'd come to rely on his presence the last six months. Not that he knew. On the rare occasion when she didn't see him, she'd felt alone. On days when she'd been able to look out the window and see him in the yard or if she glanced across the room and saw him adjusting costs for the budget or even when they'd locked gazes in the courtroom, she'd felt a certain amount of peace. Almost as if he were around, then everything would work out.

Now, as he kissed her, as his calloused hands searched the skin beneath her big sweater and her legs wrapped around his waist, she only knew one thing for certain. He belonged to her tonight. For six months she'd been practicing living in the present, knowing that was the only way she'd survive if she went to prison. One day at a time. Tanner had told her as much during some of their conversations. This moment, with his hand on her breast and his tongue in her mouth…this was a memory she'd take with her tomorrow into court and for the rest of her life.

Jess rubbed against the erection pressing between her legs and heard Tanner groan.

"Upstairs," she panted between kisses.

Breathing hard, Tanner pulled back, touched his forehead to hers with his eyes closed.

"Okay, yeah. Definitely the bedroom. But I'm slowing this train down. We've been doing this fast and hard for months and tonight I'm taking my time."

"Speaking of time…you're wasting it standing here talking."

Tanner grinned before he gave her one last deep kiss and set her down. "After you," he gestured toward the stairs and she backed up, watching him as he followed. God, he was gorgeous.

His dark eyes were bright with desire, with lust. An incredible feeling of power came over her as she made her way upstairs. She wouldn't think about tomorrow or court. She'd spend the rest of the night concentrating on Tanner.

At the top of the stairs, she started walking backwards again, wanted to keep her eyes on him for as long as possible. He was such a predator the way he stalked her. There was no way he was going to go slow. They hadn't had sex in three days…one of their longer periods since their quickies began, because they were at the whim of a busy household.

"What's the smile about?" he asked, a slow grin curving his lips.

She hadn't realized she was smiling. "You. Thinking you're going to go slow." To make things interesting, she grabbed the waistband of her leggings and pulled them off. She had to stop for a second to get them over the ankle monitor, but then she was moving again, taunting him with bare legs. "Nope, I don't see slow in our future."

"You don't think I can take my time?" he asked, following her into the bedroom.

"I think you'd like to, but you won't be able to."

He kicked the door closed without looking at it, then reached behind him and locked it.

A shiver of excitement raced down her back. She lifted the edges of her big sweater.

"Stop," he told her. "That's my job." '

Chills prickled her arms and heat flashed up her center. "Then you're slacking off, dude."

He moved toward her. "Is that so?"

She smiled and took a step back to taunt him more, but he lunged, grabbed her around the waist, spun and pinned her against the wall in a full body press. The kicker…maybe the moment she fell more deeply in love with him, was when she felt his arm behind her again, his hand searching for molding, making sure he wouldn't hurt her.

Instead of diving in for a hungry kiss, Tanner watched her, a slow grin spreading across his face. "Are you paying close attention?" he whispered. Then slowly, so slowly, he leaned in, slanted his mouth over hers and destroyed her with the softest, sweetest kiss. His lips molded to hers as his tongue slowly explored her. It was heaven. It was perfect. It was what she'd always wanted. Knowing this might be her last night with this man, she gave him everything she had, everything she was.

Jess wrapped her arms around his neck and melted into him. She never realized he had moved until she felt the bed at her back as he laid her down and ended up half way on her. "When are you going to take this sweater off me?" she muttered. "I'm hot."

"I noticed," he answered roughly as he nibbled his way across her jaw. "I'm gonna get you hotter." He traced his tongue around her ear and Jess nearly shot off the bed. His hand eased up her bare thigh, moving higher, promising more, teasing until he continued and lingered right under her breast.

She moaned in frustration and he chuckled. She tried to shift his hand higher, but he caught both her hands and locked them over her head, staring down at her with victory in his eyes. He moved against her so she felt his erection over her clit. "Tanner," she moaned. "Take off your stupid clothes. And my stupid clothes."

He chuckled again. One-handed, he lifted her sweater to uncover her breasts. She still wore her bra, but he didn't seem too worried. He kissed around the lace. Then through the lace. He tongued the stiff peak of her nipple before gently sucking it. His hot tongue stroked her over and over. God, it was torture of the best kind. Finally, he unsnapped the front closure of her bra and peeled back the cups, exposing her to the cool room air.

"You have the prettiest breasts," he whispered as he gave her other nipple the same treatment.

She was used to hard and fast, not this slow, tender assault. This reminded her of that first full night together. But this was different. Better. Because he wasn't a stranger. He was the man she loved. A man she could confide in, share her secrets with. He left no part of her untouched.

Jess got a hand free and managed to pull off her sweater. Tanner seemed too engrossed in kissing her breasts to notice. She watched as he devoured her, fascinated at the devotion he showered her with. Her nipples were plump, wet, red. Her breasts engorged and aching. It was too much. Not enough. Jess grabbed his head and forced him up as she leaned forward and took his mouth. She loved his kiss. Loved the way he sank into her with every stroke of his tongue. Somehow she rolled him over and lost her bra. Now to get rid of his clothes and her underwear.

She lifted his shirt. "Off," she muttered as she exposed the hot skin and hard muscled chest that always made her wet. He sat up, helped her get it over his head and she reached for the button on his jeans. He was everywhere at once, his lips on her jaw, her neck, his hands on her skin.

In a flash, he flipped her on her back. "Oh, no you don't," he breathed. "Nice try. But tonight, we're doing this my way." He palmed her head and proceeded to kiss her slowly. Deeply. He took her mouth with the same devotion as her breasts. His tongue played against hers in a sensual game of give and take, stroking inside her mouth, sending sparks zipping through her extremities. God, he was turning her inside out and outside in.

In two short minutes he had her panting, grasping, begging for him.

He seemed truly pleased by it all.

OH YEAH. HE HAD her right where he wanted her.

Underneath him and begging.

But she had a point. He did need to lose his clothes and her little white lace panties. In a minute. Right now he wanted to keep kissing her. He wanted to feel her tongue against his as she moaned into his mouth, wanted her nails digging into his skin as she arched against his body. He pulled back, gave them both a minute to breathe as he trailed kisses down her neck. She lifted into him, offering everything. Emotion constricted his chest. The way she gave herself made him feel whole. Made him feel worthy.

With one hand, Tanner unbuttoned his jeans. It took a little longer to get the zipper down with his hard-on pressed against it so tightly.

"Stay," he ordered softly. "I'll be right back. Don't move." In one quick motion he levered himself to the side of the bed and quickly got rid of his boots and socks. He lifted to take off his jeans and felt Jess behind him, her lips on his shoulders, her hands on his biceps.

"Thought I told you to stay put," he rumbled. But he loved that she had to touch him. Loved how she'd taken his cue and finally slowed down.

"I couldn't help myself," she whispered in his ear. "You're better than chocolate." The picture of her licking him like candy sent a fresh surge of blood to his groin. She traced her tongue around the shell and made his cock even harder. "Here, let me help you with those." She knelt next to him on the bed and pushed his jeans and boxer briefs farther down his legs. "Mmm," she purred and dropped her head in his lap quicker than he could stop her.

Stop her? Was he nuts? Why stop something so fuckingly, erotically great as having her go down on him. He hissed in a breath as she took him in her mouth and his hands threaded through her hair. She obviously enjoyed giving him pleasure. He'd had seven years less than most people and if she was trying to make up for any lost time, then she was well on her way. She gave him so much and he had so little to offer. She gave him her body with all her heart and soul. With her mouth, tongue and hands. God, how had he forgotten how unbelievably fantastic it was? But this sideways angle of hers gave this blowjob a whole new feel. She was killing him with pleasure and although he loved it, he wanted this night to be for her.

Tanner stroked his hand down her back as she continued to suck him and the answer to this particular dilemma—if he could call a fantastic blowjob a dilemma—came to him in a flash.

Forgetting about his jeans, he leaned back on the bed and gave her total access to the area she seemed most interested in. As she redoubled her efforts to blow his mind, Tanner eased the lower half of her body over his head and settled her exactly where he wanted her.

Sixty-nine. A position he'd always heard about, but never had the chance to explore. Until now.

Jess moaned on his cock as he moved the lace aside and licked into her. It was highly intimate. Enormously erotic. Something he wouldn't have wanted to do with just any woman. The realization had Tanner working harder to make her come. He wanted her on the edge. He wanted her to know that he'd do anything for her. But really…the panties had to go. Damn if he was going to take the time to push them down her legs. With a quick snap, he ripped the thin barrier to shreds and tossed them away. Much better.

She'd gotten way ahead of him on the pleasure scale, and sweat streamed off him as her hot mouth continued to suck his rigid cock. This whole experience was so much like the first night, but so different. Jess's desperation before had come from helplessness, from fear. This thing between them now was fueled by emotion. Love. At least love on his part. Whether she admitted it or not, he believed to his soul that she felt the same way. He didn't see how she could do what she was doing if she *didn't* feel the same. Tanner fought pleasure with pleasure. He used his fingers and tongue to take her to the edge. He had her so close to coming that she lost her rhythm as she moved over him.

Oh, she was close, so close, but he didn't want her to come this way. He wanted to watch her eyes, kiss her lips. He wanted to bury himself inside her and show her he was the one and only man for her, no matter how long it took before they could be together.

With a growl, he hauled her up and tossed her toward the pillows. In seconds, he lost the rest of his clothes and moved on top of her.

It took every ounce of control he possessed to slow things down again. As he covered her, his erection pressed snugly against her wet entrance, he watched her. That same foreign emotion crashed in on him a second time as he brushed his lips over hers. She moaned and grabbed his ass, tried to bring him more fully inside her. Tanner pushed a fraction. Enough to make her feel the invasion. Still he kissed her. Slowly. Deeply. With every kiss he sank more fully into her. He took his time. For every inch inside her, he withdrew and started over until he had her mindless. He couldn't take much more as he rode a wave of electric heat, skated on the edge of completion.

The smell of sex surrounded them. Her little cries shredded his control further. With another growl, Tanner thrust inside of her, filled her completely as he filled himself emotionally. Jess cried out as he moved on top of her, pumping, pushing, and she met him each time.

His mouth crashed down on hers. The intimacy struck him head-on and with another plunge she broke apart. Every muscle froze as her body clenched around him. A groan rumbled in his chest as he stroked into her hard and his own release jetted inside her.

It was monumental. Colossal. It was the most amazing thing he'd ever experienced. Being with her couldn't compare to anything else in his life. She was as essential as his next breath. She was his freedom.

Breathing hard, he collapsed on top of her. He would've moved, but Jess wrapped her arms around his back and held tight. She seemed content to take his weight. After a minute, Tanner shifted to his side and kept her close, kept them connected. He brushed his lips over hers in the gentlest of caresses.

How would he manage without her? It was a crazy thought. One too devastating to think about, so he held her close and breathed her in.

Silence stretched between them as Tanner brushed his palms over her damp skin. Just like before, they were on a clock and his chances of forever with her dwindled with every passing minute.

"I missed you," he whispered. "I missed the feel of you, the taste of you." His mouth closed over hers. Their quickies hadn't involved oral sex. There hadn't been time for each of them to take a turn and he'd been hell-bent on making sure they both got what they needed.

As she opened for him, as her tongue met his in another soft kiss he forgot everything but the way she touched him. Not just with her hands and mouth, but with her spirit.

Before he had a chance to do anything, Jess pushed him back, straddled him. As she nibbled on his neck, alternately biting and licking, he grew harder inside her.

"I don't want to sleep tonight," she breathed near his ear. "I don't want to miss a minute." She was thinking about tomorrow. About going to prison where she'd have nothing but time to catch up on her sleep.

Tanner framed her face in his hands. His eyes stung but he forced a smile that reeked of pure sex. "I hadn't planned on letting you." He slid his hands down her sides, cupped her ass and brought her more snugly against him. He took respite in the soft haven of her body as they moved together slowly. Seconds turned into minutes that turned into hours. Jess dozed next to him a couple of times, but it never lasted long as his fingers or mouth played over her skin. He'd been so good all night, keeping his emotion under wraps, but finally, near the break of dawn, he couldn't keep the words in any longer. He said them so softly, he didn't think she heard him.

"I love you."

She froze in his arms. "Don't," she said, clearly panicked.

"Why? It's true. I love you, Jess. No matter what happens today, doesn't change how I feel about you." He tightened his grip on her, pulled her close.

"We talked about this," she said, gently stroking the stubble on his jaw. "You're not—"

He shushed her with his lips. "When are you going to learn you can't tell me what to do?" he asked quietly. "You can't tell me how or what I feel. You can't tell me how to live my life." He kissed her again. "I love you. No matter what happens today, we'll deal with it."

Tears brimmed her eyes as she pulled out of his grasp. "No." She shook her head and fear trounced the soft emotion beating in his chest. "You have to live your life." She found her robe on the hook behind the door and slipped it on. "I won't last if I think you are waiting for me." She implored him with desperate eyes. "Please, Tanner, please. Live a full life. That's what I want for you." The first rays of sunlight streamed into the room and Jess walked into the bathroom and shut the door, locking him—and everything he felt for her—out in the cold.

CHAPTER 25

DAYLIGHT HADN'T BROKEN WHEN Jay gave Terry a soft kiss and pulled out of her warm body. Sweat nearly glued their skin together. He rolled onto his side. She was unnaturally quiet. Not surprising considering the day ahead. Their normal sexual banter had disappeared and in its place was silent need, wordless caresses that filled the terrifying void of the day to come. They'd always turned to each other in crisis. Emotionally and physically. This situation was no different. They needed the comfort the other provided with the intimacy that had kept their marriage so strong throughout twenty-four years.

Terry turned into him, her face shiny with perspiration, the usual light in her eyes dimmed with worry. "What will we do?" *If Jess is found guilty.*

He didn't need the clarification. Jay stroked some damp hair off her cheek. "I'll appeal."

"They'll take her away though. Today. What will we do then?"

"We'll survive. We'll visit as much as we can. We'll send her care packages. We'll explore every possible legal avenue." He shook his head, at a loss as to how to comfort his wife when he had the same concerns.

Sighing, she absently stroked his thigh as she digested his honest answer. "Do you think Jess is okay this morning?" she asked after a few minutes.

Jay still didn't quite believe they'd left her alone with Tanner all night. What if he'd convinced her to run away? An irrational part of him actually hoped for that; the side of him that couldn't stand the idea of his daughter being locked up, but that action would only make matters worse. Much worse. Nevertheless, he'd been torn leaving Jess on what was possibly her last night as a free woman. But Terry had insisted. Without being specific—because she knew he couldn't think of his daughter being intimate with a man—she'd apparently been aware of the relationship between Jess and Tanner. He'd seen no sign of it himself. His daughter was discreet to say the least. Terry too, hadn't seen anything incriminating either, but from that night three months ago when everyone had gotten home late, Terry had known. "Call it mother's intuition," she'd said. One look at Jess and Tanner had told the whole story. They'd managed to stay together since. Jay couldn't figure out when they found time together and purposely chose not to think about it.

Jess was an adult and deserved to have an adult relationship with a man. Jay didn't really have a problem with Tanner either, but Tanner closed himself off sometimes, mostly when it came time to talk about his family. Jay hugged Terry closer. If Tanner couldn't communicate, then Jay didn't see the man having a lasting relationship with anyone and the last thing he wanted was more heartache for Jess.

"I love you, you know," Terry whispered.

Looking into her eyes, Jay nodded. "Yeah. I know. I love you too."

Terry kissed him and rubbed her wicked hand high between his thighs, sending very obvious messages to his semi-hard dick. "Again?" he asked. They hadn't had sex four times in one night in a long time.

"Unless you don't want to," she said, retreating.

Jay caught her hand and set it back over his growing erection. "I always want to," he said against her lips. "You still drive me crazy after all these years. That won't ever change." He rolled onto his back and kept Terry against him, putting her on top where she loved to be. "Do your worst," he challenged. Usually when he said that Terry got a gleam in her eye and tortured him within an inch of life, but now she stared down at him with all the love in her heart plain to see. When she mounted him and he sank deep in her body, the love he felt for her multiplied for the eight thousandth time. She loved him slowly, sweetly, as only Terry could do. And when they both peaked, the feeling most prevalent in Jay's heart was hope. Hope for a new day and a new beginning.

Later, at the courthouse, his small ray of hope dimmed when he saw Jess and Tanner walking toward them in the hallway outside the courtroom. Jay hadn't expected sunshine and light, but even the friendly bond that had been so evident between them was nowhere to be found. Terry noticed it too, and gave him a look that said *trouble in paradise.*

"Tanner, can I talk to you for a minute?" Terry didn't wait for an answer. She grabbed Tanner's arm and took him toward the bench down the hall, leaving Jay alone with Jess.

"Where are they going?" Jess asked, her eyes narrowed.

"I have no idea." But as long as they had a minute of privacy... "Want to tell me what the problem is?"

Her head snapped toward his. "What do you mean?"

Jay glanced at the ceiling. No wonder Terry knew about them getting together. Jess really was a bad liar. "I mean, the wall of ice between you and Tanner is about ten feet tall. Should I not have left you alone with him last night?" All his protective-dad instincts reared to the front.

Jess rolled her eyes. "No. It's just..." she searched for an explanation and the longer it took the more Jay worried about her. "He wants to wait. If I...you know...get convicted. And I told him not to. I want him to be free and live his life."

The thought of her going to prison made him sick. His baby girl behind bars... But all she could think about was Tanner and his feelings. The trial hadn't changed her nature. She was still a people pleaser, still trying to make everyone around her happy. Jay loved her so much. His eyes stung with emotion. He exhaled and gave her the best advice he could.

It was a tough call. "Isn't it up to Tanner what he does with his life?" He got her *don't-make-this-into-a-lesson-I-need-to-learn* face that was so familiar.

"Are you on his side?" Her whisper squeaked high and incredulous.

"I'm not on anyone's side." Jay lifted Jess's chin. "If the man wants to wait for you, then it's his prerogative." He studied her tortured expression. "Is it that serious between you two?"

"He told me he loved me." Jess's eyes brightened with moisture, her voice soft.

Jay nodded and hugged her close. Didn't need to ask if she felt the same way. It was all over her pretty little face. "You have to figure out what you want, honey." Jay set her from him. "I can only tell you this…" He looked down the hall at Terry talking so seriously to Tanner. "If your mother and I were in your situation, I'd wait a hundred years. There just isn't anyone else in the world for me." Jay looked back to Jess. "If Tanner feels that way about you…I hope you'll think long and hard about how you treat the situation, how you treat him. The guy deserves—"

Jess's cell phone rang and she checked the number. "Oh, my God. It's Bobby McBride."

She answered the call, but did little talking. Her wide eyes told a story all their own. The boys rounded the corner as she spoke. "Really?" She paused. "Thank you." She ran a hand through her hair. "Thank you. Yes… Someone will call you. Thank you." She slid the phone in her bag, her face shell-shocked. "He loved it," she murmured. She looked at him, her face a mixture of elation and despair. "He finally got a chance to read it last night and couldn't put it down. He gave me carte blanche to hire the cast and crew and he wants me to direct it. He said he didn't expect me to even answer the phone because of the trial, but he's hoping for the best. If I can manage to walk out of here today, he'll fund the movie. All of it."

Jay didn't know what to say. It was great news, yes, but they had a giant hurdle to cross before celebrating a victory that might never be. "Congratulations, honey." He hugged her tight, his pride for her filling his chest with emotion he'd been trying to keep buried. He checked his watch. "C'mon, we should go inside and take our seats." He didn't have a good feeling about this. He'd barely touched breakfast, but what little he had threatened a revolt. He needed a miracle in the next thirty minutes. Because he'd already had one miracle happen when Tanner rescued the family, he seriously doubted that another was forthcoming. He motioned to Terry as they headed for the courtroom and his sons followed them in.

JESS NERVOUSLY TURNED IN her seat, surprised she didn't see

Tanner in the front row next to her brothers. He'd been out in the hall for almost ten minutes. They were about to close the doors. Had he left? Had she really pushed him away after all they'd been through? But wasn't it for the best? He did deserve a life. He shouldn't have to wait. But what if she was found not guilty? Her father's words made her think. What if their love was the real thing like her parents? Even if she did go to prison, Tanner might never find someone he cared about as much as he seemed to care about her. Real love didn't have boundaries. Hers didn't. She'd love him until the day she died no matter where they were.

Hadn't she been the one to tell him that his family loved him no matter what? That shutting them out was never the answer? Then she'd proceeded to do the exact same thing.

What had she done?

Just as panic washed through her veins, the door opened and Tanner walked in. He pocketed his cell phone and took his regular seat behind her. Relief made her sigh. Tanner deserved her honesty and she had to live with his decision to wait or not whether she liked it or not. Jess tore off a sheet of paper from her dad's notebook and wrote a short nine-word note.

As the jury settled in their seats, Jess straightened the collar of her white blouse. Per her father's request, she'd dressed conservatively in a baby-blue suit. It made her look ten years younger, which hopefully made it harder for the jury to put her behind bars. Her stomach had so many butterflies she felt sick. The next few minutes charted the course of the rest her life. The enormity of it made her dizzy.

Next to her, her father sat coolly and watched the jurors. He'd told her if they'd reached a guilty verdict that they'd most likely not be able to look her in the eye. Contrary to Tanner's belief, she wasn't brave enough to see for herself. Instead she watched the bailiff as he held open the door. She folded her note neatly into fourths, her palms sweating as the seconds ticked by.

Run. The word whispered through her brain. But she didn't. Couldn't.

Behind her, Jess felt the presence of her family. Her mother and little brothers had been there through every day of the trial.

They'd all testified and given the accounts of the three days they'd been held by Paul Facinetti. They'd made sure the jury understood that Jess had been in an unthinkable position and only acted out of fear for them.

The two officers who'd been on Facinetti's payroll had been taken into custody and the jury heard her accounts of their scare tactics. Whether they believed her enough to give a *not guilty* verdict was the question. Facinetti's trial wasn't scheduled until late next summer.

Even Tanner had testified, stressing the fact that Jess had never intended to harm Maurice, but had only wanted his help in saving her family. Her decision to trade him had only been a last ditch effort, and had he shown any compassion or will to help her, she wouldn't have kidnapped him. Nor would he have died if he hadn't drawn his gun.

Realizing that the fault lay completely at her feet, Jess had taken responsibility for kidnapping Maurice in the first place, but begged the jury to understand that it was never her intention to kill him.

The jury took their seats and the judge entered the courtroom. The nauseous feeling in her stomach got worse. Sweat slicked her palms.

The room seemed to fade as everything went into slow motion. Her life was about to change dramatically. Either she'd put this whole mess behind her or she'd spend the next ten or fifteen years behind bars.

The note in her palm nearly burned her skin. If she didn't give it to Tanner soon, she'd lose the chance completely. How quickly would they take her out of the room after a guilty verdict?

Jess turned slightly and locked eyes with Tanner. He looked as nervous as she felt. He'd borrowed a suit from Eric, but he seemed just as imposing. His future was on the line as well, and Jess understood that. He'd been helping her all along. For the last six months he'd done nothing but support her. She owed him more than shoving him aside now. Her dad was right. Tanner could make up his own mind. If he chose to leave, then he deserved her support and if he wanted to stay, then she'd thank God she had a man who loved her enough to wait.

But first he needed to know the two most important things she had to tell him.

Everyone stood as the judge entered the room. Jess handed her note to Tanner as the court was called to session. The judge asked the jury if they'd come to a decision. The foreman, an older man with gray hair, confirmed that they had, as he rose and handed a piece of paper to the bailiff who handed it to the judge.

Jess glanced back at Tanner, watching as he scanned her note.

The judge read the slip of paper. "In the matter of the state versus Jessie St. John, the jury finds the defendant...

Jess swayed, not ready to hear the words. A familiar roaring in her ears drowned out sound around her. She couldn't pass out. Not now.

"...not guilty."

The room erupted and Jess held onto the table. Had she heard him right? Not guilty? She looked at her dad about to ask what happened when the judge continued.

"Miss St. John, I can only hope that you've learned a lesson from this experience. It's always in your best interest to go to law enforcement officials in times of such crisis."

Jess nodded, couldn't say a word since she didn't have a lick of spit in her mouth. She was free?

The judge thanked the jury and lifted his gavel. "This court is adjourned." He banged the desk. Noise erupted in the room. Her dad wrapped his arms around her and one by one the rest of her family did the same until she was squished in the middle of a giant huddle.

It was really over? Six months of worry, of panic attacks, of preparing for the worst...and it was over?

Slowly, her family members parted. Tanner stood five feet away, his eyes bright with tears. "Hey." His voice cracked as he moved in front of her. Her note dangled in his hand. "You look a little shell shocked."

"I am," she admitted.

Her family backed off a few steps and followed the crowd toward the door.

Tanner pulled her into a hug. "Congratulations."

Congratulations? Nothing about her note? Her confession? She held tight until he stepped back. Frazzled nerves had her babbling. "Bobby called right before we went in. He loved the screenplay. He gave me a green light."

A giant grin split Tanner's face and just about knocked her socks off. "Looks like your dreams are coming true."

"Some of them," she agreed. But what about the dream that mattered most? She gazed up at him, ready to say the words that had been on her tongue and in her mind for the past six months. Ever since the day he'd saved her family. The words she'd written in the note but never had the courage to say before now.

"Just some?" he asked. "What if I want them all to come true? What would I have to do to make that happen?"

That was easy. "Be my partner." Three words, but not the only three she wanted to say.

"Are you asking or is that an order?"

"I don't know. Which one works better? Maybe it's both." She smiled at him, not sure where he was headed. Had he decided to leave anyway because she'd pushed so hard before? Uncertainty niggled in her belly. He hadn't mentioned the note yet. Nothing.

Jess smiled and covered up the hurt. "Tanner, you've already done so much. I couldn't have gotten through all these months without you."

"Yeah, you could. You're one of the strongest women I know. Just like your mother." He knew her trigger. Knew there were very few things that mattered to her. Her family. Him. Her chest got tight, her heart ached.

"Look, you got me thinking earlier this morning."

Oh, God. He'd decided to leave after all. The trial was over and her note wasn't enough.

"I made a phone call before the proceedings started." He looked at his shoes before glancing at her. "I called my mom."

The sting of tears burned Jess's eyes. She hoped with all her heart that if Tanner didn't stay with her, he'd at least go home to the family that loved him.

"I told her I was sorry." Tanner quickly swiped at his eyes and Jess couldn't hold back the hot tears streaking down her face. "I told her I was wrong to push her and the family away."

Jess put a hand to her mouth to hold back a sob. She

understood the courage it took for him to call home after so long. In a flash, she understood why he'd done it. If his family could forgive him then he could forgive her.

"What did your mom say?" she asked, almost afraid of the answer.

"She told me she loved me. That she never stopped loving me." His voice cracked, but he gave her a wobbly grin. "Hey, I almost forgot," he said, handing her note back.

Jess wiped her eyes. Why was he giving this back to her?

"Go ahead," he said. "Read it."

Read it? She'd written it. Jess looked at her familiar handwriting.

I'm sorry I pushed you away. I love you.

But something new was added to the bottom.

I know. Marry me.

A broken sob escaped and Jess slapped a hand across her mouth. Her heart filled to a breaking point as she looked up at him. Was he serious? She'd never felt more full or more complete. Tears filled her eyes faster than she could swipe them away.

"If we're going to be partners," he said. "I figure we should round out the whole deal."

There were so many things she wanted to say. She wanted to scream with happiness. Jump in his arms. She was a writer for God's sake and all she came up with was, "Seriously?"

He grinned. "I got your mother's permission. I should probably talk to your dad too, but he was busy talking to you, so... I want us to be together, Jess. Always." He took her hands, searched her eyes. "I love you. Say yes."

"Oh my God. I can't believe this." This was so far from what she'd expected. Instead of going to prison, all of her dreams were coming true.

Tanner shook her shoulders a little. "Jess?"

Jess leapt into his arms. "Of course. Yes. I love you too. I love you, I love you, I love you." She couldn't stop saying the words.

Tanner's lips came down over hers and—just like her movie— Jess knew the ending to her story would be happily ever after too.

Epilogue

JESS GAZED OUT THE airplane's window at the lush Colorado forest beneath. Right now it was covered with a thick dusting of pristine white snow. She loved California and its three hundred days of sun, but this amazingly beautiful sight nearly stole her breath. Christmas in Colorado. It didn't get much better than this.

"Pretty, isn't it?" Tanner said next to her. He squeezed her hand and she gave him her full attention.

"Very." She smiled, tried to defuse his nervousness. Though he'd acted cool, this trip meant more than he let on. "I like *this* view too," she said, looking into his eyes.

"You're such a sweet talker," he murmured. Then he kissed her softly.

"Only where you're concerned," she whispered at his mouth.

"You're so full of shit," he continued, but he was smiling. "You sweet talk every person you get on the phone. You've become the best producer in town on your first project. You can get anybody to do anything for almost nothing."

It was true. Whether it was the notoriety of the trial or the fact that a lot of people just liked pulling for the underdog, Jess had managed to get an A-list crew to work for nearly half their going rate. She was way under budget and everything was progressing without a hitch.

"Yeah?" Jess ignored the Hollywood speculation about the timing of her movie or her part in Maurice's death, and she couldn't control the people who approached the media to discuss his morally corrupt private life. Maurice had nearly destroyed her while he was living and she refused to let him do it from the grave.

Whether this film became a success or not, she still had the most important thing right in front of her. "Keep talking." She teased his mouth with her own. "You're making me hot."

Laughing, Tanner pulled back. His face grew serious. "Thanks for coming with me. I..." He stopped. Seemed at a loss for words, but the emotion in his eyes said it all. "I really love having your support."

Speaking to his mother that day in the courtroom six weeks ago had been a huge step for him. They'd talked a few more times and she'd asked him to come home for Christmas. Tanner wasn't sure if the invitation stemmed from obligation and he hadn't asked. The time had come to face the consequences of his actions whether he wanted to or not. He'd asked Jess to join him and she'd accepted.

"You always have my support," she told him as the landing gear groaned and settled into place. "Besides, you promised to teach me how to ski. I'm holding you to it." Jess squeezed his hand and gave him a quick buss on the lips.

The plane taxied to the gate and the door opened. Passengers grabbed their bags from overhead bins and filed in the center aisle. Tanner didn't move. He let all the passengers go by before standing up, clearly avoiding the inevitable meeting about to take place when his mother picked them up at baggage claim. Jess pulled her only carry-on bag from under the seat as Tanner lifted his own backpack and they started out.

Jess kept her feelings in check. She couldn't control anything but her love for him, and that was a free-flowing river. They were a united front in everything they did. The bond they shared matched what she saw in her parents' relationship and she refused to take it for granted.

She'd already vowed to protect him and if anyone even looked at him funny, she was going to let them have it with both barrels.

No one messed with her man.

They emptied out into the terminal and headed toward the exit.

"I love you," she told him. "No matter what happens, I love you."

Tanner nodded, his eyes bright with uncharacteristic emotion. "Love you too."

Jess hated seeing him so worried. "I know," she said, leaning against him. "And I have the ring to prove it." She lifted her left hand and let her sparkly engagement ring speak for itself.

Tanner grinned and she smiled back at him. "I'm serious when I said we're upgrading as soon as I can afford something bigger."

"And I'm serious when I said I didn't care about the size of the diamond. It's the *idea* of the ring that makes me deliriously happy." She tipped her head to the side. "Check that. *You* make me deliriously happy."

Grabbing her hand, Tanner glanced at her. "You are so getting laid tonight."

Happiness bubbled in her veins. "Mission accomplished," she murmured, linking their fingers.

An escalator ahead took them down to the baggage carousels and ground transportation. A large contingency of people seemed to be crowded at the bottom of the escalator. But not until they reached the midway point did Jess see the sign.

Welcome Home, Tanner.

The emotion that Jess had kept in check until now slowly leaked out her eyes.

A crowd of over fifty people cheered when they saw him and Jess squeezed his hand tighter. Holding the sign in front of them, five women had tears streaming down their cheeks and when Tanner got into hugging range, his mother and sisters mobbed him with unconditional love.

Jess laughed through her tears, knowing she'd written the final scene for her movie exactly right.

The End

Also by Dee J. Adams

The Adrenaline Highs Series

DANGEROUS RACE

"High Octane Awesomeness!"
> 5 stars – Laura Wright, author of *Mark of the Vampire* and *Bayou Heat* series.

"Really, really fabulous read. The mystery / suspense subplot is interesting and keeps you on your toes, the main and secondary characters are all great and likable, there is sizzling chemistry in both the primary and secondary romances, and it's well-written."
> 4.5 stars – The Fiction Vixen

Taking high octane romance and suspense to a whole other level, Adams goes green flag with a prologue that left me shaken and a story that both thrilled and chilled.
> 4 stars – One Good Book Deserves Another

DANGER ZONE

"Okay, I'll admit it. I'm a sucker for romances set in the world of movie-making. But in Danger Zone, *Dee J. Adams not only uses her years of experience in Hollywood to create a delightfully gritty and authentic world filled with insider insights; she also creates a cast of very real and likable characters. I especially loved stunt-woman Ellie Morgan's kickass, take-no-prisoners attitude, and her long-time friendship with her best-friend and roommate Ashley. As for the book's hero, Quinn Reynolds? I'm in love. This one's on my keeper shelf."*
> *New York Times* Bestselling author Suzanne Brockmann

"Highly recommended for romantic suspense fans, especially those who like stories with complex relationships."
> Marlene Harris, Reading Reality LLC
> Starred Review from *Library Journal*

DANGEROUSLY CLOSE

"Witty dialogue and unyielding suspense make for another great story in the Adrenaline Highs series. The hero and heroine are fully developed and emotionally rich, and the best part of the novel is the developing relationship between them from strangers to friends to lovers. Readers will enjoy spending time with these memorable characters."
4 stars – *Romantic Times*

"Dangerously Close is hands down my favorite book in this series thus far and it's easily one of my top picks for 2012. I was completely and utterly drawn into this story. The strong romance balanced out perfectly with the suspense element."
5 stars – The Book Vixen

LIVING DANGEROUSLY
Winner: 2014 Gayle Wilson Award of Excellence

"It has everything from the glitterati of Hollywood to a high-speed cross-country getaway—even a bit of bondage. Narrow escapes are the norm in this action-filled novel."
4 stars + Scorcher – *Romantic Times*

IMMINENT DANGER

"Loved it! Lots of romance action mystery and sex! Love the series."
5 stars – Happy Amazon Reader

"Adams never fails to deliver a fast-paced plot filled with unexpected twists and 'whoa…I can't believe that just happened' moments. Abbey & Blake's story is as deliciously sexually charged as it is suspenseful."
4 stars – Goodreads reviewer

A LITTLE DANGER

"This is the type of book where you'll want to clear some time and just sit and read it. You won't want to put it down. But be warned, it's like riding a roller coaster of emotions."
5 stars – Happy Amazon Reader

"Adams expertly writes the earthquake as a formidable villain that appears determined to keep Elena and Bill apart."
5 stars – Happy Amazon Reviewer

ALWAYS DANGEROUS

"Dee J. Adams does a great job at mixing just the right amount of excitement in with the romance and the pace of the developing relationship between Kim and Leo was perfect. They're sexy together and have great chemistry."
4 stars – Under the Covers Book Blog

"Miss Adams has a new fan in me after this, and I'm definitely planning on going back and reading all the previous titles in this series. If the final book is anything to go by, I've been missing out."
– Dirty Girl Romance

ABOUT THE AUTHOR

After graduating high school in Texas, Dee J. moved to Los Angeles to pursue acting. For twenty years, she acted in television and worked behind the scenes as an acting/dialogue coach for sitcoms. Writing happened accidentally after a vivid dream and the urging of her husband to "Just write it down." Three weeks, fourteen hours a day, and four hundred and fifty (long hand) pages later, she had her first novel. Dee J. loves writing books filled with action, mystery and love. (Not necessarily in that order.) Her experience in show business led to her narrating many of the books in the Adrenaline Highs series for Audible.com. She is the wife of a wonderful man and mother to a fabulous daughter. She's a dog lover all the way—due in part to a deathly allergy to cats—with a fondness towards Boxers and Pit Bulls. She is a member of several organizations, including Romance Writers of America, Screen Actors Guild and American Federation of Television and Radio Artists.

For more information on Dee J.'s books please visit:

www.deejadams.com